THE THIRTEENTH APOSTLE

Richard Brinsley Sheridan Mysteries

Book Three

R M Cullen

SAPERE
BOOKS

THE THIRTEENTH APOSTLE

Published by Sapere Books.

24 Trafalgar Road, Ilkley, LS29 8HH

saperebooks.com

ISBN: 978-0-85495-737-8

For my sister Patricia

ACKNOWLEDGMENTS

First of all, I would like to acknowledge the debt of gratitude which I owe to my late mother, who listened whilst I read the first draft of *The Thirteenth Apostle* aloud over our afternoon tea and who always made perceptive contributions to the development of my work. My sister Patricia continues in that vein to be a source of kindness and support as well as a great reader, I dedicate this novel to her.

My efforts have been bolstered over many years by the input of the South Manchester Writers group who never let a misused word slip by or fail to pick up on a jarring moment in the narrative. In particular I would like to thank those members who took the time to read the completed first draft and offered their fulsome feedback, making the revisions process so constructive: Liz Kolbeck for her razor-sharp points, Christine Johnson for bringing her skills as a professional editor to bear on the manuscript and Ros Davies for her encouraging remarks.

For the support of my late friend and talented playwright Ellen Fox I will be forever grateful. Carole Thomson continues to be a wonderful critic and is responsible for tasking me to describe the food and meals of the period in greater detail.

Yet again my thanks go out to my former colleague and writer Jan Weddup for his invaluable tips. He also kindly offered to write a review of the novel for the *Allotments Monthly*: 'I had to put sowing my onion seed on hold to find out who did it.'

As a historical novelist I cannot but be indebted to the numerous books which now adorn my shelves, not only biographies and general histories but those which shine a light on the more particular, whether it be Georgian plumbing or eating habits. A number I would mention are *The London Hanged: Crime and Civil Society in the Eighteenth Century* by Peter Linebaugh, *London Under* by Peter Ackroyd and Emma Kay's *The Georgian Kitchen*. There are a growing number of books which explore homosexuality in the period and I found the contributions of Rictor Norton in this area invaluable.

Lastly, my fulsome thanks go to Sapere Books for taking on my Sheridan series. My editors, Amy Durant, Matilda Richards and Natalie Linh Bolderston, have applied their sharp eyes to keeping the manuscript focused and succinct and all the better for it.

CHAPTER ONE

London, 1793

Richard Brinsley Sheridan turned down the side alley by the theatre and wove a course through the gathering prostitutes, those 'spells' who inhabited the Haymarket and other places of entertainment. It would soon be the intermission and they were waiting for clients to emerge, either to be of immediate service or to arrange later assignations.

Sheridan parried their salacious greetings with smiles and winks until his path was blocked by a young woman whose black eyes glittered with mischief.

'We hasn't had the pleasure of your company this good while, Mr Sheridan.'

'Ah, Sally…' Sheridan inclined his head politely.

'You know you've always got special rates with me,' she crooned coquettishly with the west country burr inherited from her mother.

'Sally, my dear, you are ever generous. How do you fare?'

'Middling passing, Mr Sheridan.'

He noticed that she had lost yet another tooth since last he had been waylaid. Sally had a sweet tooth. She should take care she did not lose them all or her eventual fall might be the more precipitous. For a moment he wondered whether his wardrobe mistress, Mrs Petty, might take her on as a dresser? Sally was a kind-hearted young woman who did not seem altogether cut out to be amongst these regular theatre roses. Well, he should leave that thought for another day. Mrs Petty's eyebrows had been raised enough of late.

The wardrobe mistress had found not one but two of her laundry maids were with child and both by the same flyman. Each swore that Harry Smith had promised marriage in exchange for their virtue and now it was all Mrs Petty could do to keep the girls from tearing each other apart. The philandering flyman had still not made good on either promise of matrimony. Mrs Petty moaned loudly that the jackanapes deserved the claws of her dishonoured maids. On more than one occasion she had petitioned Sheridan, bustling into his office to insist that Harry be forced to make at least one of them respectable. On second thoughts, the backstage of the theatre might be as ruinous as any brothel for poor Sally.

Sheridan entered by the stage door to the sounds of fanfare which blasted from the direction of the orchestra pit and heralded the opening of a pageant. This spectacle signalled the end of the evening's first round of entertainment. A roar and whooping assailed his ears as he found himself buffeted by a troop of sprites and fairies rushing to their cue. The children were more akin to demons, he fancied, than to flower fairies. They swirled about him and their chief mischief-maker, the little imp Edmund Carey, almost knocked him off his feet.

Mr Shaw, the stage manager, caught Sheridan by the arm with a steadying hand as he emerged from their midst.

'The devil take them!' snapped Sheridan. "Where is Monsieur Dubois? Is he not in charge of the blasted creatures?'

'Beg pardon, sir, a word.' Mr Shaw skewered him with his one good eye. 'I must warn you, sir, that Mr Kemble is in a tidy fit.' The stage manager continued by way of explanation, 'It is Shakespeare's play *Othello* we do tonight if you remember, sir, and he is all threats to not continue on, sir. His Royal Highness the Prince of Wales being in his box, Mr Kemble foresees disasters to his good reputation.'

'Mr Kemble in a fit? Mr Kemble is ever in a fit. What is the cause now, pray?'

'There is one that plays Iago, sir, Mr Marson, that has not yet arrived at the theatre tonight.'

'Marson ... Marson...?'

'Handsome young fellow — you thought him very pretty in our recent comedy.'

Sheridan threw up his arms as a stray sprite hurtled past. 'Let some other take his place. Our good Mr Kemble is too particular, he shall command the stage no less, I am sure.' He began to edge away. 'And Shaw, you must fine Mr Marson! Half this week's salary — no less!'

'It is Mr Hollingsworth what stands by to go on, sir, we can spare no other.'

Sheridan halted and lowered his arms. 'Ah.'

He did not doubt that his actor manager, John Philip Kemble, would be enraged at this prospect. 'Tom Hollingsworth. I see.'

The regular clown of the company, Tom Hollingsworth was not only too old and too short for the part of Iago, but he was wont to improvise and play up to the audience whenever he forgot his lines, which was frequent. Sheridan groaned. The damned fellow would scarce know one line of the part of Iago and would instead spend his whole time upon the stage cavorting and winking to his friends in the pit during Kemble's long and interminable dramatic pauses until the tragedy of Shakespeare's *Othello* had become little more than a grotesque pantomime.

'There must be another?'

Mr Shaw shrugged and shook his head.

Sheridan clicked his fingers. 'The young actor that was the servant, James...'

'Mr Blackett? He is but seventeen —'

'Then he should have the lines learnt by end of intermission. And here —' Sheridan rummaged in his pocket for a coin — 'give this to whoever is Prompter tonight that he might stay awake for the performance.'

'As you wish, sir.'

'And Shaw —'

'Sir?'

'Make certain that Mr Kemble does not drown his sorrows until after sweet Desdemona's fatal end.'

As if on cue, his leading actor emerged unsteadily from the actors' Green Room wearing the flowing robes of the Moorish general.

Shaw grimaced. 'I fear he is already tight as a boiled owl, sir.'

'Ah, Sheridan — very fellow!'

Kemble latched the whites of his eyes on the theatre owner.

'Kemble.' Sheridan bowed slightly. 'All is arranged. Good Mr Shaw has another for Iago. Now, I must hurry to see Bob.'

Sheridan sidled down the corridor as Kemble lurched towards him.

'Sir, you are owing my dear sister —'

'Yes, yes, it is those very accounts I must see to, be assured.'

Sheridan turned on his heel and made a swift exit.

Having reached the relative peace and sanctuary of his office, Sheridan sighed deeply and proceeded to pour himself a liberal glass of port. Kemble had reminded him that his imperious elder sister, Mrs Siddons, the greatest tragedienne of the age, was growing increasingly loud in her demands for the monies which the company still owed to her. Let her join the long list! This constant carping for payment by his actors was tedious and irksome. Would they not all be the beneficiaries when the new Theatre Royal on Drury Lane was completed? The largest auditorium in Europe. Audiences the size of which they could only dream of! How they would all clamour to perform on his new stage then, for he would give them all the chance to see their careers blaze to the very heavens. Should they not express their support and gratitude rather than constantly grasp at his coat-tails for the recompense of some paltry amount? And this when all his attention must not, on any account, be diverted from the great enterprise.

He felt a swell of self-pity. No one seemed to appreciate his efforts nor understood the great burdens which he shouldered. After the order for demolition who else must raise the finance through subscriptions for the rebuild of the Theatre Royal? Was it not he, Sheridan, who had progressed the project on a visionary scale? He who had persuaded the Duke of Bedford to buy up the surrounding land and property and sell it on in order to create a truly palatial monument to theatre and entertainment? He who had suffered the setbacks and disagreements, seen the building works delayed with costs soaring and all manner of other headaches. The business required all his wit and charm to attract and keep the subscribers. All this whilst he kept his itinerant company together. First at The King's Theatre and now presently at The Haymarket Theatre — a better stage but a smaller audience.

Sheridan sighed dramatically. He had suffered these various weighty commitments all through his wife's last illness and her final demise the previous year, leaving him with charge of their son Tom and infant daughter Mary, to whom he had given his own name despite she was Eliza's child by Lord Edward Fitzgerald. That very same lord who had then seduced and married Sheridan's newly betrothed! All this whilst Sheridan also served his party and his country as a Member of

Parliament. He gulped the last of the port. A country now at war with Revolutionary France! He stamped his foot. That Mrs Siddons and the rest of these ingrate actors should be hounding him for payment at a time like this! It was unconscionable. Sheridan sighed again and replenished his glass.

There was a rap at his door.

'Who goes?' he shouted.

'Mr Sheridan, it is I, Bob Fairbrother,' came the response.

Sheridan swung open the door. 'Come in, come in, my dear fellow.'

He embraced his young factotum. 'Friend Bob, you must save me!'

'Sir?'

'Write whatever script you will, but I must not be harried. And on no account must Mr Kemble speak with me again this month.'

Bob Fairbrother shook his head and smiled. 'There must be some little titbit, Mr Sheridan, or you shall have a mutiny.'

Sheridan regarded his informal secretary. His eyes narrowed, this was not what he wanted to hear. And yet — he felt a moment of inspiration.

'Very well. A titbit. We shall offer a bonus! All may receive a bonus as evidence of our generosity and approbation.'

Fairbrother grinned. 'A bonus but no salary. That will do it very nicely, Mr Sheridan.'

'Good man. Let it be arranged — nothing too extravagant! Now, the Prince of Wales is in his box and I must pay my respects forthwith.'

There came at this moment another knock at his door. Sheridan immediately slipped into the shadows at one side and nodded to his secretary. At this instruction the young man opened the door a fraction.

A low voice made enquiry from without. 'Sir, I look for Mr Sheridan on a matter of urgency, if you would be so good.'

'Then I must disappoint you, Constable —'

'Nicholls!' Sheridan exclaimed as he revealed himself. 'A pleasure to see you as ever.'

The Bow Street Runner bowed. 'Sir.'

'And how, might I enquire, is the beautiful Mrs Nicholls?'

'She is well, Mr Sheridan, I thank you.' Constable Nicholls paused, then added, 'And with child.'

'Aha!' Sheridan raised his glass in toast. 'I knew it should not be long. I wish you both all the inestimable joys of parenthood.' He smiled warmly at the constable whose wedding celebrations he had attended in the earlier part of the year.

'Shall you have a glass in celebration, Louis-Pierre?'

'Thank you kindly, sir, but no.'

'Ah yes, not on duty, if I remember.'

'And it is on duty, sir, that I am here.'

Sheridan frowned. 'How so?' His mind raced to the various possibilities that might bring the forces of law and order to his door.

'There is a bagnio nearby in Covent Garden and within we have found one who may be of your theatrical company.'

'That should not be a rarity I hazard!' Sheridan offered flippantly; he imagined most of his actors were beyond a passing acquaintance with the profusion of brothels on their doorstep. He laughed and then straightened as he eyed the serious demeanour of the Runner. 'But your looks tell me there is something gravely amiss.'

'And there are details of this case which are of a delicate nature.' Constable Nicholls cast a wary glance towards Bob Fairbrother.

'Rest assured, Constable, I have the utmost trust in Bob's integrity.'

Fairbrother bowed. 'Nevertheless, sirs, I must be elsewhere if you will excuse me.'

As the door closed after his secretary Sheridan turned again to the constable.

'This relates to one of my company, you say?'

'One who may be of your company. And fatally so, Mr Sheridan.'

'Ah … that is most dreadful.' Sheridan grimaced. 'An illness? An accident?'

Nicholls shook his head to both suggestions.

'Murder?'

'Most foul, sir.' Nicholls paused. 'It has been suggested the man may be an actor and I wondered, Mr Sheridan, if you would identify him.'

Sheridan flinched at the thought. 'Might I suggest my stage manager, Mr Shaw, for that task. He knows all our merry band.'

Nicholls shook his head. 'I think you will understand the need for discretion, sir, when you have witnessed the scene.'

Sheridan emptied his glass and set it down carefully.

'Very well, Constable. It seems we two are once again to be engaged with murderous deeds.'

CHAPTER TWO

To Sheridan's surprise, the bath house in question was apparently not a house of prostitution like every other bagnio of the city, but did indeed offer extensive bathing facilities. Found in the depths of an unprepossessing building hidden in the backstreets near Covent Garden, the bagnio was built on the remains of an original Roman bath house. These ruins were in the process of being restored, explained Mr Culpepper, the tremulous proprietor, who leaned heavily on his cane. There was much still to accomplish but the complex already offered a small communal pool, the *natatio*, apparently fed from an underground hot spring. Sheridan screwed his nose at the rather malodorous vapours. There were various rooms to be found, the *caldarium*, *tepidarium* and *frigidarium* — the later awaiting renovation. And cubicles in which, Sheridan was informed, various services might be offered, scrubbing, steaming, or massaging of the torso in the Turkish style. The heating was supplied by a hypocaust system proclaimed Culpepper with undisguised pride.

'We have much still to learn from the Romans, sir, such a civilized society.'

Sheridan wondered that he had never heard of the establishment amongst his circle. When he voiced this ignorance to the proprietor, the older man shifted his eyes.

'It is a gentleman's bathing establishment, Mr Sheridan, nothing more,' he murmured.

In the dimly lit area the hollow echo of the dripping water formed a constant backdrop. Sheridan appraised his surroundings. The spartan brick walls, the scarcity of

17

decoration beyond pillar and arch, and he nodded slowly in understanding. Of course, there was nothing of the feminine here, no intimations of licentiousness.

'Mr Culpepper, if you will,' Constable Nicholls enjoined.

The bagnio's owner led them down a corridor and pointed to a door with the silver tip of his cane.

'Gentlemen.' Mr Culpepper stood aside.

'No one has entered since?' asked Nicholls.

'Your watchman above has made sure of that, Constable. And I should never wish to see this sight again, sir,' he added with a shudder and backed away.

Nicholls nodded. 'We shall need more particulars, Mr Culpepper, so do not stray far.'

Culpepper sniffed. 'I shall be in the upstairs parlour, gentlemen.'

Nicholls turned to Sheridan. 'If you are ready, sir.'

Sheridan took a breath and nodded, despite his dread of what he might see.

The constable opened the door. Sheridan felt a sudden warmth come from within. There were some remnant wisps of the steam which had risen through pipes to fill the small chamber, but nothing which could hide the naked form slumped on the bench in front of them. Nor disguise the gruesome scene.

The man's throat had been cut. But that was the least of the horror. Between his splayed legs a large pool of blood had formed, having gushed from the wound that once was his manhood. That appendage now protruded from the victim's mouth — a limp and shrivelled thing.

Sheridan gagged and turned his head.

'I am sorry for this, sir. But I must ask, do you know this man?'

Nicholls leant forward and carefully raised the man's head into full view so that his fair hair fell away from his face.

Sheridan forced himself to glance again at the abomination.

He nodded. 'It is Andrew Marson.'

His stomach lurched to see the handsome features of his promising young performer so desecrated, and he now saw that on Andrew's bloodied forehead the killer had carved some sign.

'My poor Iago.'

Nicholls looked at him enquiringly.

'Iago in *Othello*. The part he should have been playing at this very time. To great acclaim, I might add. Mr Marson was an actor of immense charm but also talent. A true talent. For he could take the evil Iago and lend him a most beguiling face.'

'Thank you, Mr Sheridan. I appreciate your assistance.'

'Who would commit so monstrous an act? This is beyond anything in the ordinary way of assassination.'

'That it is, sir.'

'The bloody markings on his forehead — can you tell what they are?'

The constable shrugged. 'A simple triangular shape, it would seem.'

Sheridan nodded. 'But upside down methinks. Inverted.'

'Does it have a meaning?'

It was Sheridan's turn to shrug.

Nicholls picked up a sheet discarded on the bench which had once clothed Marson's naked torso and which he now draped gently over the corpse.

'You will capture this villain, Constable? Say that you will!'

'Now here is the rub, Mr Sheridan. I know that I may confide in you. This will not be an easy matter. In this business I will be met by the most profound silence.'

'But there cannot be anyone here who does not wish to see this killer dancing a long and lively jig on the scaffold at Newgate.'

Nicholls appraised Sheridan. 'You must know this is no ordinary establishment, sir.'

Sheridan smirked. 'A bagnio that is not a bawdy house — that is unusual, I will grant.'

'Oh, but it is a brothel, sir; one that is frequented by men who prefer the company of other men.'

Realisation dawned on Sheridan. He glanced towards the draped form of his deceased actor. 'My poor, poor fool. I did not know. Mr Marson was ever attentive to the ladies, both the females of the company and those ladies of the audience who would seek out a favourite actor. They swooned at the sight of his becoming features, you know, and he seemed to flit like a honeybee from one lady to another, sucking at their pollen, or so I fancied.'

'Men of this sort must live lives of the utmost secrecy.'

'Of course. You are right.' Sheridan paled. 'I remember well the fate of those unfortunates who were dragged to the pillory some years back.'

'Our mob justice saves its worst for these men.'

'It is a cruel fate for any man to be so inclined.'

'I have no doubt that Mr Culpepper is a Madge Cove, however fine a gentleman he may present himself.'

'If there is one thing which I have learnt in the theatre, Constable, it is that nothing is at it seems, nor any man neither.'

'No doubt he would have preferred to dispose of Mr Marson's body discretely rather than raise the alarm and draw attention to his Molly house, but that option was forestalled by one of his servants. Tobias, the attendant who happened on the scene, came straightway to the Runners in great fear.'

'The man did not haste to his master first?'

'No.'

'That is strange, is it not?'

'It is,' Nicholls continued. 'But I believe there is a plausible explanation. Your actor may not be the first to have met this wicked end. Tobias kept repeating, "It has happened again! None of us are safe!"' Nicholls sighed. 'Last month a body was dragged from the river by the officers of the new Public Office at Shadwell. A boy, perhaps sixteen or seventeen. His throat had been cut and his member removed like this.' He nodded towards Marson. 'They were unable to identify the lad and no one claimed him. At the time it was reasoned the murder might be an act of revenge, a particularly vicious one. At Shadwell it was speculated that the lad was an apprentice who had raised the skirts of his master's wife and had his manhood sliced off for his trespass. Such conjectures raised much hilarity,' Nicholls added with obvious distaste.

Sheridan's eyes narrowed. 'But you believe this to have been the work of the same killer?'

'I consider that possibility.' Nicholls turned towards the corpse. 'When I saw this scene, I began to suspect that the lad in the Thames had been tipped into the river not by the assassin who had slain him, but by those who did not want the lad's body discovered on their premises. Tobias' dread rang fresh in my ears, *It has happened again! None of us are safe!* I think by that he means that all who share the same sexual proclivities face danger from this killer.

'You think the lad may have been murdered here?'

Nicholls nodded. 'He was a catamite, I suspect. No molly house would invite the Runners within under any circumstance for fear of what we should do. Such places have been ransacked and destroyed in the past. Nor, I am sure, would Mr Culpepper wish to advertise the perils to his existing custom. No. All traces of murder would be hidden and cleared away.'

'And the assassin at liberty to do it again.' A detail occurred to Sheridan and he continued, 'Did the young lad have those strange markings on his brow?'

Nicholls shook his head. 'Not as reported from Shadwell. But the killer may have been disturbed and fled. Or, this triangle is some new unpleasant addition to his method.'

Sheridan flinched.

'If my suspicions are true, then Mr Marson is not the first victim of this killer but perhaps the second or even third such victim and I fear we may not expect much assistance from these quarters.' The constable jerked his head upward to indicate the proprietor on the floor above. 'When the watchman and I arrived all else had fled the building — no doubt when Mr Culpepper discovered the body for himself and realised that Tobias was missing, he immediately closed the bagnio. In our haste from Bow Street Tobias also slipped our grasp. And so, you see there are none to answer my enquiries.'

Sheridan gazed at the draped figure. At the pool of blood congealing on the stone floor. What a sad end was this. He tried to recall if Mr Marson had any family or particular friends who might care about his demise. All that he could recollect was that the young man had come to him from a company of travelling players based in York some two years previous, not long before the closure of the old theatre on Drury Lane.

Kemble had recognised the talent and ambition immediately, sensing in Marson something of his younger self, the same serious intent on the craft of performance, be it tragedy or comedy. Marson had been nurtured and raised within the company by the actor-manager and many times cast in roles to support Kemble. Kemble would mourn his loss. Kemble might even know something of his family history. Did he know of his sexual proclivities? Sheridan would enquire. He could not turn away from this now however much he might wish to.

'None to answer your enquiries? We shall see about that, Mr Nicholls. We shall see.'

Sheridan allowed himself a fleeting smile. He felt certain that the young constable had calculated on just such a response from him. He regarded the officer. From the first, Sheridan had sensed an affinity between them. Nicholls was quick and curious. A man of integrity but not one who was unduly inflexible. The policeman could be driven by a searing sense of justice, which was not always shared by his fellow Runners by any means, but he was also pragmatic and sanguine. Above all, however, it was his depth of feeling and humanity which had impressed Sheridan. What an unusual man he was. An outsider too. His mother being one of the French Huguenot community of St Giles. Since the troubles in France he did not doubt that Louis-Pierre had seen the ugly face of King Mob turned against all those with French connections, no matter their leanings. The execution of Louis XVI in January and the recent declaration of war from Revolutionary France had only exacerbated the prejudice.

Yes, he concluded wryly, Constable Nicholls had calculated that by drawing him in to this matter, Sheridan's own sense of fair play would be aroused and that the murder of one of his company would guarantee his interest in the business of arresting the perpetrator. Sheridan shivered. The last vestiges of warmth had drained from the small, steaming chamber.

'If you are to catch the villain who has committed this monstrous act you shall need all the answers from Mr

Culpepper you can get. If you deem that I may be of assistance in this matter, Mr Nicholls, then I am happy to oblige.'

'Gratefully accepted, sir.'

'And then, if you have no objection, I shall ask my secretary, Mr Fairbrother, to move our deceased actor to an undertaker nearby, from whence we may arrange a funeral. As I have suggested to you, Bob Fairbrother is a man of complete discretion. No one need know the particular details if you consider it would hamper your investigation.'

The constable's features creased into a frown. 'That is my chief concern, Mr Sheridan. I fear that if we trumpet this murder we may not advance with any chance of success. Unfortunately, I can expect little assistance from the officers at Bow Street; the murder of a man of this sort will be little more to them than the sauce for jest. There will be no hue and cry, they will have no care to catch the assassin, and if let loose on Mr Culpepper or this establishment may well scare any that would speak further underground...'

'What are you suggesting, Nicholls?'

'That to those beyond these walls we speak of a tragic accident.'

Sheridan regarded Nicholls keenly. Was this officer of the law really proposing to promulgate such a falsehood and expecting Sheridan to collude in the matter? A flaw in the stratagem immediately occurred to him.

'The watchman that is with you?'

'Never entered the chamber. Has not seen the body.'

'Can you be sure? When you came to fetch me from —'

'I am certain,' Nicholls cut in. Bartholomew is one of the few amongst my fellows that I can trust wholeheartedly.'

The constable's eyes searched his own. Waiting for an answer.

Sheridan cast a final glance at the shrouded form of the young actor. He felt a surge of anger along with his despair. The majority might claim that a man of Marson's tastes merited no consideration, that he had brought upon himself the wrath of God and the fires of Hell to which he would be most surely damned, but in his mind's eye Sheridan saw only a young man of grace and charm, who, to his knowledge had hurt no one nor thought ill of any other. A member of his theatrical fraternity. There would be justice for Andrew Marson. He would do his utmost to see to it.

CHAPTER THREE

They found Mr Culpepper in a small parlour up on the ground floor. The older man clutched his cane and leaning heavily on it, rose to his feet as they entered. Sheridan noticed that his rather elaborate and old-fashioned peruke was a little askew.

'Gentleman this is a dreadful and distressing business.'

'Of such disturbance that all save yourself, sir, have vacated the building, even your servants and attendants?'

'That is so.'

Sheridan clapped his hands and shook his head as if in wonder. 'I marvel at the lack of morbid curiosity amongst your servants, sir; curiosity is an attribute which I have always held to be supreme to their calling. But it seems that I must revise my opinions.'

'May I offer you some refreshment, gentlemen?'

Nicholls shook his head.

Sheridan eyed the proffered bottle of brandy with a lurch of desire but he knew it would not do to give in to temptation at this crucial juncture. With the consoling thought that he should drown a bumper later, he too shook his head, albeit rather less decisively.

'That is a kind offer, sir, but we must decline. All our wits, few as I may have, will be needed in this matter. I declare my interest. The poor unfortunate is indeed an actor of mine, a Mr Marson.'

'I am very sorry to hear that, Mr Sheridan, very sorry indeed, you may have my condolences of course. But I do not know how I may help you, sirs. I know nothing, I am afraid. Nothing at all. Nothing.'

'It is murder that we deal with here Mr Culpepper,' Nicholls interjected, 'and any little that you may recollect, however small the detail, will assist the investigation.'

'We are a simple bath house offering a number of services to our many customers. Gentlemen come and go throughout the day, there is much traffic and I have not the slightest notion how this terrible act of barbarity should have occurred on these premises.' Mr Culpepper trembled. 'Nor by whom.'

'You have no suspicions?'

'A foreigner I would say, if pressed.'

'And why might that be?'

'The act being so savage, Constable.' The proprietor explained as though this was the only natural supposition, tapping his cane vehemently on the floor to underline his opinion. 'We are visited by many foreigners. An Ottoman gentleman, I noted, has been here today and an Italian señor I believe, as well as the many French émigrés we number at present. Please be seated, gentlemen, I am afraid I must. I am most shaken by these events.'

Culpepper groped for the arm of his chair and collapsed into the seat.

'Was Mr Marson known to you, sir?' Nicholls remained standing.

'Not "known", Constable, but I do recall that the young gentleman had visited us on previous occasions.'

'At what time did Mr Marson arrive?' Nicholls pressed.

Culpepper shook his head and began to wring his hands. 'I did not see for myself, but I believe it was sometime in the afternoon.'

'Did you see him at all?'

'Once, only. He was taking the waters in the pool — it has mineral properties, very beneficial. There were maybe half a dozen gentlemen bathing at that time.'

'And what time was that, Mr Culpepper?'

'I think it was four o'clock or thereabouts.'

'Your servant Tobias came to us just before eight. That is a span of some three or four hours in which Mr Marson may have met his untimely end.'

'The gentleman was in a steaming room.'

Sheridan crossed the parlour to avail himself of a large and comfortable-looking chair. He should at least be at his ease if he could not be in liquor.

'Steaming? Is that a popular activity in your establishment?'

'One of our most popular, Mr Sheridan. It is thoroughly cleansing, sir.'

'Not sure I should care to be steamed to the colour of a beetroot myself. I noticed that Mr Marson was made quite roseate despite the blood loss. Was he so when you found him?'

'Mr Marson may have been overlong in the chamber.'

'I should say he was; damn fellow was due at The Haymarket at six-thirty for a quick turn in the opening pageant and then to appear in the Shakespeare. Mr Kemble has been most inconvenienced. Now it seems I have no cause to fine Marson after all. And come to think of it, I did remark his absence, he was normally a most punctilious young man.'

'We might conjecture then that Mr Marson met his end before six-thirty?' Nicholls proffered. 'Or slightly earlier, allowing for the time he would have given himself to dress and make his way to the theatre.'

'Odd that he should not have been discovered sooner then? Gentlemen wandering in and out about the place — or are these chambers perhaps reserved, Mr Culpepper?' Sheridan quizzed.

The older man hesitated. 'Gentlemen may sometimes wish for privacy.'

'You keep a record of reservations, sir?' Nicholls pounced. 'There should be an extra charge, I imagine.'

Mr Culpepper shifted uneasily.

'We must see the ledger, Mr Culpepper,' the constable insisted.

Culpepper sighed and then rose stiffly.

'Very well, gentlemen. If you will excuse me for one moment.'

The proprietor left the room.

'This is a damnable business, Nicholls.' Sheridan thumped the arm of his chair.

'Let us hope that the book may tell us whom we must seek for this murderous act.'

Sheridan snorted. 'Then do not be surprised if our good Mr Culpepper returns to inform us that his ledger has been stolen. He does not want poor Marson's assassin found at all, for that will bring nothing but notoriety to his establishment.'

Nicholls glowered. 'There will be no establishment without his co-operation in this matter. It shall be closed down. I shall see to it.'

Sheridan raised an eyebrow.

They heard the awkward rhythm of the cane and Mr Culpepper appeared in the doorway clutching a large accounting book.

'Ah...' Sheridan stood and exchanged a quick glance of surprise with the constable at seeing the tome.

The ledger was laid out on a small table. Mr Culpepper stood aside as the constable began to leaf through its contents. It recorded in a neat and legible hand the business of the establishment and the amounts paid. In the list for each day appeared the particulars. Nicholls hastened to the final entries and ran a finger down the inventory.

He stabbed. 'Is this the chamber where we found Mr Marson?'

The proprietor nodded.

'There are the initials A.M. marked here … and numbers — a five and two … the price? Or the time?'

'The chamber to be available for two hours from five o'clock.'

'Well, here is our fellow!' Sheridan gleamed. 'It is a Mr A.M. — who might that stand for, Culpepper?'

'I cannot say.'

Nicholls turned back through one page after another. 'All the entries are initials.'

'That is our method, Constable.'

'There must be a record, an index, of the names they signify?'

Culpepper shook his head. 'I am afraid not.'

'But damn it!' Sheridan spread his hands in confusion. 'To what address do you send the account if you have no notion who your customers are, Mr Culpepper?'

'There is no business on account, sir, everything must be settled in advance.'

'In advance, Good God!' Sheridan could not hide his astonishment. 'I wonder you do any business at all!'

The constable underlined the initials with his finger. 'A.M.? It is Mr Marson, of course. Have you not said your actor's name was Andrew, Mr Sheridan?'

Sheridan's face deflated. 'Ah, yes. Andrew Marson. But why would Marson reserve the chamber past the time when he should be expected for performance?'

Nicholls frowned. 'You think his killer had the same initials? Such a coincidence would be strange and rare.'

Sheridan wheeled about to face the proprietor. 'Do you mean us to understand, sir, that you know none of your customers by name? That you are familiar with none of them? That you recognise not one single gentleman? Come, Mr Culpepper, you must have the name of at least one fellow who has been here today?'

The older man tottered backwards on his heels as though he feared Sheridan's advance.

'There is one I have heard addressed as Mr Bumblechook.'

'Mr Bumblechook? I wonder I do not know that character. And another, sir?'

Culpepper grimaced as though straining to recall. 'Mr Strutwell.'

'Ah, that is a character I do recognise! Strutwell. Appears in Mr Smollett's novel *Roderick Random*, does he not?'

'I have not had the pleasure of reading Smollett, sir.'

'Do go on, pray, I am rather enjoying your dramatis personae.'

'Mr Peckersniff … I believe.'

'Peckersniff … Peckersniff, that I do not doubt.'

'Sir,' Nicholls cut in. 'Mr Marson's attire? He did not walk here through Covent Garden in his birthday suit I'll warrant.'

Mr Culpepper appeared to flush momentarily, perhaps at the image thus conjured, Sheridan suspected.

They were escorted below the stairs again and were led into an antechamber immediately off to the right.

'This is the undressing room — what the Romans would have called the apodyterium. My man, Tobias, helps the gentlemen disrobe and there is a wardrobe here.' Culpepper pointed to a large piece of oak furniture.

Nicholls tried the handle. Hanging within he found one costume.

'He was a man of taste, your Mr Marson.'

'Yes, I wonder that he dressed so fine on an actor's salary.'

Nicholls began a thorough search of the pockets. He extracted a linen handkerchief and then a key, shortly followed by a silver pocket watch.

'This has been well crafted, in Soho or The City I should say. See if there may be an inscription if you would, Mr Sheridan.'

Nicholls continued with his search, extracting a purse, the coins jingling as he weighed it in his palm.

Sheridan squinted and examined the timepiece by the lantern light, admiring the white enamel dial with Roman numerals. The inner side of the casing had been engraved.

Omnia vincit amor
J.B.

'Love conquers all.'

'*Et nos cedamus amori.*' Nicholls completed the phrase as he turned to Sheridan, 'Let us yield to love.'

Sheridan raised an eyebrow. Here was a constable who knew his Virgil.

Nicholls grinned. 'It is a popular inscription, sir, and my father-in-law is a watchmaker as you may recall.'

'Of course, Monsieur De Lubac.'

'He may recognise who has made this piece — and the watchmaker may have a record of who ordered and purchased it.'

Sheridan span around to Mr Culpepper. 'Do the initials J.B. ring any bells, Culpepper? Jeroboam Balderdash, perhaps?'

The older man recoiled and edged back towards the door.

'My Iago is dead, sir, and I will not be played for a fool!'

Culpepper looked startled. 'I do not know any J.B., sir. I swear to you!'

Sheridan continued to glare at the proprietor as he snapped the lid of the pocket watch shut.

CHAPTER FOUR

It had been Sheridan's original intent to spend the night at Nerot's Hotel after dining with His Royal Highness at Carlton House. He should have to send his apologies. He knew that the prince wished to discuss some matter with him, but it would have to wait. He was in no mood now to entertain either the prince or his guests. Having spoken with Bob Fairbrother regarding arrangements for the deceased and presumed on his confidence in the matter, Sheridan ordered his carriage to take him home to Wanstead. He wanted to be far from the city. The gruesome business at the bagnio had unnerved him. That final image of Andrew Marson flashed before him like a scene from a particularly ghastly Jacobean tragedy.

Indeed, the more he thought of it, the more it did seem to him that the scene had been staged. The figure arranged and disported to best effect the utmost horror in whomever should find it. In his mind's eye, Sheridan conjured the shadowy killer stepping back to admire his grisly creation.

The small chamber lit by one dim flickering lantern on the wall. There would have been swirling wreathes of steam. Resembling smoke rising from the very depths of Hell, Sheridan imagined. Yes, he nodded to himself, for the man who found Marson that would have been the atmosphere, satanic and supernatural. Smoke machines were a favourite device in the theatre and often used to create such chimerical scenes. Emerging from the mist, the man would have seen the indistinct naked figure centred on the bench. He would have had to step forward, straining to see more clearly. First, the

34

startled shock in the victim's own wide eyes. Then, the man would take a step back perhaps, not wanting to believe that the object lodged in Mr Marson's mouth could be his own manhood. But he would be drawn ever closer. And at last, his gaze would rush to that gaping wound and the whole sickening spectacle would reveal itself before his horrified eyes.

Sheridan shivered. It was a cold night, which reminded that a frost could still come even in May. He drew his greatcoat tighter around his frame. The final abomination were those markings on the forehead. An inverted triangle they had thought, but he had not cared to examine the bloody marks more closely. What were they? Not murderous cuts. The throat had been the first and fatal cut, he hoped.

The cuts on the brow surely signified something to the assassin, of that he was sure. A branding perhaps? The mark of Cain? A symbolic sign of some punishment or judgement? Or, the killer's own signature? He wanted his deadly creation to be viewed by an audience. But whom? If Nicholls was right, and Andrew Marson was not the first victim, was the assassin frustrated that his work was not more publicly heralded or on display? Nicholls had pressed Mr Culpepper to silence on the matter, he was to speak to no one, it should not reach the press. What was it that Nicholls hoped? That with the promise of discretion a witness might come forth? Was it a risk worth taking? Without a hue and cry the killer could be tempted to venture out once more. Sheridan shivered again as the carriage rattled over the cobblestones that brought him to the High Street in Wanstead.

The coachman drew up outside the house. Glancing out from the carriage window Sheridan could see the warm glow of lights within. There would be a good fire still in the hearth and he would be welcomed home with unexpected delight. He readied himself to leave all thoughts of death and murder on his doorstep and to enter instead into the life and joy of his family.

It was the sound of wailing that greeted him first as he handed his coat and hat to his manservant. Mehitabel Canning marched from the front receiving room carrying a squirming, screeching child within her firm grasp. In her wake followed the anxious nursemaid Martha biting her lip and on her heels Sheridan's son, Tom, brought up the rear, grinning from ear to ear.

Mehitabel patted the infant's back. 'Come, come child. Enough of your tears! You shall not escape us now, Mary, aided and abetted as you have been by your foolish brother, who is old enough to know better. It is time you were abed and abed you shall be!'

'Oh, Aunt Hitty you have spoilt all our amusement! We are rehearsing a most marvellous charade.' Tom sighted his father and sprang towards him. 'Pa will be most entertained!'

Mehitabel paused on the lip of the stairs. 'Dick, you are home. We did not expect you until the weekend.'

Sheridan bowed and addressed Mrs Canning by his fond, teasing nickname for her. 'Good Sister Christian, I am an inconvenience, shall I step outside my house again?'

Tom grabbed Sheridan in an embrace. 'If you do, Pa, you must take me with you! Else I shall be tongue-whipped!' He glanced back to Mrs Canning and laughed merrily.

Mehitabel shook her head but could not quite disguise the indulgent smile which tugged at the corner of her mouth.

From the library a soberly dressed young man emerged clutching a leather-bound volume. Sheridan turned towards him.

'Mr Smyth might think you should be horsewhipped, Tom. Is that not so, Mr Smyth? There has been some mischief I take it? A good thrashing, I say.'

Tom feigned shock. 'Pa! I am too old to be whipped now, I am seventeen.'

Sheridan continued to glare at the tutor. 'When King George himself insists that his sons are roundly thrashed by their tutors one must consider it a duty and a condition of employment, Mr Smyth.'

The young tutor looked momentarily stumped. 'Sir, I … I…'

Sheridan broke into a broad smile. 'But we are of a more modern and enlightened bent, do you not agree, William?'

William Smyth flushed and gave a slight bow to his employer.

'And where is the cause of all this commotion?' Sheridan advanced toward Mary. Her guardian was struggling to keep the infant of fourteen months in check.

Mary strained towards her father with outstretched arms. 'Pa … Pa…'

Her pretty face was smeared with powder and rouge streaked by the tears which ran through the paint.

Sheridan nodded to the reluctant Mrs Canning to permit him to take the child into his arms.

'And what is this strange creature, pray?' He blew a raspberry at her.

'She is Cupid, Father,' Tom enlightened. 'I have written a little comedy with Bessie. We are all to entertain you this weekend. Only Mary has not learnt all her lines yet … nor quite succeeded in her aim with the bow and arrow,' Tom added with a dramatic sigh.

Bessie Canning emerged at that moment holding the miniature weapon. She beamed at Sheridan. 'But Mary is very pretty and will quite steal the hearts of all our audience, which is only proper to the part of Cupid.' Bessie patted the infant on the head.

'Ah Cupid, where will your arrow fall? Your poor papa is quite unloved so let it be for me.' Sheridan jiggled the child until she laughed. He felt that sudden lurch of joy coupled with the pain of sadness which so often assailed his heart when he held the child. His wife had died barely three months after her birth, before which it had been agreed by all that Sheridan would claim paternity although little Mary was the daughter of his wife's lover, Lord Edward Fitzgerald. Mary should not only have Sheridan's name but all his love he had vowed. Before she died, the ever-practical Eliza Sheridan had insisted that her dear friend Mrs Canning should also be the child's guardian. A wise move it was conceded, even by Sheridan himself.

Mrs Canning flapped her hands. 'Come, Bessie, it is late, we must to our own home. I see that Mary will not be settled now whilst the Lord of Misrule is in residence again.' She nodded to the manservant to bring their cloaks.

'Mama,' Bessie whined, 'it is not so very late and we have yet to practice the duet.'

Tom nodded furiously. 'And Bessie shall need all the practice that she can get, I can assure you!'

Bessie poked at her playmate. 'Speak for yourself, Tom Sheridan.'

Sheridan glanced at the two young people and back again to Mary. 'Cupid, forsooth. Are you not meant to bring Peace and Love?'

And was love already budding if not yet blooming before his eyes? Tom, at seventeen, was avid to play the gallant, that he already knew. But here was Mehitabel's daughter at sixteen turning into a young woman before his eyes that had only ever seen her as a child and a sister to his son. The move to Wanstead had brought the two families into close and familiar proximity, but should there be more than the familial between Tom and Bessie? And how should he respond? Mehitabel seemed unaware, so perhaps he imagined the frisson between the two youngsters.

'Dick, will you call tomorrow when you rise?'

Sheridan hesitated. When would he rise? It was often the afternoon before he felt inclined to do so.

'Join us after lunch,' Mrs Canning decided for him.

Sleep eluded Sheridan and when it finally came vague horrors stalked his dreams until he awoke in a sweat. Just before dawn he rose and paced the room with a glass of port in hand. He cursed Constable Nicholls for having lured him into this affair. Andrew Marson had met a grotesque end. But given his sexual tastes, young Marson had most knowingly run the risk of a violent end. If caught and charged, the least he might expect, along with fines and imprisonment, was the pillory. That was no laughing matter. There would be no mercy from the spectators. He would be pelted with mud and offal, dead cats, turnips and brickbats. He could be seriously injured. If unlucky, he might be blinded, or even killed by the mob's enthusiasm, as had been the case on more than one occasion.

The assassin would strike again. Of that Nicholls seemed certain. He had ordered Mr Culpepper to close his bagnio for the foreseeable. That might thwart the killer in the immediate days but he was likely to seek other venues, the constable confided. The officer had taken away the ledger and other items to examine more closely. He had demanded a list of the servants and attendants, and advised the proprietor to scour his own memories more thoroughly.

What more could be done? What could he, Sheridan, do? He might offer a reward but who would come forward? None, he hazarded. For to do so might risk identification as a lover of men. No. He might only ensure that Marson received a Christian burial. To that end he had instructed Bob Fairbrother and suggested that the death be advertised within the company as a tragic accident. Bob could script the details if pressed. As for justice… That was a forlorn hope Sheridan concluded as he wheeled about the room.

He paused.

Perhaps there were one or two things he might do.

Moments later he was knocking impatiently on the door of the bedchamber next to his own. He listened at the door, knocked again and to his satisfaction at last heard sounds of movement.

A bleary-eyed William Smyth opened from within.

'Mr Sheridan?' The tutor blinked and then stared. 'Is there something amiss?'

Sheridan realised that he must present a startling appearance in his nightshirt, a glass of port clutched in one hand, but no matter.

'You're a scholar, Smyth, are you not? More than I ever was, I'll warrant.'

'Oh, I am sure you were — are — sir, I believe,' the young man stuttered and caught at a yawn.

'Yes, you are just the fellow.'

'Do you need me to dress —?'

'A triangle. But upside down. What might that mean?'

'Triangle?'

'Yes. Inverted.'

'Well…' Smyth tried to shake himself awake and then screwed his eyes, glancing quickly to Sheridan. 'Is this some sort of test, sir?'

'Matter of life and death, William.' For a moment he was tempted to unburden himself and divulge the horrors of the evening, but the earnest boyish look of the young tutor stayed the impulse.

'I see. Well … there may be a number of meanings…'

'Such as?'

'In the Hellenic tradition it is a symbol for water, a chalice you see.'

Sheridan nodded. 'Yes, well plenty of that around. And?'

William blushed slightly. 'Then also the female … you know…' he demonstrated by shaping his hands to the cleft between the thighs.

Sheridan grinned. 'Organs, genitals — yes! Pyramid would be male, erect and the other way round —' he spilt the last of his port as he aped the tutor. 'Female. Hmm. I suppose that is of interest.'

'There are other symbolic meanings, I am certain, but they do not spring so immediately to mind.' The tutor stifled another yawn.

'Thank you, Mr Smyth, I am most grateful.' He turned away and then swiftly back with an afterthought. 'If you should recollect any other…'

'Of course, sir.'

Sheridan returned to his own chamber and climbed into bed. He felt all at once overcome with a satisfying weariness as his head fell back on the pillow and before long he had drifted into sleep.

Mehitabel wanted to speak of her nephew, George Canning.

She had been as a mother to him since the death of her brother-in-law, when the boy was but one year old. He had needed a good-hearted and dependable mother, poor lad, his own being so unreliable. Sheridan knew well the nature of Mary Ann Costello, who on the death of her husband had been forced onto the stage as an actress in order to make ends meet. There were times he recognised aspects of himself in her charming disorder. Was it something in the Irish disposition? Of the artistic type most assuredly.

George was now a young man of twenty-two or thereabouts but his father's recklessness had left the boy with limited financial resources. His uncle, Stratford Canning, had recognised the youngster's potential and helped to put him through Eton, where he had distinguished himself without parallel. Then on to Oxford. Stratford had nurtured hopes that George, a young man of marked intellect and ambition, might be welcomed into the political fold despite his impecunity and the rather risqué reputation of his mother. Even as a boy, George had been introduced to leading members of the Whig party; to Fox and Burke and of course the friendship with Sheridan was of long standing. But Stratford had died when George was seventeen and since then the widowed Mehitabel had become perennially anxious in the furtherance of her nephew's future prospects.

He was presently studying the law, but Sheridan knew that the lure of Westminster was equally as strong as it had once been for him. To Mrs Canning's horror and dismay George had expressed his admiration of Mr Pitt, the Prime Minister. Indomitable as ever, Mehitabel continued to nurse a desire to see him returned to the true path of Whiggery. She was above all else a Whig. An ardent supporter of Charles James Fox through these dark and unsettled times in the cause of Reform.

If George could only be got a Whig seat in Parliament that should bring him to his senses. This, Sheridan knew, was the object of Hitty's request to speak with him. What might he do for George?

Well, little to nothing, if all the rumours were true. Not because Sheridan did not wish to mentor the young man, he would gladly do so. There had even been some possibility that the Whigs' titular leader, the Duke of Portland, might arrange a seat. But no. Neither he nor Fox nor Portland was the man to give young George what he craved because that beneficence, it seemed, had at last fallen to William Pitt. Mehitabel would be appalled if she were to know of these developments. That her nephew should choose to actively throw his hat into the ring with Pitt and the government would be anathema to her. And Sheridan was not going to be the one to tell her.

He knew from his own experience how absolute Hitty might be. When his dear wife Eliza had become expectant with child by Lord Edward Fitzgerald, Mrs Canning had turned away in moral indignation. Eliza had been distraught at the loss of this most trusted friend and the solace and strength which she habitually drew from her. It had taken all of Sheridan's art and wiles to plead with Mehitabel that she show compassion towards Eliza. He had taken the entire blame for her affair onto himself. Loudly proclaimed that it was his own neglect and his unpardonable misdeeds which had driven his saintly wife into the arms of the young Irish lord. A man whom Sheridan much admired and with whom he shared almost every political principle. All had agreed that Sheridan would claim the child as his own. Nothing reprehensible should attach to Eliza, he insisted. Mrs Canning had at length softened and relented. Not a moment too soon. Poor sweet Eliza. Sheridan felt the lump rise in his throat every time he recalled her final illness and tragic death. Thankful that he and Hitty had both been there to add comfort to her end.

No, he would not let Good Sister Christian know that, in the wake of the current revolutionary excesses in France, young George Canning had turned his back entirely upon his Whig heritage and was now become one of The Friends of Mr Pitt with the promise of a seat from Mr Pitt himself. Sheridan stifled a wry smile, some wit had remarked that men had often turned their coats, but this was the first time a boy had turned his jacket.

'So, Dick, if you might speak with George when he visits with us this weekend. You will appreciate how keen he is and what an asset he might be to Mr Fox. I know he holds you in the highest regard and listens most assiduously to all you say.' Mehitabel sighed. 'If there could be some way that George might be got into Parliament for our party despite his means being so limited.'

Sheridan opened his arms wide. 'It is always a pleasure to speak with your nephew, but I think he is a young man who has always known his own mind, Hitty. It is a serious mind, and I suspect he finds mine altogether too comical.'

There. He would not be the one to disclose young Canning's treachery to his good aunt.

Mehitabel slapped Sheridan playfully on the arm. 'You forget, I know you, Dick, and you are far more serious than you pretend.'

Yes, perhaps he *was* more serious than he pretended. Everyone thought him the fount of gaiety, the charming wit at every gathering. Few witnessed the bouts of melancholy, the turbulent sea of anxieties which lay beneath that thin veneer of insouciance.

CHAPTER FIVE

The sound of retching assaulted his ears as Sheridan stood outside the privy. He had a fair idea who might be so dreadfully indisposed. The Prime Minister had looked more ashen than was usual during the last sitting. A pallor occasioned by the forthright attacks from Mr Fox across the floor of the Commons? Or the copious quantities of wine and port which William Pitt had already consumed that day? The latter, Sheridan decided. He had noticed the slight tremor in the Prime Minister's hand and the beads of sweat collecting on his brow. And now here he was disgorging his venison pie and a bottle of claret into the privy receptacle. Well, better that than behind Mr Speaker's chair. The previous occurrence of which had turned the air of the chamber more malodorous than ever. Sheridan smiled ruefully. England was at war with France and Mr Pitt was at war with his own stomach.

Sheridan almost felt sorry for his nemesis. All politicians drank to excess but it would be the death of 'Master Billy'. It was the price to be paid, Sheridan supposed, for taking on the great mantle of power at so tender an age. God's blood, young Pitt had only been twenty-four when the king had asked him to form a government! Of course, it had been the king who had insisted — anything to keep the Foxite Whigs out of office. But here William Pitt was, still at the helm nine years later and still an arrogant pup.

Sheridan owned he was envious at so meteoric a rise. He sighed. What he could have done with such an opportunity. He longed to make his mark on history for the cause of Reform. The Foxites had almost succeeded during the recent crisis of the king's madness, when the Prince of Wales might have been regent. Those were heady days which still made Sheridan giddy to think on. He had scuttled between Westminster and Carlton House and no one had achieved greater access to the ear of the prince. He had been acknowledged then as the right hand of Charles James Fox, and who knows, his potential successor. Mr Richard Brinsley Sheridan, Prime Minister. Sheridan sighed again. Such dreams must be laid aside for the foreseeable future.

Pitt emerged from the privy dabbing his handkerchief to his lips. He looked not only pale but shrunken about his thin frame, that reminded Sheridan of nothing so much as a dried twig.

'What-ho, Master Billy, you are seasick again? These are stormy times indeed and you may not have the stomach for them, methinks.'

'I shall survive them well enough, Sheridan.' Pitt held himself straight, albeit with a slight tremble. 'The storm may be weathered and then it is those who have had mutiny in their hearts who have most to fear.'

'We are all patriots here, Mr Pitt, only some of us are more ardent in our distaste for tyranny than others.' He hoped the barb had struck home at the author of the current oppressive regime.

Pitt's eyes narrowed. 'We shall soon see the true colour of your mettle, Mr Sheridan. I bid you good eve.'

With a curt bow the Prime Minister departed. Sheridan watched his retreat with a puzzled frown. What did the fellow mean by that last riposte? Was it no more than the usual jibes, or was there something sinister to it? Sheridan was well aware there were times he walked a tightrope. The government had used the excuses of war to become ever more belligerent and repressive, a man must take care between his friends and his actions. There were government spies and agents everywhere. Since the declaration of war, the general mood in England had darkened into a climate of fear and terror.

Only that day he had heard it reported that there were Frenchmen armed with daggers on the road from Harwich to London. Alarmist, of course, sent about by some government provocateur, but the mob, and in particular the riotous King and Church gangs, would believe whatever they were told. Sheridan himself might be deemed treasonous for his espousal of the revolutionary ideals of France. That did not mean he approved of the execution of Louis XVI or the increasing violence and extremity of factions in Paris. But in wartime men lost their reason. He must be on his guard. Even within his own Whig party the divisions were becoming rife, with many rushing to proclaim their support for the war effort. It saddened Sheridan that the old clarion cries for electoral reform grew fainter by the day.

It had been a late sitting in the House and Sheridan was tempted to join various of his fellows and enjoy the company and comforts offered by Brooks's Club. But sense prevailed. He should go to his bed. He was to attend on the prince in the morning. A note had arrived earlier in the evening insisting that the engagement should not be delayed further on any account. Sheridan groaned inwardly. He had an inkling that the prince wished to call in some favour to which he would not be able to say *nay*. Some scrape to be smoothed over, no doubt. Or something His Highness wanted?

He heard the deep throated laughter of his leader Charles James Fox as that swarthy bear of a man disappeared into his carriage, the to and fro of pleasant banter amongst his peers, and he was again of a mind to follow his friends. Reluctantly, Sheridan ordered his coachman to Nerot's Hotel.

As the carriage swayed and juddered over the cobbles of the Mall his mind burned and fizzed. He was always more alive at this hour than any other. What was the point of his good intentions? He would not sleep in any case. He was not yet ready for his bed. And then a thought occurred to him. They had left the Mall behind. It was but a little detour. He knocked to halt his coachman and ordered him to the premises of Mr Lowe.

Marson's body had been removed to the undertaker by Bob Fairbrother. A swift internment had been arranged for the morrow in the mid-afternoon. It should be a short funeral service as the young actor's demise would not occasion the cancellation of the evening's performance, and those few of the company who attended would be anxious to be in time for the theatre.

For all his charm, it seemed that Mr Marson had made few real friends within the Drury Lane troupe. He had kept to himself apparently and seldom drank with his fellow thespians, but rather rushed off to other engagements at the end of an evening. Sheridan could well imagine now the company young Andrew preferred to keep in the molly houses of the city, or perhaps he had haunted the byways of St James's Park in search of a soldier.

Kemble had been taken aback by Sheridan's revelations of the man's sexual proclivities. Clearly Marson had been the epitome of discretion. Or Kemble too drunk and fuddled by his medications to notice. The leading actor and manager had been magnanimous, nevertheless.

'Poor fellow ... each to his own, I daresay. He was a fine Shakespearean. It is a loss. Nay, a tragedy.'

'Did he ever speak of family, Kemble?'

The actor shook his head sadly. 'An orphan. So, he told meh. Run away as a boy to join an itinerant company. Pantomime, acrobatics. Durham, I think he said, but perhaps it was Carlisle.'

'Durham … Carlisle — you're sure it wasn't Harrogate?' Sheridan rolled his eyes.

'Was it Harrogate?' the actor asked.

Sheridan heaved a sigh. 'Well, no family we may contact in any case.'

Kemble threw his arms out in a sweeping gesture. 'The stage was Mr Marson's home. We were his brothers and sisters.'

'Yes, all very well. Any brothers in particular?'

Kemble paused for so long that Sheridan had been about to quit the dressing room.

'Blackett.'

'Blackett?'

'Marson had rather taken him under his wing. Advising the boy on his performance and so on.' Kemble nodded. 'He did acquit himself quite admirably last night in Mr Marson's place — for one so young. A plausible Iago.'

'Anyone else Marson held a brotherly affection for?'

Kemble raised his gaze to the ceiling in an attitude of contemplation.

'Well, if a name does come to mind — at length — do let me know, Kemble.'

Sheridan had turned on his heels and departed.

There had been no opportunity to seek out the young James Blackett. An avenue to be pursued later.

But it seemed there might indeed be another who was friend to Marson. Before departing the theatre for Westminster, Bob Fairbrother had found Sheridan to inform him that the rumours of a bonus had been carefully planted and were rapidly circulating the company. Bob grinned; the prospect seemed to have quelled all cries for salaries in arrears. As an aside, he went on to mention that the prompter, Nehemiah Quail, had enquired the whereabouts of Marson's body, asking that he might be allowed to keep a vigil in the night before the funeral. Bob had seen no reason for the request to be denied. Such religious inclinations being rare within the company, he had felt it should be encouraged.

'And Marson has been discretely shrouded, sir, so that the manner of his death may not be so apparent. I have spread it abroad that he had an unfortunate slip in a bath and the injury to his bonce proved sadly fatal.'

Nevertheless, Sheridan hoped that the coffin had been nailed down, he did not particularly wish to view that countenance again or to be reminded of the various mutilations. He did however wish to speak with Mr Quail, and if the prompter should know anything of import, then tonight he might be caught off guard and in private.

There was no sign of life as Sheridan alighted from his carriage and peered down the narrow street which led to the undertaker's premises. No light from the window above the entrance. Mr Lowe, who was a pleasant fellow, and his plump wife would be safely tucked up in their bed no doubt. But there was a door at the rear of the property which let into a yard. There were stables to one end and at the other the carpenter's workshop. Here coffins for the dead and other pieces of furniture for the benefit of the living were constructed and stored. Along with Mr Marson's corpse on this particularly black night.

Sheridan stumbled in the darkness and his eyes strained as he made his way along the passage, until a sliver of moonlight slipped out from behind a bank of clouds and showed him where the opening was set in the wall. He pushed at the door. A bolt rattled in its housing. He rapped. Gently at first and then a little louder. A dog barked nearby. The stir of movement from within signalled that he had at last been heard.

'Who goes?' a thin voice came from within.

'It is Mr Sheridan… You have one of my company within. I believe Mr Quail is keeping a vigil with the deceased?' he added by way of explanation.

The bolt was released and the door was inched open by a pale-faced youth. He held up a lantern, examined Sheridan, and then nodded in recognition.

'That's right, sir, there are some gentlemen from the theatre. Mr Lowe says as I was to let Mr Quail in. I thought there be only one, but there is another that arrived with him. That is all right, is it, sir?' The boy looked anxious.

'I am sure of it. I would join them in their vigil if you would be so kind.' He wondered who the other party might be. James Blackett perhaps? Then he might kill two birds with one stone.

Flustered, the boy opened the door wide enough to allow Sheridan entry.

'Pardon, sir, of course, come inside, I shall show you to them.'

Sheridan scrabbled in the pocket of his greatcoat and withdrew a coin which he presented to the apprentice. 'Here, take this for your trouble.' Across the yard he could see a faint thread of light emanating from a window. 'But I can easily find my way and you shall return to the comfort of your cot.'

'Thank you kindly, sir.' The boy shot the bolt again and turned back towards the stable.

Sheridan headed to the rear of the premises and slipped through the entrance. All was silence. As he edged forward through the gloom, the sound of his footfall was smothered by a thin layer of sawdust. He inhaled the smells of freshly shaved wood, pine resin and the reek of turpentine. In the glimmer he could distinguish a store of timber to one side and a workbench laid out with an unfinished coffin. He groped around the timbers, seeking the source of the dim glow of light which came from further within.

The casket was open and propped on a bier to the height of a low table. In the flickering candlelight he could discern a shadowy figure seated on a cricket stool and bent over the shrouded corpse of Mr Marson. Sheridan frowned. He did not recognise the lank and greasy strands of white hair which curtained the man's face. This was not Nehemiah Quail. And what was the ancient doing? Sheridan squinted in the gloom. Surely his eyes deceived him. The man appeared to be devouring something from inside the coffin. Sucking and chewing on something. Was this —? Could this be some grotesque rite of the cannibal?

With increasing horror Sheridan's curiosity edged him into the outer circle of candlelight. Disturbed, the figure paused in his feasting and looked up sharply. Two dark pinpricks were set in a face of evil intent. Sheridan let out a strangled shriek and felt his legs buckle beneath him.

CHAPTER SIX

Aroused by the pungent whiff of hartshorn burning up his nostrils, Sheridan blinked to consciousness.

'Mr Sheridan, sir, are you all right?'

It was Nehemiah Quail who was waving the smelling salts under his nose.

Sheridan gasped and clutched at Nehemiah's coat. 'Did you see? Mr Quail, did you witness?'

'Sir, sir — you have taken fright. I am heartily distressed.'

'What was that creature?'

'If I had only known... Your visit is most unexpected... Please allow me to explain.'

'The creature...?'

Mr Quail nodded. 'I own he has a fearful aspect, Mr Sheridan, and might almost be taken for a gargoyle in this light, but it is only Silas.'

Sheridan frowned with confusion. 'Silas?'

'Mr Roden, an ancient uncle of my mother's family.'

'Uncle? He was eating...'

'Bread, sir.'

'Bread?'

'Yes, and salt. That is the traditional fare.'

Sheridan scrambled to a sitting position and looked over towards the coffin. The dreadful figure had removed from the stool and lurked in the darkness behind, but for all that Sheridan could discern the man was a ragged miserable creature. His lean and haggard features were indeed reminiscent of a gargoyle. Mr Roden wanted only the addition of one letter to his surname to denote his species.

'With a flagon of ale,' the prompter added.

'God's blood! What in heaven's name is happening here, Mr Quail?' Sheridan demanded.

Nehemiah helped him to his feet.

'My poor relative is a sin-eater, sir, and his life made such a misery in our native Shropshire that I have lately brought him away.'

'I beg pardon, Mr Quail — a sin-eater?'

The prompter nodded. 'It is an ancient custom in parts of our county, and other counties too I believe. There may be one in a village, an unfortunate usually, who will consume the sins of the recent dead in exchange for the corpse meal and some small payment. The sin-eater takes to themselves the misdeeds of others when they partake of the meal in the manner you have witnessed.'

'And so quite literally consume their sins?'

Quail nodded. 'In consequence they are oftentimes feared and abused. The country people believe that drawing so many heinous crimes into themselves, the sin-eater become as Satan, the very essence of evil.' Nehemiah shook his head angrily. 'Though to my mind it is a kind and noble act to give up one's own soul so that others may be saved from damnation.'

Sheridan peered at the ancient relic with increased fascination. 'You have engaged Mr Roden to rescue Mr Marson from the fires of Hell?'

Quail flushed and nodded curtly.

'That is indeed a kindness.' Sheridan stepped towards the wizened old man. 'Allow me to shake your hand, Mr Roden.'

Sheridan grasped the old man fervently. The sin-eater's gaunt features lightened at this unexpected gesture.

'I have interrupted you in this ceremony. Please do pardon me —' Sheridan looked back at Nehemiah — 'and let you continue.'

Nehemiah nodded his gratitude.

The relic shuffled back to his position by the casket and his nephew brought a bowl of ale, which he laid reverently on the shrouded corpse of Andrew Marson. The old man continued his repast of bread and salt and gulped down the ale, wiping his thin lips with the back of his hand. Then he stood and solemnly addressed himself toward Marson.

'I give easement and rest now to thee, dear man,' the sin-eater croaked in his strong country accent.

'Amen,' Nehemiah intoned softly.

'Come not down the lanes nor in our meadows...' Mr Roden paused for a moment as an addition occurred to him. 'Nor roam the streets of this great city. For thy peace I pawn my own soul. Amen.'

'Amen.' Sheridan joined Quail in punctuating the conclusion of the rite and very much hoped that any such ghostly apparition had been well and truly laid to rest.

'A word in private, Mr Quail, if you will,' Sheridan whispered in aside.

'Of course, sir.'

After profuse thanks, Mr Roden was dispatched to his nephew's lodgings with the remains of the flagon and more coin from Sheridan than he was clearly used to receiving in recompense for his arcane services.

Sheridan bowed a final parting. 'And Mr Roden, should you contemplate a change of career, I would be obliged if you could consider going upon the stage — your features would do devilish well in the pantomime.'

'Thank ye good sir, I shall ponder it if Satan don't take me first.'

'Let us hope the devil can wait, he does not deserve you I think.'

When Mr Quail returned from seeing his decrepit uncle off the premises, Sheridan beckoned the prompter to join him by the coffin. In the interim he had loosened the covering over the dead man's face. The young actor looked strangely beautiful in his deathly pallor, save for the gruesome markings on his forehead, which had been cleaned of blood and now more clearly revealed the inverted triangle.

Nehemiah shrank at the sight. 'What is this, Mr Sheridan?'

'I had hoped that you might be able to enlighten me, Mr Quail.'

Nehemiah shook his head fearfully.

Sheridan drew the shroud back over Marson's forehead. 'You have had no inkling as to the cause of our friend's death?'

'Bob Fairbrother has said it was an accident.'

Sheridan stared closely at the prompter.

'I do not mean you any harm or mischief, Nehemiah.' Sheridan took hold of the prompter's shoulder. 'I beg you to be candid with me. As I am now with you. Can I trust your discretion?'

Nehemiah nodded.

'You were fond of Mr Marson?'

'I liked him well enough.' The prompter blushed.

'Enough that you would go to the trouble to bring your ancient uncle hither. Why? Because you knew the depths and breadth of his sins perhaps?'

Nehemiah's blush deepened.

'You were afeared that hell awaited him. As you may also fear likewise. Am I correct?'

Nehemiah chewed at his lip.

'Come, Mr Quail. Andrew Marson was found in a bath house. One frequented by men who prefer the company of other men.'

Nehemiah swallowed hard.

'And that is why he was so savagely murdered.'

'Murdered?'

'I am sorry to impart such distressing news to you.'

'Murdered?' Nehemiah repeated with dawning horror.

'I would know who has done this terrible thing and bring that fellow to justice. Can you help us? Constable Nicholls believes our actor was not the first victim of this assassin and neither may he be the last.'

'There are others who have been killed?'

'It would appear so. Sadly, a young boy scarce sixteen or seventeen.'

Nehemiah took a deep breath. 'How can I be of service, Mr Sheridan?'

'You can tell me everything that you know of Mr Marson's history and the places he frequented.'

The prompter nodded slowly and resolutely.

They repaired to a side room in Nerot's Hotel and Sheridan ordered a bottle of cognac. He was in dire need of refreshment himself. As the brandy burned the back of his throat he felt partially restored.

'So, Mr Quail, you have known Marson since first he came to Drury Lane. Do you know anything of his history, his family?'

The prompter nodded. 'His father was a miner, in a village near Newcastle on the Tyne. He was killed in a collapse when Andrew was but a small boy. His sister died soon after of a fever and they were hard times.'

'It is a sad story, I see.'

'His mother, well his mother was transported to the American colonies. He was told it was because she was caught stealing food to feed them both. Later, his aunt with whom he was lodged said different. In a fit of spite, she told young Andrew that his mother had become a lewd woman and disgraced the family. He never forgave his aunt nor her husband for their mean ways with him. He ran away. Nine years old he was. Might have starved in the ditch, he said, but one night he sneaked into a traveller's camp for the warmth of the embers and to seek what scraps might be left in the pot. The man found him asleep by the ashes in the morning. He was a "doctor" selling potions. Quack, of course, but he took Andrew in, said he needed a new assistant.'

Nehemiah paused and drank deeply.

Sheridan replenished his glass. 'That was a kindness.'

The prompter grunted. 'Doctor Marvel? Kind?' Nehemiah shook his head. 'He demanded a show of gratitude from the first, on a nightly basis, sir.'

Sheridan raised his eyebrows in acknowledgement.

'More than three years Andrew spent with that old quack salver. Cared for each other in a manner as time went by. *Better the devil you know*, Andrew used to say.'

'So, what happened?'

'One late summer they were travelling a lonely road and were set upon by a couple of rum padders, villains of the worst sort. Andrew and Doctor Marvel were left for dead in the ditch. Only, the doctor really was done for, he'd been bludgeoned to death.'

'And then?'

Nehemiah sighed. 'Andrew made his way to the nearest town. That was a lean time, he said, when he got by on his wits and stealing a purse or two, for he was nimble in that way. He wasn't proud of it, sir,' the prompter hastened to add, 'but needs must. And he could juggle a little, Doctor Marvel having taught him to help draw the crowd when he sold his potions. Then, there was always the other ways the good doctor had taught him that he might earn his keep. You would be surprised, Mr Sheridan, how many gentlemen take fancy to a pretty boy!'

Sheridan nodded; he could think of a number of fine gentlemen rumoured to have just such tastes. William Beckford, for one, had disgraced his family and had to run to France to avoid arrest.

'Then he had the good fortune to meet with Mr Barker and his company of players. It was for his juggling and to join the posturers at first, but when he showed an aptitude for learning a part, it was not long before Mr Marson was taking a leading role upon the stage. The rest I think you know, sir.'

'Thank you, Mr Quail, that is a most illuminating history. No relatives to speak of then?'

Nehemiah shook his head. 'None that would own him.'

'No family, but were there others that might be called close? Doctor Marvel shaped the man I think, for Mr Marson had no interest in the ladies. Or did he?'

'Not that I know of, sir, though he could flatter and seduce with ease. It was all a play to him; he would laugh into his sleeve.'

Sheridan smiled ruefully. 'A part that he played handsomely, he had me for a fool!'

'He was loved by the ladies that is certain, sir, he had a charming manner.'

'But I will hazard that it was not only the ladies that he charmed. There were other suitors for his attentions? And given the expense of his tastes, he must have been the beneficiary of some largesse. Am I right?'

'It has been so.'

'The initials A.M., or perhaps J.B., do they have any meaning for you, Nehemiah?'

Nehemiah looked up sharply. 'Mr B?'

Sheridan leant forward urgently. 'Yes?'

'He showed me a pocket watch. Over a year ago, it was.'

'A very fine watch?'

'Oh, very fine, sir. I recall that he jested, "*Mr B has been Right Honourable tonight, Nehemiah*".'

'And who is this Mr B?'

'I do not know, Mr Sheridan. Andrew was ever discreet. It was Mr B and Sir W and Lord K, with him.'

'You met none of these gentlemen yourself?'

Nehemiah shifted awkwardly. 'There was one. I had a message for Andrew and I think he did not hear me knock upon the dressing room door. I entered and well, sir, a young lord had him pressed up against the wall. He was furious at the interruption. The young lord that is. He had been drinking heavily I think, for he reeked of it and cursed worse than any soldier — then slapped me hard out of the way as he made his exit.'

'But you knew him?'

Nehemiah hesitated.

'I must know, Mr Quail.'

'It was Viscount Malmain, sir.'

Sheridan's eyes widened with some surprise. 'Well, I never.'

CHAPTER SEVEN

The Prince of Wales was finishing breakfast in his ornate bedroom as Sheridan was announced. His Royal Highness lolled on the bed in a purple silk nightgown which made him look like nothing so much as a plum pudding, Sheridan thought unkindly. His younger brother, Prince Ernest, was with him perched on the edge of the bed and likewise in a state of dishabille. Sir John Lade stood by the bow window in his usual attire of riding coat and breeches, peering out to see who might be passing by.

'Sherry, at last!' the prince called, waving a croissant.

The equerry, Major Hanger, beautifully powdered as ever, half rose and returned his bow. 'Ah Dick — as rare a sight as hen's teeth to see you abroad so early in the morning.'

'Oh, I doubt it is a morning call, Hanger, rather suspect we are at the tail's end of the night before!' Sir John guffawed. 'Is that not so, Sherry? You don't look as if you've slept a wink, egad!'

'Tumbling with one of your doxies, hey, Sherry?' Prince Ernest sniggered. 'You must feel like a regular sultan, eh? A whole harem of actresses at your bidding. Lucky fellow! Any you might recommend before my brothers bag them all? One untouched, if that were possible.'

'Tish, Ernest, you are too ugly a brute.' The prince playfully slapped his brother's cheek. 'You'll excuse us, gentlemen. Sherry and I have business.'

The prince pushed himself up to the edge of the bed. His girth had increased noticeably, Sheridan marked, over the course of the year. The Prince of Whales had become a popular sobriquet in many a journal.

The others began to rise as a show of politesse.

'At ease, gentlemen.'

The prince turned to the manservant, who rushed to his side holding wide a voluminous green dressing gown embroidered in the Chinese fashion. 'Adams, fetch a bottle of champagne would you. Or would you prefer a cure for the hangover, Sherry? I believe a bowl of bull's penis soup can be very effective.' His Highness tittered as he pushed his arms into the gown.

'I find champagne to be the best cure of all after a night of excess, sir.'

'Couldn't agree more, Sherry. Two bottles, Adams.'

Sheridan followed the prince into one of the smaller and more intimate reception rooms in the state apartments. Something struck him as slightly unfamiliar.

'What do you think to the new wallpaper, Sherry? Had it sent over from China. Hand painted. The flowers, lotus, don't you know, exquisite.'

'Most strikingly floral, sir.'

His Royal Highness had gained a reputation for changing his furnishings so frequently that one scarce had time to admire one arrangement before it was changed for another. Sheridan could swear that the candelabra was also new and looked to be one made by Thomire.

The champagne arrived and they settled on the delicate Chippendale chairs, which the prince insisted were placed in close proximity. The manservant was dismissed and they were alone.

'Tête-à-tête, Sherry.'

'A pleasure as always, sir.'

'It's a fancy I've had. Thought you might be the man to assist.'

Oh dear, there was something the prince wanted done. Sheridan hoped it should not be too onerous or time-consuming a task. His Royal Highness was really the most demanding of friends, albeit the most charming.

'I am your obliging servant of course.'

'All this war and gloom.' The prince raised his glass. 'One feels one has to keep the parties going to show a bit of spirit.'

Sheridan smiled in agreement and raised his glass.

'The king and queen don't see it that way. Never have enjoyed anything beyond a game of backgammon and would be in their beds by ten at night with a glass of milk and gruel. Now with the war and Freddy and Dolphy sent to fight in Flanders, Neddy exiled to the Canadas, the court is perfect misery. My sisters' lives are frightful dull, Sherry. You can't imagine.'

'The princesses are kept very close, Your Royal Highness.'

'The queen will scarcely allow them out of her sight, damn it. And, I say this in all confidence, Sherry —'

Sheridan's nod of the head indicated that his confidence should never be doubted.

'For all the progeny the queen has produced there is little of the maternal in her nature, and I should know. York and I scarce saw the queen when we were sent to the Dutch House as boys.'

'The queen does her duty, sir,' Sheridan offered as an attempt to mollify the prince before he became too peevish, as he often would when recalling his later boyhood; he had been schooled separately with his brother Prince Frederick at the house in Kew, ill-treated and thrashed by some of their tutors.

'There have been times, I am sure of it, when the queen must have prayed the king would take a mistress, like any decent husband, to let her have a year when she was not childbearing. He is not as other men, Sherry. That business of the madness — I think it was only ever a matter of degree. If you were to ask my opinion, who has known him all my life, rather than those medical sycophants, I should say the king is still a goosecap and always was a goosecap!'

As Sheridan strained to keep from yawning, he wondered whether the prince had called for him merely to have an opportunity to rant about his parents. These were sentiments and complaints which Sheridan had listened to time after time. He felt his attention drift.

Although he had never been introduced to him, he knew Viscount Malmain by sight as he was a regular at the theatre. Often to be found in the pit with his fellow rowdies looking for an excuse to catcall or fling rotten fruit at any performer who fluffed a line or missed a cue. With Marson dead, would the young lord continue to attend? Thinking himself beyond the reach of the law? He was brazened enough. Or, was Malmain even now on a ship to Lisbon or making his way to Italy through the German states?

'— what do you think, Sherry?'

'Sir, I —' Sheridan reached for his glass of champagne.

The prince leant across and tapped Sheridan's glass with his own, his eyes gleaming.

'Just so! Here's to our success!'

'Success, Your Highness!' Sheridan concurred as his mind raced to imagine what the prince had suggested.

There had been mention of parties — was he to organise some spectacular? It would be something out of the ordinary that would be for certain, else why should the prince need his services. Where? At Carlton House? At Brighton? Had a theme been mentioned? Sheridan shuddered. Why had he allowed his thoughts to wander.

'I worry they shall never marry. And the older ones, well, they are not getting any younger.'

Ah — the prince was still talking about his sisters. So, whatever was being planned must be for their benefit Sheridan deduced.

'This damned Royal Marriages Act. The king has us all tethered with leashes so tight it's a wonder we don't all choke. And see what happens when one of us does oblige!' The prince was warming to his subject. 'There's my brother York married to our cousin Frederica of Prussia. And how long does that last? They can barely sit in the same room together ten minutes. At the time I confess to being somewhat relieved at the marriage for I thought I might be left in peace. But they are separated and not a legitimate heir to be had in the family. I believe the Duchess of York prefers the company of cats and monkeys now.'

Sheridan recalled the German princess as no beauty but he had thought her rather clever, well informed and dignified. He did not wonder she preferred the company of apes to the Duke of York.

'And when the king hears about Gussy — !'

Sheridan's ears pricked.

'*Entre nous. Entre nous.*' The prince put a finger to his lips but was clearly bursting with the need to gossip. 'The young pup has just gone and spliced himself when he was in Rome and intends to make no secret of it from what I gather!'

Sheridan's eyes widened. The king's son Prince Augustus had married without his father's permission? Yes, all hell would break at that news. And Gussy had better be elsewhere when it did. The young prince, no more than twenty years old by Sheridan's reckoning, must be either very foolish or very brave; he could be cut off without a penny, or perhaps Prince Augustus judged that as the sixth son he had little dynastic significance and might eventually be forgiven. In any event he had married for love presumably. There was a certain romance to the tale that might make for a promising play, Sheridan decided, an afterpiece; it should go down very well with a Whig audience.

'But it's Lizzy I worry for the most. You know how fond I am. I love all my sisters dearly but well ... Royal can be a little distant...'

Sheridan nodded. This was the family's pet name for the eldest daughter Charlotte, The Princess Royal.

'... and sweet Gusta so fearfully shy. It's Lizzy who's most like myself and strains terribly at the gilded cage in which they are kept and she who has risked — well...'

The prince sighed deeply and then lurched forwards again to share another intimacy.

'They petition me all the time, Sherry. But there is only so much that I can do for them.'

'You do what you can, sir, and are most considerate.'

'This is one thing I might give them!'

Sheridan looked expectantly at the prince. Only let him reiterate the plan one more time. He held his breath.

'A theatrical entertainment. The children performing.'

At last! A children's play for the entertainment of the royal princesses. Sheridan fairly bubbled up with enthusiasm.

'Sir, we have many fine child performers in the company at present, who may juggle and dance and —'

'I am sure you do, Sherry, but did you not hear me say it should be the foundling children from the Institutions which the princesses support?'

'Pardon my lapse —'

'Their Royal Highnesses are touchingly devoted to the poor motherless infants, fearing that if the king will not let them marry, they may have no children of their own. I thought we might use some of their particular favourites from amongst the girls…'

'It is a brilliant notion, Your Highness.'

'I rather thought so.'

Sheridan squirmed. 'But all non-professionals? Children? Is that altogether wise, sir?'

'Oh, damn it, Sherry! Can't be doing with being coy. I know you to be a man of honour, a man I can trust.'

'I would hope that to be the case, Your Royal Highness.' What was the prince talking about now? Sheridan feared he was losing the gist once again.

'You know it is one thing for a prince to make dalliances and possibly father a Fitzroy or two — Clarence looks set to father a whole tribe given Mrs Jordan's fecundity…'

The prince himself was not behind in that respect either, Sheridan mused. How many children had he fathered in the past dozen years? One of Lady Melbourne's sons it was rumoured, and Mrs Elliott's daughter, and of course the speculations about the prince and Mrs Fitzherbert's secret offspring.

'But the princesses are so very curtailed in whom they may meet. The queen's ladies-in-waiting are dull as ditch water — and with what men should they socialise without a chaperone? Tell me?'

'Why, *none* I fancy sir — or rather none that they should take a fancy to! Old reputable courtiers beyond concern, perhaps? A chaplain, say?'

The prince nodded. 'Yes, a few decrepits. But *None*, think on?'

Sheridan frowned, he must be suffering the lack of sleep to be so dull witted. What was the prince insinuating?

'We think we are alone, Sherry, but we are not — we are surrounded, always. Pop your head outside this door and tell me how many footmen loiter there.'

Sheridan stood.

'Sit down, Sherry. I can tell you. There will be three and another at the end of the corridor, no doubt gossiping with my valet.'

'Sir, you are saying —?'

The prince lowered his voice. 'Servants, Sherry. My sisters may make unexpected acquaintances and — well, I would hardly say friendships, but let us say there may be liaisons.'

Sheridan nodded sagaciously. 'Indeed, sir.'

'My sister is clever but giddy. None of them know anything of the world, you see. They are all so terribly sheltered, and in the circumstances become easy prey in their foolishness. It seems Lizzy at seventeen made a clandestine marriage of sorts. No legal standing, can never be spoken of, hopefully long forgotten by both parties. But before or after this masque of a ceremony, I daren't enquire, there was issue. A girl.'

Sheridan could not help but gasp. This was something beyond a scandal.

The prince took out his gilt snuffbox which Sheridan observed had on it a miniature of Mrs Fitzherbert, a watercolour on ivory by that dandified rake Richard Cosway. His Highness took a pinch and sniffed up the snuff noisily.

'Devilish difficult situation, but one way or another it was kept secret from the king and as importantly the queen. Princess Elizabeth has bouts of ill health — needs to take the air at the sea and retire to that little cottage in Kew where she may sometimes make an escape. Who should she turn to in her despair?'

Sheridan nodded in understanding. The prince may have many faults but that he was a good and kind brother could never be questioned.

'Fortunately, my sister has always had a bit of a problem with her shape, tends to the rotund. As I say, we are rather alike and very fond. Her sisters tease her; "Fatimah" they call her, over which they giggle tremendously, but useful in the circumstances.'

The prince turned to Sheridan. 'Thing is, Sherry, my fancy was that this child might perform in our little play.'

So here it was at last. The reason why the prince had need of his services for the task.

'It will be a surprise entertainment. Sometime in the autumn, I thought. And so, the whole business must be one prepared in the utmost secrecy and none but you should know the true identity of little —' the prince hesitated before divulging the name of the royal bastard — 'Eliza Ramus.'

Walking back along the corridor, Sheridan did indeed notice that there were three footmen attendant along the way and at the far corner another engaged in conversation with the prince's valet. But for His Highness' assertion, he would not normally have noticed these men, nor looked so close. He observed the valet put a hand on the footman's shoulder and shake him, the young man looked red-eyed, almost as if he had been weeping. Sheridan shrugged; it was more likely the footman had been drinking the leftover dregs from the prince's table the night before and was suffering the consequences. The lives of servants; who knew what another world of loves and sorrows lay there.

He had thought the Prince of Wales might invite him to stay for lunch but that had not been forthcoming. The artistic advisor to the prince was announced. The little dandy flounced into the room, Richard Cosway, or *Tiny Cosmetic* as he was known to the wits. He bowed obsequiously to His Royal Highness and pointedly ignored Sheridan. A new portrait by the old master Van Dyke had been delivered. The prince was at once transported away to indulge in one of his favourite pastimes, the purchase of works of art with which to furnish Carlton House.

Sheridan directed his carriage to The Haymarket and on entering the theatre sent a boy out to Mrs Hudson's Coffee House to fetch one of her steak and kidney pies. He would have an hour or two before he should need to don the face of mourning and attend Marson's funeral. Old Fletch was on the stage door.

'Let no one petition me, Fletch. I am not in the building. This is merely a ghostly apparition that you see before you.'

Old Fletch tapped his nose. 'Aye, aye, like Hamlet's father, sir, am I right?'

'Just as ghoulish. Only more so.'

There was a fresh bundle of plays sitting on his desk. It seemed every Tom, Dick and Harry fancied he could write a play. Believing that characters with names such as Phizz and Wallop only had to spout page after page of inanities to be considered a drama. Sheridan sighed. When he could be bothered to skim through one of the overwritten pieces of drivel it was the usual tired clichés. Kemble would rail at him, pointing to the growing mountain of verbiage; there might be a Goldsmith, he would exclaim, or an Aphra Behn or a new Shakespeare even — and if that were a vain hope then why not a new Sheridan?

Because only I can be Sheridan! he had replied on one occasion and that had silenced Kemble for a moment. He knew they longed for him to write another *School for Scandal*, another *Rivals*. But could he? There was a question. He had possessed such devil-may-care certainty in youth. How was it that creeping age brought with it not greater confidence in one's abilities but it's very opposite? He lifted up the manuscripts stacked on the desk and added them to a pile already tottering in the corner. A moment later the whole edifice tipped over and joined their fellows in the slush.

No, he could make better use of his time. Time he might use to reflect at last on the interesting piece of information imparted by the prompter in the small hours of the night. Viscount Malmain. Well, well... Who would have guessed. Such airs and graces as he gave himself — the arrogant cur! When everyone knew his father, the 4th Earl Crumpsall, had gambled away what little was left in the family coffers on the faro tables and was mortgaged beyond the hilt.

As the eldest son Augustus, Viscount Malmain, was the last hope, but only if he could secure a good marriage. He was handsome, that was in his favour. And he had finally succeeded. He was betrothed. He had snared the daughter and only child of new money. East India money. Plenteous amounts. Money which, it was rumoured, would secure a baronetcy for the father and looked set to buy his precious offspring an even greater title, first Lady Malmain and then, when Augustus succeeded his father, Countess Crumpsall. It occurred to him that Augustus Malmain had a great deal at stake. Enough to commit murder?

There was a rapid knocking at the door. Sheridan was not to be left undisturbed after all.

'Enter.'

Young Joseph Grimaldi bounded into the office, his features contorted with rage.

'Sir, Mr Sheridan, I will not have it! It will not do!' His voice rose, accentuating that strange meld of Italian and cockney in his accent.

'What will not do, Joey? And what is it that cannot wait for Mr Kemble's attention, is he not the manager?'

Joey raised an expressive eyebrow at that nominal title, for everyone knew that nothing would happen without Sheridan's say so, and for that reason they were beset with perpetual procrastination.

'Go on,' Sheridan conceded. 'What or who has darkened your brow to such fury?'

'Monsieur Dubois!'

'Ah.' Sheridan exhaled. He knew well that there was no amity to be had between these two performers, one a leading clown and actor of no small merit, the other heir presumptive to his infamous deceased parent, Signor Grimaldi.

'He has used me to rehearse his William Tell.' The boy touched his crown. 'And has missed my head with those devilish knives of his by only a thread of hair; indeed, I had as well been to the barber!'

'But you are here and in one piece, Joey.' Sheridan smiled to reassure. 'And the cut of your hair is very becoming.'

'I would have you know, sir, that he is a cutting gloak and if anything were to happen to me it would be no accident. When I told to him that he could have killed me, Dubois replied, "If I meant to kill you, you would be dead!" And with such a mean look, sir, I am in fear of my life.'

Sheridan could believe it. He almost admitted to his own terror of the unnerving Frenchman and should not like to be a child actor under his authority.

'Monsieur Dubois shall find another for his apple paring, how will that do, Joey?'

'There is something wicked about him, sir,' the boy spat out, but he had begun to calm and turned to quit the office.

'Joey, stay a moment.' Sheridan clicked his fingers and sat straight. It was a flash that might be an answer.

'Sir?'

Sheridan indicated a chair. Joey picked up the fresh printed playbills on the seat and sat with them on his lap.

'How would you like to have the direction of a theatrical pageant?'

'Me, sir?'

'It is for a private party and must not therefore be advertised, not even within the company, do you understand?'

'Not within the company?' The boy looked bemused.

'And so, you will have no credit for it abroad, but there will be credit where it may profit you in future.'

Joey hesitated, at fourteen years old this was a golden but nevertheless daunting proposition.

'It is not for some time. You will help me to devise the entertainment and we shall find a suitable rehearsal space and — you like children? You are good with children are you not?'

'I believe so, sir,' Joey replied, looking increasingly puzzled.

'Then it is settled.' Sheridan flapped his hand towards the door. 'We shall speak more on the matter. And Mr Quail shall assist in the management of rehearsals.'

Joey rose, playbills still in hand.

'Oh — see to their distribution will you?' Sheridan nodded to the bills.

Joey was awkwardly grappling with the door handle to take his leave when the steak and kidney pie arrived and the delicious aroma of freshly baked pastry wafted across the room. Sheridan's stomach rumbled at this reminder of his ravenous hunger. He let out a hum of pleasure. To hell with the prince's salmon in aspic and quivering mousses — nothing could compare with a good steak and kidney pie!

CHAPTER EIGHT

One could rely on Kemble for a good eulogy. Interminably long though it might be. He struck just the right sombre note and leavened it with moments of pathos. Sheridan had relayed a highly edited version of Marson's childhood to the actor-manager before the brief funeral service. After the internment the small gathering had repaired to nearby rooms hired for the occasion and Kemble rose to pay tribute to the deceased. He made much of the tragic death of Marson's father, an honest miner who had toiled tirelessly to provide for his small family. His voice gentle and mellifluous as he described the delicate but fading flower that was Marson's young sister overcome by chills and fevers and to crown it all the mother wasted away by grief to leave an orphaned boy of no more than six years old, at which climax a tear came to Kemble's own eye.

Nehemiah Quail exchanged a questioning glance with Sheridan at that particular footnote. Sheridan allowed himself a wry smile in reply. Quail bowed and smiled in turn.

Then Kemble's voice quickened and rose to the drama of adversity. An unkind uncle, the cruel beatings and the flight into an unknown and perilous world where the young boy might so easily have perished. But when all seemed lost, young Andrew Marson was met with the kindness of strangers. Those of the theatrical profession, Kemble proclaimed dramatically, fellow strolling players, they had given the young boy refuge and succour. He had been clothed by the prose of Jonson and nurtured by the verse of Shakespeare. He had grown not only in stature but in feeling, the deployment of which could hold an audience in rapturous thrall. There was a long pause whilst

Kemble held a suitably heroic stance. Then a tremulous voice and sweeping gesture. Young Mr Marson's all too sudden exit from the stage had deprived his audience of a rare talent, particularly his roles in the great Shakespearean tragedies, and his family of fellow actors must bear the loss of a dear, dear brother.

Murmurings of agreement rippled through the company and rose to a crescendo of *hurrahs* as glasses were raised.

Sheridan stifled a yawn. His lack of sleep was catching up with him although his nerves were all a jangle. He looked forward to the coming weekend in Wanstead where he would not be at the beck and call of all and sundry but might lie in bed and then play the indulgent father with Tom and little Mary. He would put all these present concerns to one side.

First, however, he must call on Constable Nicholls for their rendezvous to share whatever pieces of information they had thus far gathered.

Sheridan had found the Bow Street Runner standing at the rear of the pews as they followed the coffin out of the service to its final resting place in the churchyard.

'Nicholls?'

The constable had bowed. 'I have come to pay my respects, Mr Sheridan, and to enquire if I might meet with you this evening?'

'Of course, where shall I find you? At Bow Street?'

'I am not on duty this evening, sir.'

'Then you too may raise a glass to our departed actor. Do you know The Green Man Tavern? It is not far from your lodgings in Marylebone, I think. I shall be there at seven, they serve a good pigeon pie.'

'Right you are, sir, thank you.'

It was only after Nicholls had quit the graveyard that Sheridan's eye was snagged by another who lurked in the shadow cast by the church spire. Had the fellow just arrived or had he attended the service within? He was not of the theatre company, but as Sheridan squinted for a better view there was something oddly familiar in his features. Was he an acquaintance of Marson? A regular theatre-goer? Or...? Sheridan's mind gave vent to feverish speculation. Might this be the assassin come to gloat over his handiwork? He shivered to recall that many a villain had calmly attended the funeral of his victim.

As the parson spoke his last over the lowered coffin, Sheridan emboldened himself to confront the man in the shadows. But should he march over and demand his name and connection to Marson, or saunter across and draw forth confidences with a welcoming smile and solicitude for a presumed grief at the actor's passing? As he decided on the latter course, his path was obstructed by an oily-faced man with glittering eyes.

'Mr Sheridan, this is a sad day for the thespian arts. My condolences.'

'Ba— Brockenhurst.' Sheridan bowed but could not quite disguise his distaste for the man before him. Brock the Badger, as he had dubbed him, or simply Badger — which name he had just now almost let slip. Though in truth the fellow reminded Sheridan more nearly of one of his own characters, Mr Snake, the slithering, creeping journalist of his *School for Scandal*. Not for the first time he felt the haunting quality of his own creations. But Badger he was and this moniker suited well enough for the time Brockenhurst spent digging through the dirt. A writer of scurrilous squibs, a purveyor of gossip and defamatory pronouncements, a denizen of the gutter.

The pen-smith returned the bow but made no haste to let Sheridan pass.

'I wonder if I might have a word?' A smile smeared across his shiny countenance.

'Here may not be the place or time, Mr Brockenhurst. You see we have just now buried our friend and must solemnise our farewells before this evening's performances.'

'I will not keep you long, my dear fellow.'

Sheridan bridled at the familiarity.

'It is a piece on the late lamented Andrew Marson that I wish to write.'

'Speak to Kemble then — he was his mentor on the stage; you will find him nothing but praise.'

Sheridan made to move forward with some urgency for he could see that the stranger in the shadows was turning to depart.

'Oh, but I think that what I have to discuss is for your ears, Mr Sheridan, yours alone perhaps?' The journalist continued to block the way, his prominent nose uncomfortably close to Sheridan's own.

'Discuss? What have I to discuss with you, Brockenhurst?'

'Murder should be an interesting topic, should it not?'

Sheridan felt a lurch in his stomach. 'Who speaks of murder?'

'Sir, there is a rumour afoot that your actor's death was no accident as described.'

'A rumour, sir, is a puff.' Sheridan drew himself up. 'Mr Marson was a fine actor and does not deserve such cheap witterings merely to sell pamphlets and line your pockets.'

'Rash speculations are not my intent I can assure you, Mr Sheridan, I grieve that you would thing so little of me.'

'Think what you like, Brockenhurst, I have other griefs to attend to. If you please.'

Brockenhurst reached out a hand to stay Sheridan's departure.

'I would have you believe that I take no account of hearsay but have been told this as an absolute fact, sir.'

'Who has told you this?'

Brockenhurst sighed. 'There is a contract of confidence in this matter, my informant being fearful for his own life.'

'Your informant is mistaken, sir. Now, if you will, I shall not ask again —'

'A man may not be misled by what he sees with his own eyes.'

Sheridan paused despite his urge to break away from the beady-eyed Badger.

'Devil take you, Brockenhurst! Why has the man not made report if what he claims is true? Do you not see he takes you for an ass and pressed you for payment to boot, I daresay.'

'I believe you were taken to the scene, Mr Sheridan? For the purpose of identification. If I may have your account then none can question its veracity.'

Brockenhurst spread his hands with an expressive shrug.

Damn the fellow. Sheridan hoped his cheeks had not reddened to be so caught off guard.

'I will share no account with you, sir. You may print what you like — your damnable lies shall decorate every privy from here to —'

'Wanstead?'

Sheridan pushed the sneering hack aside.

Brockenhurst smirked and jabbed the air between them. 'I know the truth of Mr Marson —' the journalist paused to allow his revelation to penetrate before imparting a final jibe

— 'and there may be an avenging angel abroad that will finish his sort for good.'

Sheridan's ears rang with the Badger's threats even as he scoured the grounds for the lurking stranger. But that man was nowhere to be seen and then Nehemiah Quail called to him from the gate.

'Do you not join us, Mr Sheridan?'

'Of course. Lead on, Macduff.'

Sheridan ordered a jug of the Pharoah, a good stout to compliment the pigeon pie. The Green Man Tavern was not one of his regular haunts, the customers being of a lower sort, but it was a square crib by all accounts and the landlord provided a good hearty repast. The main advantage of The Green Man as a meeting place was anonymity. He glanced furtively about the tables thronged with beer-swilling apprentices, coopers and heavily jowled butchers. Sheridan hazarded he might not be so readily recognised in this establishment. He sighed at the perfect irony of this hope. Had he not sought renown? Coveted fame? It was of his own making; he had toiled long and hard for it. Sheridan the playwright and then Sheridan the politician and Sheridan the famous orator calling for the Impeachment of Warren Hastings — who in the land had not heard of him? They must be living in a cave surely.

But oh, he could wish that his features had not been so thoroughly caricatured. So that all felt they knew him. Scarcely a week seemed to pass when he did not spy some cartoon in a shop window. He owned that he might not be the most well featured of men, like many Irishmen he was wont to redden in the sun, and he was now past forty, but the cruelty of those doodles that coarsened his looks with ruddy freckles and scheming eyes. That damned Gillray worst of all! The only consolation being that Gillray spared no one; neither the king's weak chin, nor that twig Mr Pitt with his nose twitching to the heavens, nor Charlie Fox's hedgerow of eyebrows and swarthy complexion — all were equally the victims of his wicked sketches. How easily the cartoonist could burst the balloon of vanity with mockery.

But it was not all satire. Take Gillray's depiction of the French King Louis on the guillotine, blood flowing skyward from his decapitated head and crying out for vengeance, how that had stirred a show of frenzied loyalty to King George and his government. Pitt never missing an opportunity to ram home the advantage. As if to underline the current of his own thoughts Sheridan's ears pricked to the talk amongst the drinkers. It was all of the war with France.

'I hear, Ben, as your boy 'as taken the King's shilling and is a galloot now,' a thin, wiry man addressed his neighbour.

'Sails next week with a regiment that will join the Duke of York.'

'They reckon he's of the right mettle after all — not like his dumplin' brother!'

'Give me a cold iron, Davy, and I'd swing at the French myself!' a swarthy fellow joined in.

'Oh, you're just huff, Jack — where were you when we went on that shindy in Bell Lane!'

'Watch your rattle, Davy, it's a bus-napper.' Ben elbowed his companion and jerked his head towards the approaching constable.

Sheridan nodded a greeting and Nicholls took the seat opposite. Sheridan poured a beaker each of the stout and raised a toast. The men at the next table cast a cutty eye over them both for a moment and then, losing interest, continued with an imagined assault on the riff-raff army of the French, in which they took a leading part.

'Sir, thank you for —'

Sheridan leant forward urgently. 'Nicholls, I must give you warning. There is a Grub Street writer who says he knows the truth of our bagnio, says he has been informed of my actor's savage end by one who claims to have been witness to the aftermath. The story will be on the streets tomorrow and it will not be a pretty one, this pen-smith has a loathing for men of that sort. My poor Marson, his name shall be in the mud and all else of his worth forgotten.'

Nicholls was silent in thought for a moment.

'What will you do?' Sheridan pressed.

'I thought I should have the advantage longer, sir, to see if any might come forward discretely with information. There is nothing for it. I must confess my stratagem to Sir Sampson, and tell him it is a murder that we deal with — before the Grub Street rag is printed and lets the cat out of the bag.'

Sheridan nodded. Sir Sampson Wright was the Chief Magistrate at Bow Street.

'Do you risk your position at Bow Street?'

'Perhaps. But I have some confidence that Sir Sampson will support my reasoning for silence in the first instance.'

'That is well. I can speak for you if you will. I would not like to see a good man go down.'

'Thank you for your kind opinion, sir.'

'Have you made any progress in your enquiries?'

Nicholls shook his head. 'Very little I must admit. Mr Culpepper provided the list of his servants but as I suspected, all that I could trace were blind to any goings-on at the bagnio and claim to know nothing.'

'And the servant Tobias?'

Nicholls grunted. 'He has disappeared. I quizzed his landlord. He made mention of a married sister in Little Barbary but could not recall her name. That will be like looking for a needle in a haystack.'

'Tobias will want for employment. The offer of a reward for information may bring him out and loosen the other servants tongues a little too.'

'Perhaps. But if they have been involved in the disposal of an earlier victim they may fear to be caught up in the business and stand to lose more than their livelihood.'

'You are right of course.' Sheridan speared the last of his pigeon pie and mopped the gravy with a crust of bread.

'Tobias lies low for now, but his belongings are still in his rooms and he must return to his lodgings at some stage. I have told the landlord it will be worth his while to let me know when he does.'

Sheridan nodded.

Nicholls continued, 'I have had my fill of landlords today, for I have also visited the lodgings of Mr Marson.'

'Ah, anything of interest there?'

'The expense of his tastes was confirmed to me. He lived like a gentleman and had many fine possessions — but none else inscribed. Bills from tailors and the like but no personal correspondence that he kept. Nothing intimate in fact. Playscripts but no books, clearly not a man who read for his own pleasure. His rent is paid to the end of the month but the landlord wants to know what will happen with his things?'

'There being no family, I shall ask good Bob Fairbrother to gather up what there is and we shall consider what may be done then. Poor Marson, what does he leave behind? His reputation will be in tatters once Brockenhurst's story is out and however fine the cloths and trinkets may be, they are left only for his brother actors to squabble over. None will treasure his memory.'

'I have also set Bartholomew to watch the bagnio, to see who might come and go, clients thinking it still in business, and to follow anyone who might be of interest. There was a well-dressed gentleman yesterday who knocked on Mr Culpepper's door and sidled away when there was no answer, but my watchman lost him when the man then took a hackney. Bartholomew may have better luck today, but I suspect that word passes around with practiced haste.'

'I may know of someone who frequented the place.'

The constable sat forward, all keen attention.

Sheridan grinned, pleased to have something at last of substance to offer.

'A young lord who may be of more than passing interest to us, for he was observed to be an admirer of Mr Marson and actively so.'

Nicholls' eyes narrowed.

'Furthermore, his initials are A.M., the same who reserved the steaming chamber.'

'You think this may be our assassin?'

'I consider that likelihood. The young man has a hot temper and would not take kindly to anyone who would thwart or threaten him.'

'He is capable of such savage violence?'

'If cornered or brought to anger I do not doubt it, Louis-Pierre.' Sheridan lowered his voice. 'It is my conjecture...'

Sheridan paused to drink from his tankard.

Nicholls smiled knowingly. 'You have a conjecture, sir?'

'That at least one of our two victims may have tried to blackmail this lord and these murders are the consequence.'

'That is a plausible motive.'

'The earlier victim, that lad you spoke of, was a mistake perhaps, the killer thought it was the lad who sent these threats and demands for money but when they continued, he realised his error and confronted Marson. There is much at stake for this young lord, he cannot afford any whiff of scandal now for he is recently betrothed to an heiress and his family in dire need of her fortune.'

'I think you may have the matter solved, sir. Congratulations.'

'That is all very well in its way, Constable — and I forgot to mention to you the stranger I noticed lurking in the shadows during the burial. So, I may be entirely wrong to suspect Viscount M. In any case, how should we bring this young lord to justice, there is no proof?'

Nicholls pondered for a moment.

'I shall pay a call on your Grub Street muckraker; he must be made to give up this so-called witness.'

Sheridan eyed the brawny police officer with a smirk. 'Yes, you might very well be the man to persuade him, Nicholls.'

CHAPTER NINE

The joy of a comfortable bed.

Sheridan rolled over on to his back and stretched out his arms, luxuriating in the ease he felt. Almost at once it occurred to him that it had been some time since he had shared his own bed with another. He felt a momentary pang for lost loves. For his wife Eliza, whom he missed more than he could ever have imagined. What a good, sweet soul his wife had been, and he had treated her with unpardonable neglect. True the doctors had said that carrying another child might be her death and warned that touching her was like so many nails in a coffin. So, he had sought that physical comfort elsewhere.

The doctor's advice had proven all too prophetic when Eliza had given in at last to the attentions of Lord Edward Fitzgerald. For although Sheridan would allow no one else to raise blame against the lovers or to give voice to the suspicion that it was the birth of the infant Mary which had hastened her dear mother's end three months later, he knew it to be true. Eliza was gone.

The young woman who might have taken her matrimonial place, Pamela Syms, was now married to that same Fitzgerald. In retrospect, he saw his courtship of Pamela as no more than playfulness and she had clearly taken it for a mere trifling game. Sheridan felt a lump in his throat. He had not been fortunate in love. His thoughts raced to Harriet, as he knew they would. How he tried to scrape her from his mind. But to no avail. He could not forget. Harriet, Harriet, Harriet. He groaned. Now, there had been a great passion. He should love Lady Duncannon above all others to the day he died. He wondered did she still care for him? He had long suspected that it may have been his own sister Betsy who had informed on them to Lord Duncannon. Sheridan shuddered to recall the threats of divorce proceedings which had only been forestalled by the intervention of Harriet's brother-in-law the Duke of Devonshire.

Harriet was abroad now, an invalid, it was said, there had been some fit of paralysis. She was gone from his life, forever he feared. He needed to love again. He was ready for love. He was a man in want of a wife. Someone to share the comfort of this bed. And there was little Mary to think on, she needed a mother. Mrs Canning had already five of her own, she could only give so much maternal affection. And his boy Tom. Sheridan sighed. A ray of sunlight stole through a chink in the curtains. It must be passed luncheon. He should rise. But oh, the pleasure of sleeping in his own bed.

As he emerged from his rooms, he heard voices above coming from the nursery. Mary would be put down in her cot for an afternoon rest — he should seize the chance to hug her as he had arrived home too late the night before. He would surprise his little poppet and he tiptoed up the stairs with this intention. Hitty was within, but it was not the nurse with whom she was conversing. He recognised the light, tinkling laughter. It was Mrs Wallis, wife to the parson in the nearby parish. She and Good Sister Christian had become fast friends through their various charitable works.

Sheridan lingered a moment. He realised that his heart beat a little faster. Was it all his thoughts of love which caused this stir within his breast? Breast be damned, he thought, it was his groin which was roused. Cecily Wallis was a pretty blonde woman. Devilish pretty when he thought about it, fresh and rose cheeked, and not yet twenty. He had noted the sparkle of her eyes only the previous month and that delicious laughter. She seemed a young woman simply made for gaiety and parties, but she was constrained by her husband's stern demeanour when in his presence.

What a contrast was there. The Reverend Peter Wallis was the younger son of a local squire, Sir Edward. He had taken up the living at St Jerome that was in his father's gift and was a churchman through and through. Which could not often be said to be the case with these younger sons sent to study theology up at Cambridge. Peter Wallis, on the other hand, was a devout Greek and Hebrew scholar, according to Mrs Canning, and he wrote obscure tracts for publication in religious pamphlets. Sheridan recalled Hitty's surprise when this reverend had married his church warden's young daughter.

'I suppose Cecily was right under his nose else Reverend Wallis should not have noticed her at all, for his head is always in books and parchments!' Hitty had exclaimed at the time.

Sheridan had taken little notice himself then. So many other affairs had his attention in the last tragic year. Now, he wondered if a little flirtation might not be just the diversion that he needed.

'My, Mrs Wallis but you are a natural,' he heard his friend Hitty coo. 'The way you hold Mary, see how comfortably she lays her head on your shoulder.'

'She is a sweet child, quite the prettiest little thing!'

Sheridan warmed to hear his daughter described in such glowing terms.

'She has inherited her mother's beauty,' Hitty offered.

'And her father's charm and intelligence, I believe,' Mrs Wallis continued.

Sheridan heard Mrs Canning hesitate. Mrs Wallis was not to know that Mary was Fitzgerald's child, but yet she was his too

— and Mrs Wallis thought him charming! What else might she confide? It was not Sheridan's habit to eavesdrop, but when the conversation was so very pleasing...

'There shall be little ones of your own soon I should not wonder, Mrs Wallis.'

Cecily Wallis heaved a great sigh. 'I had hoped for that possibility, Mrs Canning, it is my dearest wish.'

Hitty softened her tone in solicitude. 'You are young and healthy, Mrs Wallis, it is simply that sometimes nature is contrary and conception may take longer than desired. You must not worry yourself; but should you have a concern, I have a very good doctor —'

'Thank you, Mrs Canning, but I do not know how a doctor may help, however expert, when there is no —' Mrs Wallis floundered for a moment and seemed almost tearful — 'consummation.'

Sheridan held his breath. Had he heard right? What horror was this? Reverend Wallis had not touched his wife? Was the man such a monster as to have no feeling?

'I think I am to blame, Mrs Canning. Something I have done on our wedding night seemed to quite distress Mr Wallis. I am so untutored, having no mother myself and only my father and brother. Mr Wallis has never attempted since.' Cecily allowed a sob then.

'There, there, my dear.' Mehitabel was clearly trying to give comfort. 'Here, let me take the child.'

At that point the infant Mary let out a loud wailing and Sheridan seized the opportunity to retreat down the stairs with much to think on.

George Canning arrived after luncheon on the Sunday offering profuse apologies to his aunt for his delay in joining them for the weekend.

'Of which there is scarcely any left, George!' Mehitabel picked at a piece of fluff on the young man's collar. 'I shall imagine you avoid us,' she admonished peevishly.

She turned to Sheridan, who was standing at the threshold. 'And here is Mr Sheridan most particularly desirous of your company.'

Sheridan smiled; he was not to be allowed to sidestep this mission.

'Come, George, let us take a circuit of the garden. The afternoon has turned very fine and I am in need of an airing, spending most of my life in windowless rooms.'

'Of course, sir, I should be delighted.'

When they had ventured down to the willow tree and were safely out of earshot, Sheridan cut short his tittle-tattle, brought them to a pause and looked directly into the young man's face.

'There is something different to you, George. Your lips twitch as though they might at any moment let loose a volley of laughter. Why do you strain to keep them caged? Some hidden pleasure that you do not share with us?'

George tittered nervously.

'It is something delicate? Something you may not impart to Good Sister Christian? But not, I hazard, the conquest of some fair lady — I should know the flush of that success nine times out of ten.'

'You mistake; it is my pleasure in the company of my family and friends —'

'No, George, you are not yet a seasoned dissembler, although a study of the law will provide good practice, I give you that.'

'You will tease out nothing of import, Sheridan.'

'Your mask is not so tightly fixed as you might wish, George. Consider a temporary Ally, a Coalition let us say, rather than the Opposition.'

'Confound you, Sheridan, I see now what a thorn you may be.'

'And am I right in thinking that you may feel those pricks yourself before long?'

George pressed his lips tight, as if by doing so he could resist Sheridan's wheedling.

'Pitt has found you a seat? A well-padded one it would seem since you have no funds to fight an election yourself.'

'Oh! Damn you, Sheridan. I suppose you will know soon enough. I am to have Newtown on the Isle of Wight.'

'No hustering needed at all then. You must be giving thanks that the last efforts to bring a Reform Bill came to nothing for Reform would do away with all such rotten boroughs.'

George grimaced. 'You know I would support such a Reform.'

'Only once you are safely inside Nobs House. The door might be closed, but only after you have entered. I shall look forward to your speeches on the matter.'

Sheridan was enjoying baiting his friend's nephew and he would continue a little longer before he should clap young George on the back and let him know that though the young man had chosen Master Billy over Charlie Fox, Sheridan was nevertheless proud of his advancement. Better an intelligent and penniless young lawyer at the heart of government than the many foolish sons of M'lords Bish and Bosh.

'My aunt must not know, Sheridan.' The young man's brow furrowed with anxiety.

'This will not be a secret you can keep for long, George. And then —' he sighed heavily — 'well, you know how like a tiger she is for Fox.'

'At least until I make my mark and she can see the sense of supporting Mr Pitt's government in this time of war.' George thumped a fist into the palm of his hand.

'We may all support the war. The execution of Louis was without justice or justification. But we cannot be blind to opportunities to sue for peace, war for war's sake and to excuse acts of tyranny at home cannot be countenanced.'

'You misjudge Mr Pitt.' George looked accusing.

Sheridan could see that his hackles had risen dangerously. Clearly, George had joined that circle of young men around William Pitt who hero-worshipped their Prime Minister.

'There is much we will disagree on, young Canning, over the coming years, but let us agree on one thing. That we are friends. And shall always love each other as we have since the days when I dangled you on my knee.'

George shook his head and smiled, the tension falling from his face. 'You are right, Uncle Dick, we must always be friends.'

Sheridan opened his arms and they fell into an embrace. Sheridan patted the young man on the back then and whispered in his ear, 'Well done, Canning. I applaud Mr Pitt for the recognition and appreciation of your talent — he does at least have good judgement in this one regard.'

Hitty called to them from the path.

'George, Dick, our guests are arriving.'

As the two men re-entered, Hitty took Sheridan's arm and pulled him away, leaning in confidentially.

'I see you have taken the opportunity to speak with George. I am glad of it. Thank you, Dick.'

Sheridan smiled as disingenuously as he could muster.

It was a small party of family and friends that gathered for an early supper. Aside from the Sheridans and Cannings there was the Reverend Wallis and his young wife, their neighbour Sir Arthur Ralph and Lady Isobel, both Whigs of the old sort, another close neighbour, the watercolourist Frederick Jukes and Mrs Jukes, the tenor Michael Kelly and Mehitabel's old friends, the widow Mrs Burridge and her niece Miss Campbell. Tom also had an old schoolfellow, Henry Drake, who was visiting with him from Dr Parr's school in Warwickshire.

Afterwards the gathering moved through to the salon, which had been arranged with chairs in front of a performance area. Whilst Miss Campbell played the harpsichord Sheridan slipped into the seat beside Mrs Wallis.

'A heavenly instrument, don't you think, Mrs Wallis?' he whispered.

'Oh, I do wish that I had been taught to play.' She sighed.

'Our dear Mrs Canning tells me you have a very fine voice.'

'That is kind. To your practiced ear I am sure it would seem a little thin; I believe your wife was one of the finest sopranos of the age, Mr Sheridan.'

At the mention of his deceased wife Sheridan nodded sadly. He must get that subject to one side or he should not be able to play the gallant at all.

Miss Campbell ended her rendition of Handel with a flourish and the applause was enthusiastic.

Tom, Bessie and her brother William had been absent during the concert but now appeared to one side in makeshift Roman costume whilst another Canning boy, Charles, set a screen-painted backdrop of Tuscan hills and castles.

Tom bowed solemnly to the audience and with a short prologue introduced *Propitia and Syllius*, an original comedy with contemporary arrangements by Mr Tom Sheridan and Miss Canning. He extended an arm to the side and Bessie made her entrance to take her bow and complete the prologue with a short poem. Sheridan watched the easy rapport between Tom and Bessie with a new interest.

The youngsters had devised a well-worn plot involving the Goddess Venus and her penchant for meddling in the affairs of mortal hearts. Namely the unrequited love of the clever and deserving Propitia, played earnestly by Bessie, for the callow but arrogant Syllius, with her brother William in that role, which he delivered with great enthusiasm if a little shaky on his lines. The entertainment featured plenty of familiar tunes, Miss Campbell obliging again on the harpsichord. The songs had been refreshed by comic lyrics written for the performance, there were amusing disguises and hilarious misunderstandings. Tom had taken on the plum role of Venus and for his first entrance he had transformed his appearance with an elaborate wig, no doubt borrowed from the Wardrobe Mistress Mrs Petty, and his face made up most becomingly with rouge and powder. The assembled guests gasped and clapped their appreciation. He moved across the stage with a comically exaggerated grace much to the amusement of the audience. Before he had even parted his lips, Tom had already stolen the show.

Sheridan smiled with satisfaction. His son was a pleasing young fellow, handsome and lively and clearly not without wit. Tom might very well be headed for a career in the theatre, following in the footsteps of his grandfather and father. Sheridan knew the temptations which such a path presented and Tom was already writing poetry of no mean merit. He might be the Sheridan for the new age. Kemble should be pleased with that. But Richard Brinsley Sheridan was not entirely sure that he wanted his son in the theatre. His own election to Westminster, his friendship with the prince and other leading aristocratic figures of the day had opened the door to other more illustrious possibilities for Tom which Sheridan could not have imagined at his birth. The Sheridan name might shine upon a different stage. A political rather than theatrical dynasty was a pleasing thought.

A burst of laughter and applause brought him back to the moment. Sheridan smiled. Tom was still a boy at heart, he told himself. Let him play. Let him play at theatricals. Let him play at love. Let Tom and Bessie Canning both play at love.

'How clever and comic your son is, Mr Sheridan!' It was Mrs Wallis who whispered enthusiastically in his ear, her eyes glittering with amusement. 'He does you credit, sir.'

'I am obliged, Mrs Wallis, you are very kind. I hope I shall have the pleasure of earning your credit for my own poor part one day.'

'You are already high in my esteem, I can assure you, sir.'

Was that a slight blush he detected? Might it be that this pretty young woman did hold him in some regard? Well, let the reverend continue to write his sermons. Sheridan would dust off a piece of poetry. There were plenty he had composed over the years full of sighs and longing, that would be sure to flatter the delectable Mrs Wallis.

Celestial blushes check thy conscious smile.
With timid grace and hesitating eye …

That portrait had been for Mrs Crewe, but serviceable enough to be rejigged. Or he might even consider writing something new. He stole a glance at Cecily Wallis, so young, so fresh in her unadorned beauty. It gladdened his heart to look upon her innocence and purity, for if he had understood correctly, she was still virginal. Yes, Mrs Wallis was deserving of his better efforts. He let his appreciative gaze linger longer than might be proper and so was caught unawares when he found that the Reverend Wallis had fixed him with a reproving glare.

The audience hushed as the finale approached and the Goddess Venus entered to intervene in the lovers' dilemmas. Cupid was summoned to set all right. Venus gestured towards the rear of the audience.

At the sound of a door opening the audience craned around to view the expected entrance. Gently prompted by her nursemaid, the infant Mary ran barefoot up the aisle between the seats. She was wearing what looked like little more than her linen clout, a pair of wings had been hooked over her shoulders and a garlanded band crowned her wispy blonde curls. In one hand she held a little gold-painted bow and in the other a golden arrow.

Sheridan felt tears prick at his eyes and his heart swell with pride as the audience 'oohed' and 'aahed'.

CHAPTER TEN

Viscount Malmain was sitting in the Duke of Beaufort's box and clearly working his charms on the matronly duchess. Henry Somerset, the 5th Duke of Beaufort, was not in evidence. Sheridan supposed Malmain must be a pal to one of their many sons — Lord Norborne, he would hazard. Sheridan clenched his fists but knew what he must do.

When the footman slipped him through the door, two of the Somerset boys were leaning over the rail and sniggering as they flicked orange pips on the beaus below. A scene from one of Cumberland's comedies *The Fashionable Lover* played out on the stage, but it was a restless audience and the actors were struggling to be heard above the general hubbub of conversation. Young Mr Blackett was in the part of Tyrell and Sheridan was reminded that he had not yet found time to quiz the actor on his friendship with Marson. He put the thought from his mind; it no longer seemed necessary.

'Sherry!' the duchess called aloud when she spied him.

Sheridan inclined his head and came forward to kiss her outstretched bejewelled hand.

'It is nearly an interval; I have sent out for some of Gunter's confections. You will stay, won't you?'

'Delighted, Duchess.'

'We think Miss Farren marvellous and await her next entrance. You shall see how rapt we are then. The boys are all in thrall to her of course!' The duchess smiled indulgently. 'And do you know Viscount Malmain?'

'Mr Sheridan.' The young lord bowed graciously. 'I have long wished to make the acquaintance of our greatest living playwright.'

'Oh, don't call him that, Gus dear. Sherry is all politics now and scarce likes to be reminded that he once wrote plays at all!'

'You now make a "play" of politics, Mr Sheridan?' The viscount laughed at his own joke. 'More of a blood sport these days, from what I can gather. It is all fox and hounds, but the fox is nearly run to ground. Shall you be there at the kill?'

'The fox is a cunning beast; I should not write him off just yet. But blood sports, that is your interest is it not, sir?'

'Cocking, Mr Sheridan, that is my passion. Nothing like a pair of fighting cockerels going to it! I have a mind to breed the black-breasted red if I can get Derby to part with one of his heroes and if I can afford the price! Do you follow the sport, sir?'

'It is not to my taste to see such fine creatures pecking and clawing at each other.'

'Oh, but it is their nature. And it is either that, with a fighting chance, or the cooking pot — I know what I would rather!'

'You are a fighting man then, Lord Malmain?'

'Sadly, my father will not allow me a commission or I should be even now with my brother in the 15th Light Dragoons running down the French.'

Sheridan saw a fire in the young lord's eyes; he had clearly been thwarted in his military inclinations.

'So, you are headed for the cooking pot then?'

'Oh, very droll, Sheridan. Yes, I suppose I am.' Malmain leant forward and lowered his voice. 'I must marry and shall be a cooked goose then.'

'I heard that, Gus!' the duchess interjected. 'He jests, Sheridan. Miss Harte is perfectly charming and quite the catch — Lord Malmain is entirely besotted.'

Norborne guffawed. 'With upwards of twenty thousand a year I would be too — and could even overlook her freckles!'

'You are to be congratulated, sir. I gather you are betrothed to Miss Harte?'

'How news spreads.'

'Shall we still see you often at the theatre?'

'Why, yes, of course. My future wife is a great admirer of Mrs Siddons.'

'And I hear you are a regular, Lord Malmain, backstage too, and have made acquaintance with some of my actors.'

'Actresses, I think you mean, Mr Sheridan!' one of the Somerset boys said. "Gus should have more than a passing acquaintance with them, heh what!'

'Boys!' the duchess admonished indulgently.

Malmain smiled, but Sheridan had noticed a slight slip in his sangfroid and a narrowing of the eyes.

'You will have been saddened to hear of the death of Mr Marson. Unfortunate accident in Covent Garden.'

'Marson!' The younger Somerset boy lit up with salacious interest. 'Isn't he the fellow…? No accident I read in *The Daily Enquiry* —'

Norborne elbowed him in the ribs. 'Hush, Robbie! Mama!' he hissed and rolled his eyes in warning at the potential indelicacy of mentioning the now infamous actor.

Sheridan pretended oblivion to the boys and continued to look pressingly at Malmain. 'I believe he was an actor you greatly admired.'

'A mere passing regard, sir. It is in the nature of actors to deceive and that looks to have been Mr Marson's forte.'

There was a knock at the door and the Beaufort footman ushered in the sweetmeats which had been sent from Gunter's. There were immediate exclamations of delight from the duchess, whose figure gave evidence of her sweet tooth.

'If you will forgive me, Duchess.' Malmain bowed. 'It has been a most enjoyable evening but —'

The duchess rapped him with her fan. 'We shall have an end of season ball next month and Miss Harte shall be invited and you will be forgiven for marking her card so none other may enjoy her company on the dance floor!' The duchess beamed and then returned her attention to the selection of custards and jellied fruit.

'Do you take the strawberry or the lemon, Mr Sheridan?'

As he left the theatre nearing midnight Sheridan found Nicholls falling into step beside him with his long stride.

'Sir, I am glad to have caught you.'

There was a faint sheen of sweat on the Runner's brow.

'Constable, I do not know why you consider me to be of any assistance to you at all —'

Nicholls looked questioning.

'Come join me for a moment in my carriage — we will be private there.'

They turned the corner on to Haymarket.

Sheridan groaned. 'I fear we shall never catch Lord M out unless in the act.'

'Has his lordship been at the theatre tonight?'

Sheridan stepped up into the waiting vehicle.

'Yes, I tried to —'

'Then he is not our assassin after all,' the constable interrupted.

Sheridan turned back to stare at him.

'What do you mean?'

'I have just come from an alley off Vere Street. A body found and killed with that same savagery that finished your actor.'

Sheridan ushered the Runner inside the carriage and closed the door on them.

'The hue and cry is up now, but we know not who we look for.'

'Why do you come to me, Constable? How might I be of any help to you?'

'Mr Brockenhurst avoids me. I thought you might be able to persuade him of the wisdom of co-operation now that we have another murder to deal with.'

'He is an unpleasant character, Nicholls, but I shall do what I can.'

Sheridan ordered his coachman to an address near Fleet Street.

As the carriage jolted over the cobbles towards the City, Sheridan drummed his fingers on the seat beside him.

'And this murder has just happened, when?'

'Within the last two hours I should say,' Nicholls informed. 'The man had been drinking in a nearby tavern, The White Swan. We have his name, too. He is one Thaddeus Broadhead, a labourer. One of the other drinkers found him when he was setting out for home and raised the alarm.'

'Vere Street. At ten o'clock or thereabouts?'

'It seems so. Thaddeus left the tavern at about that time, the alley is but a few minutes away.'

'Ten o'clock.' Sheridan nodded slowly. 'Then Malmain is not out of the frame, Constable. He excused himself from the Duke of Beaufort's box shortly after nine. I'll hazard my life he quit the theatre entirely at the same time.'

'And it is no great distance from Haymarket to Vere Street!' Nicholls brightened.

Sheridan blew out his cheeks. 'I fear I may have goaded him rather.'

'Sir?'

'I made some pointed remarks about Marson and this is his response I think.'

They sat in silent consideration for a while.

'That may be to our advantage, Mr Sheridan.'

'What do you mean?' Sheridan frowned. 'A man has died, some innocent man in the street it seems, taking a quiet piss down an alley!'

'Mr Broadhead may have been mistaken for … something he was not, because he simply thought to take that shortcut to his home. He may not have known the reputation of this particular alley. It is not widely known, I did not know myself until my watchman Bartholomew enlightened me. It is a haunt of men seeking brief and lewd encounters apparently, usually for payment. A fatal route for the victim tonight.'

'And if he were fumbling with his breeches to relieve himself, that action may have been dreadfully misinterpreted by the killer.'

'Dreadful not only for Thaddeus Broadhead but for his wife and children too, according to the drinking friend who identified him.'

Sheridan looked aghast. 'That is most tragic.'

They were both silent a moment in contemplation of Mrs Broadhead's loss.

'But where is the advantage you speak of in all this?'

'I mean only that this young lord seems out of all control — if he is goaded so easily as you suspect. There is an unbridled fury in these acts, a kind of bloodlust, is there not?'

Sheridan nodded. 'And in this state, he will make a mistake.'

'And then we shall have him.'

'Dear God, I hope so, Nicholls.'

'I have left Bartholomew to make enquiry at the tavern. Our assassin may have been seen by someone, lurking nearby or coming out of the alley clutching his bloodied knife. Now may be the time to offer a reward.'

'Consider it done, sir.'

'To kill in the open, in an alley, where he risked being discovered, the killer has become reckless,' Nicholls continued, an edge of excitement in his voice. 'And he has mistakenly murdered Thaddeus, believing him to be touting for business because of the location. This was no random act. The choice of place was deliberate. But he has made a terrible mistake and murdered an innocent man, which may unsettle him further.'

'In the open, yes … I wonder at that…' Sheridan murmured aloud. 'It is just a fancy, but there seemed to me something theatrical in the way that Marson's corpse was presented in the bagnio … as though he had been placed with great care … an advertisement … a warning to others … now it seems the killer wants all to see his work.'

Nicholls nodded thoughtfully. 'Not disposed of quietly, as we suspect Culpepper has done, nor kept from attention as I sought to do with your actor.'

Sheridan sat up straight.

'Perhaps it was not simply my remarks that prompted this more public display of his gruesome handiwork. What if it were Mr Brockenhurst's sensational article? Badger promised to laud our killer as some avenging angel raising the sword of righteousness against the scourge of sodomy. Do you have the article, Constable? I have not read it yet myself.'

Nicholls retrieved a folded sheet from an inner pocket.

'I only read the piece to see if it might give any clue to the witness the writer claims was at the scene.'

Sheridan shook out the page torn from *The Daily Enquiry*. He scanned it briefly picking out the main gist.

… Our readers know that here at The Daily Enquiry we will take a stand against vice and point to it wherever it may be found … as we live through an age of licentiousness and unmentionable freedoms of every kind…

… the pollution of revolution and the unchristian beliefs which have led the French to embrace their own perversions will not infect these glorious lands…

… we will stand as men against an accursed tide of despoilers, against those who would seek to weaken and corrupt our young men…

We demand not the pillory nor Newgate for these wicked lechers but,

Hang them all!

Hang them all!

… let the rotten apples in the barrel be purged…

Who amongst you will speak against an Avenging Angel who has picked up the sword of the Righteous to smite down the evil-doers in our midst?

Only last week the celebrated actor Mr A_w M_n was cut to death in a notorious club, where men disport in naked abandon, his manhood fairly sliced off and rudely displayed. It is rumoured that he was not the first nor will he be the last to feel God's sword of judgement.

Remember Sodam and Gomorrah and the fate of those debauched citizens who laughed in the face of Our Lord!

They will be shown no Mercy!

S. B.

Sheridan slapped the page. 'Do you know, I think Mr Brockenhurst may be just the man we need.'

CHAPTER ELEVEN

Nicholls had been knocking at the door with his baton for some time before a response came from an opened window above.

'Who's that knocking at this hour? The reason had better be a good one you hairy jackanapes, or this steaming pot of piss will be tipped out over your dunderhead and the turds to follow!'

'As you can hear, Mr Brockenhurst has a marvellous superfluity of words,' Sheridan chuckled. 'But I should stand well aside, Constable, or the usual deluge will be more stinking than ever.'

Nicholls looked up as he moved back from the door. 'Mr Brockenhurst, I am an officer from the Bow Street Public Office. We wish to speak with you on a matter of some urgency.'

There was a hesitation. 'What does Bow Street want with me?'

'If you will let us inside, Mr Brockenhurst, all shall be explained.'

There was a grumble from above and the window banged shut. Five minutes later the front door of the narrow house swung open and the sour-faced journalist stood before them in his nightshirt with a blanket hastily wrapped around his shoulder.

Nicholls bowed. 'Sir —'

Brockenhurst peered past the constable through the gloom. 'The devil Sheridan, is that you? Do you bring trouble to my door at this hour?'

'I rather fancy you invite that mistress in yourself, Mr Brockenhurst.'

'What do you want?' the pen-smith continued warily. 'Do you look to sue me with some false claim of libel?'

'*The Daily Enquiry* is scarce worth the effort, sir, it is already known to be a scurrilous rag from end to end.'

'I'll have you —'

'But it is a popular one, I will concede. No, Mr Brockenhurst, I have no desire to shut you down. As you know, I am a great supporter of the freedom of the press.'

'Aye, well, the people have a right to —'

'And you have a wide and varied readership from the lowliest taverns to the Lords dining hall. Some must find your fictions entertaining, I conclude.'

'So, what is it you want? Knocking me up at this hour? And with a Runner at your side.' The hack's eyes shifted uncertainly to Nicholls and back to Sheridan.

'Why, to tell you a story, Brockenhurst.' Sheridan indicated the door. 'May we?'

They were led in and squeezed into the small parlour, where Brockenhurst lit a lamp.

'Go on then, gentlemen.'

'There has been another murder tonight, sir, in an alley,' Nicholls began.

'Murder?' The journalist's eyes lit up.

'And you may be the first to print the story,' Sheridan added dramatically.

'There is some snag here — I know it in my bones — what is it, Sheridan?'

'Your *Avenging Angel* has been about his bloody business once again.'

Brockenhurst's brow creased. 'And you come to me with this?'

Nicholls leaned forward. 'Mr Brockenhurst,' , 'there is an assassin abroad, one who kills with unmentionable savagery.'

'Yes, well if those deviants kept their peckers in their trousers then they should not be sliced off!' Brockenhurst snorted.

'And so, you would incite mob justice — with all the anarchy that brings? Let God judge. If not God himself, then his anointed, those Justices vested in the authority of law to uphold the law.'

'The law's not always to be found though, is it, Mr Sheridan?' The journalist cast a placating eye towards Nicholls. 'Not your fault, Constable — we all know you haven't the numbers and you will take note that I wrote very warmly in favour of the new Public Offices at Shadwell and Shoreditch and the other Offices — and only eager to see more policing in our great city that is plagued with sins of all kinds, thievery, coining and vice.' Brockenhurst was warming to his subject.

'Yes, yes, Mr Brockenhurst, we can all agree on that, more police of the professional sort and less of the military. But my point, sir, is that your *Avenging Angel* is neither an officer of the law nor is he God's instrument. Of that you can be certain — and tonight sees the proof!'

'What do you mean?'

'An innocent man has been murdered and will be traduced if we do not act.'

'What Mr Sheridan means, sir, is that this killer has made a fatal mistake.'

'Not once but twice to my mind. Fatal for my actor. Fatal for Mr Broadhead whose loving wife is now a widow with five fatherless children who are faced with penury! And you, sir, shall write *that* story!'

Brockenhurst heaved a sigh as he deliberated, digesting this latest. 'And in return?'

'Mr Brockenhurst, this man is a danger to the general public,' Nicholls reasoned. 'It is a Monster that we deal with and no Angel. He must be stopped. And you can help us with the writing of this article. Only with his capture shall there be justice for Thaddeus Broadhead and his grieving family.'

Brockenhurst nodded. 'Then I may have all the details and speak first with the widow?'

'You may. And be the first to advertise the reward.'

'I am glad to be of service, Officer.'

'Good.' Nicholls eyed the journalist steadily. 'You will have no objection then to disclosing the name of the witness to the scene at the Covent Garden bagnio. We have two murders to investigate now.'

'I do not have it.'

'A description of the man then,' Nicholls persisted.

'I do not have that either.'

'You wrote of one who had seen with his own eyes, Brockenhurst.'

'It was a note. Stuck under my door.'

'What?' Sheridan was on his feet.

'Here…' The journalist rose quickly and scrabbled about the papers stacked on a shelf, squinting in the poor light. At last he drew out a folded piece of paper and handed it to Nicholls.

The constable perused it to the end. 'It is anonymous.'

'And this is your "absolute fact"?' Sheridan spluttered.

A look from Nicholls bade Sheridan to hold his tongue.

'You will have no objection, Mr Brockenhurst, if I keep this.'

It was not a request and the Runner refolded the note and placed it in his pocket.

*

Sheridan stayed the night at Nerot's Hotel and groaned loudly when the porter woke him as instructed at seven o'clock in the morning. But the Prince of Wales' business must be got underway. As sign of this Major Hanger had arranged an appallingly early appointment (Sheridan felt this to be some cruel jape on the equerry's part) with the governor of The Foundling Home for Daughters of the Deserving Poor, which Institution was one patronised by Her Royal Highness Princess Elizabeth and her royal sisters. Sheridan was to discuss the arrangement of a pageant to honour and entertain their Highnesses.

As he made his way to the dining room for breakfast, Sheridan asked the attendant to send out for *The Daily Enquiry*.

'*The Daily Enquiry*, Mr Sheridan?' The man looked askance.

'Yes, Darby, *The Daily Enquiry* — I have a hankering for scandal and hyperbole this morning and don't pretend you don't read the rag yourself! In fact, you may lend me your own copy, there's a good man.'

'It is not yet out, sir.'

'Well, when it is — and can you send a note to Sir Percival Jarvis, Green Street, apologies but that I may be a little delayed.'

He could not possibly face that old Tory toady Sir Percival without a hearty breakfast to bolster him for the task ahead and when he entered the dining room and saw the treats laid out on the sideboard, he knew this had been the right decision and furthermore wondered that he had not sampled the breakfast fare before now. The devilled eggs looked particularly good.

As he finished off his meal with the delicious little sugar pastries, he pondered the theory which Nicholls had postulated

— that the anonymous note might be from the assassin himself.

'*I believe you are right, Mr Sheridan, when you suggest that this man wishes to advertise his deeds. And if that is the case, then it is also the case that he has chosen Mr Brockenhurst's style of journalism in order to do so.*'

After Nicholls' description of the way in which Thaddeus Broadhead had also been laid out on the ground, as though to make display of all his mutilations, Sheridan was more convinced than ever that the assassin intended to create a spectacle. The first murders had taken place behind closed doors, as it were, but this last was outside, in a public place, albeit a narrow alleyway. Did it mean that the killer was becoming more reckless, or did it mean that he had become more emboldened? Would he seek an even more public arena for display on the next occasion? Sheridan shuddered to think of it.

What was meant by these acts? Why the display? Why the sign on the forehead? What lay behind these murders? Sheridan's initial suspicions had been that the assassinations were prompted by attempts at blackmail. If one supposed that the lad found in the Thames were the first victim, then it was a short step to supposing that the lad had imagined he might make an extra guinea by some cack-handed threat to expose Lord Malmain. And then Andrew Marson, who seemed to have had close relations of sorts with the viscount; he was an actor with expensive tastes and he may have been tempted to push too hard. Especially once he found out about the impoverished viscount's engagement to the wealthy heiress Miss Harte. Marson would know that Malmain would have an almost limitless source of funds once that marriage had been secured and his credit duly restored. The murders had been both revenge and perhaps a warning to other potential blackmailers. But why not simply cut the victim's throat and leave it at that? That had been the fatal strike, why then the embellishments?

The mutilations spoke of a kind of loathing and deep hatred. The victims had been emasculated. Their members stuffed into their mouths. Hardly a subtle reference to the sexual acts they had presumably engaged in. Then the inverted triangle, which Smyth had pointed out could denote the female genitalia.

Did this mean the victims were being cast as effeminates? Despised as such? He did not recall ever thinking Marson particularly feminine. There were certainly more dandified and effete members amongst his troupe of actors. Sheridan scratched his brow. On the contrary, although he was strikingly handsome, Marson had always struck him as possessing a very masculine demeanour. He had questioned Nicholls about Thaddeus Broadhead's appearance. The labourer was short but well built, his hands rough as one would expect, and his features made ruddy by a life labouring out of doors. A typical working man by all accounts. It was puzzling and it nagged at Sheridan.

His thoughts were interrupted by the return of the attendant with a copy of *The Daily Enquiry*.

'Thank you, Darby my good man, I shall leave it here for you when I've finished.'

Darby sniffed and bowed curtly when dismissed.

'My dear Sherry!' It was one of the Friends of Mr Pitt who hailed him with such infuriating familiarity. Charlie Long, one of the Cambridge set with whom the Prime Minister still surrounded himself like a moat.

'I almost had to look twice, sir, being astounded to see you abroad so early!' The fellow Member of Parliament chuckled gleefully.

'Long — are you not seeing double in any case? You haven't been supping brandy all night with your good friend?' It was a reference to the witticism posted in a Whig paper some months back. The occasion when Pitt and his drinking companion Dundas had staggered into the House like a couple of old soaks.

I cannot see the Speaker, Hal, can you?
What! Cannot see the Speaker, I see two!

'Rather suspected you had written those lines yourself, Sherry, but seems *The Daily Enquiry* is more your level of news and journalism these days!' Long pronounced the word 'level' with relish, perhaps intending some punning allusion to The Levellers.

'If Mr Pitt had his way, we should have no freedom of the press at all but simply his own philosophy and propaganda disseminated from on high. So, for all it is a dreadful, scurrilous rag — but one which I have a singular cause on this occasion to peruse — I say, "Hurrah for *The Daily Enquiry*!"' He raised the folded paper and waved it in the air.

Sheridan rather enjoyed the number of shocked faces which turned his way at this outburst. Such snobbery one encountered, even in the matter of newspapers.

CHAPTER TWELVE

He was on his way now to the offices of the East India Company to call on Mr Henry Ramus. He would not be expected. No preparatory letters of introduction or intermediary as with the estimable but exceedingly dull Sir Percival Jarvis. No. He was on his own with this meeting and he must act with all delicacy and diplomacy. Not least because he knew so little of the family and the circumstances surrounding little Eliza. He presumed there must be some settlement for the upkeep and raising of the child. Who had managed that, he wondered? The prince? But was it sufficient? Were all parties happy with the arrangement? Members of the Royal Family were not notable for their alacrity when it came to discharging their debts or financial obligations. Sheridan may very well be entering a hornet's nest.

What did he know? The equerry, Major Hanger, was also a confidante in this affair, although out of delicacy he had never once mentioned the name of Her Royal Highness, and he it was who had acquainted Sheridan with the bare outlines. The child was five years old. Her father, George Ramus, was a son of Nicholas Ramus, a senior page to the king. The Ramus family hailing originally from Switzerland by some accounts and having entered into the king's household with the arrival of the queen. Members of the family seemed to hold numerous positions within the household, including barber to His Royal Majesty. A sister to George had even married a baronet, Sir John Day.

He had imagined this George would be a strapping young fellow who had, with the carelessness of youth, stepped over the boundary which should have existed between a servant and mistress. To his surprise it seemed that George Ramus was some years older even than Sheridan himself, and more than twice the age of Princess Elizabeth at the time of the — how should he think of it? Not affair, as such, if there had been some form of highly irregular and clandestine 'marriage'. *Liaison*, he decided, would have to suffice. The princess cannot have known what she was doing at seventeen, this fellow George Ramus had taken advantage of her naivety, of her sheltered upbringing in the queen's secluded court and her complete lack of knowledge of the world. Had George perceived some advantage to himself?

Little Eliza had been adopted by her uncle, Henry. Clearly, George's younger brother knew the parentage of his niece. What sort of man was Henry, Sheridan wondered? He was about ten years George's junior and industrious, by all accounts. He hoped that he would be dealing with a sensible man and not a schemer. Her Royal Highness' relation to the child would always be vociferously denied if any of the Ramus family dared to claim that connection. They could not but expect consequences if they even threatened to make so bold a move. It occurred to Sheridan that blackmail was a very precarious pursuit. Particularly if one did not wield the greater power and force.

He was reminded of the known trick amongst thieves, where one grabbed a well-dressed young man on the street and shouted out accusations that he was a sodomite to the poor fellow's bewildered astonishment. Then, the accomplice, acting like a gentleman passer-by, advised the poor dupe to pay five or six guineas to settle the matter quietly. Many a victim, Sheridan felt sure, had paid over at least a guinea or two rather than face that heinous accusation, be it true or not. But a number of rogues had been caught at this trick and the law had dealt very harshly with them, not least for attempting to extract monies with accusations which were dubbed a calumny.

Here he was again drifting into thoughts of the Malmain business, as Sheridan now thought of it, when he should concentrate all his energies on the prince's play, the gift to His Royal Highness' sisters.

Sir Percival had agreed that the performance was, in principle, a perfectly splendid idea. It would not only enable the Institution to honour and hopefully entertain Their Royal Highnesses, but also allow the dear children themselves to show their appreciation of the great benefits they received at The Foundling Home. The little dears could demonstrate their well-being and display a variety of talents to their benefactresses.

He really was a most pompous old toady. When the discussions had then centred around rehearsal schedules and where they should take place and who should be involved, Sir Percival had begun to nitpick and become a stickler for propriety. The children should need chaperones. The girls should not be coached by anyone who was not beyond reproach. He emphasised that the moral education of their charges was of primary import to The Foundling Home for Daughters of the Deserving Poor. What assurances could be given in this regard? Sir Percival had eyed Sheridan with some scepticism and ferocity, as though anyone connected with the theatre was likely to be of dubious moral probity. To be honest, there were some grounds for that concern, Sheridan reflected.

Sheridan had attempted to mollify and charm the governor. Assurances were made. The welfare of the girls would be his utmost consideration and so on and so forth, all the while he wondered whether he might persuade the unquestionably respectable Mrs Siddons to make an appearance at the start of the rehearsals for a small remuneration. He could count on her discretion in the matter, although the same could not be said so confidently of her reprobate of a husband. He should have to emphasise that the theatrics were meant as a surprise and supposed he might have to pay Mrs Siddons some of her salary also.

And where would the money to pay for this all come from? The prince magnificently offered this and that, but Sheridan knew full well that no monies were ever likely to come back into his own pocket. He remembered others who had organised parties and events based on the Prince of Wales' expressed wishes and who had ended up footing the entire bill. He should have to borrow and fund the whole thing himself, and it could not look a cheap production. Really, he could do without the expense at this present time. The costs of the rebuild of the new theatre at Drury Lane were soaring. He shivered to even think of the precipice of debt before which he now stood. There had also been the expense of the lease for the previous temporary residency of the company at The King's Theatre — that had been something of an outrage on the manageme

nt's part to take such advantage of their homeless situation. In truth, he felt that he was being fleeced on every side.

His carriage drew up at the East India Company House on Leadenhall Street and he was about to open the door and step down when he recognised a figure emerging from the building. He sat back into his seat, keeping the curtain drawn aside. What business had Viscount Malmain here? And then he saw that the young lord was escorting an older gentleman in his wake and offered him his arm to lean on down the steps.

Sheridan raked his memory. Mr Harte of course, the future father-in-law, saviour of the Crumpsall fortunes. Malmain helped the East India Company grandee into a waiting carriage and followed in behind.

The sight of Malmain unnerved Sheridan. The viscount looked so pleasant and gracious. He looked ordinary, dare he admit it, for all he had a good tailor. It was difficult to imagine that only the night before the fellow had slit a man's throat down an alley and then mutilated the body. Experience had taught Sheridan, however, that men who committed murder rarely looked exceptional.

There was nothing apparently exceptional about Mr Henry Ramus. He worked as a junior clerk for the East India Company. The clerks were better known as 'writers', which appellation Sheridan found childishly amusing. Mr Ramus was rather taken aback when his superior brought him into a side room and introduced him to the Honourable Richard Brinsley Sheridan, indicating that the noted playwright, theatre owner and Member of Parliament wished to have a word with him privately.

'Forgive me for seeking you out here, Mr Ramus, but you will understand when I broach the business that I could hardly call on you at your home.'

Sheridan gestured Henry Ramus to a chair. Reluctantly the younger man took it.

'What is that business, sir?' He looked puzzled.

'Your family have an established connection with our esteemed Royal Family, I believe?'

Ramus nodded warily. 'My father has long been a faithful servant of King G

eorge.'

'Just so.'

Ramus entwined his fingers nervously. 'How may I help you, Mr Sheridan?'

'You have an adopted daughter, I believe?'

The clerk's eyes narrowed. 'Of what concern is that to you, sir?'

'A delightful young girl, I am sure.'

Henry Ramus pursed his lips.

Sheridan faltered. Mr Ramus would not be drawn, it seemed. Perhaps he should be more direct.

'Mr Ramus, I am preparing a children's entertainment. It is at the request of my royal friend the Prince of Wales.'

There was a flash then of something like hostility in Henry Ramus' eyes.

'His Royal Highness should like to entertain his sisters with a presentation by children who are not trained theatricals; he rather fancies that his royal sisters would be delighted by the innocent and guileless performances of quite ordinary children. But children with some connection to Their Highnesses perhaps, the children at a Foundling Home which they patronise, the offspring of esteemed servants —'

Henry Ramus stood suddenly. 'Pardon me, sir, but I fail to see how I might help in this matter.'

'Your daughter, Eliza —'

'Eliza?' Ramus straightened. 'Eliza is unavailable and unsuited for your theatrical, Mr Sheridan.'

'On the contrary, Mr Ramus, I believe your daughter might truly shine and of course there should be some token of gratitude for your daughter's time and any inconvenience caused.'

'Beg pardon, sir, but I must wish you good day, I shall be wanted at my desk.'

Sheridan rose also. 'I don't think you quite understand, Mr Ramus.'

'Oh, I understand perfectly, Mr Sheridan.'

Henry Ramus looked him squarely in the eye. 'My daughter is no one's puppet or plaything, royal or otherwise. I bid you good day.'

With that the writer nodded sharply and left the room.

Sheridan sighed. He could kick himself for making such a hash of the task. How could he have anticipated that he should meet a man of such apparent integrity. And at the East India Company of all places. Oh dear. He should have to think of something and quickly. The prince would not be disappointed in this matter, for if he were, Sheridan's credit might be swiftly and perilously debited.

CHAPTER THIRTEEN

At his invitation, Mrs Canning had brought the Reverend Wallis and Cecily to Haymarket along with Tom and Bessie for the evening's entertainment, which would include Mr Kemble's noted performance as Brutus in Shakespeare's *Julius Caesar.* Cecily expressed herself thrilled in anticipation and delighted with the views from the box which Sheridan had arranged — the Duke of Devonshire being absent that night and the box made available. He was all attention to the party's comfort and welfare; fruits were sent for and bottles of champagne and ratafia.

'This is very considerate of you, Mr Sheridan.' The reverend bowed rather formally. 'My wife and I do not often have occasion to visit the theatre. I can seldom spare the time, as you may imagine. But *Julius Caesar* is a favourite of mine and to see Mr Kemble in the leading role of Brutus is a rare privilege.'

In the box opposite, Sheridan caught sight of young George Canning making an entrance and then being presented to the Duke of Richmond, a member of Mr Pitt's cabinet. The duke was attending the performance with his wife and her sister, the sculptress, Mrs Damer. And was that one of the government whips, Charles Long, he could see hovering at the duke's shoulder?

'Is my nephew George with the Duke of Richmond?' Mehitabel squinted through her eyeglass across the auditorium. 'I believe it is. What is he doing with that old traitor?'

'Good Sister Christian, you know the duke is not a bad sort even though he left the Whigs bereft and joined the enemy!'

Mehitabel pursed her lips. 'I do not know how you can make so light of betrayal, Dick.'

'Sadly, it is quite the fashion since Mr Burke's dire pronouncements on the Revolution in France have sent shivering cracks through our ranks. But see, the duke is with his sister-in-law, who is as devout a Foxite as you yourself.'

'Mrs Damer?' Mehitabel sniffed with distaste. 'I wonder she still shows her face in the theatre.'

'Ah yes…' Sheridan lowered his voice. 'There was a scandal of sorts.'

When was it? Four or five years previous? Rumours which had linked the tall, angular sculptress in a rather salacious way to one of his own actresses, his Queen of Comedy, Eliza Farren. No one within the company had taken the nonsense seriously for one moment. They were all too aware of the dedicated virtue of that actress in the pursuit of her designs on the equally constant Lord Derby. Everyone knew that Derby only waited for the death of his disgraced and discarded wife in order to claim Miss Farren as his future countess. The idea that pretty little Eliza Farren was frolicking beneath the bedsheets with Mrs Damer was patently ludicrous, no matter how striking the sculptress might be. Nevertheless, the actress had tantamount gone into hiding rather than face the crude catcalls coming from the audience in the pit.

Rather strangely, Sheridan had discovered that the origin of this sapphic calumny was none other than William Siddons. That wretched husband of the Muse of Tragedy. He had prayed that this did not signal warfare between his two leading actresses. The casting about of anonymous slanders and the distribution of malicious epigrams a new way to exact revenge for some slight, real or imagined. He did not approve of such fabrications unless, of course, he himself were the source.

Sheridan smiled to himself. Yes, he admitted he had been guilty of fanning a flame between Miss Farren and that contending Queen of Comedy, Dora Jordan, with his anonymous pieces speaking of a feud between the two women and alluding to them as 'The Rivals', a playful reference to an upcoming production of the play. Thankfully, nothing further had appeared from William Siddons, nothing at all from the Farren camp that he knew of, and he had quite forgotten all about those Sapphic allusions until Mrs Canning had reminded him.

He supposed it was this Marson business and the notion of attraction between those of the same sex which now brought these memories more sharply into his mind. How those rumours and snide references must have hurt and damaged the two women he could well imagine. It was in the nature of gossip and rumour to be malicious. Wasn't that at the very heart of his play, *The School for Scandal*? Society enjoyed nothing so much as a delicious scandal, conversation could be so very dull without it. Sheridan wondered if the tittle-tattle about Mrs Damer might surface again. He should not be surprised. The Press were currently obsessed with impure relations between women. The Sapphic slurs against Marie Antoinette had been renewed with unbridled gusto in Paris and only added to the clamours for her trial. That poor, friendless French queen who was all too likely to be following her husband to the guillotine. As Sheridan gazed at Mrs Damer in the opposite box, he very much hoped that any future aspersions on the good sculptress would not include Miss Farren. Eliza Farren's star had continued to rise and the profits of the company could well do without another hurried absence from the stage.

His eye drifted back to George Canning, who was clearly basking in the duke's attention. Sheridan had no doubts that a young man as gifted as Canning would go far if his origins might be overlooked. At that moment their eyes locked and George became aware that he was being peered at from their box. He made a swift and awkward bow towards both his aunt and Sheridan.

During an interval, George and Charles Long arrived at their door. George clearly could not ignore the presence at the theatre of his aunt and cousin.

Bessie gave him a disingenuous embrace. 'Why, don't you look handsome and distinguished, cousin Georgie!'

Mehitabel patted his shoulder. 'We did not know you would be here tonight, nephew, and keeping such elevated company.' She cast her eye across the auditorium to the Richmond box.

Charles Long's interest in joining their party had not been so obvious to Sheridan until it transpired that Long had been up at Cambridge with Reverend Wallis and was grasping the opportunity to renew acquaintance.

'Wallis, my dear fellow! You were always meant for the cloth. How well it suits you.'

The reverend seemed to flinch under the bright spot of Long's attention.

'Do you see our good friend, Mr Pitt? Were you not in the same lodgings together at one time? I rather remember you were always on his coat-tails.'

Wallis shook his head. 'I don't doubt our Prime Minister has too much of the affairs of state to be troubled by the old friendships of youth.'

Long smiled. 'On the contrary, Wallis, William likes nothing better than to have old friends about him from his Cambridge days — we are quite the merry band!'

'Please, do send Mr Pitt my warm regards.' The reverend bowed stiffly.

'You are now ensconced at Sir Edward's living, I believe? I hear it is a fine church. How gratifying it must be to sermonise to one's own family!'

Wallis introduced his wife and Charles Long raised an appreciative eyebrow.

'Mrs Wallis, I am entirely delighted to make your acquaintance.' He bowed low.

Cecily Wallis pinked.

'For a moment, Mrs Wallis, I took you to be some pretty ingenue of Sherry's, for you look far too young and fresh to be a married woman.'

'We are not long married, sir, and I am nearly twenty.'

'Delightful! And delighted to make your acquaintance, Mrs Wallis.' He bowed again and then grasped the reverend on his shoulder. 'We must renew our friendship, Peter, or Reverend, should I now address you, sir? You cannot keep such a charming wife hidden away in Woodford.' He turned to young Canning at his side. 'Isn't that right, George? I wonder you don't visit your aunt more often?'

'If I might enjoy Mrs Wallis' company, perhaps I should.' The young man bowed courteously to the reverend's wife.

Was that a faint flush on George's face? Sheridan allowed himself a smile of amusement. Had young Canning also noticed the delectable charms of Mrs Wallis? The young lady herself was clearly flustered by the gallantry now focussed on her, but she was also thoroughly enjoying the attention of the urbane Mr Long and handsome George Canning.

'We wish that he would, sir,' Mehitabel contributed lightly. 'But his business with the law keeps my nephew much occupied.'

'Oh, George is very much preoccupied at the moment, Mrs Canning, I can vouch for that. There is a certain matter on the Isle of Wight which takes all his interest.' Mr Long smirked and Sheridan caught the warning glare which young George then directed to the Friend of Mr Pitt.

When the two gentlemen had left the box, Hitty turned to Sheridan in an aside.

'Whatever is George doing with that Pittite scoundrel?'

'Oh, you know that George finds his mind expanded by listening to the opinions of all parties. He is a well-rounded young man.'

'He may play at devil's advocate but only let him be saved from The Pitt!' Mehitabel allowed herself a little congratulatory chuckle at her own witticism, she so rarely found a bon mot in the moment.

The orchestra had struck up and the merry tune signalled a comic interlude.

Sheridan excused himself from the party. There were theatre matters which he must attend to.

'You are never at your ease, Dick, but always restless.'

'I am sure, Mrs Canning, that you are the only one of my friends to be of that unique opinion. I am castigated on all sides for idleness, don't you know.'

She tutted and tapped him with her fan.

He bowed to the rest of the gathering, but Tom and Bessie were already leaning over the rail and tittering at some business of Joey Grimaldi's on stage. The reverend's eyes were trained on the Richmond box where Mr Long was once again ensconced — but not young George, Sheridan noted.

The only member of the party who expressed any misery at the loss of his company was Cecily Wallis; she turned to him with appealing eyes.

'Oh, must you leave us so soon, Mr Sheridan?'

She really was most winsome, he decided.

'Would that I could stay, Mrs Wallis, to enjoy your favour.'

Emboldened, he reached for her hand and with a bow pressed his lips to her soft, white fingers. Mrs Wallis eyes widened and she blushed to her roots. He smiled conspiratorially. It was a matter of moments and no one else had seen the gesture.

As Sheridan made his way through the narrow corridors backstage, he found the young actor, James Blackett, in his path. He was dressed in a Roman toga and cloak, his face painted for the part of Mark Antony. Sheridan appraised that the Wardrobe Mistress, Mrs Petty, had added some padding to the shoulders of the costume to lend a more manly and soldierly profile to the lad, who was of a slight build.

'Mr Sheridan. Might I have a word with you in private, sir?'

'If it is about your salary then you must speak to the Treasurer.'

Sheridan made to pass.

'Another matter entirely, sir.'

'Ah, you would that I would "lend you my ears", is that it? But what if I am neither Friend, Roman nor Countryman, Mr Blackett?'

James Blackett looked a little exasperated.

'Mr Sheridan —'

Tom King came out of his dressing room carrying a Roman gladius. He swiped the short sword from side to side as he approached.

'Let us have no conspirators here!' he declaimed and punctuated his decree with a grin when he stopped in front of them.

'Beware young Blackett, our illustrious proprietor is a notorious schemer!' King sneered. 'And I should know, I was his manager once!'

'Mr King, you know yourself that running a company of this size is not for the faint-hearted. But scheming? Sir! Retract at once!' Sheridan glared ferociously at the actor. 'But for the fact that you are *not* a gentleman I would challenge you to a duel!'

James Blackett looked with growing alarm between the two men, who were squared off against each other.

Then both broke into great peals of laughter and Sheridan punched his old friend in the chest. He turned to James Blackett.

'Now that Mr King has restored my good humour, you may have five minutes of my time, Mr Blackett. Follow me,' he commanded, knowing the young actor would be fast on his coat-tails.

He was reminded yet again that he had not yet questioned the eighteen-year-old about any knowledge he might have about Marson. The prompter had claimed that the murdered actor had been the lad's friend and mentor within the company.

'Mr Sheridan, the season here is almost at an end —' Blackett began hurriedly once they were inside the office.

'And? I am sure you will be wanted at The Haymarket for the summer. You may rest easy.'

'That's just it, sir, I should rather be elsewhere.'

'Oh? Are you not happy within our merry band?'

'Oh! Yes, sir. It is everything that I could have wished for and Mr Kemble has been most considerate, but...' He trailed off.

'But what, Blackett?'

The young actor flushed. 'I am frightened, Mr Sheridan. I think someone may be watching me, following me...'

'I usually find those skulking fellows to be a creditor. Ignore them. It is the only answer.'

Blackett shook his head. 'I have no debts, sir.'

Sheridan leapt playfully into an attitude of astonishment. 'Then you are a subversive, sir, and undermine our economy which, don't you know, runs entirely on credit. It is your duty, particularly in this time of war, to run up as much debt as you can!'

'Mr Sheridan, I came to ask you for a letter of recommendation to Mr Monroe of a company in Edinburgh which I thought to join.'

'And quit the best theatre in London? Are you quite mad?'

'I am afraid, sir.'

Sheridan nodded and assumed a sympathetic expression. 'It is the death of your friend Mr Marson which has unsettled you, James?'

'Yes,' Blackett mumbled.

'You have no doubt read the scurrilous and lurid reports in *The Daily Enquiry* of debauchery and murder at a nearby club?'

'Yes, sir.' The young man flushed again.

'I understand your concern, and believe it or not you have my sympathy. I concede, the reports are true in this, it was a savage murder. Nothing justifies such an end.'

'I read there is an Avenger abroad and I fear —' The lad floundered.

'That you may be singled out, James?'

Blackett gave an imperceptible nod. 'Last night I was sure I was followed again on my way home to my lodgings. On the instant, I changed direction and hurried towards a nearby inn where I knew there would be men within who should hear me cry out if I were attacked. My heart was racing, sir, but I stopped to look behind and see who pursued me.'

'And you saw jack-a-lantern himself, I presume?'

James offered a weak smile. 'A man halted in the shadows when he saw that I stopped. He was dressed in black. Like a crow. His hat was pulled low but I could feel his eyes on me, Mr Sheridan.'

'A gentleman? Well, might he not have paused simply because he thought that you might turn and attack him?'

James shook his head. 'He came towards me then, and I felt myself frozen to the spot. If a couple of fellows had not tumbled from the inn at that moment I do not know what might have happened. The gentleman gave me such a strange look when he passed by me that I cannot get his eyes from my mind. He seemed of another devilish world…'

Sheridan regarded the young actor with bemusement. James Blackett had clearly worked himself into a state of absolute dread and in his febrile imagination conjured all manner of demons and avenging angels in pursuit of him. Well, so be it.

'Of course, you must go to Edinburgh. It is a miserable, dour and grey city but your reference from me shall glow so brightly that Mr Monroe will wonder where you keep your halo.'

'Thank you, Mr Sheridan, thank you.'

'Before you go to your cue —' Sheridan grabbed the young man by his padded shoulders — 'believe me when I tell you that I would do anything toward the capture of Marson's assassin. If there is anything you felt that you might confide to me that might throw some light, then I beg you please to tell me. It will be divulged only with those who share our great desire to catch this *Avenging Angel* and to see him punished.'

Blackett hesitated and then, encouraged by the gentle persuasion in Sheridan's eyes, blurted out, 'I know that he was married, sir.'

'Married?'

Had he heard right? This was something unexpected altogether.

'Not in the usual way, a man and a woman, but to another man, that was his husband. I have heard of such ceremonies but never witnessed one. Andrew swore me to secrecy, but confessed that he had never known such love.' The young actor continued to gabble nervously. 'We had a similar history, he and I, Mr Sheridan, he knew it at once when we met. That is why he could confide in me. That is all I can say, sir.'

'Thank you, Mr Blackett, for your candour. I shall write the letter of recommendation forthwith. Now, go you forth to bury Caesar.'

He had scarcely put quill to paper when there was another call on his time, but one which he welcomed with alacrity.

'Good to see you, Louis-Pierre!'

'Sir.'

'May I offer you a libation? I was just about to pour myself — but no. You are on duty?'

Nicholls assented.

Sheridan poured himself a bumper of brandy.

'What must I prepare myself for now, Constable? You have a habit of imparting unwelcome or disturbing news.'

'On this occasion, Mr Sheridan, I hope I arrive with an answer to one of our puzzles.'

'Which one? There are so many?'

Nicholls allowed himself a small smile.

Sheridan leant forward.

'You will recall the pocket watch that we found amongst Mr Marson's clothing.' The constable extracted it from his pocket and opened the backing. 'Last week I found time to show it to my father-in-law, Monsieur De Lubac, who is himself a watchmaker of some repute.'

'And?'

'He examined the piece with every care. It is a simple verge pocket watch in silver pair cases but the workmanship is very fine, he said, and could be the work of only a handful of his brother watchmakers. He then found the maker's mark was hidden in the mechanism.'

Sheridan saw the gleam come into Nicholls' eyes; he had clearly discovered the maker.

'And now you have the name?'

Nicholls nodded. 'A Mr Inigo Hughes of the City of London. Today I have met with Mr Hughes and he recognised the piece as one that he had made some two years ago. I said that my object was to return the valuable item to its owner. Mr Hughes agreed that he would consult his ledgers and identify who that might be, as he could not recall who the gentleman was after this length of time, and his order books being so full for watches of a similar type.'

'Our Mr J.B.?' Sheridan clapped his hands and rose to his feet. 'Do not keep me suspended, Constable!'

Nicholls shook his head. 'Not J.B., sir. Indeed, Mr Hughes insisted that the inscription was not by his hand, nor noted in his ledger. Some other must have been employed for that task.'

'I see. But who commissioned the watch? That must tell us who gave it to Mr Marson. The inscription done later and the initials with some more obscure significance than a name.'

'Sir Jonas Soersby.'

'Judge Soersby?'

'The same, sir.'

Sheridan sat back down heavily. Sir Jonas Soersby, notable High Court Judge and soon to be a Justice of the King's Bench. Here was no stranger to Sheridan but a man with whom he had conversed and dined and been entertained over the course of some seventeen years. This was an answer so bewildering he must absorb the revelation and gather his thoughts into some order of response.

Sheridan's late wife Eliza had been well acquainted with Lady Priscilla Soersby. They had been girlhood friends in Bath before either had married. Miss Clary, as she was then, had been musically inclined and a great admirer of the Linley sisters. It was Sheridan's wife, and her sister Mary, who had been the celebrities then, the leading sopranos of the day. Priscilla Clary's friendship had blossomed with Eliza in particular. On her marriage to Sir Jonas Soersby, Lady Priscilla had taken up residence in their Mayfair house during the season and renewed the friendship with Eliza. He recalled her laments that Sheridan no longer allowed Eliza to sing in public. The two friends were frequent visitors together to the opera house. And although there had been a slight estrangement in the final years, he recalled the very genuine tears which Lady Soersby had shed during Eliza's funeral at Wells Cathedral.

The friendship between their wives had inevitably brought Sheridan and Soersby within each other's orbit, but it had never been more than polite acquaintance on the part of the two husbands. Like himself, Soersby was a man in his forties, but with an aloof and distinguished air, something Sheridan had never managed to project even when he tried. Sir Jonas had a reputation for being stern, but not a 'hanging' judge. On the last occasion of their meeting, Soersby had enthused about the prison settlement at Botany Bay and advocated transportation as preferable in most cases. Though many considered that to be a death sentence of another sort. They had little of shared interest and their spheres of connection had seldom brought them any closer. Sheridan was a Whig and frequented Brooks's Club. Sir Jonas did not hold strong political allegiances but was a government man by inclination and a member of White's Club.

Sheridan was so astounded by Nicholl's revelation that he could not but question it. What could the Justice possibly have to do with Andrew Marson? Despite Lady Priscilla's love of music and the theatre, Sir Jonas was seldom to be found in those arenas himself. And as for the other — that he too might prefer the company of men? Sheridan, for all his worldliness, shrank from that thought.

'You are acquainted with Sir Jonas, sir?'

'I am, Nicholls. I can only imagine that there is some simple error here, some mistake in Mr Hughes' ledger…'

Sheridan was beginning to wish that he had not allowed himself to be dragged into the murderous business in the first place.

Nicholls paused in thought.

'Might I suggest that we both call on Mr Hughes and ask to examine the record for ourselves, to be quite satisfied and certain with this information.'

'Yes, let us do it tomorrow. I cannot see how I can rest easy until the matter is clarified.'

Nicholls looked at the watch, weighing it in his palm. 'Mr Sheridan, if it does prove to be Judge Soersby who has ordered this timepiece, I would very much welcome the opportunity to discuss the matter with you and perhaps seek your advice and guidance before I act further on the information.'

A loud rapping at the door was followed by the entrance of Monsieur Dubois without invitation. He ignored the constable and glared directly at Sheridan.

'Monsieur Sherrie — Hercules has not eaten. Is *non habitual*. Is *mal*.'

'Monsieur Dubois —'

'I call the doctor — and you will pay!'

'Sir.' Nicholls rose and nodded to Sheridan. 'If you will excuse me, I shall be wanted at Bow Street now and must take my leave. I hope to see you on the morrow.'

'You will, Constable Nicholls, you will.'

Dubois held the door wide for the Bow Street Runner and continued to regard Sheridan ferociously.

'Hercules is —'

'Yes, Dubois, Hercules is sickening and will not eat his hay. Actors may come and actors may go, but a good horse — do whatever must be done and the money will be found, do assure our good horse doctor.'

Dubois made a loud sound of satisfaction and left the room, slamming the door behind him. Sheridan wondered, not for the first time, why he had been persuaded to grant Dubois supervision over the theatre's stables and menagerie of animals for a ridiculously extravagant addition to his salary. But the Frenchman had a real care and sympathy for the creatures which was often missing in his relations with fellow humans.

Alone at last Sheridan refilled his glass and exhaled long and loud. His mind raced. The timepiece in Andrew Marson's possession could not have been given to the actor by Sir Jonas Soersby, of that he was certain. The inscription, *Omnia vincit amor* — Love conquers all — should be from a romantic admirer, surely? And the initials J.B. did not equate with J.S.

No. It simply could not be.

CHAPTER FOURTEEN

Nicholls had taken him to that part of the city well known for its horologists to visit Mr Hughes. The little man raised himself from his workbench and eyed them through his loupe, the magnifying piece wedged into one eye socket.

'I have already given the information, Constable.'

'We would see for ourselves, Mr Hughes. If you please,' Nicholls added, attempting a smile of persuasion.

'This is most inconvenient; I am a busy man. Can you not take my word?'

'Such fine work, Mr Hughes, it is most marvellous,' Sheridan intervened. 'I commend you on the detail and I believe your watches keep excellent time.'

'I should think they do, Mr Sheridan!'

'Your orderbooks are very full, I believe, sir, but would you have room, do you think, to include the making of a piece in time for November?'

'November? It is … possible.'

'I would be most indebted. It is my son's birthday, you see. He shall be eighteen. The age at which Time becomes important to a man. Children, I find, have no sense of time whatsoever and neither should they — it is of no significance to them, for they think it will last forever and see no need to parcel it up into hours and minutes.'

'Well, I could manage it.'

'And an inscription? I thought it might say, *Time Waits For No Man* — as my own did, a little tease of Mr Fox from whom it was a gift, before it was stolen.'

Mr Hughes nodded and with a little grumbling under his breath, ordered his boy to fetch the orderbook for the first half of 1791 from his archive.

Nicholls withdrew Marson's timepiece from his pocket in readiness and Mr Hughes scanned through the entries until he stabbed his finger at one.

'See, here it is. Silver verge pocket watch. Full plate fire gilt movement with round pillars. Pierced and engraved cock, silver regulator disc. Plain three-arm steel balance, blue steel spiral hairspring.' Mr Hughes sniffed and stabbed again. 'White enamel dial with Roman numerals, blue steel beetle and poker hands.'

Sheridan and Nicholls both peered at the details of the entry to doubly assure themselves that the description of the watch was indeed matched to the account of Sir Jonas Soersby, though what a 'silver regulator disc' might be neither had a notion.

It was there in black and white. There could be no mistake, it seemed.

'Thank you, Mr Hughes. Sir Jonas Soersby is an esteemed friend of mine and I am sure that he will be delighted with the return of such a valuable piece.'

'Quite so, Mr Sheridan.'

'*Tempus fugit*, Mr Hughes. Time flies and so must we. We thank you again for your good grace.'

On the journey back to Bow Street, Nicholls sat opposite Sheridan. He rubbed at his face and Sheridan could see the weariness and strain written there. This murder had involved the constable in some very difficult decisions.

Nicholls had been forced to confess to keeping his masters at Bow Street in the dark as to the murderous scene at Mr

Culpepper's establishment. He had recorded the death at the bagnio as an unfortunate accident. Only when pushed by the imminent scandalous report in *The Daily Enquiry* had he hastened to the Chief Magistrate at Bow Street and explained the omissions in his original account and the reasoning behind his silence. He had been fortunate to have a sympathetic ear from Sir Sampson. But many of his police colleagues had not been so understanding and his position within their ranks was made tenuous.

It seemed the business now took yet another treacherous direction. Nicholls faced the prospect of questioning a senior man, a baronet and a judge. Sir Jonas Soersby would not take kindly to be being quizzed in this way by a lowly Bow Street Runner. It was almost impossible to consider. Sheridan's expression softened in sympathy as he eyed his young friend, for he had begun to think of the police officer in that regard.

'Let us talk through the predicament we have arrived at, Louis-Pierre. I believe you wished to ask my advice. I am not certain that I can give you advice of any worth in these circumstances, but I may provide a friendly ear at least.'

'Thank you, sir. I am most grateful.'

'Let us consider firstly what we know for fact.'

Nicholls nodded. 'The fob watch was found in the pocket of Mr Marson's waistcoat.'

'A fact we can agree. But what proof, if any, do we have that it was Andrew's watch?'

'Your prompter has said so, has he not?'

'He has said that Andrew received a fine watch from a Right Honourable Mr B. and showed it to him; and he has said that this was above a year since.'

'We must check it is the same piece.'

Sheridan nodded. 'Yes. It may not be the same one. Though we admit the likelihood that it is.'

'I shall find him at the theatre.'

'Mr Quail did not know who Mr B. was. He said that Andrew referred to all his admirers by an initial. Further, he described Mr B. as the Right Honourable.'

'Meaning a gentleman of rank.'

'The son of a baronet? A Member of Parliament? A Justice? We cannot know. But Mr Quail implied that when Marson referred to this gentleman as the "*Right Honourable*", it was in the tone of a jest. That may be because Mr B. is either a man of rank but may not be *honourable*, or he is a man who is not of rank but has such pretensions.'

'We do know that this timepiece was made by Mr Hughes and that it was made for Sir Jonas Soersby.'

'Yes. But without the engraving.'

'We do not know that Sir Jonas commissioned the inscription.'

'The initials of his name are J.S. and not J.B.'

'We do not know that Sir Jonas gave the watch to Mr Marson,' Nicholls concluded.

'Precisely. Now, let us speculate.'

Nicholls smiled.

'You smile, Nicholls?'

'Because, Mr Sheridan, I do believe you are enjoying this.'

'Constable, the act of murder is, I believe, foreign to our natures.' He flicked a hand between the two of them. 'It is a mystery. And if we do not relish and enjoy the solution to that mystery, why, then we might only have recourse to weep, and our tears will not help the dead.'

Nicholls' smile widened and Sheridan could see that his spirits had lifted a little.

'Speculation. The watch may have been stolen,' Sheridan began.

'Or lost then found by someone else.'

'Speculation. The inscription may have been commissioned by someone other than Sir Jonas.'

'Speculation. This man may have the initials J.B.'

'Speculation. The initials signify something other than a given name.'

'Speculation. Sir Jonas Soersby gave the timepiece to Andrew Marson.'

'Speculation. The Judge prefers the company of men.'

'Speculation. Sir Jonas Soersby was being blackmailed.

'Speculation. Sir Jonas Soersby was being blackmailed by Andrew Marson.'

Nicholls gulped. 'Speculation. His Honour murdered Mr Marson.'

They were silent within the cocoon of the carriage. Outside, there was a cacophony of noise from sellers and callers, carters shouting at those pedestrians in the way, the neighing of a horse, the ringing of a bell, the shouts of drunken soldiers. Sheridan felt a resonance with his own jumble of jarring thoughts. The game of speculation had not dispelled anything of the confusion. There seemed only one way forward, which Nicholls then voiced.

'All this speculation may only be clarified by asking for the answers directly.'

The two men looked at each other. How should that be possible? Sheridan knew that neither he nor Nicholls could with any ease question Sir Jonas on who the pocket watch was made for and why. Because if, just if, the watch had been a gift from Sir Jonas Soersby to the actor Andrew Marson, that could only mean one thing. Some degree of intimacy. The thought was outlandish. The potential for insult made him pale.

Sir Jonas would have no option but to lie. He must know by now of Marson's murder and he would say that, yes, the watch was one that he had ordered but that it had been lost or stolen and he was very sorry to find that it had been found amongst the possessions of a murdered man. And no, he knew nothing of the inscription and would express a curiosity to know what the inscription was. If, on the other hand, the judge were speaking the truth and the watch had indeed been lost or stolen, how should he or Nicholls ever be truly convinced of it?

'There seems little point in questioning Sir Jonas. Any connection to Andrew Marson will be denied.'

Nicholls nodded a slow assent.

'A judge of the High Court might not take kindly to being interrogated by a Bow Street Runner in a matter that involves not only murder but sodomy. You might find your advancement at Bow Street mysteriously hampered, Louis-Pierre. I should not like to see that happen.'

Nicholls had voiced within the game of speculation that Soersby could be the killer. Sir Jonas might have as much reason as anyone if he had been intimate with the actor. Sheridan realised that he had locked himself into a fixed idea about Viscount Malmain and that perhaps he needed to consider the case more widely.

It seemed that they were at an impasse again.

The carriage had stopped outside the Bow Street Magistrates' Court when they were hailed by Mr Brockenhurst.

The journalist's article about the tragic murder of Thaddeus Broadhead had garnered wide circulation and his outcry in support of the widow Broadhead and her family had brought an excited response. Shocked well-wishers had rallied around to collect funds on her behalf and Brockenhurst was urging for the purchase of apprenticeships for her two sons. The affair had become something of a cause célèbre for *The Daily Enquiry* and its readership.

'Constable Nicholls! Mr Sheridan! I am glad to have found you.'

Mr Brockenhurst paused to recover his breath as he reached the door of the carriage.

'Mr Brockenhurst, I read your last piece and must admit that I was moved almost to tears by your description of Mrs Broadhead —'

'Mr Sheridan, Constable —' the journalist gasped for breath. 'You have been sadly mistaken. Very mistaken. I am all of a quandary!'

'Whatever is it, Badger? You are quite unsettled.'

The journalist was so busy extracting a folded page from his pocket that he did not at first register the use of the nickname.

'Here. You must read this. Where is the truth to be found, I ask?'

Nicholls opened up the page and allowed Sheridan to peer over his shoulder from his seat within the carriage.

The letter to the Editor of *The Daily Enquiry* claimed that Thaddeus Broadhead might be a married man with five children but it refuted that he was an innocent. He was an habitual frequenter of such alleys. Which made him that most vile creature of all, a man who hid behind the skirts of a woman in order to disguise his true nature. The assassin had indeed been acting with the Sword of Righteousness in his hand like an Avenging Angel.

The note was unsigned. From an inner pocket Nicholls withdrew the earlier missive and put the two pieces of paper side by side, glancing quickly from one to the other.

'The same paper, I would hazard. And the same hand — the similarities in the crossing of the letter T and the curve of the S is distinctive. Here is our Anonymous again.' Nicholls looked pointedly up at Sheridan, both knowing what that might signify.

'Spreading his false accusations yet again.' Sheridan turned to the Grub Street hack and shook his head. 'You cannot print this, Mr Brockenhurst.'

'Mr Sheridan!' Brockenhurst shook his head in turn and laughed. 'I am a journalist!'

'It is unproven slander.' Sheridan waved to the letter dismissively. 'Whilst Mrs Broadhead still grieves and her children face empty plates. Think what your writing does for them. Think what good you may do.'

Mr Brockenhurst looked uncertain.

'If the proof of these claims about Thaddeus comes forward then by all means print, Mr Brockenhurst. I should be the last man to stand in the way of truth.'

The pen-smith pursed his lips and shook his head as he grappled with the appeal to his better nature against the tug of his Grub Street instincts.

The tussle was clearly proving a difficult one.

'Sir,' interjected Nicholls, 'the Bow Street Office would wish to speak with the man who writes these letters. He claims to have knowledge of the happenings at the bagnio and to know hidden details of Mr Broadhead's life. How does he come by this information? Because he is privy to these murders? Because he is acquainted with the assassin?' Nicholls tapped the letters. 'Why does he write to you, Mr Brockenhurst?'

The journalist looked momentarily puzzled. 'Because he wants the truth to be known.'

'And if you do not print the information in this second letter?'

'He will write again.'

'And the more he writes, the more he may attempt to offer greater proofs to persuade you to print. The more he may reveal himself.'

Brockenhurst pointed at the letter. 'Or he may simply take his claims to another newspaper!'

'That is a risk, but I believe he has chosen you to be his mouthpiece, sir.'

Brockenhurst's eyes narrowed.

'And if we find this man — there may be the bigger story!' Sheridan offered.

'If this man is brought out then I shall want that story exclusive.'

'It shall be all scooped up for you Badge— Mr Brockenhurst.'

'Very well, I shall delay — for now. Good day to you gentlemen.'

Sheridan heaved a great sigh of relief as they watched the journalist scurry away.

'If we are right and these letters come from the assassin, then he may be pushed to write again, Mr Sheridan,' Nicholls voiced hopefully.

'Let us hope so, because his other course may be to answer the silence of *The Daily Enquiry* with another murder.'

CHAPTER FIFTEEN

They were at the end of the parliamentary sittings in June and true to his word Brockenhurst had not published the allegations made in the anonymous letter against Thaddeus Broadhead. He had instead continued a heartfelt and moving campaign for the assistance of Broadhead's impoverished widow and her children, which appeal had captured the imagination of a sympathetic public. To Sheridan and Nicholls' disappointment, Anonymous had thus far sent no further missives to Brockenhurst, dashing their hopes of gaining more insight into the man who sent them. On the other hand, he had clearly not taken his claims to any of the other scurrilous rags; for which they were thankful. The anonymous letter-writer appeared to have reined in his horns. If he was also the assassin, as Nicholls suspected, that activity too seemed to be in abeyance. But Sheridan did not dare to think the ghastly business was at an end. Someone had gotten away with murder, not once but twice and even thrice — or more. Sheridan had become convinced that the killer was highborn, an aristocrat. The thought that a man like Viscount Malmain might feel himself above the law and beyond the reach of justice needled at him.

Despite his attempts to put the affair out of mind, images of Andrew Marson's injuries continued to haunt him, even as he sat through the pressing debates of the day. He eyed Mr Pitt sitting across the House from him. His lean figure and pointed features seemed to him to have become increasingly hawkish and predatory. After the debacle of the Regency Crisis, Pitt's position of power now seemed unassailable. The advent of war had served only to increase his stranglehold as the Whig opposition found themselves in disarray. Pitt had only to speak of the nation's security and the constant threat of French invasion in order to introduce one draconian measure after another. The opposition seemed powerless to resist the assaults on freedoms which had until very recently been taken for granted.

The Whig party were at a crossroads, splitting under the strains of divisions over the response to the Revolution in France and the subsequent war. Sheridan's countryman, Dr Edmund Burke, had published his *Reflections on the Revolution in France* and truly put the cat amongst the pigeons. Suddenly, to be a supporter of the reformist aims of the revolution and to wish for a greater fairness and equality in the British Isles had become akin to expressing the views of an out-and-out traitor. The Whig tradition had always stood for limitations on excessive royal power and a respect for parliament and representation. But these principles had become increasingly fractured by issues of loyalty and national security. Sheridan himself had endured being caricatured as a *sans-culotte* traitor for his championing of The Friends of the Liberty of the Press, his defence of societies like The Friends of the People, and the relish with which he continued to vociferously discredit the government's use of coercion.

His own relationship with William Pitt, he acknowledged, had become increasingly bitter and personal. A decade earlier, Pitt had taunted him with his theatrical origin, his career as a poet and playwright. He had praised his "*dramatic turns and his epigrammatic points,*" then sneered "*But this is not the proper scene for the exhibition of those elegancies*". Sheridan had struck back immediately with the retort that were he ever to write for the stage again, he would attempt an improvement on Ben

Jonson's character of the 'Angry Boy' in *The Alchemist*. To his delight, the name *Angry Boy* had haunted 'Master Billy' for all these years since.

Yes, there was no love lost between them. His thoughts still on the murders in the bagnio, Sheridan was reminded that he had on more than one occasion inferred that the Prime Minister himself might prefer the company of men. Deliberately cruel jibes, he realised. They had been designed to undermine the leadership of the king's chosen minister — Sheridan had referred to him as *a minion of the crown*, in an allusion to the Duke of Buckingham, rumoured to have been the male lover of King James I. Then, Sheridan had not seriously considered if what he charged might be true. Insults were part and parcel of that cut and thrust across the floor of the House. Now, he wondered.

William Pitt the Younger was not married. At thirty-four that might not be considered too remarkable for a man. But there had never been any talk, serious or otherwise, of a mistress or romantic interest of any kind. Pitt and his friends had put it about that the demands of high office were all-consuming. Such demands had not curtailed the lust of other political leaders. He had heard it mooted that power itself was an aphrodisiac of sorts and he could well believe it. Was Pitt truly celibate? Like some papist clergyman? Or, and this was a new thought, if his sexual proclivities did incline towards other men, must he deny himself? It should be too dangerous a secret to try and keep hidden. Sheridan regarded Pitt with a new interest. What might that do to a man? He himself had rarely, if ever, denied his lustful urges — tempered them perhaps, as with Eliza when the doctor had advised that she should bear no more children. No, he had always been a passionate man. How should it be to deny all gratification for the sake of being the First Minister? Sheridan shuddered. It was not something he could imagine for himself.

He felt a momentary stab of pity for his adversary. Which fell away as Pitt rose to make his usual assaults on Charles James Fox, that amiable, shambling hulk of a man who sat to Sheridan's right.

Sheridan emerged from the buildings of Westminster in the wake of Charles Long to find that waiting for this particular Friend of Mr Pitt was young Canning. George had recently been informed of his success in the election at Newtown on the Isle of Wight, without any necessity for him to even meet his new constituents. Sheridan smiled wryly. Canning was clearly champing at the bit to insinuate himself into the inner circle around Mr Pitt and was here continuing his courtship of Mr Long. George acknowledged Sheridan with an almost imperceptible nod before the two young men set forth, no doubt to discuss current government strategy.

'George!'

Sheridan caught sight of a young man running across from the Green and waving his hat to draw Canning's attention. Canning turned as his name was called out again and he visibly stiffened at the approach of the youngster.

'George! How glad I am to have found you!' The youth caught at his breath. 'I was told at your lodgings that I might chance on you here.'

George nodded curtly. 'Charles.'

The young man arrived in front of Canning, forcing him to come to a halt. Mr Long hovered alongside. Sheridan felt sure Long was intrigued to know who this threadbare interloper might be who hailed George Canning with such familiarity. That interest would only be piqued further when he should find out who the young man was. This was one of Mary Ann Costello's sons by the actor Samuel Reddish, and therefore George's half-brother. Sheridan had never heard of there actually being a marriage, although the actress had used the title 'Mrs Reddish'. Indeed, Mary Ann Costello had but lately married a Mr Hunn of Plymouth without scandalous cries of bigamy.

Young Charles Reddish held his hat in his hands. 'Congratulations, George! I have just heard and I am most delighted that I have this opportunity to extend my own heartfelt compliments,' he gabbled, smiling broadly. 'We could not have imagined that one day we should have a Member of Parliament in our own family! Mother will be most especially delighted to hear of this news.'

As he drew up to the trio, Sheridan could see the desperate tightness now set around Canning's jaw. The young would-be politician was embarrassed by this ambush and knew not how to extricate himself in front of the inquisitive Long without suffering further humiliation.

'Canning!' Sheridan slapped George on the back and grasped his hand in a vigorous handshake. 'Let me congratulate you again on your election to the House. The voters of Newtown, who I hear mostly amuse themselves with catching fish, have done their duty and have netted themselves a goodly sized cod. I look forward to our debates whenever you will take up your seat and you can count on me to cast a sharp hook on the end of my line!'

Sheridan then turned to the young intruder and extended a hand. 'And this is young Mr Reddish if I am not mistaken?

'Mr Sheridan.' The youth bowed.

'Well I do declare, you are quite growing!'

'A tad.' The young man looked discomfited at the insinuation that he was still a boy.

'I am heading even now to The King's Head.' Sheridan placed a hand firmly on the youngster's back, guiding him away. 'Come, you must join me, for I am sure that George has business with Mr Long. We shall raise our own toast to the Right Honourable Mr George Canning and you must tell me all about your dear mother, Mrs Hunn...'

Charles Reddish continued to look almost longingly over his shoulder towards his brother. *He wants money from George, that is his business here*, Sheridan mused.

'Does she reside still in Plymouth? I believe she has a new enterprise and has lately developed an eye ointment. Extraordinary.' Sheridan glanced back to Canning and Long. 'You will excuse us, gentlemen, I trust.'

'Sheridan, Charles.' George bowed to each. 'Good day and thank you for your kind felicitations.' As their eyes met, Sheridan could read the gratitude that was written there.

Well, it was a small favour he might extend. He recalled the fits of both nerves and excitement which he had experienced in his own first days elected to Westminster and all those subsequent sneers and jibes which he had faced as 'a player's son' from the sons of earls and dukes. How very much more trying for George Canning to be the son of an impecunious actress of very questionable reputation.

CHAPTER SIXTEEN

It was the end of June and the Prince of Wales was in Brighton at the Marine Pavilion, where he had been instructed by his doctors to bathe in the sea for the benefit of his health. Sheridan had arrived that afternoon and been informed that he was to join the prince on the beach at his earliest convenience.

The sun was still high in the sky as Sheridan laboured his way across the pebbles towards the bathing huts and the entourage clustered at the water's edge. A light breeze ruffled his lightly powdered hair but was insufficient to dissipate the heat of the sun, which he could even now feel burning his brow. Beads of sweat were forming there and already pricking at his eyes, and he could feel a dampness forming in his armpits and the small of his back. He was tempted to take off his coat, a light blue silk for the summer, but he could not present himself to the prince in a state of dishevelled undress.

A pair of Sir John Lade's hounds ran towards him, tongues hanging out and sleek coats already wet from the sea. They ran around him in circles, a greeting and an invitation to do likewise. Something of their simple enjoyment of the salty tang in the air was infectious. Sheridan paused and allowed himself to inhale deeply of the briny smells, to hear the rhythmic slosh of gentle waves on the pebbled beach, and to be dazzled by the brilliant light shimmering on the calm surface of the sea. Further out he could see the red sails of a local coaster plying its trade. Jumping from one foot to the other, he removed his shoes and stockings. He could at least save them from being ruined by the seawater. The feel of the smooth stones beneath his bare feet brought him back to a moment of childhood. He took in another deep breath of the salt-laden air and imagined himself seven years old again allowed to run on the Strand at Sandymount, Dublin Bay glittering like an encased jewel on just such a summer's day.

His Royal Highness was emerging from the bathing hut which had been dragged into the shallows. He was dressed in a calico bathing suit of a pale green with discreet stripes. His powdered hair had been tied back with a dark blue ribbon. What flesh was exposed looked plump and pink. Already in the water, Major Hanger dived beneath the rippling waves and re-emerged tossing tendrils of loose hair from his handsome face. He was clearly buck naked.

The prince dipped a toe into the water and winced. 'Damn me, sir, but it's cold!'

'Not a bit of it, Your Highness, it is lovely when you're in!' Hanger replied. He flipped onto his back and bobbed on the surface, allowing sun and sea to caress the length of his taut body.

Sheridan had reached the water's edge and dipped his toe into the froth. A gentle wave broke and ran up around his ankles. Sir John greeted him with a raise of his riding crop. He was dressed in the usual riding gear topped with the wide-brimmed hat of a country squire. His boots were stained with a rim of seawater, but he had taken off his jacket and untied his cravat.

'Lovely weather, eh what, Sherry!'

'Sherry! Is that Sherry?' the prince screeched and strained to peer around the side of the bathing hut to where the two men were standing at the shoreline.

Sheridan bowed. 'Your Royal Highness.'

'Sherry — you will join us.' It was not a question, but a command, as Sheridan well knew. 'See, Hanger has quite purged his excesses of last night in the salty brine.'

'As will you, sir, if you will ever take the plunge!' the major called out with his typical impertinence.

The equerry stood and thrashed at the water beside him, sending a delicate spray up and over His Royal Highness' podgy feet.

'Blaggard!' the prince cried out and, dipping his foot into the sea, kicked an answering spray into Hanger's face. 'Sherry, come and help me show this rude fellow a lesson!'

A footman had approached Sheridan and stood patiently by to help him divest himself of his clothing.

As he removed his blue silk coat he glanced at the man. There was something familiar in the tall man's features. Of course. Sheridan remembered where he had first taken note of him. He was that young footman in the corridor at Carlton House who had seemed red-eyed and anguished in company with the prince's valet — being comforted or berated, Sheridan had not been certain. But now on closer inspection he recognised another occasion when he had seen this young man. He was the stranger who had been lurking in the shadows of the church in the graveyard at Andrew Marson's funeral.

'Shall I take your coat, sir?' the attendant asked politely.

'Do I know your name, fellow?'

'Matthew, sir.'

'Matthew…' Sheridan nodded. 'I believe I do know you.'

'I should not think so, sir, only that I serve His Royal Highness.'

Sheridan held out his blue silk coat. 'You skulk about at funerals do you not?'

The footman flushed and fumbled, dropping the coat to the pebbles.

'Beg pardon, sir.' The footman stooped swiftly to retrieve it and delicately flicked at the silk to remove any sign of debris.

Sheridan loosened his cravat.

'You did attend the burial of my actor, did you not?'

'I … I happened by, sir.'

'Happened by?'

'It was my day off, sir.'

'And you just stumbled into a graveyard? To pass the time, Matthew? To have a picnic?'

Sheridan handed over his neckpiece and began to pull out his shirt.

'I … I recognised some of the funeral party, sir.'

'What do you mean?'

'Mr Kemble, sir, and others of the theatre company.' The footman shifted as Sheridan looked with expectancy for further elaboration. 'I often attend His Royal Highness at the theatre and on my day off I will sit in the Gods, sir.'

'I see. You are a regular at our entertainments, an admirer of Mr Kemble?'

The footman nodded.

'And of Mr Marson?'

The young man bit his lip and nodded again.

'You were sad to learn it was he that we buried?'

The footman remained silent, struggling to control the emotion which rippled beneath the surface of his smooth, handsome features.

Sheridan handed over his shirt.

'I have taken a particular interest in the circumstances of Mr Marson's death…'

Sheridan began to divest himself of his breeches and watched the footman closely.

'I believe that you too may have such an interest.'

'Sherry! Where the devil are you?'

The prince still hovered at the edge of the bathing hut.

'At half-mast sir!' Sheridan called in return.

'Well, let loose the anchor, there's a good fellow.'

He let his breeches fall about his ankles and stepped out of them.

'Should you wish to tell me anything, in strictest confidence, Matthew, then you know where to find me.'

Sheridan turned and dashed into the sea, yelping loudly as the waves slapped his thighs and the cold waters rose up around his torso. He was as a boy again and he dived beneath the next languid wave's approach, kicking into the swell. He resurfaced, gasping and blinking the salt from his eyes, the cold sea waters prickling at his extremities. Sheridan shivered but felt invigorated and alive. He wondered that he did not partake of sea bathing more; the benefits being so evidently wholesome. Whooping, he headed towards Hanger and upended the floating equerry. Hanger splashed about and coughed up seawater.

'Oh, well done, Sherry!'

Sheridan turned to the heir apparent. 'Jump in, sir, and we may finish him off.'

His Royal Highness clenched his fists and, thus emboldened, leapt off the final step of the bathing hut. Sheridan smiled; it was not for nothing that his royal friend was dubbed the Prince of Whales.

Exhilarated by their high jinks in the sea that afternoon, the prince continued in the mood for pranks and games. The party that evening was intimate, a mere forty guests for dinner. The atmosphere was jolly and the conversation lively.

Sheridan had been seated next to the Comtesse De Grignord. She was a plump and attractive émigré from Paris whose husband the comte was currently fighting with the campaign in Flanders. The couple and their two small children had fled France after Louis and his queen were captured and brought to the Tuileries. They had likewise disguised themselves as butler and servants, but had been more fortunate in the route of their flight than the French Royal Family and had managed to reach the Netherlands before seeking refuge across the Channel. The comtesse had quickly ingratiated herself into the Prince of Wales' circle and shared his enthusiasm for chinoiserie.

As the party toyed over the rich display of desserts, the Prince of Wales suggested they might leave the table and have a séance, the fad being fashionable again.

'We might call up the Cock Lane Ghost that would not appear for my grandfather and teach that spectre a lesson in manners,' he hooted.

The notion was met with an enthusiastic response and the party retired to the small salon where the chairs were arranged in a circle and the order given to snuff the candles.

A lone violinist was directed to provide a 'celestial' atmosphere to the proceedings. The chandelier was lowered and one servant made busy snuffing out the lights there whilst another glided around the room extinguishing the wax candles set around the walls. Each addition to the darkness was met with gasps of anticipation and stifled laughter.

The Prince of Wales was always an excellent mimic and relished opportunities to perform. He took this occasion to ape the stentorian tones of the artist Philip de Loutherbourg, who was noted for the mesmeric séances which he had begun to hold in his home in Hammersmith. As de Loutherbourg had also designed theatrical sets in the past, Sheridan knew him well and had to admit that the prince gave a fair impression and might also match the portly old Frenchman in girth as well as tone. Others in the gathering who were familiar with the style of de Loutherbourg's séances tittered or softly clapped their appreciation.

'Spirit, we call to thee, we pray you visit us from that other side beyond the ties of this earthly domain and beg you make appearance amongst us … speak again from your place beyond the grave … bring us light and healing…'

In the dark Sheridan slipped away from his seat and began to tiptoe across the Persian rug. He paused to assure himself of his position. Yes, there was Mr Hancock to the right with his wheezing breath, and to the left he heard the nervous titters of the comtesse. He adjusted his course a smidgeon and waited for his cue from the prince.

'Is there anybody there?'

At which point Sheridan leapt into the lap of the Comtesse De Grignord. The good lady promptly let out the most blood-curdling shriek. Responding gasps and shouts rippled around the assembled circle to be met by the booming gales of laughter from the Prince of Wales.

Later in the evening the dancing was got underway with His Royal Highness leading the opening cotillion in partner with Mrs Fitzherbert. Sheridan stood aside. He felt uncommonly weary, too weary to undertake the effort of making love to any of the ladies present, none of whom stirred his fancy in any case. Beside him, Sir John was talking about a racehorse he had been training with a view to running him at Newmarket.

'Capital creature. If you want a sure thing, Sherry, you will not go amiss if you wager your guinea on Corsair.'

'Not against my nag, Lade! I'll lay you fifty.' The prince lurched between the two men; his breath sweet with the maraschino cherry brandy he favoured.

''Scuse us, Lade. Need a word with Sherry.'

The prince laid a hand across Sherry's shoulder and led him to one side.

'That little business we discussed,' the prince slurred. 'The theatricals for my sisters — how do they progress?'

'We audition at the Foundling Home next month, sir, and I am assured by Sir Percival that the girls will show very willing as they are most diligent at all their lessons.'

'And do they sing and dance?'

'That has not been on the curriculum, sir, but I believe they sew and embroider very neatly.'

'Embroider, do you say? Well, that should be a good start I suppose. And who shall instruct them?'

'Mrs Siddons has agreed to impart general tips for deportment and delivery on the stage.'

'It shall not be all tragic, I hope?'

'Oh no, sir. Rest assured our theme shall be all celebratory.'

'You will let Hanger know when there is a rehearsal I may attend, I should like to see this little Ramus girl for myself, before the event, so to speak.'

'Of course, Your Royal Highness.'

The prince clutched tight at Sheridan, breathing into his ear.

'You don't speak a word to anyone who she is.'

'On my honour, sir!'

'I daren't even tell my brothers.'

'Quite so, sir.'

'Let it be soon, Sherry.'

Dear God! What should he do about Eliza Ramus? Or, more particularly, her adopted father and protector, Mr Henry Ramus. A veritable Colchian Dragon guarding his Golden Fleece. Sheridan had briefly toyed with the idea of engaging one of the young girls within his own company to pass for the royal offspring. But it would be a risky venture and should the Prince of Wales discover the fraud, it would be an end. He should be placed beyond The Pale and might as well return to the boggy homelands of his O'Sheridan forefathers. He had placed this dilemma in some dark recess of his mind. Now he must bring it into the light and hasten to find a solution. Either that or admit his defeat. An option not to be countenanced.

Whilst his own stomach churned with queasy anxiety, it seemed that the heir to the throne's preference for the sickly-sweet cherry brandy was having a similar effect. The prince suddenly paled, heaved and staggered to one side. An attendant rushed to his aid and was greeted with a disgorged fountain of the evening's excesses.

Sheridan rolled over in his bed and groaned. Damn his head. He had tried to retire at a reasonable hour but the prince, revived by the vomited release of his over-indulgence, would have none of it and had him dragged out of his supine state to continue dancing into the very early hours. Sheridan had somehow found a second wind and continued to three or four in the morning, flirting with the Comtesse De Grignord to atone for having given her such a fright at the séance. But he must pay for all this now. A hammer had lodged in his head and would not let up its infernal strike upon the anvil of his brain. His mouth tasted stale and dry. He groaned again as a chink of light sliced across the crumpled sheets.

'Good morning, sir, or should I say afternoon as we are now at midday.'

It was the footman Matthew who turned from drawing back the heavy velvet curtain sufficient to be seen.

'I am to inform you that His Royal Highness plans an excursion to the Downs this afternoon. The Comte De Palmon is to be shown how to play cricket.'

Sheridan groaned again.

The tall footman poured a glass of water and brought it to his bedside.

'Shall I send for your man, sir?'

'I suppose I must…' Sheridan rubbed at his eyes and sat up against the pillows.

The footman hovered.

'Sir. Yesterday you mentioned an interest in Mr Marson…'

'Yes.' Sheridan reached for the water and gulped it down. He shook his head vigorously, as though trying to dispel all ills that might be lodged there, and felt awake at last. 'I would know why he was murdered and by whom, and I would see justice done.'

'There are those who would claim that justice was served in his killing.'

'Not I.'

'What should I tell you, sir?' the young attendant murmured.

'I am told that Andrew had a man that was his *husband*.'

The footman's eyes widened.

'I am thinking that man might be you, Matthew.'

The footman nodded as, pressing his lips tight, tears sprang to his eyes.

'I do not pretend to understand the nature of such relationships. Nor do I wish to.' Sheridan waved his hand in the air. 'And for ought I know, perhaps it was you who killed my actor in a fit of conjugal jealousy?'

Matthew's head jerked up and he shook it vigorously.

'But he was consorting with another, or more than one, was he not?'

'Why do you say that, Mr Sheridan?'

'You did not keep him in the latest fashion or present him with a finely tooled watch, inscribed in Latin — did you Matthew?'

'Andrew kept nothing from me,' the footman asserted with a touch of pride. 'I know the pocket watch of which you speak, Mr Sheridan. That was from a previous admirer, before we became attached.'

'And did he tell you the man's name?'

Tears rolled down Mathew's cheeks. 'What will become of me?'

Sheridan thumped the bed. 'What sort of husband are you? Don't you want to see Marson's assassin hang? We need to know of anyone who might hold some grudge. Who was this benefactor?'

Matthew shook his head and gulped down another sob.

'Did this man dispense with Marson or was it the other way?'

'After our ceremony, Andrew promised he would see him no more.'

'And the man was angry?'

Matthew shrugged and sniffed, wiping his nose on his cuff. 'I don't know, sir. He said we must not talk of it again.'

'The man, who was it?'

'He would not want me to tell…'

'Andrew is dead! And so too may you be if you will not divulge.'

He should strangle the watery-headed booby himself if the footman did not speak up.

Matthew looked fearful, his lips quivering and Sheridan felt a pang of guilt for giving him the jitters, but only for a moment.

'A name, Matthew. Whisper it to me.'

The footman swallowed. 'Sir Jonas Soersby.'

CHAPTER SEVENTEEN

Sheridan was shortly to remove his family to the country villa on the river at Isleworth for the remainder of the summer. Before that date he had thought to have a last gathering of friends in Wanstead. It was arranged that a convoy of barouche and open carriages should take the party to nearby Epping Forest where they might enjoy a visit to the ancient earthworks, a game of rounders on the Flats, after which refreshments should be provided followed by a stroll in the shade of the great oaks by any who wished.

Sheridan had thrown out an invitation to the excursion to the Soersbys, with little expectation of a reply in the affirmative. He was both surprised and a little nervous when they were pleased to accept. It appeared that matters of business had delayed their usual seasonal return to the estate in Somerset, and that they should have their son Frederick with them. Mehitabel was delighted, relishing the opportunity to become reacquainted with Lady Priscilla. Together, she hoped, they might share some treasured recollections of Eliza Sheridan.

Various of the neighbours were to be included in the party; Reverend Wallis and his wife of course, the Jukes, old Mrs Burridge and her niece Miss Campbell, the recently retired Colonel Branson with his son Phillip, a naval lieutenant returned on leave from the West Indies. Apologies were given on Mrs Branson's part but she must visit an old aunt as previously arranged.

Joining them would be Sheridan's old friend and playfellow Richard Tickell with his young family. Tickell had been married to Eliza's sister Mary Linley, who had similarly died of consumption, and he was now wed again to a striking young woman, twenty years his junior. Sheridan rather feared that he had neglected this old friendship of late. They had once been inseparable. The excursion would be a means to make amends.

Other reconciliations might also be facilitated. George's presence had been requested and Sheridan hoped that there would be opportunity for aunt and nephew to overcome their differences. Canning had written to inform Mrs Canning of his election to the seat at Newtown, a seat which he assured her placed him in obligation to no one other than Mr Pitt and, he further boasted, the whole business not costing him a single farthing. Mehitabel's frosty reception of this news had been ameliorated only in part by soft words from Sheridan. Good Sister Christian had conceded at last that the success of her nephew's long-held desire to enter Westminster merited some celebration, however grudging.

The morning of the excursion proved as fine as Sheridan could have wished for. He drew back his bedroom curtain and surveyed a blue sky scattered with the odd puff of wispy white cloud. His satisfaction was laced with a sliver of dread. There had been no particular plan in his mind when he had extended the invitation to Soersby. He could scarcely confront the Judge at a picnic in front of friends and family, with children running about beneath their feet. So, what had been in his thoughts? To renew the connection, he supposed. To see the man for himself. Unguarded. To look afresh and consider him. Consider what Sheridan himself had once deemed outlandish. With the knowledge which he now possessed would he be able to discern in Sir Jonas any tell-tale signs of his lust for other men? Would he be able to read in his manner the potential for brutality and death-dealing? And if he *could* imagine any of these possibilities, what on earth was he to do about it?

Such a bright and enticing day to be laced through with such dark thoughts. Sheridan shook himself with annoyance. It had been a foolish error to invite the Soersbys. Today he would be all charm and gaiety and his only concern would be the entertainment and pleasure to be provided to his guests.

As if to remind him of this object, the animated buzz of children burst onto the landing outside his bedroom door, their laughter and excited voices tumbling down the stairs. The Tickells had arrived to stay the evening before and the children could now be heard below as the bustle of preparations were got underway. He could make out Tom commanding which bats and balls and other playthings were to be loaded into the waiting cart.

The servants scurried about organising the packing of the hired wagon with the marquee which should erected, chairs for the elderly, table for the buffet, rugs and blankets for those who would spread themselves on the sward. In a second wagon there were plates to be carefully packed along with tumblers, wine glasses, knives, forks and spoons, teacups and saucers, the three teapots and not forgetting the lump sugar. Panniers and baskets of food and bottles of cordials and wines and all the extraordinary paraphernalia it seemed was necessary in order to dine outdoors in a natural country setting with the illusion of rural simplicity.

The bell at the door rang and Mrs Canning arrived with her own tribe in tow to add to the general melee. Sheridan must put all thoughts of murder to one side and arrange his features into a perpetual smile.

Sir Jonas, Lady Priscilla and their son arrived promptly in their barouche for the scheduled departure. Sheridan went out to greet them warmly. Lady Priscilla surged forward and clasped his hands.

'Oh, Richard we are so very pleased to see you. It has been far too long and the last occasion one of such sorrow when we bid that final farewell to dear Eliza at Wells Cathedral. You look well. I am glad of it. And Tom is quite the young gentleman now!'

'As is your own son!' Sheridan bestowed a beaming smile at a handsome boy of fifteen. 'You are at Eton, Frederick? And I believe you are to be a colleger?'

'Yes, sir.' The boy pinked.

'You must be very proud of your boy, Sir Jonas, he is a credit to you.'

Soersby smiled at Frederick and in that moment his chiselled features softened with affection. 'A father could not be more so.' He patted his son's back and then extended his hand. 'It was good of you to invite us, Sheridan. A reminder to us all that we should not let the ties of friendship slip too long.'

The hand that held his own was warm and strong and the words which accompanied the gesture seemed full of sincerity.

'And what a glorious day we have to celebrate that most worthy of bonds — *vive la fraternité*!' Tickell advanced on the new arrivals with arms outstretched.

Sheridan stood aside for a moment to watch as old friendships were rekindled and new introductions made as the rest of the party assembled. He took some satisfaction in the general mood of gaiety and good humour. Then, galvanising himself, he rushed to ensure that all were settled comfortably into the various transportation.

The Soersbys would travel in their own barouche to the Forest and could accommodate two others. It was suggested that Miss Campbell and Bessie Canning accompany them.

Sheridan could see that this arrangement was already pleasing to young Frederick, who was markedly captivated by Bessie's vivacity. Tom appeared to have noticed this interest also and lingered by the side of the barouche on horseback, entertaining the occupants with his usual playful humour.

Sheridan handed old Mrs Burridge into his own carriage alongside the reverend and the delightfully fragrant Mrs Wallis. The Tickells had arrived in their own carriage and four, but Tickell's daughter squeezed in beside Cecily, the young girl having formed an instant attachment to Mrs Wallis. When all were seated Sheridan gave the order to advance and the convoy set off.

By the time the party had walked the short distance to the designated picnic site, the marquee had been erected and preparations for luncheon were well underway. Rugs had been spread out about the grass and chairs arranged for the older members of the party under the wide shade of a spreading beech tree. Drinks and cordials were dispensed and toasts raised to the host, to the perfection of the weather, to the freshness of the air, to the views to be had and to the splendid luncheon which they awaited with eager anticipation. First, however, there should be the games.

Teams were organised for the main event, a game of bat and ball. They were to be reds and blues and each side to sport a ribbon accordingly on their shirts. Lieutenant Branson was chosen captain to the Reds, with Soersby as his vice-captain, while Richard Tickell had command of the Blues with Tom as his second. Sheridan himself had proffered his services as the referee, which position seemed most appropriate for the host and he assured everyone that all would be fair play. The position also allowed Sheridan the opportunity to observe the party. And in particular, Sir Jonas Soersby.

He was, Sheridan had to concede, a fine figure of a man. Robust and manly with strong features, which were not without refinement. He clearly led an active life, as Sheridan recalled, enjoying country pursuits on his estate in Somerset when he was not sitting in Sessions. Soersby entered into the game with obvious relish and a competitive spirit. A coin was tossed and Tickell chose to bat first. The Reds were deployed about the field and Soersby offered himself in the outfield. This proved to be a wise choice on the captain's part. Not only could Sir Jonas judge a ball's trajectory and place himself in readiness for the catch, but those balls which he retrieved he was able to toss back to the inner fielders with a marvellous accuracy. He was left-handed, Sheridan noticed, which rather disorientated the bowlers on the other team when he came in to bat. Soersby made full use of any and all advantage.

There was only one contested moment in the game which came when young Frederick Soersby, having received the throw-in from his father at second base, gleefully called Tom out. Tom began at once to protest that he had touched the base before the ball was caught.

Sheridan sighed. He could not be seen to favour his own son, but on the other hand Tom was in the right by a matter of a second. What was an umpire to do? He could claim that it was too close to call and the shot might be taken again? But that should disrupt the rhythm of the game and lend an altogether too serious tone to the sport.

'Apologies, dear boy, but Frederick is quite right — you are dismissed, banished to the sidelines! But consider the advantage.'

'Advantage, Pa?'

'Because you have failed to work up a sweat, my dear Tom, you may mingle pleasantly and fragrantly with the ladies. I am sure that Bessie is longing to hear you explain the rules of the game.'

Sheridan wondered if his son had caught his sly wink.

Tom shook his head and grinned, then turned and proffered a hand to Frederick. 'Well fielded, Soersby!'

The Reds went on to victory, despite a valiant effort by Tickell and a surprising performance for the Blues from the Reverend Wallis, who was not only a nifty batsman but remarkably nimble and fast on his feet.

As his guests gathered with lively chatter outside the marquee, Sheridan surveyed the luncheon table with a glow of satisfaction. There were loaves of household bread, still warm to the touch, and tin loaves and butter curls. There were cold meats of various kinds. Four roast fowls, a joint of cold roast beef, and a tongue. Pastries and pies. Venison, ham and pigeon. Small birds aplenty, plovers and wheatears. There were quail's eggs, mousses and seasonal delicacies such as asparagus tart. Baskets overflowed with salad leaves and cucumbers. At the centre of the table was laid a great platter of one of Sheridan's own particular favourites, a salmagundi whose recipe he could recite as well as any poem. The thought tickled him.

Oh Salmagundi, Salmagundi, glorious Salmagundi!
Chopped poultry, boiled eggs and anchovy,
Mix well with capering capers, olives gaily,
And from the good rich earth a host of fungi!
Enchant our taste buds with sweet addition
Raisins and blanched almonds in profusion.

Virginia potatoes — pray do not stint!
Petite pois, forsooth! — More than a hint
With currants, be they red and white.
Oil and vinegar shall wrap all tight
In a queenly dish of heavenly delight.
Oh Salmagundi, Salmagundi, glorious Salmagundi!

His mouth salivated. Of course, he should have to hold back and ensure that all his guests were served first. But perhaps he might now whisper in his servant Robert's ear to hold back a goodly portion just for him.

There should then be a course of deserts. Stewed fruit, with cinnamon and ginger, well sweetened, plain biscuits to accompany. Cheesecakes, a plum pudding, sponge cake, jellies, fresh fruit, pears, apricots and plums. A variety of cheeses. And then another favourite delicacy, strawberry fritters. He hoped there should be enough of them, for they were a favourite of the children too.

As he scooped up the last of his salmagundi with a satisfying smack of the lips Sheridan found himself addressed by Mrs Tickell. She was a pert young thing, this second wife, a little too enamoured of herself and her appearance Sheridan could not help feeling.

She leaned in towards him as though sharing a confidence. 'Such pleasing company, Mr Sheridan, it is quite the social occasion. I tell Tickell that we should throw more parties down at Hampton Court and where more pleasant for a picnic than by the river. I do enjoy the intrigues, don't you? I see that Lieutenant Branson has been paying most particular attention to Miss Campbell.'

'He seems a fine fellow, though I have scarce made his acquaintance — the sea is a demanding mistress.'

'She is that, Mr Sheridan.' Mrs Tickell fluttered her fan and lowered her voice to a conspiratorial whisper. 'But I observe there is another here who might wish that the object of his gallantry were a mistress equally demanding.'

'Of whom do you speak, madam?'

'Why, Mr Canning, of course.' The young woman's eyes gleamed.

'George?'

'Have you not noticed that he has been most solicitous of Mrs Wallis? He perceives an opportunity — for her husband seems to ignore the poor creature entirely, and they are not long married I believe.'

Sheridan glanced across the party and spied George Canning carrying a plate of strawberry fritters, which he presented with a flourish to the young reverend's wife. She made a show of delight and dipped into the fritters.

George and Mrs Wallis? Sheridan felt a sudden acute sensation of envy. Oh, to be a young man again, instead of one past forty.

CHAPTER EIGHTEEN

After luncheon the party broke up to stroll to the various beauty spots and points of interest in the vicinity. George and Tom, Frederick and the tutor, Mr Smyth, were to accompany Mrs Wallis, Mrs Tickell and Bessie on an expedition to the nearby Iron Age works. The Jukes and Miss Campbell were walking with Hitty's eldest son and the Tickell boys to the lake. A number of the ladies preferred to remain at the picnic site, keeping an eye on the younger children or to take their ease under the shade of the old beech tree. Reverend Wallis clutched a book with the expressed plan to find some quiet place for reading and reflection, but had been waylaid in conversation with Sir Jonas on the subject of Botany Bay and whether or not there should be effort made to civilize the new territory and the indigenous peoples who had been encountered there.

Tickell took Sheridan to one side and asked that they might have opportunity of some words alone. Sheridan looked between his old friend and the retreating figure of Mrs Wallis. He had been piqued to a sense of rivalry with George by Mrs Tickell's earlier comments and it had been his intention to continue his own play of gallantry with her. The general air of frivolity had enlivened her features in a most enticing manner and Cecily Wallis seemed intent to escape from under the shadow of her husband. The walk to the ancient mining site, without the dampening presence of the reverend, would have been an ideal opportunity to ingratiate himself further into her affections. Instead, he could see that young George Canning had managed to place himself by her side with every show of solicitude.

Sheridan tore his gaze away from the alluring Mrs Wallis and turned a kindly face to his old friend.

'I should like nothing better, Tickell. Let us take an amble into the woods. There is a clearing where you may find the Gifford Oak. Have you ever beheld the Gifford Oak? A fine, ancient specimen. Almost as broad as it is tall. It is not so very far.'

They headed along a path which took them into the trees and they were soon beneath the verdant canopy of the forest. The sun, high in the sky, strained through the broad foliage overhead so that one could see the veins pulsing through each leaf and creating a pleasing dappled shade. The rustle of branches, faint scurries in the undergrowth and the variety of birdsong spoke of a world living and breathing. It was soothing to the mind, Sheridan conceded, to be away from the daily clamour of the streets of the city. His wife had loved to be in the countryside, she had preferred its tranquillity, the slow and steady pace of life. Sheridan took in a deep breath of the earthy woodland smells, so different to the stink and soot of London. It did him good, he knew. And yet it would never be his natural setting.

Tickell paused and turned his head to where a thrush had trilled into song. He struck an attitude and declaimed,

'*The Nightingale, of birds most choice,*
To do her best shall strain her voice:
And to this bird, to make a set,
The Mavis, merle and robinet
The lark, the linnet, and the thrush,
That makes a choir in every bush.'

They were silent a moment, listening to the summer chorus which had joined with the songbird.

'Drayton. I had a master was very fond of the poet and that poem in particular,' Tickell explained. 'Do you think of Eliza, Dick?'

Sheridan smiled ruefully. 'Eliza can never be far from my thoughts when I look on the children, and when I hear such a bird in song I am minded of her sweet voice.'

Tickell nodded. 'It is the same with my dearest Mary.'

'You think of her still?'

'I am haunted…'

Sheridan frowned.

'…by memories of our great happiness,' Richard Tickell continued in explanation.

'I did not think you would marry again, Tickell. You had sworn so vehemently that you would not.'

Tickell sighed. 'Men are inconstant, I do not doubt. A man needs a wife. My children have need of a mother.'

'The new Mrs Tickell is scarce more than a child herself.'

'True. Sarah is young and sometimes I think that marriage to her is all a diversion.' Tickell threw his arms wide. 'And perhaps I led her to a greater expectation of my worth.'

Sheridan caught the note of desperation in his friend's voice.

'No one can doubt your worth.'

'She would be Mrs Tickell with a coach and four.'

'Ah, so I saw when you arrived. Four horses?' Sheridan shook his head in mock wonder. 'You would look well alongside a duke, I should say.'

'She has insisted; though we do not need such an extravagance and she has no knowledge of the costs which result. I try to talk with her, Dick, but anything that is serious she will simply not acknowledge.'

Sheridan felt he could not but agree. Mrs Tickell shied from the serious as from something ugly and repulsive. Earlier in the day he had overheard Tom's tutor remarking that Mrs Tickell was, '*eminently handsome, but without mind in her countenance or anywhere else.*'

'Mrs Tickell is a very pretty adornment, my dear friend, and anyone can understand why you should love her, but I suspect that in dear Sarah there is an absence of mind. Which should be of no consequence, of course, in a beautiful woman.'

'I confess to moments of despair.'

'It is that perennial mathematical problem, Tickell, of monies in and monies out and the difference that lies between. It is one, alas, that I am well acquainted with and have yet to find the solution.'

'I petitioned Mr Hastings and he has been most generous.'

'Hastings?'

'You know he is not a bad fellow, Dick. I know all the arguments for his impeachment, but one must allow that the affairs of India and the way things are done by the governor there must of necessity be other than they should be in a civilized society such as ours.'

'We shall not speak of the trial of Mr Warren Hastings, I am plagued by Burke on the matter as it is, but rather I shall gladly acknowledge his kindness to you, Tickell.'

Tickell sighed. 'But it is not enough to cover all. And I cannot return to him again.'

'If I could help, I would, you know that my dear fellow.' Sheridan placed a hand on his friend's shoulder. 'The truth is the new theatre has me mortgaged to the hilt, far, far beyond anything a sensible man would venture — but my hopes are high that once we are opened all will be recouped! Then you shall not want for my largesse, Tickell. In the meantime, I must daily play at cat and mouse with my creditors.' Sheridan laughed to lighten the mood. 'You should see how nimble I have become at avoiding their traps — but I have felt their whiskers on my tail nonetheless!'

Sheridan performed a little jig to illustrate and Tickell could not help but chuckle.

'You must tell your pretty little wife that two horses shall do very well, and I know many a countess who should be glad of two. And does she not have her dowry to help you? You must be firm, Tickell — there is half your expense at a stroke.'

Tickell nodded in sage agreement.

'It is good to see you, Dick. Our games this morning were a timely reminder that *play's the thing*! I have let the blue devils in when I should show them swiftly to the door. We will manage.'

'All will be well.'

'That ends well.'

'We will have no ending's my friend, only new beginnings, just as you have now with Mrs Tickell.'

'And shall you marry again, Dick?' Tickell regarded Sheridan with sly amusement. 'I thought you were much taken with Pamela Syms? I wondered that you let that Irish Romeo, Fitzgerald, rush her to the altar first.'

Sheridan shook his head. Had he ever seriously considered himself betrothed to Pamela? Looking back now on the events of the previous year, it seemed to him that he had entered one of his own comedies and might be dubbed Sir Ludicrous Lovedupe.

'It was all a fizz, Tickell. We took delight in the tittle-tattle of the gossipmongers but it was for our amusement only.'

'But you should marry again, Dick, it does not suit you to be alone. You have too much care and should have someone care for you, preferably a woman who is not already married!'

'Ah, but who that is young and singular shall care for an old dolt like me?'

'You must allow yourself to be taken seriously.'

'Now you do jest.'

And they both burst into sudden laughter. Sheridan warmed to see the old familiar twinkle in Tickell's dark eyes.

They came to a small clearing where the buzz of insects was loud in their ears. In front of them stood an enormous oak tree in full leaf. The sun was beginning to dip in the afternoon sky and cast a halo about its form.

'There it is, the Gifford Oak, King of the Forest. Reputed to be over three hundred years old.'

'I have a *hunch* this giant fellow was an acorn when our namesake fell at Bosworth Field!'

'And now the hunch *back* must turn around, dear Tickell, for the lovely Mrs Tickell will wonder where you are. Whilst I must gather up all our guests and see them safely returned to civilization before they are magicked into woodland boars and toads by the nymphs and sprites who dwell in these places.'

'Should Puck be near —'

'I will know you as the one with the ass's head, Tickell.'

Sheridan moved about the glade. 'We might find some twigs and make a headdress, you shall be Oberon, King of the Faeries —'

'And you shall be the Greene Man and we can make mischief when we —'

'When we —?'

'Over there, Dick — against the oak, is that Lieutenant Branson?'

Sheridan peered across to see a man slumped against the great girth of the oak. He had been hidden entirely when they first entered the glade.

'He has fallen asleep perhaps?'

Sheridan's friend grinned and picked up a long twig from the forest floor. 'Then I shall Tickell him awake!' he whispered as he made an exaggerated play of tiptoeing towards the naval officer.

Sheridan smiled at his friend's buffoonery. Glad to see his mood so lightened.

As Tickell poked at the man's protruding shoulder, the figure slid to one side and in that instant Sheridan knew that something was horribly amiss.

The body had been propped against the giant oak tree, the legs splayed out displaying that bloodied absence. In sliding down the trunk, the head now fixed Sheridan with a startled gaze. The member had fallen from the gaping mouth and Branson's high forehead sported the sign of the inverted triangle.

Sheridan could hear Tickell retching nearby. 'The devil … the devil!' his shocked friend was exclaiming between each gagging motion.

Blood still trickled from the slit throat. Sheridan's eyes narrowed. One side of the triangle was missing. The killer had been disturbed. Perhaps alerted by the sound of their approach along the path, their burst of laughter. Everything in the scene spoke of a very recent event.

He spun around. The assassin might be here still, watching them from forest. Sheridan imagined that grim figure, lurking, bloody knife still in hand, shrouded in obscurity, gloating at the scene which their arrival had created. An audience of one. Oh, what a stage was this, and he seemed fated to play a leading role in this vile drama. Would that poor Tickell could have been spared the 'supporting character'. A tempest of anger and dread assailed him.

'I know you who you are!' Sheridan felt the boom of his own voice reverberating in his breast.

A stillness answered.

A breeze rustled through the greenery.

A bird called. And another.

Sheridan's gaze slowly circled the small glade.

'Foul Fiend! Through the sharp hawthorn blows the cold wind. Foul Fiend. That has crawled from the pit of hell!'

In the western sky the sun slipped behind an approaching cluster of cloud and the light dipped into shadow.

Tickell was at his shoulder, wiping his mouth with a linen handkerchief.

'Dick, let's away — there is some strange and vicious highwayman prowling these woods.' His voice trembled with fear. 'We must raise the alarm and return in numbers. Nothing can help Lieutenant Branson now.'

Sheridan took a breath and nodded. Tickell was already pulling him away.

As they hastened back along the path towards their party, Tickell cast a sidelong glance at Sheridan.

'When we found poor Phillip, I felt that you had — that you had seen something like this before, Dick?'

'Yes.'

Tickell started. 'The devil —?'

'Say nothing. But I believe we have a killer in our midst.'

'You are saying this is no highwayman then?' Tickell's frown deepened.

Sheridan gulped. 'And — oh Tickell, it is I who have invited him into our company.' Sheridan slapped a hand at his head. 'Fool! Fool! Fool!'

'You know who might have committed this atrocity?'

Sheridan nodded. 'A devil as you say. A devil who wears a mask of kindness and respectability. But now — now I see the true monster that he is!'

'Who is this monster?'

Sheridan hesitated. Should he disclose all to his friend? What should be said when they re-joined the party? How should he impart this horror?

'I think it best you do not know, for now. We must have everyone to safety and with as little alarm and distress as is possible. You must think of your wife and children.'

Sheridan stopped, a plan forming in his mind. Tickell turned back to him.

'Dick, what is it?'

'This, if you will agree.'

'Go on.'

'I shall wait here on the path. You will return to the party — we must be no more than ten minutes off. You will say merely that Lieutenant Branson has met with an accident and that I have stayed with him. You will direct the colonel and...' He thought for a moment. 'Reverend Wallis, yes, the reverend must come. Then my servants, Robert, should be sent to fetch a doctor, and discretely tell Robert to alert an officer of the law and to return here also, he may take Tom's horse.'

'Might this not be a matter for Soersby? He is a Justice.'

'No.' Sheridan paused, was this the right course? 'He has his family here. Send my sincerest apologies to all our guests, but I may be delayed some time.'

Tickell heaved a sigh. 'You are right. You are right. This is the thing to do. We shall wait for you in Wanstead.'

'You must play a part, Tickell.'

'I know. It is hard to cast that horror from my mind's eye, but I shall do it, Dick, you may rely on me.' Tickell clasped his fist, emboldening himself for what lay ahead.

'I do, old friend.'

Tickell then turned a face of concern. 'But you, Dick? Will you be safe from this madman?'

Sheridan picked up a fallen branch and broke off the offshoots so that it more resembled a stout club.

'You forget, Tickell, I am a man who has fought two duels.'

Tickell nodded. 'I'll grant that was bravery but also foolishness since you had no skill in the matter.'

'I had right — and God's favour.' He looked up, hoping that some divine presence was watching over him still.

Tickell hesitated.

'Go,' Sheridan urged. 'Say nothing to anyone of what you have seen.'

CHAPTER NINETEEN

As Sheridan waited, he began to imagine what he should say to Colonel Branson. How he might prepare the bluff old soldier for the death of his youngest child, the only son, and in so gruesome a manner. He dreaded the moment when they must arrive at the corpse and the father should see for himself the cruel mutilations inflicted on his beloved boy. He was a military man who had served in the wars in the Americas and in the field against the French before that, and had no doubt seen all that war could do to the body of a man, but nothing would prepare him for the malicious acts he would witness on the body of Lieutenant Phillip Branson. Had the colonel read the lurid reports of those other murders of Andrew Marson and Thaddeus Broadhead? Would he know of the slur which had been attached to Mr Marson? How would he react to that possibility?

Come to think of it, did this murder suggest that the young naval officer may have been another of that inclination? Recognised by the killer as such? The anonymous letter to Brockenhurst had been adamant that Thaddeus Broadhead was one. Sheridan stretched his mind back over the day that they had had. From what he could recollect there had been no apparent recognition between the Soersbys and Phillip Branson, they had been introduced as entirely new to each other. But might Sir Jonas and Phillip be so practiced in deception that any previous acquaintance would be instantaneously concealed?

Or, had something occurred in the course of the day's outing to suggest to Soersby that Phillip might be of the same persuasion? They had been on the batting team together and had established a quick and easy camaraderie.

He tried to recall in the time after lunch before he set off with Tickell what others of the party were planning. He seemed to remember that Phillip had offered to join Miss Campbell and the Jukes on the walk to the lake. William Smyth had also been of that group, he was almost certain. He could question the tutor later. And Sir Jonas, what direction had he taken? Perhaps, he had not yet left the picnic site? He vaguely remembered that he had noticed him in conversation with Reverend Wallis and George, or had George joined Mrs Wallis and Bessie? Oh, it was all too unclear. Of one thing he felt certain, Mehitabel's expressed plan was to stay behind with Mrs Burridge and Lady Caroline and watch over a couple of the younger children who were tired and sleepy after lunch. He might discretely ask her what she had noticed.

The sound of a broken twig and disturbed undergrowth came from the thickets to his left and jerked him back to the present. For all he knew the killer might be skulking still; he had imprudently dropped his guard. Sheridan reassured himself as to the weight of the short, thick branch in his hand and peered into the foliage. A young fallow buck darted out across the path in front of him. He leapt back with alarm. The creature disappeared into the forest on the other side.

'Sheridan!'

It was Colonel Branson who advanced.

'What has happened? Where is Phillip?' The old gentleman glanced around, his anxiety growing as he could not see his son and then he looked at the branch clutched in Sheridan's hand.

'Are you attacked? Is that it? Mr Tickell would say nothing, only there has been an accident and I came straight. Where is my boy?'

Reverend Wallis emerged on the path behind the colonel, a little out of breath. 'Mr Tickell suggested I might be of some assistance and I am glad to help in any way. He has sent me with a blanket.'

'Thank you, Reverend.' Sheridan nodded to Wallis.

'Colonel, I do not have words adequate but I must prepare you —'

'No...' Branson shook his head. 'What has happened, you must tell me, damn you!'

Sheridan tried as gently as he could to recount the discovery. As soon as the colonel heard mention of the Gifford Oak he hastened up the path, Sheridan on his coat-tails attempting to describe the scene that they would find, knowing that nothing could communicate the full horror of what lay ahead for this distraught father. He was relieved to see that Reverend Wallis was keeping up with them and, from the expressions which flew across his face, that he had the gist of Sheridan's account.

The colonel was hunched on the ground, his head clasped in his hands, heaving as though sobbing, although no sound came. Reverend Wallis helped Sheridan to lay the body out on the ground and then stood over the sad corpse and spoke words of blessing and prayer.

'Let all sins be cast out. Go now to that better world and meet thy maker. Amen.'

'Amen.'

They stood a moment in reflective silence.

'I am glad you are here, Wallis,' Sheridan murmured. 'Distressing as it must be for you also.'

Wallis nodded. 'It is a time of devils; the shadow of Hell is cast upon the earth.'

'Well some demon certainly walks the land. We nearly had him, Tickell and I, but he must have heard our approach and taken flight.'

'You saw him, heard him?'

'No.' Sheridan shook his head. 'This fiend moves like a ghost.'

'But you knew you had disturbed him?'

'Wallis, see these markings on the forehead.' Sheridan pointed. 'There should be a third line to complete the triangle.'

'How do you know this?'

'You do not read *The Daily Enquiry*?'

The reverend looked blank.

'No, of course not! You would know nothing of such low and lurid reportage; it is not my usual reading matter either. But alas, I have seen this scene before.'

The reverend looked askance. 'There has been a similar horror?'

Sheridan nodded. 'One of my actors, I was called to identify him.'

'You are a watcher, Mr Sheridan, to the present evil that is upon the earth. Perhaps, the Lord has chosen you to bear witness.'

Sheridan shuddered. 'No more, I pray.' He could wish that the reverend were not so religiously minded, but supposed that this was a natural consequence of the profession.

'This triangle, it is inverted...'

Sheridan nodded. 'Smyth has told me that it signifies the female parts. There is too the emasculation. The men are no longer men. Some such meaning may be read here, I believe.'

Wallis twitched. 'This insinuates what? That the victim you mentioned, your actor, was impotent? A eunuch? Is that what *The Daily Enquiry* claimed?'

Sheridan grimaced. 'That he was "a sodomite". And I fear may make similar slander against Lieutenant Branson.'

'You don't think the lieutenant was a…' The reverend looked astounded.

'The killer thought so.'

Reverend Wallis retrieved the blanket and placed it neatly over the body of Lieutenant Branson.

Sheridan shrugged. 'It is altogether strange. I have wondered whether this assassin means to leave a message or a signature and I am no clearer.'

The reverend eyed him keenly. 'You have taken a particular interest, Mr Sheridan?'

'I could wish that I had not.' Sheridan sighed. 'I do not like to imagine what lies in the mind of the man who can commit these savage acts.'

'I suppose it is in the nature of one who creates fictions and tells stories to imagine what another might think and do.' Wallis looked at Sheridan with compassion. 'I see now that that may be a curse as well as a blessed art.'

'There you have it, Mr Wallis. But neither of us may truly imagine the torment which the good colonel experiences now. I have asked Tickell to send my man Robert for a doctor as well as an officer of the law.' He lowered his voice. 'Sadly, it is Branson who will have greatest need of the doctor and I hope that he shall have laudanum with him.'

They turned now towards the colonel.

It seemed the old soldier sensed the attention and, forestalling their assistance, he staggered on to his feet. All colour was drained from his face but he drew himself straight.

'Gentlemen.' The colonel swayed. 'Gentlemen…'

The reverend moved swiftly to his side. 'Colonel Branson, perhaps you should sit again?'

'No. Let me say what I must say.'

'Sir?' Sheridan prompted.

'This murderer is no ordinary villain. No cutpurse nor highwayman has done this. I have heard tell of a similar assassination in a bath house in London. It was some while ago and that the man killed was a known lover of men. The mutilations, the defacement, underlining that suggestion. Should —'

The colonel swayed again and Wallis took his arm to steady him.

'Should Mrs Branson ever hear our son described in such terms — it would destroy her entirely. Gentlemen —' he looked to each with a pleading gaze — 'my wife must never know of this. If there is a way that the manner of our boy's death might be kept from common knowledge, I must find it! Do you see?'

'I do, sir, and you may trust that I will hold this close,' Sheridan reassured.

Colonel Branson turned to Wallis, looking for the same assurance.

The churchman hesitated.

'Wallis?' the old man pressed, desperation in his low voice.

The reverend squeezed the older man's arm. 'I will say nothing.'

'I am grateful to you both and for your kindness. Who has been sent for?'

'My man will have called for Dr Slocombe —'

'Slocombe? Good. Slocombe is a friend … a good man … he will understand.'

'And I have sent for an officer of the law, but we cannot know who may come and they shall want only to catch the murderous villain.'

Branson nodded tightly. 'As do I.'

CHAPTER TWENTY

Dr Slocombe finished examining the body. He was a man of sixty or thereabouts and he declared that he had seen it all in his professional career, but nothing quite as this.

'Phillip was a fine young man, Branson. A son to be proud of for his courage and his honour. This is a terrible end. Most dreadful. You have my deepest sympathy.'

The colonel nodded in appreciation.

'If it is some little consolation, I can tell you that I believe the throat was cut first, from behind, there are no signs of struggle or defensive cuts as one might expect if Phillip had faced his attacker. Death would have been quick and sudden, he would scarce have known what was happening.'

'That is a blessing,' the reverend remarked.

'One other observance — the man that did this favours his left hand. The deepest cut is to the right of Phillip's neck. I would say, too, that the killer was of at least the same height, perhaps a little taller.'

'That is most useful, Slocombe, and will surely assist those who hunt for this villain.' The colonel patted the doctor on the back.

Sheridan had paled at this observation. The assassin was left-handed. An image returned of Sir Jonas Soersby striking out with the bat. The ball soaring over the heads of the fielders. That powerful swing of his left arm. And then Lieutenant Branson standing at last base as captain of the Blue team, waiting to offer a congratulatory embrace. The grins and cheers all round. The camaraderie between the two men. Could Sir Jonas really have hugged Branson so close and then mere hours later have killed him with such savagery? Sheridan struggled to swallow the lump in his throat and force down the bile. What a foolish, dangerous game he had played to invite the judge to this gathering.

Slocombe shook his head sadly. 'I dearly hope they catch this fellow. For all the precision and care of his method, there is undoubtedly a deranged mind at large and he may kill again.'

'He has already done so, or so I am led to believe,' Wallis contributed. 'May there not be some purpose in these acts?' he added.

'If there is, it is a devilish one!' the colonel exclaimed.

The doctor nodded. 'Voices in his head, perhaps. It is something I have witnessed in a patient — voices that issued orders and directives he imagined came from a divine source. It is a form of madness that can prompt a man to unusual acts. The man I speak of tried to kill his own wife.'

'Dr Slocombe, you should know that one of my actors was murdered, in every way identical to this butchery — with the suggestion that it was because he preferred men to women. That is what is reported in the newspaper. That should not be said of Lieutenant Branson. For his poor mother's sake, if for no other reason.'

Slocombe's brow creased. 'That is ill. Very ill. Such a slur against an officer who served in the king's navy and at a time of war it is unpardonable. Edward, my dear friend...' The doctor turned to Colonel Branson and clasped his shoulder.

'What can be done?' The colonel shook his head in anguish. 'A magistrate or a constable shall be here presently. He must report what he sees and then the details are public and stories will begin that will spread this vicious poison. My poor boy ... and my good wife whose heart shall be broken not once but twice over...'

'No man here desires that your wife should be so tormented, Colonel Branson,' Sheridan insisted.

The doctor pursed his lips in thought. 'We shall keep Phillip covered with the blanket and the Justice or the constable may see simply that his throat has been fatally cut. I shall add nothing further to that observation.' He sighed. 'I shall then write a report to the coroner. It could be hypothesised that all cuts to the body were sustained in the attack, perhaps received as Phillip tried to dodge his attacker's knife. The verdict of unlawful killing is beyond question.'

'And there shall be no less a hue and cry!' the colonel added firmly. 'The villain is somewhere hereabouts and may have been sighted. The devil, but he shall be caught and I would hang him myself!'

Sheridan's manservant Robert arrived on horse at that moment, followed closely by a parish constable.

The long shadows of a summer's evening approached. The barouche, which had been sent to collect Sheridan and Reverend Wallis, passed along the main thoroughfare of Wanstead and Sheridan was startled to ecognize a familiar figure. Stepping into the late sunshine and shielding his eyes, Viscount Malmain emerged from a curiosity shop with a smiling young woman draped on his arm. Sheridan passed close enough to see that the young lady's powdered face thinly disguised a rash of freckles. Miss Harte, he could only assume, with her chaperone in train and on the arm of her betrothed. He strained his neck to keep the couple in sight.

'You know Miss Harte, do you, Mr Sheridan?' asked Wallis.

'No, no.'

'She is betrothed to Viscount Malmain. Perhaps it is the young lord that you recognise? Is he the young gentleman who escorts Miss Harte? I have not had the honour of an introduction to his lordship yet.'

'Yes, I am acquainted with Malmain. Does Mr Harte reside in this vicinity?'

The clergyman nodded. 'Mr Harte has purchased Holbroke Hall within my parish. He has recently added another wing to the house and the gardens are now quite restored and much improved upon, I would say. There has been a new orangery built and he plans to grow pineapples. Mrs Wallis and I had tea in the gardens only last week with Miss Harte and her father. I may have the honour of officiating.'

'Pardon?'

'At the wedding.'

'I see. When is the happy occasion?'

'All parties are keen that it should be soon. The end of the month has been mentioned. Mr Harte offered that his gardeners assist my own to improve the general appearance of the church grounds, which I consider very generous and most welcome. Our humble church is not often graced by dignitaries of such note. The viscount's parents, the Earl and Countess Crumpsall, of course, and I believe the Duke and Duchess of St Albans may number amongst the guests…'

Sheridan listened with half an ear to the reverend whilst he boasted of the grandeur of the upcoming matrimonial event. His mind tumbled with the revelation that Viscount Malmain was at this moment in Wanstead and may earlier in the afternoon have very well been riding in the vicinity of Epping Forest. The young lord may even have known of Sheridan's planned excursion there. Might be acquainted with Lieutenant Phillip Branson. The lieutenant had only recently returned from duty in the Indies and there might be some reason why he should presently pose a threat to the viscount.

Thoughts of how he might discover Malmain's movements that day scuttled through Sheridan's mind, but nothing other than intrusive questioning of servants and the like presented itself. He felt himself floundering. He had so convinced himself at the first that Malmain was behind these murderous acts. Then the discovery of the provenance of the watch in Marson's possession had equally convinced him that Sir Jonas might be responsible for these crimes. Which man was it? Or, could it be both in partnership? The idea inflamed his imagination. It was not beyond possibility that Viscount Malmain and Sir Jonas Soersby should know each other, given their rank In society, or for them to have learned that they each had the same shame to hide. Both men with reputation and standing at stake were a prey to blackmail and extortion — perhaps from the same source?

There was a thought. Three men dead. Andrew Marson, Thaddeus Broadhead and Phillip Branson. Aside from sharing the same sexual proclivities, were these three men connected in other ways? Could they have conspired together to squeeze the Justice and the young lord?

'Mr Harte has a keen regard for planting. Naturally, I daresay, his own interests being in tea,' Wallis was saying. 'My wife and I were delighted to try the Darjeeling from Mr Harte's own plantation only last week.'

'You foresee no obstacles or objections to the marriage then?'

The parson's eyes widened. 'I should think not, Mr Sheridan, I gather it is a union welcomed on all sides.'

They had arrived at the rectory attached to the church of St Jerome. Mrs Wallis emerged as the barouche clattered over the driveway in front of the house. She wore a look of abject concern.

'Mr Wallis, Mr Sheridan. What news? We have been all in dread. I have Mrs Burridge and Miss Campbell within to stay for supper.' She looked to her husband as though seeking to placate him. 'They insisted we should not part until we know what the accident is.'

'My dear, it is the worst news.'

Her hand flew to her mouth.

'I am sorry to report that Lieutenant Branson has been attacked and killed by some brigand in the forest. The militia have been called out to scour the area.'

Mrs Wallis gasped and stifled a cry.

'There is even talk —' her husband continued, as he stepped down from the gig — 'that there may be French spies or agents in the neighbourhood and that seeing the uniform and Lieutenant Branson alone the French took the opportunity to slay him.'

Tears pricked at Mrs Wallis' eyes.

Sheridan wondered that Wallis did not offer an arm of comfort to his wife, but on closer acquaintance he had surmised that the clergyman was not a man for any great show of feeling.

Reverend Wallis turned to him and bowed. 'Thank you for delivering me to my house, Mr Sheridan. You must be anxious to see your own family.'

Sheridan nodded. 'A tragic and brutal end to a day which had seen so much of gaiety. I offer my thanks for your support, Reverend, and in such distressing circumstances. Colonel Branson will be forever grateful, I am sure. Mrs Wallis, I am grieved that we end our day in such sorrow.'

The carriage moved off and Sheridan prepared himself to deliver an edited account of the dreadful events of the day to all who would be gathered at his house. Mrs Canning, he knew, would be particularly distraught on behalf of Mrs Branson, who had been an early friend when Hitty had first arrived in Wanstead from Putney. He worried too for Richard Tickell. His friend had seemed more pressed by cares than usual that day and the horror of the scene which had met them at the Gifford Oak would only have added to his melancholy.

Alone at last, Sheridan allowed that he too was shaken to his very core by the events of the afternoon. Dark thoughts nagged and scratched at his mind. He felt the presence of the Angel of Death lurking in the shadows all around, taunting him. He did not wish to see that face again, but knew that it would haunt him through his dreams and into his waking hours.

CHAPTER TWENTY-ONE

In the days that followed the disastrous expedition to Epping Forest and the sad funeral of Lieutenant Branson, Sheridan was glad of the distractions occasioned by the move to the villa in Isleworth for the remainder of the summer. The hue and cry which had arisen in the wake of the murder of the lieutenant had not abated. A wave of panic swept through the areas neighbouring the Forest. Increasing speculation that the assassins were an advanced guard of an imminent French invasion fanned the flames of alarm. The public mood was jittery and restless. To date, however, all that had been rounded up were a handful of local poachers and a couple of itinerant hawkers. As his carriage departed Wanstead, he noted the increased presence of the local militia on the streets and the arrival of a troop of Light Dragoons.

Sheridan was almost grateful for other distractions too. The rebuild of the Theatre Royal on Drury Lane had been beset by delays and obstacles. The previous year having been one of the wettest anyone could remember and then a cold winter, works on the foundations and structure had suffered any number of delays. Workmen had stopped yet again for a time in May in some dispute. In consequence he had been on tenterhooks that the subscribers to the new theatre project would make their scheduled all-important second payment. One-hundred-and-fifty-thousand-pounds' worth of debentures had been issued and taken up by the public. He himself had continued to borrow heavily and was mortgaged to the very hilt.

Everything was staked on success. The project could not — must not — fail. He had to keep assuring himself that the investment was sound. More than sound. The order to demolish Old Madam Drury was to be embraced not as an occasion for mourning — for who would miss the faded auditorium and subterranean world of peeling dressing rooms and reeking cellars — but rather a cause for celebration, the chance in his lifetime to create a theatre that should be the wonder of Europe. One that he would make his own, not a creaking monument to antiquity haunted by David Garrick and the like. Finally, at last, the project progressed. He inwardly gave thanks for the persistence of his architect, Henry Holland, and dashed a note to him.

... I have been very impatient to see you — but I have not plagued you 'till our difficulties are really over. Here is money Plenty — and all my Hopes are now on your super-natural exertions. Pray meet me tomorrow at Hammersley's at two. I shall come to Town on purpose and will now give my whole mind and time to this business.
Yrs
RBS

Well, that was not strictly true. His mind, it seemed, could never be solely on one item of business. There was also the small matter of the entertainment for the Royal Princesses. There could be no further delays. To begin with, a round of auditions was scheduled to take place at The Foundling Home for the Daughters of the Deserving Poor.

Mrs Siddons condescended to attend and to contribute to proceedings. She was welcomed with great ceremony by the Warden Mistress of the establishment and by Sir Percival himself. A light luncheon of stuffed capon and braised artichokes had been prepared and a number of local patrons were included as guests at the dining table. It was apparent that all assembled were in thrall to the great Muse of Tragedy and had seen one or another of her renowned performances. She accepted all their idolatry with her usual gracious hauteur.

'I shall never forget the moment, Mrs Siddons, when you entered upon the stage in the role of Lady Macbeth —'

Sheridan smiled to see the theatricals gathered at the table surreptitiously spit over their left shoulders at mention of this forbidden and ill-omened name.

Mrs Siddons, in response, quoted the lines from *Hamlet* frequently used by actors to offset the curse of The Scottish Tragedy. '*Angels and ministers of grace defend us!*'

Sir Percival was for a moment perplexed but then continued his gushing adulation. 'That moment when you set down the candle, the washing of hands as though from an invisible ewer, so perfectly capturing both horror and remorse. "*Here's the smell of blood still: all the perfumes of Arabia will not sweeten this little hand.*" Why, madam, I was chilled to the very bone! To have seen your performance in that character is an event that I shall never forget.'

Sheridan inwardly sighed with satisfaction. The old Tory might more easily be persuaded now to allow the rehearsals to take place in the spacious rooms near Vauxhall which he had rented for the purpose and where the staging and props were to be built and gathered. He had already explained to Sir Percival that the proposed entertainment would involve a number of other young girls patronised by Their Royal Highnesses and the rehearsal location would be to the convenience of all.

They were waited on by a couple of the older girls of the establishment; scrubbed and neat in simple grey, they served the various luncheon courses with admirable skill and grace.

The competence and deportment of the young women were praised by the assembled diners as evidence of the Home's continued success in the training of these deserving daughters of the poor. The Warden Mistress puffed herself up and was pleased to announce that both of her charges were shortly to be placed in good and reputable households. One presently to Mrs Fitzhenry in Mayfair — the older girl bobbed a curtsey in acknowledgement of the congratulatory looks bestowed on her — and the younger girl was to join the household staff of the wealthy tea merchant Mr Harte at Holbroke Hall in the autumn. Murmurs of approval circulated the table. It appeared that Mr Harte was noted for his philanthropical endeavours and had become a recent benefactor of the Home.

Sheridan's ears pricked at the mention of Holbroke Hall and he wondered if this girl, Jane, might be useful to him in some way.

Various of the guests remained to observe the afternoon's proceedings, which took place in the dining hall. The plain wooden tables and benches had been stowed to the side and seats arranged in front of a small performance area. The smell of cabbage and something which Sheridan thought might be tripe, however, lingered disturbingly in the air.

Sir Percival was ensconced beside Mrs Siddons. Sheridan and Mr Quail, who had been introduced as the manager for the pageant, sat to the great lady's left. The girls to be auditioned were lined up in nervous rows along the side. Sheridan had already decided that Eliza Ramus would be appreciably the youngest of the troupe. He had therefore stipulated that the girls to be seen that day should be above eight years of age. Some of them were so shrunk and thin, however, he could not imagine them above five or six in years.

After half an hour of nervous caterwauling and recitations from the King James Bible, Sheridan had yet to add a name to the list in his hand. He sighed. The general public, and he included the prince in that number, were simply unaware of the plethora of skills required for performance at a professional standard, or how many years of practice and devotion to the craft were necessary. And children upon the stage? Why, they must be trained from the cradle, nay from the womb itself! He had heard an actress swear that her offspring had learnt his first tunes when she had sung her ditties full big with him. Audiences loved to see a child perform. Singing, tumbling, dancing sprites and fairies were ever popular. There was a certain kind of gentleman, rather too many he admitted to himself, who relished the ballet interludes when young girls in scant costume cavorted across the stage.

All this talent needed to be schooled, it seldom arrived fully-formed on the stage, and he himself had sometimes winced to see the draconian methods used by the likes of Monsieur Dubois and Signor Grimaldi, to shape the children of the company in their charge. Still, there was no denying that the hours of strenuous training and exercise had produced many an audience favourite, not least Grimaldi's own son, Joey. And now Sheridan was expecting that same young Joey to work miracles with these unfortunate creatures. How on earth were they going to conjure up anything approximating an entertainment for the Royal Princesses?

Nothing should matter, however, if he did not secure little Eliza Ramus.

When he arrived home to the Isleworth villa that evening, Sheridan found two messages had been brought to him from the theatre. The first was a message from a Matthew Simpson.

He puzzled over the name for a moment until he ecogniz that this was the footman in the Prince of Wales' household. The *husband* of Andrew Marson. He scanned the note again.

Sir,
  I beg your indulgence.
  On reflection I find that there is something further which I would wish to impart in the strictest confidence concerning events earlier in the year. I should be available on the coming Thursday and could meet Mr Sheridan at a time and place of Mr Sheridan's choosing.
  Your respectful servant,
  Matthew Simpson

Well, he might be able to make the request fit with his plans. Sheridan had arranged to take Tom and his friend Harry to see *The Siege of Valenciennes* at Astley's Royal Grove. This spectacular was the talk of the town. Bringing to vivid life the siege which had lately taken place to the end of July as part of the Flanders campaign led by the Duke of York and their Hapsburg allies. The successful outcome had been deemed a great Allied victory against Revolutionary France. York had been declared as a saviour by the population of Valenciennes. Accounts had even emerged that the townsfolk had trampled the revolution's tricolour underfoot and then hailed the Duke of York as their *King of France*!

Sheridan had chortled at this titbit. He imagined that the Prince of Wales should have an opinion on that. York and the younger princes had each in succession been allowed an active military or naval career. Despite the Prince of Wales' pleading with his father, the king had denied the heir to the throne any and all such opportunities at every turn. Now here was his younger brother York, who might be on a throne before him!

Without a thought for the imprisoned dauphin, a number of French émigré aristocrats in London were in all seriousness plotting to place the Duke of York on the vacant throne after the defeat of the Revolution. Sheridan shook his head wryly. The Prince of Wales would feel himself slighted and betrayed, an impotent booby. Much as he loved his brother Freddy, His Royal Highness would listen to the clamours for the regal elevation of his younger brother with increasing frustration. The Duke of York to become King of France? Well, that would be something to see and York might have to make up with his monkey-loving wife in the event, for she would be queen and they should need to make a new dauphin.

Sheridan dipped his quill into the inkpot and scribbled a note for Matthew Simpson, inviting the footman to meet him at Astley's Royal Grove. An entrance ticket should be left at the booth for him. He wondered what more the footman had to tell him. It occurred to him that he might also take the opportunity to enquire whether Mr Simpson was acquainted with or knew anything of Lieutenant Branson, or Thaddeus Broadhead for that matter.

The second note was from Nicholls. The attendant at Mr Culpepper's bagnio, Tobias, had returned to his lodgings in the night. A watchman had been alerted and seized the missing servant. Nicholls was keeping him in a cell in Bow Street and was confident that he might snitch on his former employer and reveal something of the goings-on at the bagnio.

Sheridan tapped his desk as he tried to decide whether or not to rush to Bow Street or to leave the visit to the morning. His curiosity had the better of him and he called for his carriage again. Crossing the entrance, he was met by Mr Smyth and Tom returning from an afternoon stroll by the river. He apologised and begged leave, but he should not now be joining them after all at their neighbour's whist party that evening.

Tom groaned. 'Pa, it seems I must apologise for your absence on a daily basis! I am become quite expert in the art of apology.'

'Practice makes perfect and it will stand you in good stead, my dear boy. You will find that apologies will form half of your correspondence at the very least.'

'What event of national importance must I quote now as your excuse?'

'I go to assist in the apprehension of a brutal and villainous assassin.'

Mr Smyth let out an involuntary titter.

Tom merely rolled his eyes. 'Pa, I shall have to give something more plausible.'

'The king considers me for an office in his beneficence and so I am called to dine with His Majesty at Windsor.'

Tom looked agog. 'Really? What office?'

'Polishing his buckles — what do you think?'

'Oh, Pa!' Tom slapped his thigh in annoyance.

CHAPTER TWENTY-TWO

One of the watchmen was emerging from the Bow Street office as Sheridan's carriage drew up outside. He bowed as Sheridan stepped down.

'Mr Sheridan, you are here to see Constable Nicholls perhaps?'

'Bartholomew, isn't it? Yes, I have received a note from Mr Nicholls. Was it you who seized this servant Tobias last night?'

The watchman nodded. 'Yes, sir. Tobias attempted to creep up to his room but it was a warm night and the landlord could not sleep, he had his bedroom door ajar and heard the intruder, then sent a boy to fetch me. I arrived in the very nick of time. Tobias was stepping out of the building with a sack of his possessions.'

'Excellent. And does this piglet squeal yet?'

'The constable is right now persuading him, sir.'

'Perhaps I might add some encouragement.'

'Then let me show you to them, Mr Sheridan, before I get about my duties.'

They turned into the building and Bartholomew picked up a lantern. He nodded to a fellow officer of the law and led Sheridan down into the bowels of the building. They stopped before a thick door and rapped loudly.

Nicholls ushered Sheridan within whilst Bartholomew took his leave.

'Mr Sheridan, I did not expect to see you this evening. I hope you are not inconvenienced?'

Sheridan shook his head. 'You have denied me the pleasure of being trumped and losing at whist.'

'You are welcome indeed.'

Sheridan peered beyond the constable into the far corner of the dim cell, where he could see that a slight and trembling figure had been clapped in chains.

He nodded. 'Good evening, Mr —?'

'Tobias Bloomer,' Nicholls supplied.

'Mr Bloomer.' Sheridan smiled broadly. 'I believe that you are going to be of the utmost assistance to this sad investigation, are you not?'

'I know nothing, sir, nothing,' Tobias averred and latched his eyes on Sheridan as though he might hold the key to his release.

Nicholls sighed wearily. 'At present, Mr Bloomer does not appreciate the benefits of cooperation.'

'Ah.' Sheridan glanced quickly to the strained countenance of his friend. The young constable had clearly been thwarted in his attempts to glean any useful information from the former bath house attendant. Sheridan knew that Nicholls would refrain from extraction by means of threat and violence unless no other course presented.

'If I may be so bold, Officer... Might this be because Mr Bloomer does not see a mutual advantage? He fears that in speaking out he may be forced to incriminate himself in matters of a criminal character.'

'I believe he does have that fear. And rightly.' Nicholls clenched his fist.

'So, he may risk the noose, or worse, transportation to Botany Bay.'

'I beg you would help me, sir. You would not see an innocent man condemned,' the hapless servant whimpered.

'Would that I could help you, Mr Bloomer — if you are truly innocent I should consider it my duty. But who may swear to that?'

'Sir?'

'Shall your master, Mr Edward Culpepper, say that you are a man of good character? Shall we send for him? Shall he say that you are beyond suspicion?'

Tobias gulped.

'After all, were you not the one to first discover Mr Marson? You beheld the savage scene by your own admission.'

'Horrors I saw…' Tobias moaned.

Sheridan turned to Nicholls. 'Did you not see blood on his hands, Constable?'

Nicholls nodded in affirmation.

'Therefore, who is to say that it was not Mr Bloomer who has murdered my actor? Then, with all the guile of a true villain, run straight to Bow Street so that the officers of the law might not consider it was he that did it in the first place. At the very least Mr Bloomer would be a co-conspirator.'

Nicholls nodded slowly. 'That is a theory worth deliberation, sir.'

'Mr Bloomer, it is most probable that you will hang at Newgate. Indeed, I believe it to be beyond reasonable doubt — whether you speak or no.'

'No … no…' Bloomer whimpered.

'On the other hand…'

Sheridan paused for effect, sustaining it for almost as long as Kemble had been fabled to do after uttering the immortal lines, *'To be, or, not to be…'*

Tobias Bloomer held his breath and leant forward in hopeful expectation.

'On the other hand, Mr Bloomer here may have been sorely abused. An unwilling participant to felonious activities. He is, after all, only a servant at the bidding of his master. Which begs the question, should the *loyal* servant be held culpable? Should the *loyal* servant pay for the misdeeds of the master? How shall a *loyal* servant refuse his master's command and not risk his very livelihood?'

Nicholls drew himself up and rubbed his chin. 'Hmm ... you present a worthwhile argument there, Mr Sheridan.'

'Yes ... yes...' Tobias sobbed.

Sheridan turned to the trembling man but addressed himself to Nicholls.

'In which circumstances, if I may suggest, Officer, and speaking as a former magistrate myself, I think the law might look kindly on an otherwise loyal servant should that fellow be persuaded by his conscience in the service of justice to divulge the wickedness of his master. Let it not be forgotten that it was Mr Bloomer who came to Bow Street to alert the officers of the law of this murderous crime and should he continue his help in the investigation, why, then such a man might be granted a level of immunity and released from custody.'

Sheridan could not help but feel a degree of satisfaction at the outcome of the interview with Mr Bloomer, and not a little for the part which he had played in encouraging the lamb to bleat. And how he had bleated! All the while disclaiming any responsibility for what had passed. It was as Constable Nicholls had first suspected. There had been a similar murder at the beginning of April.

According to Tobias, Mr Culpepper had been thrown into a frenzy of panic when the lad's body had been discovered on the premises one night, naked and mutilated.

'He was known to us as Johnny, sir. I never knew his surname. He was an urchin off the street. One of the many one sees about Covent Garden. There was never any talk of family — I daresay he had none. Mr Culpepper used him for errands and the like and I suppose he was always about. Underfoot often as not. As time passed, he ingratiated himself with some of our customers. He would help about the bath house.'

'Who was there on that day?'

'There was much coming and going on that day, sir. And Mr Culpepper, he insisted that the customers were never referred to except by an initial, Mr R or Sir D, if you follow, sir. Indeed, the gentlemen employed the same system of address amongst themselves. I only knew that the murdered man, Mr M, was the actor Mr Marson because I had seen him for myself on the stage at Drury Lane.'

'You are saying you could not identify any man that might have been present on either day of the murders?'

'No, Constable, on my honour.'

'Mr Culpepper did not report the murder of the lad, John?' Nicholls asked.

'No, Constable. He expressed the opinion that it would bring unfavourable attention to the establishment and that all our livelihoods would be affected if the baths were closed down. He was also of the opinion that the lad would not be missed by anyone. Further, he said the lad would have starved long ago were it not for Mr Culpepper's good nature and whilst John's end was unfortunate, he had lived well with us to that point. Or some such similar words.'

'What course of action did the good and kind Mr Culpepper propose in the circumstances?' Sheridan quizzed.

'That we might wrap the body in a sheet and slip him into the Thames at the dead of night, sir.'

'And you did as you were bid?'

Tobias nodded with an expression of contrition. 'I knew it was wrong, Mr Sheridan, but Mr Culpepper would not have the stain of murder on his house and I must do as I am bid. I said a prayer as we slipped poor Johnny into the river, sir, much as they might with a burial at sea.'

'That was most considerate of you, Mr Bloomer.'

'I heard he was dragged out near Shadwell.'

Nicholls nodded.

'He did get a proper burial then I hope?'

'In a pauper's grave.'

Tobias looked relieved. 'A Christian end at least.'

'Your master did not think it important to catch the villain who has done this grisly deed?'

Tobias sighed heavily. 'It could not be imagined that such an act would be repeated, and Johnny was dead, nothing would bring him back. But then … I stepped into that chamber where Mr Marson was and knew straight away that none of us would ever be safe.' He shivered. 'I pray God you catch the villain.'

As they ascended the stone steps from the cells, Sheridan addressed the constable. 'You will arrest Mr Culpepper now, Nicholls, this very night, will you not? And he must tell us which men have used the services of his establishment.'

The Bow Street Runner grimaced. 'That bird has flown, Mr Sheridan. Or rather, his ship has sailed. From the little I gather, he has abandoned his property and slipped my net of watchers and barkers. Mr Culpepper will have had assistance no doubt from one of his wealthier customers; they will have clamoured to aid his flight, fearing what he might divulge otherwise. The cove will be in some safe haven in France or possibly the Americas by now.'

'Oh dear.' Sheridan shook his head. 'I fear this is a game of advance and retreat at every step.'

'That is three men that we now know are killed in similar fashion, all in the space of so many months. I do not think this fiend will stop.'

'Four men, Mr Nicholls. I may include another.'

He proceeded to recount the circumstances of Phillip Branson's murder in Epping Forest. Nicholls listened with interest as Sheridan relayed the facts, reacting with concern at his invitation to the Soersbys to join the excursion.

'Mr Sheridan, I appreciate your desire to help in this matter, but I would not have you put yourself in the path of danger with so brutal a killer at large. This man would not think twice to kill anyone who gets in his way.'

'Thank you, Constable, but it was poor Lieutenant Branson whom I placed in jeopardy. If I had had any inkling that the beloved son of our neighbour might be a target I should not have ventured in this way. I confess his death weighs heavily upon me, Mr Nicholls. I cannot wrest those final images from my mind. I am haunted and all the more determined that this madness must end.'

Sheridan finished his account by detailing his later sighting of Lord Malmain within the vicinity of the fatal happenings.

'That is a fortunate coincidence, Mr Sheridan. We had put all our suspicions of that gentleman to one side, perhaps too hastily.'

'Yes, though his appearance muddies the waters yet again.'

Nicholls shook his head. 'The field is narrowed, sir. Up to this point the assassinations that we know of have been within a small circle, the bagnio in Covent Garden and a street at no great distance. For all our speculations the murderer might be anyone in this great teeming city — and that is to find a needle in a haystack. But this murder at Epping must point to Sir Jonas Soersby or Viscount Malmain. We know now who we deal with. One or other of these gentlemen.'

'Or both together.'

'They know each other?'

'That I do not know. But this I do; they share much in common, a connection to Andrew Marson, and a great deal to lose should their secrets be exposed.'

As they stepped out into Bow Street, Sheridan paused and looked up at the cloudless night sky teemed with stars.

'We cannot stand idly by waiting for another murder to occur in the vain hope of catching this fiend in the act. I for one must do something. You still have the pocket watch?'

Nicholls nodded.

'Then allow me to return it to Sir Jonas. He shall tell me how it came to be with Andrew Marson. It is likely that he will lie and say the piece was stolen or mislaid, but if he lies, I do believe I shall know it, because I know him. And he shall know that I know. And he shall know that he is watched.'

Nicholls shook his head. 'If he is the killer, you alert him and place yourself at risk, Mr Sheridan.'

'If he is our assassin, he may as likely hesitate if he knows he is under suspicion and might even call a halt to his murderous rampage. That is surely worth the risk.'

As he pulled himself up into his carriage, Sheridan called to his coachman to take him to Brooks's Club. He was in need of a bumper of brandy, or maybe two.

CHAPTER TWENTY-THREE

Sir Jonas had gone to his estate in Somerset for the summer. Sheridan would have to await his return to London along with the rest of society. In the meantime, he was intrigued to discover what it was that Matthew Simpson wished to impart at their rendezvous and his mind raced with various possibilities. But he still had a day or two before the meeting with the footman at Astley's. He felt himself distracted, ill at ease and unable to settle long at any activity.

He tried to write, sitting at the desk in his study which looked out across the lawn and gardens down to the river, shimmering in the summer heat. There was always something to catch his eye and his interest; a boat on the river, a heron on the bank, or when his children were at play. That afternoon, it was a game of pall mall between Tom and his friend Harry. The sounds of mallet on ball drifted up to the house through the open window and Sheridan found himself following their play. Tom cried out as he struck the round boxwood ball with an almighty whack and then whooped in delight when it flew through the iron hoop. Sheridan half rose and punched the air.

He sat back and picked up the sheet in front of him. He had attempted to jot down some ideas and half-formed sketches for the royal entertainment. Thoughts about what might amuse and delight the princesses came and as quickly went, for they must be within the performance capabilities of the ragtag girls he had finally mustered from the Foundling Home. He toyed with the notion that it should be a pantomime so that the little chicklets would have no need to open their mouths and declaim at all. He doubted that Their Royal Highnesses would understand much of what the girls would say anyway, given the variety and strength of accents which they presented. Never mind the stuttering and hesitations and lack of performance. It was enough that they must be taught to sing in some manner harmonious. A pantomime then. Which one? In the Italian tradition or something fresh? Then the question, should he include any breeches parts? Or should they all be female characters? An Arabian scenario? A tale involving the exotic princesses of the seraglio engaged in sharing stories amongst themselves in the tedious hours awaiting the arrival of the sultan. The heroine might even be named *Fatimah*. Or should that setting be too risqué?

Sheridan sighed and loosened his cravat. The day was too hot for sitting at one's desk. He strained across his papers to catch sight of the boys. Harry was concentrated over his ball; he then swung back and let fly the mallet. With deadly accuracy his shot caught Tom's ball and cannoned it from the arena whilst his own stopped in front of the hoop. Oh, a crafty shot. Well played, Harry. The boy grinned widely and Tom made a show of waving his mallet about in mock rage and then laughed.

There was a creak at the door, which had been left slightly ajar. He turned to see little Mary poking her face around the frame. She squealed with delight when she sighted him and rushed across the carpet. He opened his arms wide and she clambered up on to his lap. The nursemaid appeared on the threshold, frowning, a bead of sweat on her brow.

'Miss Mary, come away and do not disturb your father at his work!' Martha bobbed a curtsey. 'Sorry, sir, Mary is in a lively mood after her nap.'

'Then allow me to entertain her for a while, good Martha, and you should take your ease. It is much too hot today to be chasing this rapscallion about the house and garden. But before you rest you might have a glass of lemonade each sent up.'

'Yes, sir.' Martha bobbed and retreated.

Mary had already turned her attention to what was on the desk. When Sheridan looked down he found that the infant clasped a pencil in her chubby little hand and was busy making marks and scribbles on his text. He laughed ruefully. Mary had appreciated the worth of his ideas, which was to be scribbled all over and made the base for amusement. He picked up his pen and joined her.

'What shall I draw for you, Mary?'

'Doggy, doggy!'

Sheridan proceeded to sketch a dog in the blank space of the page, much to his daughter's delight.

'Woof, woof!' he exclaimed, drawing a speech bubble from the dog's mouth to write in the sounds of barking.

'Woof, woof!' she replied, jabbing at the cartoon creature with the pencil.

It was a slow progress over Westminster Bridge. The bridge itself and the streets at either end were clogged with vehicles, chairs with chairmen shouting and pushing their way through the throng, carts coming in from the countryside laden with produce, carriages, horses, hawkers and people on foot. Many were heading towards the popular Astley's Royal Grove, Sheridan noted, as his carriage approached. *The Siege of Valenciennes* was the show everyone in London wanted to see. Tom was leaning out of the window, hallooing everyone he ecognized and many he did not, flushed with excitement. Sheridan felt his own anticipation mounting. This was what people desired. To see real events enacted and brought to life in all their spectacular glory. Horses, fire, cannon, huge backdrops and sets that could make you feel you were actually present to watch a great battle or some historic action like the storming of the Bastille; various representations of which had been a huge success some four years previous.

He had once feared that Philip Astley's equestrian extravaganzas were competition to the patented theatres. Now he sensed that Astley's variety shows, rather than stealing audiences from the theatre, had brought out more people ready to pay for such entertainment, and his shows with their inclusion of pantomime and posturers had whet the appetite of this new audience for more and more such spectacles. Sheridan's new Theatre Royal would have the largest auditorium in Europe and a stage great enough to accommodate all his grand and bold ideas. These people crowding the streets south of Westminster Bridge should soon — next spring all being well — be heading north up to Drury Lane.

The old riding school and amphitheatre had been revamped some years previous to provide a roof over the heads of the spectators, allowing a continuance of performances into the winter months and during inclement weather. The new interior retained a sense of the exterior, with its sylvan decoration, painted foliage and fake greenery adding to the illusion, and the building had soon been dubbed The Royal Grove. Astley had also added a theatrical stage, allowing for more elaborate sets and enhancing the spectacle. Boxes and galleried areas expanded to accommodate the growing audience. What an industrious and ingenious fellow the former Sergeant Major was, Sheridan mused, and quite the hero! Aged over fifty, the amphitheatre's owner had recently reenlisted in the 15th Light Dragoons following the outbreak of war with France. His role, aside from that of a horse-master renowned for his skills in breaking and training horses, was clearly to inspire the troops. Sheridan looked about the thronging crowd as his party walked towards their box and rather missed the presence of this giant of a man who could stand out in any crowd.

'Ah, it is every Tom, Dick and Harry I see!'

Sheridan swung about to find Charles Long in their path.

The fellow MP smiled pleasantly at Sheridan.

'Mr Long, you are mistaken.'

'Oh, how so?'

'It is a *long* and therefore rather tedious story, I am afraid.'

'What-ho, Sherry! I apologise, gentlemen.' He bowed to the boys. 'I should never think you ordinary, on my honour. It was an unpardonable but irresistible tease.'

'Long may you continue, sir, to fall short of wit,' Tom rejoindered merrily.

The young MP grinned. 'Quite right. I shall never scale the heights of a Sheridan. So, let me fall back in defeat and rather let us enjoy the spectacle of the Duke of York's resounding success into Valenciennes. I hear tell they would make him King of France!'

What a popinjay Charles Long was, but nevertheless, Sheridan found he could not entirely dislike him.

The show did not disappoint. Aside from the usual mix of comedy, music and tumbling, Astley's son John commanded the stage with his astonishing feats of equestrianism. Then, the saga of the siege itself quite took one's breath away. The re-enacted skirmishes were thrillingly realistic. Cavalry broadswords swept down from side to side as horses charged and thundered past their box. Both Tom and Harry leapt to their feet when the cannons started to blast, smoke filling the arena. One could almost be in Flanders and smell the acrid fumes of the battlefield. The noise was deafening in the enclosed space. It was as he put his hands to his ears and instinctively turned his head that Sheridan became aware of the figure waiting patiently at the threshold for admittance to the box.

'Matthew, welcome!' he greeted, or rather mouthed, as nothing could be heard above the din coming from the arena.

The footman bowed. He was out of livery of course, it being his day off. Regardless, he still presented a very neat and handsome aspect in his well-tailored suit. He really was a very good-looking young man, almost beautiful, Sheridan realised, with his long dark lashes and smooth skin.

'We shall not be able to talk here. One moment.' Sheridan called into the ear of his manservant to inform the boys, if necessary, that he should be gone a short while. His man gave the merest nod in acknowledgement. No one ever expected Sheridan to tarry in any one place for long.

With the booming cannons still resounding in his ears, Sheridan led Matthew out of the building and across to the riverside where they paused to enjoy the slight breeze, which lifted off the Thames and cooled the air.

'There is something more you wish to impart to me, Mr Simpson? Something which will help in the hunt for Mr Marson's killer?'

'I do not know if it will go so far. If what I tell you shall demonstrate the kind of man you deal with and can play any part in bringing him to justice, then I shall be very glad of it.'

'Why have you hesitated to come with this information before? It is three months or more since Andrew was assassinated and a full month since I spoke with you in Brighton.'

Matthew bit his lip and then emboldened himself. 'Sir, you must know that men of our sort live in a hidden world. It is a world where all must wear a mask, where discretion and subterfuge go hand in hand. The newspapers would have us in a quaking fear because there is a killer abroad who targets us. But such fears are nothing new! Our lives are lived in constant fear. One wrong move and we may face the pillory or noose. Our only safety is to guard each other as best we can. The very worst we can do is to betray another.'

'And that is why none will talk to the Bow Street office?'

'Our best defence may be silence.'

'But you will speak?'

'As far as I dare, Mr Sheridan. For Andrew.'

'Go on.'

'There is a house in Holborn, near the Inns. It is where I first met Mr Marson. And loved him from the start. The press speaks of our carnal desires but none speak of love! Do they imagine that love is something foreign to us?'

Sheridan heard a note of anguish in Matthew's voice. He had to confess that he himself had never thought of love as part of the equation. He regarded Matthew afresh. When young Mr Blackett had revealed that Marson was 'married' to another man, Sheridan had taken it as some jest, a parody of a wedding, not a union which could be considered in any way true. Now he reconsidered that perhaps the emotions ran as deep as in any other union.

'It was one night, in February. The country had learned that the French meant to make war on us and that topic was on every lip. That is until a man arrived, an old official recently retired from the East India Company's service. He had managed a factory there he told us. We were taken aback because he was accompanied by a Hindu servant, dressed in

217

colourful, flowing robes and adorned with jewellery. We were confused because naturally women are not permitted into our club premises. Simon, for that was the official's name, laughed to see our expressions.'

The footman shook his head and smiled at the recollection.

'But you will tell me this was indeed a man?'

'When we heard the account from Simon, it seemed to us that his companion was neither man nor woman. Apparently, it is not uncommon in the countries of Asia where they are known as Hijras. These Hijras may be born with some natural defect of the male organ but if not and in any case once they have proclaimed themselves as Hijras they are emasculated entirely.'

'Eunuchs then,' Sheridan surmised.

'In a way. But they have desires, they desire men and engage in a ritual marriage to one of the Hindu gods, I cannot recall his name. In consequence, Simon told us, they are considered semi-divine. It is believed that they have special powers allowing them to bless or curse others.

'Simon came to us that night because he had heard that marriage ceremonies might be arranged in the house and he wished to marry his servant. He confided that he intended them to live as man and wife.'

'A marriage took place?'

Matthew nodded. 'In our own fashion. Without a church. But there is a ritual of sorts and words of blessing. The Hindu spoke little English but was prompted by Simon when they came at last to the vows. Andrew and I were reminded of our own ceremony.' The footman paused in reflection.

Sheridan wondered where all this was leading; colourful as the story was, he could not yet discern any significance.

'Sorry sir, you are wondering what the relevance may be of this tale? It is this. There is a room set aside, a bedroom where newlyweds may lie.' Matthew flushed. 'The Hindu entered to make ready and the old East India Company man said he would have some air. He ventured out of the rear door, where there is a small courtyard. The rest of us were engrossed in celebration of the event and some time passed before we noticed that Simon had not returned. Andrew said he should go and see that the old man was all right.'

Sheridan's eyes narrowed. 'And what had happened?'

'Simon was lying in the dirt, his throat had been partially cut and he was bleeding, but he was still alive. In one hand he held a sharp and vicious-looking knife which he must have wrestled from his assailant. He tried to speak but the injury prevented him from doing so. He waved towards a wall and Andrew took him to mean that the attacker had escaped in that direction. There were a couple of barrels up against it, the wall would not have been difficult to scale.'

'Did he survive?'

'There was one in our company who revealed himself as a surgeon. He managed to staunch the flow and bandaged the old man as best he could, he was a tough old goat, unconscious by then but breathing still. The Hindu was brought down and started a kind of wailing and keening, which threw us all in a panic. Someone went abroad to find a carriage. Simon's address was found written on a letter in his pocket and, well, we bundled him into the vehicle and directed the driver thither.'

'Is there more?'

Matthew sighed. 'The events preyed on my mind. After some days I went to make enquiry. I had remembered the address. The door was answered by an elderly woman; Simon had a sister, it seemed, who had come to nurse him. She was a pinched-faced woman who would not invite me indoors but she did say that it was hoped her brother, whose name I learnt was Thacker, would recover and she prayed they would catch the thieving cut-throat who had attacked him. But I do not believe this was the work of an ordinary cut-throat, Mr Sheridan.'

'No? You imagine this was the work of the same villain who murdered Andrew?'

The footman nodded.

'And he might have likewise mutilated Mr Thacker if that old fighter had not knocked the knife from his hand.'

Matthew paled and Sheridan placed a hand on the footman's shoulder.

'Thank you, Mr Simpson, for coming to me with this information. Well, well…' Sheridan shook his head. 'If this is the same man. He is the very devil.'

'From the deepest pit of Hell, sir.'

'But I am all at a loss again as to what impels him! This attack on the East India Official, that does not smack of vengeance.'

'Sir?'

'I confess, Mr Simpson, that I had thought this business might all be one of blackmail. Each victim in one way or another presenting a threat to this man. Their deaths a brutal retribution. But —'

'You thought Andrew to be a blackmailer?' The footman stiffened in horror.

Sheridan looked at Matthew squarely. 'Was he?'

'No!' Matthew's brow creased. 'No, sir. He was not.'

'You are without any doubt?' Sheridan pressed.

The footman feature's hardened. 'He was a good man.'

'Even good men can be prey to temptations. Particularly if he thought the other were not a good man. And Mr Marson's life had not always been easy — he had done what he must in order to survive when he was younger.'

'Mr Sheridan, I must object to your insinuations.'

'Well, we may never know.' Sheridan softened. 'Let us give Mr Marson the benefit of doubt, for he is not here to defend himself. But if your suspicions are right, Mr Simpson, and the attacker that night was the same man who murdered him, then this killer seems to act at random. Or, to some design that I cannot yet comprehend.'

The footman nodded in agreement. 'I fear I will never see justice for Andrew.'

A thought occurred to Sheridan. 'The killer must have been of your company within the house that night.'

'That thought has presented itself to me,' Matthew concurred.

'Did you notice anything particular? Any absence whilst Mr Thacker was outside taking the air?'

'It was a lively gathering that evening and I cannot be certain of everyone's movements. There were a number of gentlemen unknown to me. One who, I cannot say I heard him speak, was dressed soberly and had a serious mien. Another that was not long arrived in the city and wished to make acquaintance with all.'

'Who can you name?'

Matthew shook his head. 'Sir, sadly that is more than I can say, as I have explained.'

Sheridan frowned in irritation. 'Can you say who was *not* there then? Sir Jonas Soersby, for example?'

Matthew looked hesitant, then nodded slightly.

'Viscount Malmain?'

Again Matthew moved his head almost imperceptibly.

Sheridan shook his head in confusion. 'Neither man was there? Are you sure?'

'There are some who will wear a mask when they enter the house.'

'Egad!' Sheridan huffed. 'I may as well be lost in a maze — going around and around in circles and never finding the way out!'

Matthew looked at his feet and muttered, 'You may try the cottage named Samsara at Heath's Green and find an answer there.'

'Thank you. Thank you.'

'I must take my leave now, sir.'

'Of course. It was good of you to give your time.'

'Good day, Mr Sheridan. I pray your constable catches him.'

The footman bowed and turned to leave.

Sheridan watched the footman until he was lost amongst the crowds milling towards the river crossing. His mind fizzed as he thought over the events which the footman had described. Could this really be the same attacker? It might simply have been some passing rogue in the alley, who, hearing the old gentlemen in the yard, had scaled the wall and seized the opportunity to threaten him with a knife and steal from him, not anticipating a man such as Simon Thacker would resist and put up a good fight.

Then again, what if it was their assassin? Slipping out into the yard to attack Mr Thacker whilst the rest of the company was distracted. For how long had these attacks and killings been happening? Dr Slocombe's conjectures came to his mind. At Epping Forest the doctor had spoken of a derangement he had observed, unfortunates who were compelled to violent acts by voices from within their own minds. With so many murders, this might very well be the work of an unhinged mind.

Sheridan fed a ravenous Tom and Harry their fill of beef and gravy at a nearby chop house and listened to their excitable recounting of the scenes from *The Siege of Valenciennes* which he had missed. Afterwards he dispatched them in his carriage home to Isleworth. He then made his way in a chair to Bow Street in search of Constable Nicholls.

The Runner was not to be found and Sheridan was writing a note to be left for him when the sound of shouting and ruckus tumbled through the door. Bartholomew held a young barefoot lad by the scruff of the neck, an arm wrenched behind his back.

'I ain't done nothin', you pig turd!' The youth continued to kick and protest.

Nicholls entered behind and scowled. 'Desist now, Tuck, or you will be charged with assault as well as with thievery.'

'Not me, Mr Nicholls. I was just helping the gentleman! Trying to earn an honest farthing, I was.'

'You are no honest link-boy but a Glym Jack and were leading that gentleman into an ambush.'

'Nah, nah — how was I to know them footpads was down that alley!'

Bartholomew smirked. 'Because I recognised one of the coves that fled as your own father, my lad! Come on, Tuck, it's the magistrate for you.'

Nicholls broke away on sighting Sheridan. 'Sir? You have some news?'

'I do not know yet if it will signify.'

'We can but see, Mr Sheridan. I also have news of interest.'

'Then pray, speak first.'

'Tobias Bloomer, Mr Culpepper's servant. The magistrate has had him arrested and charged with the murder of Mr Marson and the young lad John. He is even now being held at Newgate.'

'This cannot be! You and I have little doubt that Tobias is no killer.'

'There is more.' Nicholls stared solemnly at Sheridan. 'He is to go before Judge Soersby.'

Sheridan paled.

CHAPTER TWENTY-FOUR

Samsara was a neat but sizeable cottage set in its own grounds not far from the Heath. There had been a light summer downpour and the steam lifting off the lawn and garden borders smelt rich and sweet with a floral fragrance. The sunlight seemed to gleam more brightly, as it often did after rain. Sheridan took in a deep breath as Nicholls rapped upon the door. This was where the retired East India Company manager had planned to have his twilight idyll with the Hijra. And a very charming spot it was.

They were shown through to a comfortable parlour where they scarce had time to sit before a large, bustling woman dressed in quilted cap and widow's weeds entered. They rose.

'I am Mrs Wallowes. I believe you gentlemen wish to speak with my brother, Mr Thacker?'

Nicholls bowed. 'I am an officer from Bow Street, ma'am, and this is Mr Sheridan.'

Sheridan inclined his head politely.

Mrs Wallowes stiffened. 'What is your business?'

'We wish to speak with Mr Thacker, ma'am.'

'I know that much, gentlemen, but on what matter do you wish to speak?'

'Mrs Wallowes, your brother was attacked, grievously, in February —'

'Yes, and you have never caught the villain!'

Sheridan noticed the look of consternation on Nicholls' face at this reprimand when the attack had never been reported in the first instance.

Sheridan stepped forward. 'Ah, but we may apprehend him very shortly! Mrs Wallowes, Constable Nicholls here merely craves a more fulsome description of the attacker to be sure we make the right arrest.'

'Then you have come in vain, sirs. My brother is not well enough to receive visitors. He has lost the use of his voice as a consequence of the assault. Further, he grows weaker with a chest infection and we do not expect him to be with us for very much longer. You are too late to be of any comfort to him. Only the good Lord may offer him solace now.'

Mrs Wallowes picked up a small bell to ring for the servant, no doubt to show them to the door.

Nicholls looked hurriedly across to Sheridan.

'Ma'am, if we might nevertheless be admitted to see your brother, I assure you we will not presume long on his time. Your brother's condition only confirms how pressing it is that we capture the cut-throat who has done for him. Mr Thacker need not speak, only nod or shake his head or give some other sign which may be crucial in this matter.'

Mrs Wallowes hesitated, then replaced the bell on the small table. 'Very well. But if my brother should become at all distressed —'

Sheridan raised a hand of reassurance. 'Have no concern, dear Mrs Wallowes. Your brother is well served by your care and devotion, of that I am in no doubt, and we shall endeavour not to jeopardise your good offices.'

'Mr Sheridan? That name seems familiar. You look to be a gentleman, sir, are you a magistrate?'

'I have been a magistrate, ma'am, but on this occasion my interest is simply in the capture of the same villain who I believe responsible for the fatal injury of an associate of mine. An informant indicates there may be a potential connection.'

'You are a diligent friend, sir.'

'I trust so, ma'am.'

'Follow me, gentlemen.'

Mrs Wallowes led them up to the landing above and then paused.

'Sirs, you may know that my brother was in charge of a factory for the East India Company and a long time in their service at Masulipatnam where, naturally, he had many Indian servants. On his retirement he chose to bring one of these servants back to England.' Mrs Wallowes bristled with displeasure. 'A woman. He has claimed she is his spouse, but of course how can that be? She is not even Christian! And she scarce speaks one word of English. How my brother thought she might be accepted as his wife here in this neighbourhood, I do not imagine!' She laughed with disbelief. 'I can only believe the infernal sun may have got to him.'

Sheridan proffered a small smile.

'Once my dear unfortunate brother has departed this world, I shall see that this Lakshmi is put on the first ship and returned whence she came.' Mrs Wallowes grunted. 'She nurses him well enough, I daresay. He will have no other at his bedside! I say this to prepare you, gentlemen. Wait one moment.'

Mrs Wallowes knocked peremptorily on a door and entered without waiting for a response. Moments later she re-emerged and nodded to Sheridan and Nicholls.

'My brother will see you. But please do not tax him long, for he must rest. I must attend to the household. I will send the man up shortly, he will see you out.'

Sheridan bowed to her retreating back.

*

Simon Thacker lay propped up on pillows in the middle of a large four poster bed which had been draped with silks. His face was gaunt, his breathing shallow and laboured. By the bedside stood the Hijra, draped in reds and vibrant orange. She placed her hands together as though in prayer and bowed a greeting to Sheridan and Nicholls as they came into the room. It was, Sheridan decided, impossible to consider this vision of beauty as anything other than female. Her skin was glowing and smooth, her glossy dark hair scraped back beneath a head shawl. The kohl around the eyes, the reddened lips and the mark on the forehead all seemed to contribute to her undeniable allure. She was bejewelled. Bangles of gold, some studded with rubies. A necklace of fine filigree. Earrings likewise and dripping with tiny pearls. Most disconcertingly, a gold ring through the left nostril was attached to the earlobe by a delicate chain. Sheridan could not help but stare in fascination for longer than was polite.

All about the bedroom were displayed evidence of Mr Thacker's long years in India. Framed scenes painted on silk of men in turbans and women in flowing robes, hanging tapestries densely patterned and intricate, ivory trinkets and carvings of Hindu gods. The room was a profusion of colour at odds with the ordinary simplicity of the rest of the cottage. And that smell? Sheridan felt himself intoxicated. He looked about for the source. A stick of incense burned, heady and fragrant, in front of a statue of a creature half man and half elephant. There seemed to be some offering there, a plate of fruit and other edibles. A shrine to the god Ganesha.

'Mr Thacker, we thank you for agreeing to see us. I am Constable Nicholls of the Bow Street Public Office and this is Mr Richard Sheridan.'

Sheridan's wandering attention was brought back to the business in hand. He bowed.

Simon Thacker made a peculiar grunting sound.

'We wish to speak with you concerning the man who attacked you in February at the house near Holborn.'

Mr Thacker frowned and looked suddenly anxious.

Sheridan stepped forward. 'Do not be alarmed, Mr Thacker. We have no intent to expose the proclivities of that gentleman's club. Nor do we wish to cause any distress to you, sir, or your lady wife.' He inclined his head towards the Hijra. 'Mrs Thacker, delighted, I am sure.'

For a moment the eyes of the Hijra lit up on hearing herself so addressed. Simon Thacker reached out a hand across the quilt and his helpmeet placed her own above it. Sheridan noticed that the long, tapering hand was painted in an intricate pattern with some dark ochre. She really was a most strange and ravishing creature.

'I understand from your sister, Mrs Wallowes, that you have lost the power of speech, Mr Thacker, as a consequence of the assault. I am sorry to hear of it, sir.' Nicholls stepped closer to the bed. 'We come on you suddenly and without warning, but Mr Sheridan and I believe that the man who tried to kill you has assassinated others, perhaps as many as four or more. This murderous rampage must be stopped. Might you answer some questions, sir, with a nod or a shake of your head?'

Mr Thacker emitted the strange grunting sound again and nodded. His eyes, shrunk into their sockets, strained to open.

Mrs Wallowes is right, Sheridan thought, *her brother is near his end.*

'The man who attacked you — did he come from over the courtyard wall?'

Mr Thacker appeared to shake his head.

'He came from within the house?'

The old man nodded, his eyelids closing.

Nicholls and Sheridan exchanged a look; here was progress of a sort.

'Did you see the man?'

Thacker opened his eyes, seemed to hesitate, and then nodded.

'Would you recognise that man again?'

The East India manager looked uncertain.

'It was dark — perhaps he was in shadow? The light of the house behind him?' Sheridan hazarded.

Thacker nodded.

'Did he attack you straightway?' Nicholls continued.

Thacker shook his head.

'Did he speak to you?' Sheridan leant forward, hardly daring to breath as he watched the invalid nod in response.

Thacker grunted and began to scratch at the quilt.

Puzzled for a moment, Sheridan then exclaimed, 'A pen! Mr Thacker wishes to write.' He mimed paper and pen and looked hurriedly about the room for the implements of communication.

The Hijra seized his meaning and presented a letter which was sitting on the bedside table, pointing to the blank page at the back. Nicholls withdrew a pencil from his pocket. A tray was found and propped up so that Mr Thacker might have a surface to write against.

Gently the Hijra placed the pencil in her master's hand. With effort his hand began to move across the page with a jerking motion.

Sheridan strained to interpret the scrawl.

I shal hav

Nicholls shook his head. 'What does it say, Mr Sheridan? I cannot make it out.'

pity on me

The final word declined on the page and the pencil slipped from Thacker's trembling hand.

'I shall have pity on me.' Sheridan frowned. 'What can it mean?'

Thacker grunted and shook his head. The Hijra placed the fallen pencil back into the old man's hand and supported his arm. With a great effort he added an 'n' to the last and then collapsed back into the pillows.

'I shall have pity on men.'

Thacker nodded.

Sheridan looked to Nicholls. The constable shrugged. Neither of them, it seemed, had any more notion of what was meant.

The Hijra was now mopping the brow of the retired Company man. His eyes remained closed.

There was a light rap at the door at that moment and the promised manservant appeared on the threshold. He said nothing, but his intent to show them out of the house was clear.

'Thank you, Mr Thacker, we are most obliged.' Nicholls nodded and headed towards the manservant.

'Just one more question if you will, sir.' Sheridan hung back. 'The knife when it came — was it in the left hand?'

There seemed to be no response forthcoming and Sheridan was about to take his leave when the old man grunted and nodded.

'Good day, sir. Good day, Mrs Thacker.'

Sheridan bowed to the Hijra and was rewarded with a most exquisite smile.

CHAPTER TWENTY-FIVE

Sheridan slid off the slick and lithesome body and collapsed spread-eagled on the grubby sheets. He scarcely cared to think when the tavern's laundry had last been washed. He felt his face flush with the exertion of their coupling as he blew out his breath. Really, he had been living like a monk this long while and was very nearly out of practice. He grinned with satisfaction. What a fool he was to have so neglected his own needs. He should have more care of himself. It was the Hijra, he admitted to himself, who had aroused his dormant desires so that when he had encountered Sally in Haymarket, something of her dark features had mirrored that forbidden fruit.

Sally clambered astride him and beat a tattoo upon his chest.

'Good ride was it, Mr Sheridan? You was givin' it some. You look all done in, sir!'

'A fair old gallop I would say, Sally, as good a ride as I have had in a long time.'

She laughed and jiggled about on top of him as though he were now the one to be ridden. Her full breasts with their dark nipples bounced up and down against her taut skin and he reached up to cradle them. He let out a low pleasurable moan and Sally laughed the louder. She leant over him and playfully twisted the hair on his chest. But he was not ready to be brought on again so soon.

He opened his arms. 'Come lie here a moment, mistress mischief.'

She slipped into the crook of his arm and he held her companionably. After a little while he saw that she had dozed off. Well, let her rest. He might sleep too. And he did.

He awoke with a start as an early dawn stole through the windowpane of the room in the eaves. Sally lay snoring softly beside him. He should rise and dress and take himself to Nerot's Hotel, but felt himself in the grip of an overwhelming lethargy. What would be the point? His attention was always wanted. A ceaseless treadmill. He embroiled himself in this business and that. He scurried about. The theatre. His actors. Raising monies for Drury Lane. The business of Parliament and his party. The constant stream of petitioners from his constituency in Stafford — and further afield! Then to be drawn into the search for this mysterious assassin. But what did he achieve? What progress did he make?

After the visit to Mr Thacker he had felt more than ever that the Marson affair was all shrouded in impenetrable darkness and he could see little to light their way forward. *I shall have pity on men.* What on earth did that mean? He sighed and slipped his arm out from under Sally. She snorted and turned the other way. His arm was stiff and numb. It tingled as he massaged the blood back through his veins. He groaned. And then there was the prince. The matter of Eliza Ramus could be postponed no longer. Rehearsals were due to commence in the following week and whilst they might begin without her, she should be needed very shortly.

He had written to Henry Ramus, discretely, nothing that might be used in any inflammatory way. Merely to apologise for the indelicacy of his first approach and to suggest that Mr Ramus might take time to reconsider the matter which had been discussed. There had been no response. A week had passed and there was still no answer. He rather suspected there would never be a response. He had briefly considered the subterfuge of setting another girl in Eliza's place, but that had been short-lived as a notion. Whatever way he looked at it, Mr Ramus must be persuaded.

Sheridan had sought to find some chink in Henry Ramus' armour. Some way to dent the man's determination that Eliza should not perform in front of any in the Royal Family. So far, that armour had proved impregnable. It seemed that the East India Company writer was a man of the utmost probity. Major Hanger had ascertained that Henry Ramus appeared not to gamble. He drank to no great excess. He did not have a mistress or visit the ladies of the street. Damn it all, his only vice was his obsessive devotion to his work and to the East India Company!

A thought occurred to Sheridan. There might be his weakness. Any slur that might damage his reputation and standing with the company would surely strike fear into Mr Ramus. Gossip and rumour need not be true to create such a damaging threat, as he well knew. Indeed, the less truth involved the harder the slander should be to refute.

Sally stirred beside him, reminding him of her presence. He gazed on her tousled features and felt a tenderness sweep over him. He should do something for her before that prized bloom of youth began to fade inexorably.

As though she had read his mind, Sally stretched out and yawned widely.

'You still here Mr S?'

'Yes, Sally, and I have a great hunger — what do you say to eggs with bacon and a crust of warm bread with a great slab of butter.'

Sally's eyes widened with pleasure. 'I should say that'd be billy-o.'

'Come, get dressed. There is something I would discuss with you.'

Later in the day Sheridan called in at Carlton House. The prince had returned from three days in the country near Newmarket after a surprising run of luck on the racetrack and was in a further tizzy of excitement, for he had been met by unsettling news. It appeared that his youngest brother, the eighteen-year-old Prince Adolphus, had been captured at the Battle of Hondschoote just days before. His Royal Highness made much of the drama.

'Dolphy attached to the Hanoverians, you see, on the Field Marshal's staff.' The prince moved some condiments around on the dining table to illustrate. 'Well, seems von Freytag led his men straight into a town —' the prince trotted the salt and pepper along the cloth, the salt being the young Prince Adolphus by Sheridan's reckoning — ' — Rexpoede, I think, anyway, the place had already been captured by the French — they'd advanced so damn fast, caught our fellows unprepared.' The prince moved a sauce boat, namely the French, on top of a bowl of figs to signify the victory. 'Freytag blunders in.' The pepper pot was bounced into the figs, followed by the saltcellar. 'Bit of a scuffle. Dearest Dolphy wounded in the process…' The prince took hold of the curved spoon from the sauce boat and whacked the saltcellar. 'But by gad he put up a fight by all accounts before they were taken.' The prince demonstrated with a tussle between the saltcellar and the spoon, salt scattering over the figs in the process before the cellar was laid on its side.

Sheridan started. 'Prince Adolphus is a prisoner of the French?'

His Royal Highness smirked. '*Was* a prisoner of the French! Doubt they even knew who they had. He and his aide-de-camp Scharnhorst made a break for it and managed to escape! Good on Dolphy! Plenty of spirit, that boy. Old Freytag had to wait for Walmoden to turn up and rescue him. Bit of a wheeze in the end, they even took the town back!'

The prince concluded his tale by picking out a ripe fig, dusting off the salt and sinking his teeth into it.

'Well that is good news, sir.'

'Would that it were all so jolly,' the prince slurped. 'My brother York has had to withdraw from Dunkirk.'

'Damn it, sir! After the success at Valenciennes I understood Dunkirk should have been an easy matter for the Duke of York.' Sheridan shook his head. There would be plenty to discuss when the new session of Parliament opened.

'It's all a blasted shambles, Sherry. I blame the government — my brother blames Pitt. Where were the guns that were promised? Where was the naval support! He's in an absolute blazing fury! It must be clear to everyone by now that Mr Pitt may be an *Angry Boy* but he is no war leader.' The prince grunted and held up his sticky hands. An attendant rushed in with a bowl of water. 'The time has come for change. The country needs men of sense and foresight.'

Men who would be willing to treat with Revolutionary France, Sheridan thought, *and give succour to the more moderate factions in that country before the Republic was drowned in a sea of blood*. It pained him to see the high ideals initiated by the four years of revolution being trampled underfoot by the more extreme elements of the Jacobins. Burke's predictions of savagery had been all too prescient when it came to the Paris mob. But then, that held true of any mob worked up to a fever by unscrupulous demagogues and political agents. One had only to think of the riots in Birmingham the year before, or further back to the Gordon Riots.

Sheridan excused himself from the rest of the evening.

'I offer heartfelt apologies, sir. Nothing would please me more than to play at faro and the like with the present company, but I have matters of a family nature which call me away, if Your Royal Highness will permit.' Sheridan had learnt that talk of family was often a useful card to play when looking for excuses.

'Family yes, egad, one must have a care. Talking of which — Major Hanger tells me that we shall attend the rehearsals tomorrow week.' The prince winked rather lopsidedly, having already imbibed more than the usual.

Sheridan bowed. 'It shall be a great pleasure, sir, to welcome you.'

'Thought I would come incognito, Sherry, don't want to unsettle the children.'

Sheridan wondered for a moment what that incognito might be. 'As you wish, sir, but Hanger will inform me of the disguise I hope — so that I shall recognise you?'

The prince laughed, clearly tickled by the notion. 'Yes, Sherry, could be embarrassing if you were to make a faux pas, hey what?'

On the journey back to Isleworth, Sheridan reflected on how narrowly disaster had been avoided. He had ventured to Leadenhall Street that afternoon and requested to speak with Mr Ramus. After some moments the gentleman had appeared before him. Sheridan replayed the meeting as his carriage jolted over the cobbles.

'Mr Ramus, I am obliged, sir.'

Henry Ramus bowed curtly. 'I do not think we have any further business, Mr Sheridan. I thought that I had made myself clear on the matter.'

'Do you have a window nearby, Mr Ramus, that looks down upon the street?' Sheridan smiled warmly.

Henry Ramus frowned, disconcerted by the request.

'There is something that I would show you.'

Reluctantly the writer led them to one of the tall windows on the first floor which gave an outlook over much of Leadenhall Street. It was busy at that time of day with the to and fro of traffic between Gracechurch Street and Lime Street, produce from the local meat and fish markets and goods from the company's own warehouses, which were located at the rear of the offices, which trundled passed on carts beneath their view. Sheridan rapped on the windowpane. On the pavement opposite a female figure looked up and waved. Sheridan returned the salute to Sally, who had been fitted out in a plain but becoming costume by Mrs Petty the Wardrobe Mistress.

'What is this, Mr Sheridan?'

'Why, I understand it is your wife, is it not, Mr Ramus?'

The writer snorted. 'That is not my wife, sir! I have never seen the lady before in my life!'

'Then you are a bigamist?'

A colleague passed near to where the two men stood and catching the question darted a look of surprise at his fellow writer before he moved on about his business.

Ramus lowered his voice. 'Sir, I must object most forcibly to this pretence and ask you to leave.'

'Mrs Ramus finds that since you have abandoned her and left her near destitution, she has had no recourse but to search you out. Unless I can persuade her otherwise, I do not doubt she will be at the door presently to petition you herself.'

'Then I shall call for the Runners to have this woman arrested for her calumny.'

'Do you really want there to be such a scene in this revered temple of commerce? Think on it, it matters little whether the woman speaks false or not, a seed of doubt will have been sown.' Sheridan turned at that moment and bowed to a stiff-looking gentleman who emerged from an inner office. Ramus likewise bowed. They waited for the official to disappear through another door. 'And in front of your employers, Mr Ramus?'

'Mr Sheridan, do you try to blackmail me? Are you sunk so low, sir?'

It was low. Sheridan felt it, and the ruse made him uncomfortable. He sighed. 'Believe it or not, Mr Ramus, I am trying to help you.' He nodded to the figure below. 'This little charade is only to demonstrate to you how precious and yet fragile a man's good reputation may be. I should not like to see you maligned, nor your employment jeopardised.'

Ramus coloured. 'You may try!'

Sheridan softened. 'Do not be foolish, Mr Ramus. Neither you nor I can afford it.'

'It is a form of tyranny,' Ramus muttered.

'I may agree with you there…'

They were silent a moment.

'You will take care — we are grown very fond of Eliza.'

'I see that, sir. I promise I shall take the very greatest care of Eliza, as though she were my own daughter, and it shall all be a jolly game to her.'

Henry Ramus stared at Sheridan. 'I fear they may take her from us.'

'Have no fear. On my honour.'

On his honour.

Sheridan reflected on that promise as his carriage passed through the gates of the villa in Isleworth. What did his honour amount to? What could he possibly do if the prince or his royal sister on seeing Eliza became determined to make her a ward? Well, he would not think of it now. His honour was intact for the moment, however precariously.

Sheridan was in his library scanning the shelves, hoping that some form of enlightenment might leap out at him. He had jotted some notes on the Marson business and was worrying over the words spoken to Thacker by his murderous assailant, *I shall have pity on men*. Not one book had spoken to him yet. Neither Shakespeare nor the King James Bible, those normally most voluble of tomes.

There was a knock on the door.

'Enter.'

William Smyth appeared in the doorway.

'Ah, Mr Smyth, come in.'

'I saw the light under the door, sir, and although the hour is late thought I would pay my respects before I retire. I have just returned from a trip to Liverpool to visit my parents.'

'I do hope that you had a pleasant stay and that your parents are in good health?'

'Thank you, sir, they are both well.'

Sheridan noted the slight strain in the tutor's response. No doubt his father's bankruptcy earlier in the year had taken its toll. That same bankruptcy which had forced William Smyth to leave Cambridge and to seek employment as a tutor. 'You have eaten?'

'On the road, sir.'

'Good fellow.' Sheridan waved the hand holding his notes towards the tutor. 'Pour yourself a glass of brandy and you may replenish mine.' Sheridan tapped the spines of the books on the shelf in front of him with the finger of his other hand.

'I shall have pity on men.'

'Pardon, sir?'

'I shall have pity on men,' Sheridan repeated. 'What the devil does it mean?'

Smyth poured the brandy and taking up Sheridan's glass, moved towards him.

Sheridan reached out and took a sip. He smacked his lips. 'Welcome back, Smyth. From the lips of a murderer should it not be — *I shall have no pity on men?*' Sheridan shook his head and muttered to himself, 'Thacker has misheard, surely.'

'I shall have pity on men...' Smyth's brow creased in concentration. 'I have read it.'

'Oh yes?' Sheridan skewered the young tutor with a beady eye.

Smyth nodded. 'I believe it is apocryphal. The word of God, or Christ rather, for I believe it goes something like ... *My Father will give unto them all the life, the glory, and the kingdom that passeth not away ... I shall have pity on men.*'

'Apocryphal?'

Smyth nodded slowly. 'It comes to me ... it is an oddity...'

'Odd? How?'

Smyth held a finger up. 'Yes. It was a Revelation to be kept secret. At the end of all, after the prophesised wars, plagues and tribulations and moral disintegration, Christ's Second Coming and at last the Final Judgement at which each man is consigned to either Heaven or to Hell — and in the text the punishments of Hell are rather too vividly described in all their horror and brutality — well, then there is a postscript if you like, sir.'

'How do you mean?'

'The prayers of the righteous in Heaven will eventually save the sinners in Hell. God will take pity.' Smyth nodded. 'That's it. In Eternity. All men will be forgiven.'

'All will be forgiven?'

Taken aback, Smyth laughed nervously. 'All, sir.' The tutor warmed to his subject. 'That is why the Revelation was to be kept secret. Else why should men bother to be good at all?'

'But it isn't a secret — you know it.'

'Yes. But it is a lesser known and arcane text, sir, buried for centuries and kept from most eyes. But a theologian or scholar might have stumbled on one of the versions in the original Greek — just as I did. And there are those who would suggest that these visions, which are attributed to Peter —'

'Peter?'

'The Apostle,' Smyth clarified. 'These visions have an unreliable source, a Roman follower, and are not to be considered seriously as any part of Church teaching.'

'Final Judgement...' Sheridan waved his notes about, thinking aloud. All forgiven. Then why act in judgement, as an Avenging Angel?' Sheridan stabbed at the names which he had jotted down.

'You list the Apostles here, sir?'

'What do you mean?'

'Not all, but you have Simon, John, Andrew, Thaddeus, Philip — and you have a question mark at James, though do not say whether it is the Elder or the Younger.'

Sheridan stared at the page on which he had written out the names of the killer's victims or potential victims. 'James Blackett would be the Younger.'

'Blackett?' The tutor looked puzzled.

'The other names? What are the other names of the Apostles?'

'Well, if the Simon here is the Canaanite, then there is also Simon, whom Jesus called Peter, James the Elder of course, Bartholomew, Thomas, Matthew and Christ's betrayer, Judas Iscariot.'

Sheridan's eyes widened. 'This is altogether too biblical.'

'And Matthias — he is often forgotten.'

'Who is Matthias?'

'The thirteenth Apostle.'

CHAPTER TWENTY-SIX

Sir Jonas Soersby had returned to his home in Hanover Square, leaving his family behind at the country estate in Somerset. On learning of this, Sheridan felt the time had arrived to confront the judge. He was relieved that Lady Priscilla would not be in residence; it would make his mission that much easier to accomplish. He hastily wrote to Sir Jonas asking that he might call on him at his convenience. The reply came by return to suggest the following afternoon.

Sheridan now approached the house in Mayfair, fingering the pocket watch which Nicholls had reluctantly placed with him. The constable had expressed himself uneasy about Sheridan's intention. He would have preferred at the least to accompany Sheridan to Hanover Square. But his police duties prevented it. Since the arrest of Tobias Bloomer the Bow Street Runner's days had been taken up with the day-to-day demands of policing in the capital.

The urgency of Sheridan's desire to visit Sir Jonas was further prompted by Mr Brockenhurst and his renewed campaign in *The Daily Enquiry*. The upcoming trial of Mr Bloomer had allowed the Badger plenty of opportunity to dwell on the case and to express his vitriol. Rumours that sodomy was no longer considered a crime by the Republican government in France led the pen-smith to warn against the imminent dangers of moral decay should the same ideas be spread in England. He enjoined every good Christian Englishman to stand up against the invasion of vice. The revelation of the earlier murder at the Covent Garden bagnio of a young lad named John was grist to the mill. The lad had been lured in off the capital's streets by men who were unscrupulous predators. The youth's innocence had been defiled and this might be the fate of any of the nation's young men unless immediate action was taken to rid the land of this accursed obscenity.

Gone, however, was the rhetoric about Avenging Angels. The brutal assassinations of John the catamite and Mr Marson, a noted actor and member of Mr Sheridan's company, had been committed by a servant of the bagnio. Sheridan pursed his lips to see his own name segued into the article. Mr Brockenhurst continued in this vein with mounting relish. The assassin, one Tobias Bloomer, had become corrupted and inured to wickedness of all kinds in the service of his diabolical master, the proprietor Mr Edward Culpepper. A man who had tellingly fled to France! The Badger then expanded on his satanic theme. He went on to describe the murders as ritualistic sacrifices performed as a central part of a devil-worshipping cult. The hidden subterranean lair of the bagnio was depicted in lurid detail. Its Roman-style baths an apposite setting for the acts of gross indecency which took place there and which were so reminiscent of the Roman Empire in the depravity of its decline. The arcane symbols carved into the victims flesh served as yet further evidence of the devilish nature of the proceedings. And so it went on, each issue of *The Daily Enquiry* adding yet another salacious detail to the scene.

Sheridan sighed. The unfortunate Tobias Bloomer had been found guilty before he had set one foot in front of judge and jury at the Old Bailey. An innocent man would likely hang and the judge who would don the black cap and pass sentence would be none other than Sir Jonas Soersby. The very man whom Sheridan now suspected of being the real perpetrator of these unholy crimes. The man whom he was about to call on with every play of civility.

The butler escorted Sheridan to the library where Sir Jonas was ensconced in a comfortable chair reading *The Times* newspaper. The judge stood to greet him.

'Ah, Sheridan. How good of you to call on me. I know you are a most industrious man of affairs even when the House is not sitting. So, I am honoured.'

'The honour is mine, sir.'

'The new theatre on Drury Lane comes along? I believe it will be without rival. Beyond *The Rivals*, heh what?' Soersby added by way of a rather weak allusion Sheridan thought, but then the judge was not in the business of wit. He was engaged in the far more serious matters of life and death.

'It is kind of you to see me, Soersby. I trust that Lady Priscilla and the children fare well?'

'They are in Bath. The girls love to dance, Lady Priscilla enjoys the concerts and Frederick makes conversation with many influential new acquaintances.'

'I have always found that in Bath all tastes may be satisfied.'

'Shall you have tea? I have rather taken to imbibing lapsang souchong in the afternoon; I find it conducive to the digestion, you know. But you may prefer claret? Port?'

Sheridan hesitated. Should he put aside his loathing of tea, and of lapsang souchong in particular, as a matter of politesse. The judge was a sober man. He should be sober also. 'I should be delighted to join you in a bowl of lapsang souchong. They say that tea in the afternoon shall soon become de rigueur.'

Sir Jonas nodded to his butler and they were left to make idle chitchat about the progress of the Duke of York in the Flanders campaign and the narrow escape of Prince Adolphus near Dunkirk until the tea arrived, was poured and set before them.

Soersby took his first sip of the lapsang souchong with a smile of satisfaction and then his face clouded. 'My dear Sheridan, do you have any more news on that tragic business in Epping Forest? I feel so very greatly for poor Colonel Branson and the terrible loss of one's only son. Phillip was a first-class young officer, a very solid type I should say, and to come to such an unpleasant end is most unfortunate.' He grimaced. 'Cut down by common highwaymen — I do not subscribe to the theory of a French vanguard. Do you hear anything? Have they caught the villains yet?'

'There is no progress in the matter I am afraid, Sir Jonas.'

'Not all murderers may be brought to book. As I well know.'

Sheridan raised his bowl of tea and allowed a silence to hang between them. Was Soersby hinting at his own position beyond the reach of law and justice? His ability to commit the most criminal of acts with impunity?

'Not in this world perhaps.'

Sir Jonas looked up in surprise. 'You are right in that regard, my dear fellow. In the next life we shall all be judged.'

'Even the judges?'

'The judges most particularly.' Soersby proffered a thin smile. 'So often the officers and guardians of the law are called upon to cast that first stone. But none of us would say we are without sin ourselves. Do we, in passing judgement, transgress Christ's teaching?' The judge sighed. 'Perhaps we do and thus compound our own tally of sins.'

'Something like the offices of a sin-eater?'

'A sin-eater?'

'One who ingests sin for the greater good of us all.'

'Yes,' Soersby nodded, 'that is well put, Sheridan. The officers of the law willingly partake of the transgression. We ask, how should the world run itself if we do not task ourselves with the judgement of our fellow citizens? How should good governance survive? The lives of all would be as Thomas Hobbes warned, "nasty, brutish and short". I have always rather tended to agree with the Hobbesian view of the world.'

'You do not believe in the innate goodness of man then, Sir Jonas? Our common humanity?'

'Perhaps I have seen too much of wickedness from the bench at the Old Bailey.'

'When all is shadowed in darkness it must be difficult at times to recognise the innocent. Those who stand before you falsely accused.'

Sir Jonas shook his head. 'There are few indeed who are entirely innocent, believe me, Sheridan. I do not doubt that there may be occasional errors in judgement, but none that should give me cause for sleepless nights. I find my conscience continues clear.'

'No doubt. But…' Sheridan replaced the bowl on the table, he really could drink no more of the abhorrent tea.

'But? You have some reservation, Sheridan? I have sensed that this is no mere courtesy visit, my dear fellow. You have some matter you wish to discuss with me? Pray, do feel free to express yourself.'

'Tobias Bloomer.'

'Tobias Bloomer? What is your interest in Tobias Bloomer?' The judge replaced his own empty bowl and then looked across with a show of sudden comprehension and sympathy. 'Of course, Mr Marson was an actor of your company.'

Sheridan regarded Soersby keenly. If the judge had once gifted Marson with an inscribed pocket watch as a token of his love, there was little indication of that feeling now. No telling tic or nervous hesitation. Either that love had turned to another, more deadly emotion, or Sir Jonas was devilish good at controlling his outward appearance.

'You can be certain that Mr Bloomer will hang for his crime, Sheridan.'

'No, sir.'

Sir Jonas looked confused.

'I very much desire that Tobias should not hang.'

'I am bewildered, Mr Sheridan. Why ever not? He has murdered Mr Marson in the most grotesque fashion.'

'He is not the killer.'

'Mr Bloomer has already confessed to tipping the young lad John's body into the Thames.'

Sheridan nodded.

'He was the first to find Mr Marson — that is a well-known ploy of the assassin.'

Sheridan nodded again.

'And yet you express yourself with a marvellous surety?'

'That Tobias Bloomer is complicit in a great many crimes I do not doubt, but he is not the man who has murdered young Andrew Marson.'

The judge stroked his chin and Sheridan felt his piercing gaze peel through the outer layers of his carapace.

'I believe you have spoken with Mr Bloomer at Bow Street, after he was apprehended. You wished for an account of what had happened to your actor. I would hazard that Mr Bloomer took the opportunity to work on your good nature, Sheridan.' The judge leaned forward sympathetically. 'He has convinced you that it was all the work of Culpepper, no doubt. I fear that Mr Bloomer is a plausible rogue who has hoodwinked you, sir.'

'Unless Tobias Bloomer was also in Epping Forest on the day of Lieutenant Branson's murder, which I very much doubt, then he cannot have committed these crimes.'

'What are you suggesting?'

'Bloomer is not the man who acts with such savagery. He is not the man who declares *I shall have pity on men* before he pulls the knife.'

Soersby shook his head. 'Are you saying that Lieutenant Branson was also murdered in the same fashion?'

'Yes, sadly. I am a witness. But all who saw that abomination shall deny it for Mrs Branson's sake.'

'But then by whom and for what reason?' Sir Jonas pressed.

'You may deduce, Soersby. I believe the killer may have been amongst our own party.'

'I am at a loss for words, Sheridan.'

'I should like to see the real perpetrator brought to justice.'

'As would I,' Soersby insisted and then his hawkish eyes narrowed and he looked thoughtful. 'But consider you are mistaken. The murder of the unfortunate Lieutenant Branson may have been a mere facsimile.'

Sheridan's brow creased. A copy? What could Sir Jonas mean?

'The press has not withheld the gruesome details of the bagnio murders or of that man in the street, Thaddeus Broadhead. Far from it. *The Daily Enquiry* in particular has gloried in descriptions of the mutilations and barbarity of the crimes. There are villains, Sheridan, who make a play of murder and these evil men may well have found a devilish inspiration in the reports of what Bloomer has done in Covent Garden.'

Sheridan paused, he had not considered such a scenario. He had to admit that the theory held a convincing air about it.

'I know you to be a man of feeling,' the judge continued. 'And I admire your pursuit of justice. But I fear you have been set upon the wrong track.'

Sir Jonas sat back in his chair and crossed his long legs. It was clear that he considered all discussion on the business of the murders now closed.

Sheridan fingered the arm of his chair as he sought to find the right way forward. He had made a play to proclaim Tobias Bloomer's innocence. It was the least that he felt that he could do whilst that wretched servant languished in the jail at Newgate bereft of friends and with no one to speak for him. He had revealed the circumstances of Phillip Branson's death in Epping Forest. It had been his intention that by intimating the assassin was amongst their number on the excursion, he might unsettle Soersby. To no avail. The judge had deftly side-stepped the confrontation. How like a lawyer. Sheridan felt a sudden wave of nausea. Tobias Bloomer would hang. And then? Then Sir Jonas Soersby might desist from his murderous acts in order to allay all suspicion and that would be the end of the matter. There would be no justice for Andrew Marson. Any reasonable man would, however reluctantly, accept the inevitable.

Sheridan, however, knew himself to be sadly lacking when it came to reason. He had fought not one duel, but two, with the same man, Captain Matthews, and had been lucky to survive the second encounter with his life. He had eloped with Elizabeth Linley when he had not the means to support her and had incurred the wrath of his father in consequence. He had taken one hair-raising risk after another with the Drury Lane theatre and must constantly dodge his creditors. No, he was not a reasonable man.

Sheridan stood. 'I do apologise, Sir Jonas, I have presumed largely on your time. I shall take my leave.'

Soersby rose abruptly. 'Not at all, my good fellow. I appreciate your … your taking such interest in the matter. You must have been very fond of Mr Marson.'

Sheridan nodded. He withdrew the timepiece from where it nestled in his waistcoat pocket and held it out before him.

'*Omnia vincit amor.*'

All at once Sir Jonas paled.

With care Sheridan placed the watch on the occasional table.

'Good day, Soersby. I can see myself out.'

CHAPTER TWENTY-SEVEN

Eliza Ramus was not at all as Sheridan had envisaged. He had pictured a sweet-natured, dainty and pliable little girl. He was ill-prepared for the plump five year old who ran into the rooms at Lambeth all lively, confident and thoroughly unruly. By contrast, the girls from the Foundling Home for Daughters of the Deserving Poor were altogether too meek and lacking in personality. Within five minutes of her arrival, three of their number had been reduced to tears by Eliza's pulling their hair or poking at their ribs.

Sheridan could not imagine what Henry Ramus had told his wife about the stratagem which had been employed in order to ensure the child's attendance, but Mrs Ramus regarded him and the assembled company with undisguised suspicion. Whatever she had been told did not endear her to those present and she appeared to abdicate all responsibility for Eliza's behaviour and making no apology when the child, on being introduced to Sheridan, stood before him and stuck her tongue out. He wondered briefly if she had been taught to do so by her adoptive father. Sheridan could immediately detect glimpses of the Royal Hanoverian temperament and an inbred desire to rule rather than to be ruled. In short, the child was a brat.

On the sidelines he caught sight of Joey Grimaldi grinning from ear to ear. Well he would soon have the grin wiped from his face when he should try to direct the girl.

The first part of the production involved a ballet featuring Titania the Faery Queen surrounded by her various little imps and faeries. The conceit being that Titania would cast her spells and conjure up the spectacle which was to follow. Titania was a perennially popular character well calculated to please Their Royal Highnesses, for which role the oldest and tallest foundling girl had been chosen. She was unfortunately at an age when the tender skin of the face can erupt into a pustulating mass of red and raw pimples, but a thick layer of white paint should render her presentable for performance, Sheridan had been assured.

The trio of musicians struck up a sprightly air and Joey entreated the girls to prance about the hall as they please. The limp and wooden response soon had him calling a halt on the music.

'No, no, no, no! Why you so sad, bambini? You are fairy! You are happy. You have no care. Your life, it is all a game. Watch!'

He nodded to the musicians and they struck up the tune again. Joey somersaulted into the centre of the room and began to dance with exaggerated step, pulling funny faces and then tripping over himself and landing on his bottom, looking comically bewildered until one or two of the children began to titter into their sleeves and then, unable to contain themselves, to laugh openly at his prat falls. Soon one girl after another had burst into a contagion of uncontrolled laughter. The chaperone from the Home looked aghast until she too caught something of the infection and clapped a hand over her mouth in an attempt to subdue her guffaws. In this hysterical state Joey began to move amongst the girls, twirling one child around and lifting another high into the air until they were all spinning and leaping and following him about the room as though he were the Pied Piper of Hamlyn leading the children away to some other enchanted world. And the children were as under a spell. Their faces, which had previously seemed grey and dull, were flushed and their eyes glittered. Sheridan found that it touched him to see these children so transformed by something as simple as laughter and dance. The Pied Piper was a role, Sheridan concluded, which suited Joey Grimaldi very well and might be an idea for a new pantomime at Haymarket.

The tune became ever faster and livelier as the musicians caught the mood of abandon. Even Sheridan found that his foot tapped on the floor and that the tug of music was about to sweep him up from his chair. Eliza Ramus, who was not cast to be a part of the ballet, could contain her high spirits no longer, and slipped from her adoptive mother's grasp and ran screeching into the swirling maelstrom. Once in the centre she jumped up and down, screaming ever louder as though she were at the very centre of a vortex. Joey's grin widened, if that were possible, and lifting Eliza, he raised her up and over his head to sit draped about his shoulders. From this vantage position Eliza might look down on all the other girls as Joey continued to weave between them. Her noise ceased immediately and from her lofty height she gazed with open delight at the dancing faeries who teemed and swarmed beneath her.

It was into this scene of magic and mayhem that Sheridan was startled to see a corpulent figure enter through the doorway, swathed in scarlet cassock and tippet. Skirting around the imposing figure Mr Quail hastened to Sheridan's side.

'It is His Royal Highness, but I am to tell you that he is now the Archbishop of Carlton,' Nehemiah whispered.

Sheridan rose and approached His Grace, who had been followed by his accompanying retinue. This naturally included Major Hanger gamely rigged up as a clergyman, albeit one with a rather rakish air and rather too much powder. Matthew, he noted, was amongst the attending manservants.

The musicians, aware of the new presence in the hall, brought their feverish tune to a sudden and climactic end. After a moment of silence, the spinning foundling girls all flopped onto the floor as one. Only Joey remained standing at the centre with Eliza Ramus perched on his shoulders. The little girl's face was pink with excitement. She beat a tattoo on his head and cried out, 'More! More! More!'

The prince smiled beneficently and clapped his hands. 'Bravo, bravo!'

Sheridan bowed to the royal visitor. 'Your Grace, Archbishop, welcome to our rehearsals and for the interest that you take in the girls of the Foundling Home for Daughters of the Deserving Poor.' He turned to the room. 'Children, we are visited today by His Grace the Archbishop of Carlton. He has seen with his own eyes how well you may dance. Now, I am sure that His Grace should like to see how well you curtsey.'

The girls jumped to their feet and bobbed up and down in a pleasing display of reverence, as they had evidently been taught to do in front of visiting dignitaries. Joey, meanwhile, had lifted Eliza from his shoulders and returned her to the ground. She leaned back against him and, sticking her thumb in her mouth, regarded this interloper who had taken all the attention from her with a frown of annoyance.

The prince expressed himself delighted with the curtsies and then turned to Sheridan with an urgent whispered aside, 'Which one is she, Sherry?'

'Your Grace, allow me to introduce to you our youngest performer, she is only five years of age, little Miss Eliza Ramus.'

Joey nudged the child in front of him but she shook her head and clung to his breeches.

'She is a little shy, methinks, Sherry. I shall go to her.'

In a balloon of scarlet, the prince glided towards the child. Eliza promptly hid herself behind Joey.

The prince smiled indulgently. 'Are we to play at peekaboo, Eliza my dear?'

It seemed so. As the prince crouched and moved about the figure of Joey, seeking to catch Eliza's eye, the plump child edged around her hero, attempting to keep herself from view. The prince swung the other way in an effort to outwit her.

'Peekaboo!'

Eliza yelped and backed away, still clinging to Joey's breeches.

The game continued in a frenzy of swing and turnabout until, emboldened by the spectacle of the jolly man in his silky red dress, Eliza darted out and knocked the black velvet catercap from his head. With a shriek of glee she then ran towards her mother's skirts.

'You are the piggy, the piggy, the piggy!' she yelled after her.

The prince stood up, beaming from ear to ear. 'Well, I declare, she is like to my sister as a pea from the same pod!'

Mrs Ramus, who clearly knew perfectly well who this costume disguised, clutched Eliza to her bosom.

Major Hanger sighed and with his usual languid air turned in an aside to Sheridan, 'Blood will out, Sherry.'

It was almost with a measure of relief that Sheridan made his way towards the courts at the Old Bailey. He might still catch the end of the trial of Tobias Bloomer. But that travesty may be already done and dusted. He feared that the hearing would be short and decisive. The mood of the populace having been worked to a fever pitch by the press, and not least by Brockenhurst's rabid campaign in *The Daily Enquiry*. The clamour was loud for a hanging.

The Badger was indeed the first person whom Sheridan encountered as he squeezed through the crowd in the spectator's gallery. Journal and pencil in hand, the pen-smith was busy taking notes of the proceedings.

'Ah, Mr Sheridan!' The Badger glimpsed him from the corner of his eye and pounced at his elbow. 'The jury are conferring. They will not be long about it, methinks. I believe that you interviewed Mr Bloomer shortly after he was arrested and heard his confession. May I quote you, sir?'

Sheridan shrugged him off. 'I heard no confession of murder, Mr Brockenhurst. You may quote that.' Sheridan hesitated, he would sooner quiz anyone than the Badger, but needs must. 'Has there been a defence?'

'Tobias Bloomer has been forced to represent himself,' Brockenhurst sneered. 'None other would plead for him. He has been unable to call forth any witnesses on his behalf. The vipers' nest is all cleared out, it would appear. The case is open and shut. You may know that *The Daily Enquiry* has engaged Mr Farthingale as lawyer for the prosecution, on good Mrs Broadhead's behalf.' Here the Badger turned to a plain woman wrapped in a shawl who was standing at his side with two sallow youths. 'And he has made short work of Mr Bloomer's bleating. The man speaks of obeying the order of his master, Edward Culpepper. He lauds himself as a loyal servant. Can you credit such a defence! It is clear to everyone assembled that the two were in it together, for he has nothing to answer to the charge that he aided in the disposal of the lad's body into the river. That alone has signed his death warrant.' Brockenhurst turned to Mrs Broadhead. 'Which will be some small comfort to the wife of Thaddeus Broadhead and to his sons who are here present to see that sentence delivered on the wretch.'

'I would prefer to see the right man hang.'

'Mr Culpepper is fled to France, devil take him.'

'I do not believe that he is the right man either.'

Brockenhurst lowered his voice. 'You still think of those letters, Mr Sheridan, those that spoke of an Avenging Angel? I have concluded that they were all a nonsense written by some crackpot noodle! Either that or it was one of Culpepper's coven, attempting to divert suspicion from their number.'

'Have you received any other letters?'

Brockenhurst snorted. 'One that spoke of a murder at Epping Forest. When I made enquiry, it was true that there had been a death reported. Of a young naval lieutenant. But the talk was all of highwaymen or French agents. Nothing of sodomy. And the murder at such a distance from these other crimes in Covent Garden, it strained connection. I knew then that this Anonymous had as likely simply read of the Epping incident in the *Gazette*. I tore it up as a piece of fiction, Mr Sheridan — just as the other letters were.' He lowered his voice. 'All the insinuation about Thaddeus Broadhead —' he glanced briefly towards Mrs Broadhead. 'Damn lies, sir. A vicious slander against a poor working man and his family.'

Sheridan raised an eyebrow that Brockenhurst should speak so righteously when slander and defamation were the bread and butter of *The Daily Enquiry*. 'You must pass them to Constable Nicholls, Brockenhurst, they are still of interest.'

'As you will, sir, if only for amusement.' Brockenhurst gave a curt bow and turned his attention to the widow at his side.

Sheridan pushed into the gallery, looking for a space from which to view the courtroom below.

'Mr Sheridan.'

To his surprise, Sheridan found the Reverend Wallis at his shoulder.

'Reverend.' He nodded a bow. 'What brings you to this circus? I would not have imagined it was entertainment to your taste.'

Reverend Wallis looked pinched with disgust. 'Decidedly not, sir, but I have lately had a visit from Colonel Branson.' Wallis leant in, conspiratorially. 'The poor man begged that I might attend the trial of Mr Bloomer and report back to him in confidence. For obvious reasons he felt that he himself could not be seen here.'

'That is a kind office then.'

Wallis looked about the crowded space with hauteur. 'This trial is quite the cause célèbre. I had not expected such a crush nor to find familiar faces from amongst my acquaintance. Your presence, of course, is understandable.' He bestowed a smile of condescension. 'You too must have the interests of Colonel Branson and of course that actor of your company. But it is certainly noteworthy to see who of the quality are pressed amongst the crowd. Though I daresay I should not be so astonished to see Lord Frederick nor Lord Augustus, the infamy of this case is naturally a draw to young men of fashion and sport. Viscount Malmain has a passion for blood sports, cocking and the like, you know.'

'Malmain?'

Wallis raised a finger and subtly indicated the area behind him. 'He is in the far corner. I have not presumed on our acquaintance, having officiated so recently at his wedding, you may remember. I should not wish to occasion any embarrassment for his lordship in discovering him here.'

'Whereas your religious office and duties may excuse your presence in most arenas I should suppose, Wallis.'

'The Lord's work is everywhere required.'

'Quite so.'

'I hardly credit that this Mr Bloomer has been responsible for the acts spoken of here.' The reverend shook his head dismissively. 'He is a nonentity to my mind.'

'I would say that we are in agreement on that, Wallis.'

'I believe the journalists, of even the most respectable newspapers, have taken licence to write whatever fantastical story so pleases them and their assertions of satanic rites and the like have been regarded as incontrovertible truth, without any shred of evidence that I have heard, only hearsay and speculation.'

'You do not favour that interpretation of these murders?'

Wallis stiffened. 'It was God's fury that smote down the sinners of Sodom and Gomorrah. We are in such times where we may feel God's wrath again. Everywhere one looks, one may see portents of...'

Sheridan nodded along, it seemed the good reverend was about to launch into a well-worn fire and brimstone sermon and clearly still favoured the Avenging Angel scenario. Sheridan allowed the words to pass over him as he scanned the far corners of the gallery to catch sight of Viscount Malmain. Did the young lord attend out of a prurient interest to see what should happen to Andrew Marson's killer? Or might he still be in the frame for that same murder? It should count that he was oftentimes in the vicinity. Matthew had not been able to identify Malmain as present at the house in Holborn — but had the footman not said that a number of the visitors on that occasion wore masks of disguise? Soersby or Malmain; both may have been present on the night of the attack on Simon Thacker.

The young lord was a hothead and had a relish for violent sports. Sir Jonas Soersby, by contrast, was a man of refinement and even temper. Whilst it seemed true that Sir Jonas had bestowed gifts on Mr Marson and may have been unsettled when the actor threw him aside in favour of a footman, did that make him a likely murderer? Malmain had shown an equal interest in Marson, according to Nehemiah Quail. That had been an odd incident, when Sheridan thought back on it. Were Malmain's attentions invited by Marson or had the actor been forced by the young lord? Murder might come easily to such a man as Malmain.

To Sheridan's mind the question came back to whether there had been threats of blackmail. That might turn any man to murder should the stakes be high enough. If only there were some evidence of blackmail to be had. By the young lad John, by Andrew, Thaddeus, Phillip and the East India Company man? The list of victims was long. Too long. Sheridan shook his head. What had the tutor Smyth said? They are all named for Apostles. Coincidence? Apostles of whom? Who was their Christ figure? There was a mystery here that was deeper than he could fathom.

'…revolution and war. They say the Irish are likely to rise up. And the French have declared that they will support any who do so. It is an age of madness and chaos, Mr Sheridan.'

Sheridan heard his name spoken and turned his attention back to the clergyman. 'Indeed, Reverend.'

'Mr Pitt has become a veritable tyrant.'

'It is not wise to say so aloud, Wallis. I have Parliamentary Privilege so I may insult the Prime Minister on a daily basis across the floor of the House. But you my dear fellow must be wary. Agents are everywhere and may easily misrepresent you. To be labelled either a Reformer or a Rebel has become a matter of minute degrees of interpretation. One title may still occasion respect, the other send you to a prison colony on the other side of the known world. I thought you to be a friend of Mr Pitt? Were you not at Cambridge together?'

Wallis bridled. 'Our paths diverged, Mr Sheridan.'

There was a murmur amongst the assembled spectators. Judge Soersby had re-entered the courtroom and the usher signalled his presence by banging a staff loudly on the floor. All stood until the judge had seated. Sheridan inched towards the rail, straining to see around those impeding his view.

'Beg pardon,' he muttered as he elbowed his way forward.

One man of the jury remained standing. The foreman held his hat in front of him like a shield.

'Mr Guppy, have you and your fellow jurors agreed on a verdict?'

'Yes, m'lud.'

'On all counts?'

'Yes, m'lud.'

Judge Soersby eyed the jury with his steely gaze. 'And how do you find the defendant, Mr Tobias Bloomer?'

'Guilty as charged, m'lud.'

A high-pitched wailing came from the defendant's bench but was drowned out almost immediately by the cheers and hurrahs from the spectators' gallery.

CHAPTER TWENTY-EIGHT

The hullabaloo began to subside in anticipation of Judge Soersby's judgement. The wailing from the bench continued, however, until it was the only remaining sound. Tobias Bloomer looked wildly about the courtroom.

'I should not hang!' he cried out. 'I have hurt no man, nor wouldn't. You can ask anyone!'

A shout came from the public gallery. 'Then why are they not here to speak for you, you mewling rogue?' This was followed by loud guffaws.

Judge Soersby rapped at his bench. 'Order! I will have order!'

The chortling petered out.

Soersby turned to the man in the dock. 'Tobias Bloomer —'

Tobias' eyes gleamed narrowly. 'I have held my tongue, Your Honour. I am no snitch.' An officer of the court made to lay hold of him. 'But I can name names,' he shouted for all to hear.

At this declaration an enthralled silence fell over the courtroom.

Sheridan's ears pricked with anticipation. Might they now at last learn who was Mr M and who was Mr B or Mr D? His glance shot to Judge Soersby. Sir Jonas seemed frozen in the moment.

'There is one that works at The Stamp Office! There is a surgeon, another that is a coal merchant, one again who is a magistrate!' Tobias called out as though this litany were all that stood between him and the gallows.

The court officers laid rough hands on Mr Bloomer, hoping to shake him to silence.

Murmurs had begun to ripple through the spectators in the public gallery.

'And some as I see here present,' Tobias cried out. 'A lord amongst them!'

At this Soersby rapped loudly and called to the officers. 'Take him down below! Mr Bloomer shall be sentenced in absentia if he cannot respect the sanctity of my courtroom.'

Sheridan's eyes darted to the corner of the gallery. Yes, there he was. Viscount Malmain edging himself backwards through the throng. Sheridan pushed against the forward surge of the crowd and placed himself across Malmain's trajectory. When the young lord turned, it was to find Sheridan blocking his path and regarding him with a keen eye. The viscount's features were taut with supressed anger.

'You do not stay to hear the sentence, Lord Malmain? Where is the sport if you do not wait to the finish line?'

'Out of my way if you please, Mr Sheridan.'

'I am sorry to stand in your path, sir, but as you can see, I am somewhat hemmed in.'

Malmain glared.

'Devil take it what a scrimmage! All are agog to know who this lord might be!'

'That you, Sheridan?'

It was one of the younger Beauclerk boys, Lord Frederick, who was fast gaining a reputation as something of a scoundrel. From the stagger and smell of him, the young scion of the Duke of St Albans was already well in his cups. He clapped Malmain on the back.

'We're making a run for it, aren't we, Augustus? In case this mob start thinking the "lord" referred to by that snivelling wretch in the dock is either of us! What larks! I vote we shake our tallywags and go find a couple of Covent Garden flower girls to show just what manner of men we are!' The young Beauclerk tottered and slurred, 'Care to join us, Sheridan? You must be able to recommend a good doxy or two.'

'Not on this occasion, gentlemen, but do not let me stand in the way of your lust.' He directed the last to Lord Malmain.

The viscount replied without taking his eye from Sheridan, 'You are right, Freddie, let us enjoy a couple of flower sellers, I am bored with all this talk of sodomy. They should all go hang!'

Sheridan bowed. 'But I must not let this encounter pass, Lord Malmain, without congratulating you on your recent nuptials.'

Frederick Beauclerk spluttered and chuckled. 'Why do you think Gus here has need of a well upholstered doxy! The Harte girl may be damnably rich, but she is deuced poor in other ways!'

'Tish, Freddie,' the viscount admonished. 'You speak of my wife, Lady Malmain.'

'Apologies, of course, my dear fellow. No disrespect intended. Lovely girl.'

'Then have a care, Freddie, or I shall have to challenge you to a duel.'

Beauclerk clapped Malmain on the back again and pushed him forward past Sheridan. 'Tally-ho, Sherry!'

Judge Soersby, meanwhile, had been reiterating the charges which had been laid against the defendant Tobias Bloomer and the verdict of the jury assembled. He had now moved on to his summation.

'…that Tobias Bloomer is guilty of conspiracy and that he is an accomplice in these dreadful crimes is beyond any reasonable doubt.' The judge looked about his courtroom to murmurs of agreement. He waited for a hush. All now were expectant that he should place the black cloth on his head to signal the sentence of death.

The judge regarded the assembled with imperious command. 'I am minded, nevertheless, to give heed to the defence. Mr Bloomer claims to have been a faithful servant, blinded by his loyalty to Mr Edward Culpepper, the proprietor of this infamous den. It is Mr Culpepper who is the true malefactor. Mr Culpepper has put himself beyond the reach of our justice. He has abandoned Mr Tobias Bloomer to suffer in his stead. Mr Bloomer has expressed his remorse for not coming forward to report the murder of the lad John. But he did come forthwith to the Bow Street Public Office on discovering the assassination of Mr Marson. He knew, that by doing so, he revealed the heinous offences which had taken place under his master's roof. Taking all into consideration, I hereby sentence Tobias Bloomer to be transported on the next fleet to the prison colony at Botany Bay and there to remain for the term of his natural life.'

Soersby stood and left the courtroom as the public gallery erupted with shouts and catcalls, hissing and booing.

'Well here's a fine how do you do!' It was the Badger, close to Sheridan's ear. 'We all know Sir Jonas is one to favour transportation — anyone would think he had shares in the colony! — but here was such a hanging case as couldn't be denied! There'll be an outcry, mark my words!'

Sheridan did not doubt it. Not least because Brockenhurst would fill the pages of his scurrilous rag with his cries of outrage, peddling his disgust that the London mob were to be deprived of the spectacle of a hanging outside Newgate. Judge Soersby would not be popular. He should have a care.

Mrs Broadhead had commenced to heave with sobs.

Brockenhurst turned to her with expressions of solicitude. 'There, there, good Mrs Broadhead. Be assured, the villain will never arrive at the colony to live in ease and comfort, I can vouch for that. It is you who may take comfort. Some sailor will surely tip him overboard in the dark of night and Mr Bloomer shall drown horribly.'

Sheridan heaved a sigh, whatever the future held for Tobias Bloomer it would not be a welcome one. The servant might one day wish he had been hung in preference. Sheridan wondered if he or Nicholls might be able to gain access to speak with Tobias again. The attendant seemed ready and willing to divulge his secrets now. Perhaps he would even name some of the men who had been present on that fateful day at the bagnio. One of whom might be their assassin. If the men who were bathing that day could be interviewed by Nicholls, their accounts might reveal some telling detail which would point to who the real killer was.

But then what? Another trial? If the finger pointed towards either Lord Malmain or Sir Jonas Soersby as the perpetrators then it should get no further than to be dismissed out of hand as a gross calumny by the first Justice they should approach. This trial had put an end to the case. Why should anyone pursue the business any further? Sheridan had already given the matter more attention than he had the time to spare. In his heart he knew that justice had not been done, but his part in the hunt for it must be over. It would be pointless to continue. Sheridan nodded, pleased with himself. He had made the decision to desist from further interest.

The gallery was beginning to thin as the general public realised that the drama was finally at an end. There were mutterings of disappointment at the outcome but also excited hums of conjecture as to which names the defendant might have revealed had he not been manhandled from the court.

'Do you think the surgeon might be —?'

'George, you know someone at The Stamp Office, do you not?'

'Let him try to name me and I shall have his tongue out!'

'I am sure that young fellow in the corner was the son of the Duke of St Albans. First-class cricketer you know, I've seen him play, tremendous underarm bowler and handy with the bat.'

'God's blood! A blaggard such as Tobias Bloomer, you could not believe one word that came from his lips, he should name any man he liked for the sheer devilment of it!'

Emerging from the Old Bailey Sheridan spied the Bow Street Runner approaching the building. Here was a test to his resolve. He should slip away before he was sighted by Nicholls or face being drawn in to some further scheme of action. He had turned to do so when he found Revered Wallis behind him.

'Reverend.'

'Mr Sheridan.' The clergyman was pulling on his gloves. 'I fear Colonel Branson will be most disappointed.'

'Disappointed that there is no confession of guilt? Or that there is no execution?'

Wallis stiffened. 'Disappointed that Tobias Bloomer is clearly not the assassin. Nor Mr Culpepper, who is so decrepit that he must walk with the aid of a cane.'

'Ah, so you believe the true killer walks free?'

'And will strike again.'

'Why do you say that? Should he not desist now that there is another found guilty in his place?'

The reverend smoothed out his gloves. 'He is a messenger. I thought you had understood that, Sheridan? You have been a witness to his work on more than one occasion.'

'And what is the message, Wallis? It is that I cannot fathom! A revenge or a deterrent to blackmail?' Sheridan rubbed his brow. 'Perhaps I have sought to find complication where there is none. The solution is right under my nose. And one may find his face in every other man who walks the streets of this city and who would not consider it a sin but an act of divine justice.'

'We must not fear the end which is upon us but place our trust in God.' Wallis bowed his farewell. 'Do we see you return to Wanstead, Mr Sheridan?'

'Next week. I hope we shall soon have the pleasure of your company, Reverend, and your charming wife. Do please extend my felicitations to Mrs Wallis.'

Wallis bowed again and set off with his quick stride.

And now it was too late to evade the constable.

'Ah, Nicholls.'

'Sir.'

'It is all over. Tobias is to be transported. Culpepper proclaimed the true villain.'

The Bow Street Runner nodded. 'The order is already given for Mr Bloomer to be taken out to one of the prison hulks in the Thames.'

'Where he may sing for all he likes with none to hear.'

Nicholls nodded. 'I hear he threatened to name names.'

'He got no further than a list of professions — a coal merchant, a surgeon, a lord.'

'No one is to visit him.'

'It would not matter. His word counts for nothing now.'

'Our business is finished then?'

'There was never any chance of success in this matter, Constable. We ventured into a world which is all hidden and masked in secrets and lies.'

'I thank you for your assistance, sir, nevertheless.'

'I shall always admire your persistence, Nicholls.'

Sheridan held out his hand and the two men clasped each other in parting.

CHAPTER TWENTY-NINE

Sheridan felt a great weariness descend on him as he arrived home to Wanstead. It was not merely the lateness of the hour after a prolonged sitting at the House in the new session of Parliament, he was a creature of the night in any case. The weariness was not so much physical, more it was a general malaise, a weariness with his life, an emptiness, an unfilled void. He felt his world increasingly turned upside down and his ambitions narrowed.

The events of the last year in France had been of such an excess of brutality that few found cause to praise the actions of the National Convention in Paris. Neither was it safe anywhere in the British Isles to speak in favour of the Revolution whilst this reign of terror lay at the heart of the movement in France and showed no signs of abating. Only that day he had received the news of the inevitable execution of Marie Antoinette at the guillotine. It had followed a humiliating trial which had seen the erstwhile French queen accused of incest. Justice, fair play, even reason itself, all seemed lost. In these times Sheridan knew he must call on all his reserves of principle to stand firm, to continue to believe in a better and more equitable society untainted by privilege and corruption.

Where once the calls for Reform, the judicious extension of the franchise, abolition of the rotten boroughs and Catholic emancipation had been embraced by a broad cross-section of the political elite, the tide had turned from liberty to tyranny. Instead of heralding a great dawn of rational and enlightened thinking across Europe with the overthrow of ancient and archaic privilege, the declaration of a Republic in France had caused the enthroned heads of Europe and their governments to cling together ever more tightly. They would use whatever means necessary to defeat the French and to stamp out the threats to their own sovereignty. Now, more than ever, to speak of liberty and the rights of man risked imprisonment and charges of treason.

Despite the risks involved, there had been an upsurge in the creation of radical societies. People wanted change. They did not want the present war to destroy their own hopes for an enlargement of the franchise and constitutional reforms. A convention had been called in Edinburgh, but three of the leaders had been arrested. The principals, Muir and the Unitarian minister Palmer, had recently been sentenced to transportation on the grounds of some archaic Scottish law. Sheridan despaired. The government, it appeared, was really beginning to scrape the barrel in order to find ways to silence legitimate protest. How long would it take before they sought to silence him?

He wondered how much Mr Pitt and his spies knew of his own connections and correspondence. For some time he had been certain that his letters were opened and read. A number, he felt sure, never reached their destination. Pitt would have been informed of the extent of his support and friendship for Thomas Walker, president of the Manchester Constitutional Society. Only the previous year he had praised Walker in Parliament as a respectable character and a man of sense. He had signed his petition on electoral reform. That summer, Sheridan had been outraged to learn of the arrest of Walker and six others in Manchester. The men had been arrested, on the 'evidence' of an informer, with conspiring to overthrow the government with force of arms and aiding a French invasion. The very idea was preposterous. Sheridan would not be bullied into deserting Walker; he would continue to support his old friend against such calumnies.

His stomach lurched. He knew he was something of a funambulist. Wryly, he pictured himself high above a stage swaying on the precarious tightrope trying to keep his eyes focussed ahead whilst down below lurked The Pitt ever ready, with open jaws, to devour him should he lose his balance and fall. Mr Pitt had eyed him that afternoon in such a manner that he had felt himself a marked man. For the first time he had begun to wonder if his days were truly numbered. In the past, Sheridan had always made jests and underplayed the dangers which he faced. In truth he had never seriously considered the possibility that his liberty could be taken from him. He had felt shielded from real harm by his friendships with the prince, Charles James Fox and those Whig peers who were amongst the highest in the land. But when it came to it, was there any such surety?

He knew that in many quarters, even amongst men of his own party, he was considered an Irish adventurer, who had risen too high already. Well, perhaps he was. Perhaps that was all he had ever been and his ambition that he could make his mark on history was all a phantasm. And yet. He knew himself to have worthy ideals that he held dearly and with sincerity. He had never been a placeman nor sold out politically for monetary gain or advantage despite opportunity and despite the temptations to ease his financial plight.

No. He was a man of integrity and principle. And he should never be afraid to support his friends and to speak out against oppression. He resolved to visit Muir and Palmer when they were moved to imprisonment in London prior to transportation, a sentence which everyone knew to be a death knell. Muir and Palmer should know that he did not consider them seditious traitors but martyrs to the just cause of liberty.

As Sheridan climbed the stairs, he saw that there was a light in the library still. When he entered, he found William Smyth by the fire engrossed in reading from a selection of texts at his side. Sheridan crossed the room and with the poker broke the crust on the coals to stir the fire back into life. He picked up the scuttle and shook a few more coals onto the hearth.

The tutor looked up earnestly. 'I have been considering the triangle, sir.'

'The triangle?'

'The inverted triangle. The one which was carved onto your actor's forehead.'

'That business is concluded, Smyth.'

Smyth observed Sheridan with a knowing shake of the head. 'Only truth and justice will bring it to an end, sir.'

Sheridan sighed. 'They are in short supply these days.'

Smyth carried on regardless. 'I have considered that if the victims being named for the Apostles is no coincidence, then it is possible that the inverted triangle signifies a chalice, but not any chalice — *the* chalice. The Holy Grail.'

'And what then would that mean?'

'Well, the cup was used at the Last Supper, where all twelve Apostles were present — until Judas Iscariot slipped away to betray Jesus for his thirty pieces of silver. According to scripture, Jesus performed a miracle at the meal. The wine which his chalice contained was transformed into the 'blood of Christ' and was to be henceforth drunk in his memory. It is the central sacrament of the Mass alongside the transformation of bread into the body of Christ.'

'I still don't understand how this might relate to the murders.'

'The hunt for the Holy Grail is one of our most enduring quests. And why is this chalice so coveted? Because it is believed that the Holy Grail contained the gift of eternal life.'

'I don't follow. What is it to do with the deaths?'

'That's just it, sir. I suspect that your killer sees these deaths as a gateway to eternal life. The Apostles are again being martyred in order to hasten the Apocalypse. There should be an Anti-Christ in his configuration. And I do not think that he will stop until he has achieved his objective, to bring about the end of days, the Second Coming and the Last Judgement.'

'But why? For what reason?' Sheridan shook his head in exasperation.

'So that they may be forgiven.'

Sheridan froze. 'He wishes all sodomites to be forgiven and saved from the fires of Hell?'

Smyth's eyes gleamed. 'The killer is a sodomite.'

Sheridan's mind whirred. 'Who cannot bear to live with his sin.'

'Exactly. He thinks the end of the world is nigh and he a part of bringing it about. Because then, all shall be judged, one man sent to Heaven, another to the torments of Hell; but if the hidden Revelation to the Apostle Peter is true, as this man must believe, then —'

'God shall have pity on all men. They shall be forgiven and live forever in Heaven.'

'That is the eternal life promised by the Holy Grail.'

Sheridan clapped his hands. 'Well done, William, I am almost persuaded — were it not so very fantastical!'

'It is a rather abstruse theory, I concede.'

Sheridan reached out for the decanter on the table to pour a glass of port.

'If you are right, then we have not seen the last of this assassin.'

Whatever explanation lay behind the fiend's motives, Sheridan already had the uneasy expectation that the man should not be able to stop himself from killing again. And, for whatever reason, Sheridan seemed to have been chosen to be present. What had the Reverend Wallis said that day in Epping Forest? *The Lord has chosen you to bear witness.* He had repeated something similar outside the Old Bailey and he too had been convinced that the killer would strike again.

CHAPTER THIRTY

The Drury Lane Theatre Royal company had reassembled for the new theatrical season at The Haymarket and the aristocratic families of the *haut ton* were out in numbers. Not least drawn to the spectacle of the very noticeably pregnant Mrs Jordan. This would be her first child with the king's third son, the Duke of Clarence, since becoming his official mistress. Great fun was to be had with the arrival of a little 'Jordan' offering opportunity for ribald puns, Jordan being vulgar slang for a chamber pot. Dora Jordan took it all in good humour and insisted that she might perform right up to the point of delivery. Sheridan rather suspected that the duke's debts rendered Mrs Jordan the necessary breadwinner of that household.

He had invited the Canning family to stay at the Grosvenor Street house for a few days so that he and Tom might escort Hitty and three of her youngsters to the theatre and the Assembly Rooms. As the crowds began to gather in the foyer of The Haymarket Theatre, Sheridan cast an eye around to see who might be present. There was his leader, Fox, in company with Mrs Armitage and others of the Whig party, including the ever-loyal Lord Derby. By the stairs he spied Charles Long paying court to the Duke of Richmond as usual. Sheridan was beginning to wonder if the young politician had a fancy for the duchess. His attention was then caught by the entrance of the wealthy tea magnate, Mr Harte, and the greetings and congratulations offered to the couple in his wake, Viscount Malmain with the new Lady Malmain on his arm.

Malmain. He must not lose sight of Malmain in all his speculations. The conviction of Tobias Bloomer, and in absentia Edward Culpepper, had allowed the assassin to feel himself safely beyond the grip of the law or the reach of justice. It grieved Sheridan to acknowledge that this might be the case. And here was Mr Harte approaching him in a very friendly manner.

'Mr Sheridan.' The tea merchant bowed his head slightly. 'We look forward to the opening of your new theatre. Next year, I am assured. And fully confident of its success we are persuaded to become a subscriber.'

Sheridan bowed in turn. 'Much obliged, Mr Harte.'

'You have met my son-in-law, Viscount Malmain?'

Malmain looked askance at Sheridan.

'Always a pleasure, sir.' Sheridan forced himself to bow to the young lord. A new subscriber was not to be sniffed at, not with the rising costs of the new auditorium interior.

'I am most delighted to make your acquaintance, Mr Sheridan, I do so love the theatre!' It was the new Lady Malmain who smiled broadly, her powdered face little disguising the warm spread of freckles across nose and cheeks.

Sheridan found himself unwittingly charmed.

The orchestra had started up and people were thronging through the open auditorium doors to find their seating. Sheridan continued his tour of welcome and then made his way to the box where the Canning family had been installed.

'Where is Tom?' he enquired.

Bessie Canning unclasped her fan. 'Oh, he has deserted us already, Mr Sheridan. Tom can never be still. He has seen an old friend from Dr Parr's school but I rather imagine it was the sister who caught his eye.' She rolled her eyes.

'Ah, I see.' Sheridan nodded and wondered if there was a little whiff of jealousy in the air.

Sheridan himself could never be still for long either and after he had satisfied himself that the evening's opening programme was a success with the audience, he made his way along the corridor and through the door into the backstage area. As he emerged from the passage which led immediately to the wings, Sheridan spied a familiar figure.

'Ah, Mr Roden, is it not?'

The sin-eater nodded. The ancient relic was dressed in the costume of a demon and with the addition of his make-up, which Joey had undertaken to teach the old man how to apply, he looked every inch an apparition from hell. Sheridan felt sure that he should be a great favourite with the audience. One glare from those piercing eyes would stay the hand of any rowdie in the pit who might think to hurl a rotten egg or a turnip.

'I am delighted, sir, that you have decided to join my company for the new season.'

Roden grasped hold of Sheridan's arm in alarm. 'Good sir, he has passed right by me. Close, as I could touch him. I thought that he had come to take me at last. I wait always in that expectation.'

'Whom do you speak of, my dear sir?'

'Why, the devil,' Roden replied, as though this should be no surprise. 'Only, it is not me he has come for tonight. But he brings Death with him, someone is to die.'

Sheridan smiled reassuringly and patted the old man's hand. 'It will be an actor in a costume, like yours. You will know them all soon. I should hazard it was Monsieur Dubois, who always looks like he might kill someone.'

Really, he hoped the old man would not continue with talk like this, he would unsettle the performers, who were a superstitious lot at the best of times.

Roden shook his head vehemently. 'No, sir, this were no actor. I have seen the Angel of Death and this man is his instrument.'

Sheridan nodded. 'Then let us hope he will quit our theatre forthwith and take his business elsewhere —'

A troupe of imps scampered towards them in the narrow space. Edmund Carey at their head as usual. The little boy screwed his face grotesquely and waggled his fingers at both Sheridan and Mr Roden before barging his way towards the stage. The rest of his rapscallion band sniggered in pursuit, one brave enough to stick out his tongue in passing.

'— for we have devils enough as it is.'

Roden would not be deflected. 'He followed a boy, not littl'uns like these, but a handsome lad — who had a look of you, sir.'

'Tom?'

Well, Tom might be searching for him or have some other business backstage. Tom had always treated the theatre as his second home.

A low horn sounded from the orchestra. Nehemiah Quail appeared anxiously from his prompter's position and looked towards them. He beckoned to his ancient uncle.

'I believe that is your cue, Mr Roden. Break a leg, as they say.' Sheridan grinned. 'That is the theatrical's way to say, good luck!'

The door to his office stood open, lantern light throwing a man's shadow out into the corridor. Who should be in his office? Bob Fairbrother perhaps, though he seemed to remember that Bob had another engagement. Tom. It was Tom; and with that realisation came a sudden and overpowering presentiment of danger. Sheridan raced to the door and hurtled into the room.

'Tom!'

He gasped. There was Tom cowering in the far corner, his face quite drained of colour and between father and son stood Viscount Malmain. In whose hand was clasped a most vicious and deadly blade.

Sheridan did not need to think twice. Even as Malmain turned to face him he threw himself full force at the young lord and crashed him to the floor. The knife skittered from Malmain's hand into a pile of discarded playscripts. The two men grappled, one on top of the other. Sheridan with his hand to the younger man's throat. Malmain kicking and thrashing from underneath. Sheridan thrust his free hand out towards the knife and with a great effort managed to press his fingers around the handle before the stronger man tossed him over. As the viscount reached towards him, Sheridan shuffled away on his back, jabbing the knife at his attacker.

'Pa! Pa!' It was Tom who cried out.

Malmain caught Sheridan's wrist, staying his hand. Sheridan felt all his muscles straining against the superior power of the younger man. Was this to be the end? For himself? For his boy? It could not be.

'Tom! Tom — you must run!' Sheridan yelled, his face livid with effort.

'No, Pa! Pa — it is this gentleman who has saved my life! He has rescued me from attack!'

Sheridan looked with bewilderment into the eyes staring down on him. Malmain nodded furiously.

'Drop the knife, Sheridan. Your boy is safe.'

'That is why he had the knife, Pa — he took it from the reverend.'

Sheridan frowned.

Tom moved towards him. 'It was Reverend Wallis that attacked me.'

Comprehension began to dawn on Sheridan. He loosened his grip on the blade and let it drop with a clatter to the floorboards.

Malmain stood up and brushed himself down.

'It was fortunate I heard your son's cry, sir. That madman was set to slit his throat.'

Sheridan scrabbled to his feet in an ungainly fashion and looked at Tom. 'How? What has happened here?'

'I think Mr Wallis was following me, Pa. I was searching for you in your office and then he entered. I thought nothing of it at first. He greeted me and I him. Perfectly civil. I said I had not known he was of the party that night and he should join us in our box.' Tom's brow creased. 'And then he said I must not doubt.' Tom shrugged. '"Doubt what?" I said, for his words were a riddle to me.'

'And then?' Sheridan urged.

'He said, "I have seen you in the guise of Venus and your true nature. Thomas, you must doubt no more." Still I was perplexed. And then he said —' Tom struggled to remember — 'what did he say...?'

'I shall have pity on men,' Sheridan finished for him.

'Yes! Those very words! What can they mean, Pa?'

'That he is the most dangerous of men.'

Tom nodded slowly, the shock still registered on his young features. 'He took that blade from a sheath beneath his coat.' He pointed to the thin knife on the floor, which glittered in the light of the lantern.

'Sheridan, we waste time! This madman must still be in the building!' interjected Malmain.

Sheridan was gazing at the knife. 'There is blood on this knife.' He looked over to his son. 'Tom, are you injured?'

'Not I, Father.'

Sheridan turned to Malmain and saw the trickle of blood bubbling from the slash in the viscount's waistcoat.

'It is nothing. A scratch as I took the blade from him.'

'Nevertheless —'

Malmain cut in. 'If he did not pass you — then he has fled in the other direction. Where does that lead?'

Sheridan shook himself. Unless Wallis had crept back and passed this door when he and Malmain were grappling on the floor, which they or Tom surely would have noticed, then Wallis must go upwards.

'He has gone up. Up into the building. He might go across the top of the stage and descend again.' Sheridan gathered himself. 'Tom, go at once to Old Fletch and let him raise the alarm — he must send at once for Constable Nicholls at Bow Street.'

Tom sprinted towards the corridor.

'And no one must be allowed to leave through the Stage Door,' Sheridan called after him — although it would be more likely that Wallis should try to regain the auditorium. There he could steal out through the thoroughfare of theatregoers; there would be a throng waiting for the reduction of ticket prices for the latter end of the evening's programme.

Malmain was already at the door and heading in the opposite direction. Sheridan reached the threshold in time to see him sprinting up the narrow, creaking stairs.

When Sheridan reached the level high above the stage, he found Lord Malmain had been stopped in his tracks. Harry the flyman held a cudgel and barred his way.

'Devil take you! Out of my way, damn you!' the young lord was shouting, to no avail.

Harry stood solid. He was a great oak of a man, well known for his prowess in the boxing bouts held at Marylebone Fields.

Sheridan paused to catch his breath. 'Harry — Harry, has any passed you?'

'None would pass me that had no business here, Mr Sheridan!'

'No one has tried to cross above the stage?' Sheridan pointed behind Harry to the narrow door which led to the flies and walkways from where great canvases might be dropped and unfurled onto the stage below.

'No, sir.' The man shook his head. 'But the door did open, maybe five minutes past, I called out and then none came through.' Harry's eyes narrowed. 'Is something amiss, sir?'

'My boy has been attacked.'

Harry grabbed a lantern. 'Then he must have continued up. The villain is hiding in the eaves!'

They ascended a short flight to a narrow landing, where a ladder had been placed through the trap above.

'The trapdoor is never left open, sir. Someone has gone this way.'

The flyman scrambled up the ladder with surprising agility, Malmain hot on his heels.

'Have a care!' Harry instructed as they gained the attics. 'There is no flooring, only planks laid out for access.'

All three emerged onto a small island of boards laid out around the trapdoor. Harry raised his lantern into the vast darkness. It was a fetid and dusty space under the great beams and eaves of the theatre's roof. Lines of planks could be seen running in various directions, laid out across the floor joists.

'You must watch your step or you may find that there is nothing between you and the stage itself.'

'That should be an unexpected entrance!' Sheridan could not resist, though his nerves frayed to their very ends.

'I see no one.' Malmain shook his head in frustration.

'He is here,' Sheridan murmured.

Harry pointed to their right. 'There! See, the dust on those planks has been recently disturbed. He has crawled this way.'

Malmain nodded. 'You are right! Light my path!'

'Hold a moment, Malmain,' Sheridan commanded. 'We have him trapped. Let us wait for help to arrive.'

Reluctantly, the young lord deferred and they were silent a moment.

A silence which was punctured abruptly as they heard a resounding thumping coming from the farther end of the eaves.

'What the devil?' Harry exclaimed.

Then came the sounds of something brittle being smashed.

'He breaks through the roof!' Sheridan cried out in amazement.

CHAPTER THIRTY-ONE

Sheridan felt the planking wobble beneath his feet. He fought for his balance but was sorely tempted to drop to his knees and crawl as Wallis must have done. The Reverend Wallis. His mind could scarcely take in the revelation. That it was the quiet, serious clergyman of good family, a neighbour, a man who had dined at his own table who had attempted to kill his son Tom. Reverend Wallis who had slain so many men and in so brutal a fashion. Here was not the fiend that his imagination had conjured but a rather plain and sombre man who should never be noticed in company. And yet, he was that monster. How was it possible that Wallis had lurked unseen and unrecognised right under Sheridan's nose? There must surely have been signs that he had missed? Intimations of a deranged mind.

As they drew closer to the source of the commotion, they could see that the slate tiles of the roof had been broken through and lay splintered all about. A gap had been created between the rafters, enough for a man to pull himself up and out onto the roof itself. As they reached the opening a heavy rain fell on their upturned faces.

Sheridan made to pull himself up into the gap in pursuit.

Harry stayed his arm. 'In this rain it will be hazardous, you could slip, sir.'

'He is up there!'

'Sheridan, your man is right,' Malmain cut in. 'It would be foolish. Even I am not so reckless — and you know me to be a reckless fellow.'

'Up there he shall remain until we have rope and ladder and may safely follow.'

'He cannot escape now,' Malmain assured Sheridan before he turned to the flyman. 'Harry, we shall stay and guard this point whilst you fetch the necessary tools.'

Harry nodded. 'I shall leave the lantern; I am used to scrabbling in the dark.' He grinned broadly. 'We shall have the villain don't you worry, Mr Sheridan.'

Sheridan held the lantern to guide the flyman as far as the light would allow and then he and Malmain were quite alone, save for the madman who skulked above them in the night.

They were silent for some moments.

'Thank you, Malmain. I cannot thank you enough, from the very depths of my heart.'

'I did only what any man would do.'

'You saved my son from certain death and risked your own.'

Malmain smiled. 'Truth be told I enjoyed the skirmish, sir, heats the blood! I am only angry that I did not manage to hold him. This Wallis is a slippery varlet.'

'Slippery in more ways than one.'

'Why should anyone want to kill your son?'

Sheridan regarded Malmain keenly. 'He had seen Tom in a play, a charade, dressed as Venus, rather fetchingly; I believe he thought that one day he would be a sodomite.'

The young lord blew out his cheeks. 'Is this the man who has murdered Andrew Marson?'

Sheridan nodded. 'I have no doubt.'

Malmain rubbed at his brow. 'I never believed it was that servant Tobias or his master, Culpepper.'

'Neither did I.'

Malmain eyed Sheridan narrowly. 'You suspected me, sir, did you not?'

'Yes. I confess I did consider you, Lord Malmain. Until today.'

Malmain barked a short laugh. 'I cannot pretend surprise that you might think me a villain. I am a scoundrel. You know that very well. It is clear to all society that I have married an heiress for nothing but her fortune.'

Sheridan's expression concurred.

Malmain smiled. 'Thankfully my wife, Lady Malmain, is not a fool. She knows her father to be a parvenu. Once the marriage terms were all agreed she was perfectly frank with me. She never expected that I should love her and she certainly has no intention of loving me. To be honest, Sheridan, my wife is most convivial, and we rather enjoy each other's company. We have agreed to be good friends, and once the necessary heir is produced she is perfectly content that we make our own arrangements. I am the most fortunate of men. I shall make it my duty to see that she is admired and respected. Lady Malmain has a keen interest in pugilism, would you believe it?'

'You are something of a fighting man yourself.'

'I own I have a temper.'

'You struck one of my company.'

Malmain shifted uneasily. 'I see. That is how you knew my relation to Mr Marson. I should have apologised. I will apologise to Mr Quail. It was unpardonable. I was angry. I do not excuse it. Mr Marson and I — there was a passion; only he would not give up that footman — with all that I had to offer him!'

The two men lapsed into silence. The rain had ceased and a sliver of moonlight crept out from behind a cloud in the night sky.

'I should like to see the man who killed and mutilated Andrew brought to justice. But Sheridan —' Malmain looked up through the gap in the roof — 'if I should lay my hands on this fellow again, I cannot be held responsible for my actions.'

Sheridan did not doubt it.

Malmain turned back to Sheridan. 'I recognised him, this Reverend Wallis.'

'Recognised him?'

'When I sighted him this evening across the theatre foyer, I realised that he was a man I had seen at a gentlemen's club in Holborn. That particular evening, February I think, there was another newcomer, a manager from the East India Company, and he was attacked and near killed — fortunately for him, there was a surgeon in our midst. It had happened outside at the rear of the building and most thought it to have been some passing rogue that climbed the wall. I don't know why, but I had the strangest feeling that the would-be assassin was one of our own number and, looking about, I noticed that the other stranger, the man in black, had slipped away without farewell.

'When I saw him again this evening here, I don't know why, Sheridan, but I followed him. Curious, I suppose, as to who he was. Then intrigued to notice that he appeared to be following a boy. Your son, Tom, it transpires. When he followed into the backstage area I had a presentiment that he meant the boy some harm.'

'I thank heaven for your presentiment, Malmain.'

They heard men's voices then coming up through the trapdoor.

Malmain leapt up eagerly. 'Here is Harry.'

Lanterns threw deep shadows into the eaves as the men approached. Harry in the lead with Mr Shaw, the Stage Manager, and following in their wake a group of stagehands carrying ropes and ladders. All was the business of rigging and preparation then. One end of a strong cord was tied off to a beam and the other end tied around Harry's torso. The flyman was cautiously lifted out of the gaping hole. Squinting from below, Sheridan could see Harry raise his lantern and look about until he gave the nod that the immediate area was clear. One by one the stagehands followed Harry out onto the roof carrying the rest of the ropes and ladders with which to scramble over the steep sides of the roof of the Haymarket Theatre.

Sheridan found that his heart was thumping in expectation that at any moment they would apprehend Wallis. The clergyman would be trying to hide amongst the chimney stacks. Would he put up a fight? The knife had been dropped in the struggle with Malmain. Surely, any attempt at resistance would be futile.

After what seemed an age Harry dropped his head through the jagged circle of broken tiles.

'He's gone, sir.'

Sheridan shook his head in disbelief. 'Gone? We heard him breaking through the roof. How can he be gone unless he has thrown himself to the ground?'

'I do believe he has leapt onto the next building, sir. The gap is not such as any one of us would attempt, it would be a desperate feat — but a desperate man might just do it, Mr Sheridan.'

Sheridan beat his fist into his palm. 'Or a man who believes himself to be an Angel.'

Tom had been sent to the house in Grosvenor Street with the Canning family, they were all staying there for a few days to enjoy various entertainments of the new season. The lad himself had suggested that he remain discrete about the identity of his attacker — indeed perhaps not even mention the attack at all — worried that it might alarm and distress Mrs Canning.

'After all, Pa, I am not hurt — unlike Lord Malmain!'

A local doctor had been sent for and Malmain's wound cleaned and bound. The young lord all the while making light of the slash across his lower ribs.

'You see — it is a mere scratch!' he had exclaimed to the doctor who insisted he raise his shirt.

Sheridan could see that Viscount Malmain was already a hero of giant proportions in his son's eyes and the two had parted with a great show of friendship.

After Malmain's departure, Tom turned to Sheridan with a woeful expression. 'Poor Reverend Wallis, he was not himself, Pa. I do believe he has some illness that has temporarily deranged him. We must pray that he is found safe and that his health may be restored.'

Sheridan nodded at his good, kind boy. 'Let us hope so. And you are right, there is no necessity to unsettle our Good Sister Christian, not tonight.'

The Stage Manager arrived at his door to assure him that the theatre had been secured. A section of sail-duck had been stretched over the gap in the roof and a lock put on the trapdoor.

'I've set an extra night watchman to be certain we have no intruders, sir.'

'Thank you, Mr Shaw.'

From outside Sheridan could hear the shouts and laughter of the audience as it disgorged onto the wet streets of the city. Unaware of the drama which had been taking place behind the scenes.

At last he was alone in his office. Alone to contemplate the horror of what might have been. Sheridan's fingers trembled as he poured himself another glass of brandy and the spirits splashed across his desk.

Another thought occurred to him. Was Wallis right in his prediction? Could young Thomas Sheridan be destined to be that way inclined? How should one know? Was it something a man was born to or was it a choice? If it were true, how should he feel about Tom? His boy, his son. Colonel Branson came to mind. At Epping Forest he had sensed that the old soldier knew of his son's sexual proclivities, and his grief was none the less for it.

There was a sharp rap on his door.

'Enter!'

It was Nicholls. The young constable caught at his breath. 'I am sorry to be delayed, sir. I believe there has been an attack?'

'Right here, in this office. My son was threatened with murder.' Sheridan indicated the knife which had been placed on display.

Nicholls shook his head in concern. 'How is your boy?'

'Much shaken, though he tries hard not to show it.'

'All the talk, as I came through at the Stage Door, was that the villain fled through the roof, that he broke through the very tiles to effect his escape.'

'And must then have leapt like a creature with wings to the next building.'

'You have a description from your son?'

'More than that, my dear fellow. Much more.'

Sheridan recounted all the events of the evening and watched as Nicholls' eyebrows rose with each new revelation.

'So, this is our assassin?'

'Most assuredly. *I shall have pity on all men.* The Reverend Wallis has cast my boy as Doubting Thomas and added him to his list of 'Apostles'. He is entirely deranged and yet has all his wits about him. That is a dangerous combination.'

Nicholls frowned. 'He knows himself unmasked now. Where should he go?'

'His house is near Woodford. A rectory. He may risk a return there for some reason, to fetch something, monies?' Sheridan shrugged. 'Otherwise, I am at a loss where he might hide himself. His wife may know? Or his father, Sir Edward Wallis, or his older brother…?'

'They may all be interviewed on the morrow, at first light. For now, it is late, sir. You must sleep. I shall have a description sent to all the ports in case Reverend Wallis should try to flee the country and a man dispatched on horse, post-haste, to keep a watch on the rectory — in case he should present himself.'

Sheridan nodded slowly. 'We shall have him. At last, we shall have him.'

CHAPTER THIRTY-TWO

The intermittent rain of the night had given way to a bright autumnal dawn. The rising sun catching the oranges, yellows and reds which now outnumbered the fading green. Through the early morning ground mist Sheridan spied a shepherd out of doors gathering in his flock. The carriage moved at a steady pace through the countryside to the outskirts of the parish of St Jerome and the church steeple came into view.

'We are passing Sir Edward Wallis' estate but naturally it makes sense to visit the rectory first,' Sheridan suggested.

Nicholls nodded in agreement.

They drew up in front of the entrance to the neat Georgian rectory house. Nicholls descended the carriage and looked about for his watchman. No one showed themselves.

'Bartholomew? Where is the man?' Nicholls muttered impatiently.

'Come, my dear fellow, he shall be somewhere at hand. We shall have his report after we have made our enquiries within.'

Sheridan was already striding to the front door and pulled the bell. Within moments it was answered by a stout woman in black. The housekeeper. The good lady informed them straight away that the master was not at home.

'He is often about parish business, sir.'

'It is Mrs Wallis we would speak with. Might we present ourselves to your mistress?'

'Mrs Wallis is indisposed, Mr Sheridan.' The housekeeper glanced at Constable Nicholls, no doubt wondering what a Bow Street Runner might want with their household.

Sheridan's brow creased with concern. 'I trust it is not a serious indisposition, madam. Has a doctor been sent for?'

The housekeeper looked slightly diffident. 'Not so serious as to require a doctor, sir. Do you wish to leave a message for the master — or the mistress, Mr Sheridan?'

'My good woman, this is a matter of great urgency but some delicacy. If there should be any way that Mrs Wallis could give us even ten minutes of her time…'

'Oh, well, sir, I don't know…' The housekeeper hesitated.

Sheridan smiled gratefully and was already moving in through the half-open door before the housekeeper could bar his way.

'Most appreciated. Mrs Champ, is it not?' Sheridan prided himself on an excellent memory for names; it had proved advantageous on numerous occasions.

Mrs Champ nodded, clearly flattered at this personal address. 'Well, I suppose I can only ask. You may have to wait a little while, sirs.'

'With pleasure, Mrs Champ.'

'If you will step this way, gentlemen.'

She led them to a cosy parlour where a good fire had been banked up and then excused herself.

Sheridan made himself comfortable by the fireside while Nicholls clapped his hands behind his back and paced about the rug. It was whilst he was at the sideboard that his eyes narrowed and he picked up a sheaf of papers.

'What have you there, Nicholls?'

'Notes for a sermon, I think…' Nicholls scanned through them with increased interest. 'And I am certain that this is the hand of our "Anonymous". There is the same style in the crossing of the letter T and the curve of the S is quite distinctive.'

'It is as we suspected. The assassin has tried to advertise his deeds in *The Daily Enquiry*.'

After some ten minutes the housekeeper re-entered with a maid carrying a tray of refreshments.

'Mistress welcomes you, Mr Sheridan, and says that she will be down shortly. And you are to have tea and cake whilst you wait.'

'Tea! How delightful!'

Mrs Champ flushed. 'It is Ceylon, sir, Mr Harte at Holbroke Hall sends it over to us. It is from his plantation.'

'Ah yes, I have enjoyed Mr Harte's lapsang souchong.'

Mrs Champ looked worried for a moment. 'Would you prefer —'

Sheridan raised his hand. 'My preference is always for the Ceylon, good Mrs Champ, and the cake looks most delectable.'

'It was my mother's recipe.'

'I hope it is not a secret recipe, Mrs Champ, or I shall have to tease it out of you, and you should know, I am a master of the tease.'

Indeed, the cake was sweet and moist and most delicious. Sheridan found that he was ravenous and but for decorum's sake might easily have polished it off. Tea, he had to admit, was beginning to grow on him; there was something comforting to be found in the earthy taste of the oriental leaves.

When Mrs Wallis entered, he could tell at once that she was not herself. She was not only pale, but also had a nervous, distracted air. He leapt up immediately to greet her with solicitous concern.

'Mrs Wallis, pardon our intrusion when you are not yourself, it is most considerate of you to see us and I would not have pressed were it not for the seriousness of the matter.'

She nodded and took his proffered hand as he led her to a chair by the fireside.

'Mr Sheridan, what is so urgent? And you have brought a gentleman from Bow Street, I gather.' She nodded towards the constable.

'Mrs Wallis, allow me to introduce Constable Nicholls, who, I might add, is also my friend.'

'You are welcome, sir.'

'We do not wish to keep you any longer than is necessary, my dear.' Sheridan still held her hand in his.

'It is my husband? Something has happened to my husband?' She looked suddenly alarmed. 'There has been an accident of some sort? Tell me at once gentlemen!'

'In a manner of speaking. Your husband is not hurt,' he assured hurriedly, patting her hand, 'but he is unwell.'

'Oh!' Mrs Wallis' other hand went to her mouth.

'Let me elucidate. Mr Wallis came to The Haymarket last night. I believe he may have known that I should be there with my son and the Canning family…'

Mrs Wallis looked confused. 'Why would he go to Haymarket?'

Sheridan was finding the conversation harder than he had imagined. Was there any right way to tell a woman that her husband was a savage killer? Particularly when she seemed in so delicate a condition herself.

'I do not know, my dear, but I fear he may have experienced a fit of madness.'

'Madness?' The young woman jerked her hand free.

'He attacked my son.'

'No, no, that cannot be … there is some mistake, some misunderstanding…'

'With a knife.'

Mrs Wallis shook her head with incredulity. 'Mr Wallis would never hurt anyone. All he cares for is his books!'

Nicholls stepped forward. 'Madam, we have reason to believe your husband has acted in this way on previous occasions.'

'He is ill, undoubtedly. And that is why we are here.' Sheridan softened his tone. 'Mr Wallis clearly needs help. A doctor. Did he return last night?'

'I … I do not know. He had not returned when I retired. And then —' she flushed slightly — 'we have separate rooms, so as not to disturb me, he is so often out at all hours on parish business.'

'He ran from the scene at the theatre in much distress. We are, as I have said, very anxious to find him.'

'Of course, of course!' She rose, her features frantic. 'We must ask the servants. And if he returned — then whence he has gone this morning.'

There was at that moment a sharp knock at the door and Mrs Champ burst in without invitation.

'Please, madam, the boy says the constable is to come at once into the garden! Mr Selwyn has sent him.' She turned to Nicholls in explanation. 'That is the gardener, sir.'

Mrs Wallis made to follow but Sheridan stayed her where she was. 'My dear Cecily, you must wait here.'

She nodded. 'You are right. I feel a little faint.'

'Good Mrs Champ, please tend to your mistress,' Sheridan instructed as he and Nicholls rushed from the room.

The scene which accosted them by the large fishpond at the rear of the property was a painfully familiar one to both Sheridan and the Bow Street Runner. Mr Selwyn had warned the stable lad and the other servants to keep their distance, to stray no further than the garden lawns, and then he led Nicholls and Sheridan along a path through a thicket of trees to the grisly spectacle. Nicholls, hardened as he was to such sights, heaved into the undergrowth. Sheridan shut his eyes and let out a low moan.

The gardener, a well built and weather worn man of middle-age, slapped his hat against his thigh. 'This is the devil's work! What does the devil do here in church property?'

Nicholls recovered himself and wiped his mouth with a handkerchief. 'Mr Selwyn, you might fetch some canvas or sacking and send for a wagon. Mr Bartholomew was from Bow Street; we shall return him there.'

The gardener nodded and went to fetch material to cover the mutilated corpse.

'Is there no end, Mr Sheridan?'

'Your man, Bartholomew, must have tried to apprehend Wallis.'

'To his cost. I should not have sent him alone; I sent him to his death.'

Sheridan caught the anguish in the young constable's voice and tried to assuage his guilt. 'You could not have known this outcome. Bartholomew was set to watch, not to arrest.'

'He was ever a diligent officer.'

'He has put up a fight by the looks of it. See he has been slashed, here and here, and his hands also.'

Nicholls steadied himself. 'We must speak with the servants.'

Only the stable boy had seen the reverend when he had arrived in the early hours on horseback. Wallis had asked that his chestnut mare be rubbed down but kept ready and the boy then told not to wait up but to return to his cot. When the lad woke at first light the mare was gone. None of the other servants reported seeing or hearing their master but their quarters were in the attic and if they had not been called for would not have heard him. The master had his own key and was often abroad at strange hours. It was a part of his office and duties, all assumed.

Sheridan took Nicholls to one side. 'I am concerned for Mrs Wallis; she seems in a fragile state. Now is not the moment to tell her of this murder or question her further.'

'It will be abroad soon enough.'

'Let her be with friends and family when she is told.'

'She may know where he is hiding, Mr Sheridan. He is her husband. Mrs Wallis may be hiding him,' Nicholls pressed.

Sheridan shook his head. 'No. The marriage is not so intimate, Nicholls. Sweet Cecily can have no notion of her husband's true nature.'

'She is with child. A woman in such a condition may go to any lengths to protect the father of her unborn babe.'

'With child?'

'I cannot be certain of course, sir, but I am familiar with all the early signs of the condition, her pallor, her tremble of nausea —'

'Ah yes, you are of a large family.'

'Fifteen, sir.'

'And your wife, her time must be close.'

'My mother stays with her. She is in good hands.'

'Your mother must know all there is to know of childbirth.'

But Mrs Wallis? With child? The constable could be wrong. If what Sheridan had overheard earlier in the year were true, then the marriage had yet to be consummated. Unless Wallis had finally risen to his duties as a husband. But Sheridan somehow doubted this to be the case. The Reverend Wallis he now brought to mind seemed altogether too disturbed for normal relations.

'Whatever the cause of her indisposition, let us go gently,' Sheridan pleaded.

Nicholls hesitated. 'Very well,' he agreed at last. 'Only that I know such a shock might cause her to lose the child. But we must know where to look, Mr Sheridan!'

'I shall urge Mrs Wallis to return for the moment to her father's house, and then let us proceed forthwith to Sir Edward. We may be blunt with him, I can assure you.'

CHAPTER THIRTY-THREE

A shot rang out from near a copse of trees, followed by another and another. Here and there wreathes of morning mist were still rising from the damp sward in front of Cranby Hall, the home of Sir Edward Wallis.

'I daresay that will be Herbert. I believe Cranby is noted for its woodcocks and he shall be out hunting every day now that the season has started.'

'Well, we have hunting of a different order, Mr Sheridan.'

'That we do, Officer.'

'Will the father be of the shooting party?'

'No. You shall see.'

Nicholls shared a glance with Sheridan as they were ushered into the reception room. Sir Edward came towards them in a bath chair pushed by a manservant. A rug covered his lap, but one could nevertheless quite clearly discern the absence of his right leg. That side of his face was also horribly scarred.

'Mr Sheridan, what the devil do you do here? And in company with a Runner?' The squire cast a derogatory eye over both men.

Sheridan bowed respectfully. 'It is in fact the devil that we seek, Sir Edward.'

'None of your damn riddles — what's your business? And I hope it is not to solicit a subscription to that blasted theatre of yours! We're at war, man — this is no time for tomfoolery.'

'Murder is never a comic diversion, I think you might agree, sir.'

Sir Edward looked suddenly caught on the back foot.

'Murder? What has murder to do with me?'

Nicholls stepped forward. 'We search for your son, Sir Edward.'

'My son? My son?' the old squire fumed, and slapped his hand on the arm of his bath chair. 'Who lays such calumnies on James Herbert Wallis?'

'It is your son, the Reverend Peter Wallis, whom we seek, sir.'

Sir Edward stared at them both open-mouthed.

'We have come from the rectory —' Sheridan began.

'Where one of my men lies dead — brutally slain,' Nicholls finished, a cold thread of anger running through his voice.

The squire's eyes narrowed. 'And you claim this is the work of my son, Peter? Do you have proof? Do you have a witness?'

Sheridan and Nicholls were silenced a moment by the enquiry.

The old man laughed without mirth. 'The boy has never fought in his life. He could not even raise his fists to defend himself at his school! Never mind know one end of a gun from the other.'

'He has proved himself very handy with a blade.'

Sir Edward shook his head. 'No. There is some mistake. The boy is a mealy-mouthed sop. I had meant him for the dragoons — but he never showed a jot of spunk and has his mother's piety, God rest her. My younger boy is a man of the Church and, heaven forbid, a devout priest to boot — with his interminable sermons! Could have gone into politics at least — the only fellow he ever talked about was that boy Pitt when they were up at Cambridge.' Sir Edward looked accusingly at the Bow Street Runner. 'You are telling me that Peter has killed a man?'

'He has murdered, sir,' Nicholls replied, hoping to accent the difference between a killing which might be accidental and a murder which was not. 'Some five or six men, maybe more.'

'And attacked my son Tom, Sir Edward,' Sheridan added to underline his interest. 'That is irrefutable.'

The squire continued to glare from one man to the other before he finally responded. 'Then he must be mad.' Sir Edward nodded. 'Yes, he has clearly lost his mind.'

'That is what we suspect, Sir Edward.'

'My wife's family. She'd an uncle of unsound mind.'

'Perhaps you might know where he would go, Sir Edward?'

'Well, not here! He should have no hiding here, of that I can assure you, gentlemen!'

'I do not doubt that, Sir Edward.'

'Is there anyone with whom he might seek refuge?'

'Always an odd boy, when I think of it. No friends to speak of. Except young Pitt, as I said. But he should hardly be knocking on the door of our Prime Minister! And I believe that connection did not last beyond the university, more's the pity.'

'A place then, sir? Somewhere he might feel safe?'

Sir Edward looked blank. 'There is no place that springs to mind.'

Nicholls addressed the squire. 'We shall not detain you any longer then, sir. If your son should contact you —'

Sir Edward grunted. 'He is no son of mine, Constable. Not anymore. Good day, gentlemen.' He nodded curtly to his manservant and was wheeled away.

Both men remained locked within their own thoughts on the journey back to the city. Sheridan suspected that Nicholls was thinking firstly of his man Bartholomew and how he should break the dreadful news of his death to the aged parents with whom the watchman had lived. Secondly, he should be feeling the frustration of knowing not where to look for the culprit. An alert could be put out amongst the snitches and conks of the city. But how likely was it that the Reverend Wallis would secrete himself where ordinary villains lurked virtually untouched by the officers of the law in the slum rookeries of St Giles and Saffron Hill?

Perhaps, having gathered funds and some few possessions from the rectory, Wallis was headed for the coast to try and catch a ship to take him abroad. On horseback he might aim for Harwich or Tilbury. Harwich he should have to stop overnight and rest his mount, but Tilbury he might get that far in a day if the mare were not too tired and he did not push her unduly. By that night, Sheridan calculated, Wallis might find himself a berth and be heading for Ostend or Rotterdam on the early morning tide. Their only hope in that case was that the description which had been dispatched might alert a diligent sea captain, but there were always those who, for a fee, were less scrupulous.

Where else would the reverend go, if not abroad? Why, against all sense, would he stay? All Sheridan's instincts told him that Peter Wallis had not fled the country. Why? There was one simple answer. He was unhinged. Sheridan felt, however, that other reasons might compel him to stay. These murders. There had been a design, some plan however fantastical. He recalled fragments of the conversation in Epping Forest. The reverend had at one point asked, '*May there not be some purpose in these acts?*' Almost as though he longed for that purpose to be recognised and even applauded.

Bartholomew had been set to watch the house. Seeing Wallis departing, he must have been tempted out of his hiding place to confront him. There had been a struggle. Wallis may even have been injured, it occurred to Sheridan. But Wallis had prevailed with his deadly blade. Why had he then not made haste away? His need to escape being more urgent than ever. Why had he taken the time to drag Bartholomew's body all the way to the fishpond and inflict those mutilations which had become his signature?

Was it because Wallis recognised the watchman? He had an apostolic name, Bartholomew, albeit his surname. Could it be that the officer of the watch had always been an intended victim? Did that mean that he was also another who preferred the company of men? He lived with his elderly parents. He was not married. And something else jangled in Sheridan's memory. There, it came to him. Bartholomew had known that the alley where Thaddeus Broadhead was assassinated was one frequented at night by men soliciting other men. A fact not commonly known. Nicholls had not been aware of it, though he knew the streets of the city as well as any Bow Street Runner.

Sheridan broke the silence and leant towards Nicholls. 'Mr Bartholomew preferred men, didn't he?'

Nicholls jerked from his reverie. He looked at Sheridan and nodded slowly. 'I believe that may have been the case.'

'One of the reasons you trusted his discretion in the matter of the bagnio?'

'Yes.'

'Wallis will not flee abroad. He will return to the city. He will have been emboldened by this assassination.'

'I don't follow you, sir.'

'Bartholomew was always in his plan. That the watchman should have stumbled across his path last night and that Wallis was able to overcome him, he will have read as a signal that he should continue with his insane mission. He will have felt it was a sign from God.'

'What is that mission?'

'To act as a harbinger of the Apocalypse, to hasten the End of Days.'

'For what purpose?'

'So that he may be forgiven. That they all may be forgiven.'

'Forgiven?'

'Because he too prefers men, but has been unable to live with that sin. And then he found the Revelation made to Peter the Apostle and it —' Sheridan stared at Nicholls with realisation — 'offered him hope.'

Nicholls continued to look bewildered.

'The rest is madness, of course,' Sheridan continued, his mind aflame. 'Fuelled, perhaps, by the days we live in. Revolution. War. The streets of Paris overflowing with blood. The riots in Birmingham. And then his insane idea that by slaying the Apostles once again, he shall hasten the end. And an Anti-Christ. Smyth said there should be an Anti-Christ.'

'Who should that be?'

Sheridan shook his head, trying to wrestle an idea forth.

'Soersby? Could it be Soersby? He is a judge. Jonas? Does the name have a meaning? Smyth would know.'

'Gift from God.'

'Yes — just as Christ was!'

'We must send word to Sir Jonas then, to be on his guard.'

'At once.'

Nicholls glanced from the window. 'Here is Bow Street. I will bid you good day, sir. There is much to do.'

Sheridan heaved a great sigh. He was exhausted by the events of the previous twenty-four hours. He should return to the house in Grosvenor Street, be charming to the Cannings, and make sure his dear boy had recovered sufficiently from the shock of the attack. It made him queasy to think how close to disaster Tom had been. He would forever be indebted to Malmain.

There was one visit he must make, however, before he should reach home. He ordered the carriage on to number ten Downing Street. He would chance that Mr Pitt would be at home and that he might be granted an audience with the Prime Minister.

When he arrived at the door he was informed by the manservant that the Prime Minister was in a meeting and that he was not receiving visitors that afternoon. Could he take the gentleman's card? Damn the fellow, he knew very well who Sheridan was.

'No. I shall see him soon enough, I daresay, across the floor of the House.'

The manservant bowed with condescension and closed the door in his face.

Two weeks had passed and there had been no sighting reported of the Reverend Peter Wallis. There had been little in the press other than an appeal. The Reverend Wallis, it was written, had disappeared from his home and was believed to be in a state of mental disturbance and confusion. His family hoped for his safe return. Should anyone have information on the clergyman's whereabouts there would be a reward.

Nicholls had explained that they could not hope for more in the reportage. Tobias Bloomer was already convicted in the bagnio assassinations and Sir Edward had rightly pointed out that there were no witnesses to the murder of the watchman, Bartholomew. Despite his threats to abandon his son, Sir Edward Wallis had conveyed to Bow Street through a lawyer his intention to sue for slander anyone who claimed otherwise. He thinks only of the family's good name, Nicholls concluded. But it was decided amongst his superiors that the old squire's threats should not be put to the test.

Sheridan wondered if Wallis had gone abroad after all. He hoped that might be the case. He would be glad to have been wrong in his assumption that madness would hold the clergyman to his mission. Sheridan would as soon forget the whole business, now. He had noticed a nervous tic in Tom for a few days after the events at Haymarket and then the boy had returned to his usual blithe, good humour and fully convinced by the story that the good reverend was in the grip of some temporary derangement. Mrs Canning meanwhile lived up to their fond name for her, Good Sister Christian, and was full of solicitude, for Mrs Wallis in particular.

'How difficult it shall be for a woman so young to find her husband declared insane and perhaps in need of an asylum.' She shook her head sadly. 'I have arranged to visit with her presently. George shall be here and he has insisted on accompanying me, which is very considerate of him, for I know it shall be a distressing occasion.' Mehitabel wrung her hands. 'I worry for dear Cecily's future. It is unlikely that the living at St Jerome can remain with Mr Wallis, there shall need to be a new vicar appointed, and then where shall they go? Oh dear!'

Sheridan also planned to call on the young Mrs Wallis as soon as he could manage, but any spare time which he had available was consumed by the fast-approaching royal entertainment. For the same reason he had abandoned his intention of quizzing Mr Pitt. He had briefly imagined that, given the earlier friendship whilst they were young men at Cambridge, the Prime Minister might be able to throw some light on Wallis' character. Might even know of somewhere the missing clergyman could seek shelter. He had then reconsidered. That connection was ten years in the past and likely to have been tenuous. All his attention must now be given to the performance of Eliza Ramus.

CHAPTER THIRTY-FOUR

The three older princesses had been invited by their eldest brother, His Royal Highness the Prince of Wales, to a luncheon and entertainment at Carlton House. The prince had satisfied himself that even his parents would have approved of the select guest list as he felt sure there would be some sneak who would report back to them in any case. He wanted any scrutiny of the proceedings to be kept to a minimum.

The luncheon, characterised by the usual assemblages of game, fish, mousses and aspic, finishing with a desert course of blancmange and towering croque-en-bouche centred around an artfully sculpted meringue of the Prince of Wales' feathers and fleur-de-lys, was a short and simple affair by His Royal Highness' standards. He was keen to gather and muster the guests into the ballroom without delay for the main event. There he proudly announced that the entertainment was to be provided by various young girls as an expression of their unbounded gratitude for the patronage provided by his beloved sisters, Their Royal Highnesses, Charlotte, Augusta and Elizabeth. Each of the sisters expressed themselves surprised and delighted. Princess Elizabeth most convincingly, thought Sheridan, considering that she had been secretly primed for the occasion.

Sir Percival Jarvis had composed 'a few words' to open the proceedings and embarked on an interminably dull prologue in praise of the Foundling Home for Daughters of the Deserving Poor. Sheridan, having anticipated that there should be some such posturing, chose a moment when Sir Percival paused to draw breath in order to signal the musicians to an opening fanfare. Sir Percival grimaced but had little option other than to be seated.

A woodland scene had been created using canvased flats already available from the theatre's stock and Mr Quail had shown a great aptitude for the set dressing. The girls entered in procession, dressed most charmingly as forest nymphs and fairies. They commenced to spread a veritable cascade of flowers and gold-painted leaves in the path of their Queen Titania, the long train of her shimmering gown carried by the smaller girls. The Music Master had settled on a humming tune, with the advantage that no verses needed to be learnt, which created a pleasing, almost ethereal sound as Titania progressed into the centre of the performing area. The audience clapped their appreciation. Sheridan had to concede that Titania was remarkably striking. The tall, thin girl with pimples had been transformed by the wonders of make-up and costume into a willowy, translucent creature, gossamer wings attached at her shoulders, crowned with a silver wig and a coronet of mistletoe.

The fairies then began to skip and dance around their queen in a playful ballet. Sheridan marvelled at what young Joey had managed to achieve with the children as they jumped and twirled and froze into attitudes and tableaux in time to the music. One of them even managed an impressive somersault and another had been taught to walk on her hands.

Mr Quail had hit upon the idea that Titania should carry a large book of spells. With the added bonus that she could then read all her lines from the pages in front of her. He had taught her how to do this without neglecting the audience. After each line of verse she would raise her long swan-like neck and look towards the prince or glance along the front row of spectators. Her voice was thin with a trace of the Limehouse docks in her accent, but she had clearly embraced the opportunity which had been given to her to aspire to a career where she should play the part of a maidservant on stage rather than the more onerous occupation in life. The prompter had taken this aptly-named Sylvia in hand and she had proved to be an arduous student under his tutelage. Mr Quail had begun to petition Sheridan to find his protégé a place within the company. If all went well with the day's entertainment, Sheridan was minded to consider the request.

The conceit of the production was that Queen Titania should conjure up a pageant of the 'royal women' of England for the admiration and entertainment of her guests, the audience. The first great queen was introduced with a wave of her hand.

A fanfare heralded the arrival of Boadicea driving a small chariot pulled by a miniature pony. The child dressed as Boadicea held a spear in one hand and the reins of the chariot in the other. Two smaller girls were on either side to represent the warrior queen's daughters, but also more crucially to wedge their 'royal mother' in place so she should not fall back out of the chariot.

There were oohs and aahs from the assembled guests. The royal princesses looked enchanted and the prince was beaming with his own sense of reflected glory. Sheridan felt almost tempted to relax. As the little pony completed its third circuit of the stage area without mishap, Sheridan spotted Matthew in position at the rear of the ballroom and edged towards him. He waited for the transition to the next spectacle, a winter scene and a mime depicting the daring escape of the Empress Matilda from a besieged Oxford Castle and her crossing of the frozen Isis camouflaged by a white cloak.

Sheridan leaned in towards Matthew and spoke under his breath. 'You should know that the man responsible for Mr Marson's death is now known to us beyond any doubt.'

A flicker of acknowledgement shifted across Matthews features as he maintained his statuesque stance.

'Unfortunately, he has escaped the clutches of Bow Street and they are prevented from raising a hue and cry. This man, Wallis, has in all likelihood left the country.' Sheridan sighed. 'I am sorry that we have not managed to deliver the justice that Andrew deserved.'

Matthew was still a moment as he digested all that Sheridan had conveyed.

On the stage Titania was intoning the final epitaph for the valiant Plantagenet Empress, '*Here lies Henry's daughter, mother, wife, great in all three, her son the glory of her life.*'

'He may still be here.'

Sheridan shrugged. 'Who knows. Perhaps in hiding somewhere.'

'Someone has been following me, sir.'

Sheridan felt his skin prickle. 'You have seen him?'

Matthew shook his head almost imperceptibly. 'I have felt him.'

Sheridan considered this new development as he watched the arrival of Good Queen Bess. Attired with a silver breastplate over her white velvet dress, whitened face and a red wig of tight curls, the Good Queen processed slowly before the dramatic action in the background. Joey, who had always shown a great relish for the mechanicals of production, had devised a puppet show depicting the defeat of the Spanish Armada. Rippling waves and miniature galleons and ships of war tossed about whilst little puffs of smoke denoted blasting cannons and thunder rumbled and cracked to deafening effect.

This latter provided by a thunder sheet behind the scenes which the girls had vied to operate. At last the rumble of thunder faded and Titania was allowed to impart those famous lines delivered at Tilbury as the royal queen took centre stage.

'... *I know I have the body but of a weak and feeble woman, but I have the heart and stomach of a king, and of a King of England too, and think foul scorn that Parma or Spain, or any Prince of Europe should dare to invade the borders of my realm.*'

The speech was met with rapturous applause and the stamps and hoots of agreement from the prince were soon taken up by all the men of military mien. In this time of war, under threat of invasion from Revolutionary France, the scene was calculated to stir the blood of any good English patriot.

Sheridan took the opportunity of this distraction to look closely at the young footman. 'You cared for Andrew and I know that he cared greatly for you, I have heard as much.'

Matthew flushed.

'It is a good deal to ask of you, Matthew — but can you help us to catch this man? It is he who follows you, I am sure of it.'

'I would do anything if that were possible, Mr Sheridan.'

The noise from the assembly had reached a crescendo and Sheridan now looked back anxiously towards Good Queen Bess, frozen in a startled attitude by this sudden raucous display from the spectators in front of her. Titania clutched the book of spells and made a vain attempt to proceed with her next lines. Sheridan wondered if he should intervene in some way. Just as he was about to rush to the front, he saw someone wearing a horse head mask caper on to the stage. It was Joey, Sheridan realised from the physique. The horse regarded the audience, tossed his mane and knocked his foot on the floor loudly in the manner of a prancing stallion. The prince waved his hands to indicate that his party should quash their patriotic ardour for the moment.

Joey's horse then proceeded to turn his back, flick a tail, wiggle his rear and play coyly with the audience until all attention was his. He approached the frozen queen and began to nuzzle against her until the girl relaxed and reached out to stroke his head and mane. The horse then bent down and clearly whispered an urgent command to the girl to jump on his back. Then, with a rousing circuit Good Queen Bess was cantered off the stage leaving the audience full of chuckles and smiles.

'When might you next be free?'

'Tonight, Mr Sheridan.'

'Then tonight it shall be. I will have officers from Bow Street follow and I shall join them.'

'I am willing.'

'We shall hope that Mr Wallis lurks in the shadows. Be assured that no harm will come to you, Matthew.'

A time was agreed.

'I shall send a note when all is arranged at Bow Street. Tonight then.'

The young footman looked emboldened. 'Tonight, sir.'

The pageant had proceeded on to the Glorious Revolution and the daughters of James II, Mary with her regal consort William of Orange — the one breeches part in the spectacle — and finally Queen Anne. The pantomime was reaching its climax. Which was all leading to the entrance of Eliza Ramus. Sheridan sidled his way to the front row and slipped in beside the equerry, Major Hanger.

'Rather well done, Sherry, given your players.'

'Thank you, Hanger, it has not been without incident.'

The musicians struck up the music for 'Rule, Britannia!' and the excited prince beckoned a hush from his guests whilst Titania intoned the lyrics. All were expectant. At the second verse a small figure emerged at the back of the stage.

While thou shalt flourish great and free:
The dread and envy of them all…

Five-year-old Eliza Ramus, in simple robe and wearing the helmet of classical times, carried a small shield emblazoned with the cross of St George in her left hand and in her right the trident to symbolise her conquest of the seas. To the delight of the audience this small heroic figure sat astride a great shaggy-headed lion.

Rule, Britannia! rule the waves:
Britons never will be slaves…

The lion — or rather the miniature pony thus disguised — moved forward at a stately pace. Eliza looked from side to side with a beaming smile, all pretence of seriousness soon forgotten. Sheridan glimpsed the Princess Elizabeth clutch her hands in front of her in sheer delight.

Still more majestic shalt thou rise,
More dreadful, from each foreign stroke;
As the loud blast that tears the skies…

It was at this point that someone backstage inadvertently knocked into the thunder sheet. The sudden bang and clatter startled the pony, whose vision had been somewhat impaired by the huge mask, and he skittered to one side. Eliza dropped the shield and grabbed the mane, further blinding the poor creature as the mask rode up his face. The pony, now thoroughly frightened, twitched and bucked, skittering again. Eliza lowered the little trident as she grasped the beast with both hands and whooped with excitement. At this sound the creature began to charge towards the front row, the points of the trident aimed squarely at the corpulent middle of His Royal Highness, the Prince of Wales.

Rule, Britannia! rule the waves…

Sheridan's heart leapt into his mouth. He watched, to his horror, a tragedy in slow motion. The beast jumped from the short platform with a bucking swerve and young Eliza Ramus, still whooping with glee, was catapulted from that ruler of the animal kingdom into the lap of the sovereign-in-waiting.

Britons never will be slaves…

Eliza gazed up from her soft landing with surprise into a face that she recognised. She grinned mischievously. The trident, still clutched in her small hand, hovered below the nose of His Royal Highness.

'Peekaboo!' she exclaimed with delight.

Sheridan held his head in his hands, vowing to remind himself never to work with children and animals ever, ever again.

The musicians had stopped, caught in a moment of horrified hiatus, but their leader struck up again into the chorus.

Eliza squirmed off the royal knee, grasped the royal hand and yanked her royal uncle up to the edge of the stage. She stepped up, insisting the prince follow her. Bemused as he was, the prince obeyed. Still clasping his large hand in her own pudgy little one the child faced the audience and yelled out the chorus, stamping her trident on the boards. His Royal Highness gamely took the cue and joined in, straightening Britannia's helmet as he did so. He waved a hand in time to the music and everyone assembled rose to their feet to join three rousing repetitions of the chorus.

'Hurrah!' the prince cried and there came an assembly of answering cheers.

He then indicated to little Eliza that she should take a bow.

The infant prodigy duly obliged with a very fetching curtsy.

Their Royal Highnesses were escorted by their princely brother, Major Hanger, Sir Percival and Sheridan along the line of girls and the various accompanying chaperones. The princesses thanked all the children and adults in their own particular manner. The Princess Royal tending to the haughty and condescending, Princess Augusta, painfully shy and stammering, the Princess Elizabeth glowing and fulsome with praise to all concerned. As the latter finally came abreast of Mrs Ramus she smiled sweetly at the matron and then at Eliza who was clutched to her side.

'Eliza, is it not?' The princess stooped down and chucked her under the chin. 'That is my name too.'

Eliza starred at the princess and seemed mesmerised into an attitude of uncommon sweetness.

The Princess Elizabeth smiled and then turned to the girl's guardian. 'What a precocious child, so full of gaiety and spirit!'

'Isn't she, Lizzie — just a delight!' the prince concurred.

'I would that she were mine —' the princess stroked the child's cheek — 'I should love her dearly.'

Mrs Ramus stifled a gasp of alarm.

'You will take very great care of her, will you not, Mrs Ramus?'

Relief swept across Mrs Ramus' features and she bobbed a curtsy. 'Yes, Your Royal Highness, it is my pleasure.'

The princess looked down at the little girl again. 'I do hope we shall meet again one day, Eliza, perhaps when you are quite grown up; I should very much like to see how you shall turn out.'

And then the Princess Elizabeth turned away from the performers to re-join her sisters, who were being conducted to their awaiting carriage. As she did so, Sheridan caught the gleam of an unshed tear in her eye, and for a moment felt that his eyes might water too.

CHAPTER THIRTY-FIVE

Before quitting Carlton House, Sheridan had sent an urgent message to Constable Nicholls at Bow Street. He had then made apologies to His Royal Highness — family matters, wished that he could delay but he was sure the prince would understand and before any objection could be raised he had bowed low, stepping backwards all the while and excused himself from the party.

He hurried up the Mall and made his way immediately to the theatre and went in search of Mrs Petty the Wardrobe Mistress. She was not to be found in her usual lair, but abroad haranguing a tailor whose work she had found shoddy and not up to her usual exacting standard.

'Oh, you should 'ave heard her, sir! "*They think*," she says, "*because it is for the stage that it matters not that the hems are tacked instead of stitched proper!*" It was one of the laundry girls, Hannah, who laughed heartily and jiggled the baby at her breast. 'Oh, he'll feel the back of her tongue, all right.'

The infant boy already had the pugilistic look of Harry the flyman about him, Sheridan mused. As did his half-sister, born only weeks later to another of the laundry maids, who now entered with her babe cradled in one arm and a basket of shirts wedged in the other. Neither woman had been brought to the altar yet, Mrs Petty had reminded everyone who would listen. Then it had come out at last. Harry was already married. A wife in Bermondsey long deserted with the care of two offspring. The laundry maids had dropped their animosity and rivalry and come together to bewail their fate. They were now fast friends and considered lodging together with Hannah's mother so that the infant siblings might be better cared for.

'Anything I can help with, my lover?' It was Sally, who had been installed in the company as a dresser, much to Mrs Petty's initial chagrin. Sally's good nature had, however, worked its charms on the old woman and she now would not have a bad word spoken of her new protégé.

'Ah, Sally! Yes, you may very well assist. I have need to go abroad in disguise this evening into Covent Garden.'

'Ooh! Wha' have you been up to, sir?' Sally gave him a roguish smile.

'As it happens, my dear, I shall be stalking a dangerous assassin and it is imperative that I should not be recognised.'

'You are a one, sir — assassin indeed!'

Sheridan concurred; it was his fate never to be believed in his acts of valour.

Sally chuckled and then looked towards the stock of costumes. 'Well, if it's not some courtship you are after —' she shot a quick glance at him to double check.

Sheridan shook his head. 'No romance I can assure you, my dear. Romance is dead to me, or rather I am dead to Romance, one of us is seriously ailing in any case.'

'You'll need to blend in then... I'd go for a lumper or a ticket-porter, sir, one as looks as he's finished his labours for the day and 'as been drinking 'is wages at the Rose and Crown... What d'you reckon, sir? Or is that too much of the lower order?'

'I declare that sounds tip-top, Sally.'

When Sheridan arrived at Bow Street to meet with Constable Nicholls, his way was barred by an officer at the door.

'What d'you want, you seedy lumpkin?'

''Ere to see Mr Nicholls.' Sheridan tugged at his slouched hat, his bearing equally slumped. 'Tell 'im Dick's 'ere.'

The officer sniffed and pulled a face. 'Rather him than me!' He turned and shouted back into the building. 'Tell Nicholls there's a stinking cull out here asking for him. And you ain't coming any further.' He pointed at Sheridan.

It had been Joey's idea, after he had applied the dirt to his face, to smear Sheridan's hat and jacket with a jar of fish oil. The advantage being, the boy had suggested, that along with his badge, Sheridan could pass for a Billingsgate man and none would want to get close enough to examine his features. Sheridan had to admit it was a devious ploy.

Nicholls emerged and regarded him with undisguised disgust. 'What is it, you rogue? Be quick about it, I have business to attend to.'

'Begging your honour's pardon, it's only him as would be godparent to your first born.' Sheridan straightened himself up and winked at the constable.

'Mr Sheridan!' Nicholls looked startled and then began to laugh. 'I own it is a good disguise, but can I ask you to stand a little further off, sir!'

Matthew Simpson emerged from the tradesman's entrance at the rear of Carlton House and sauntered up towards the Strand. He was followed at a discrete distance by Nicholls and his fellow Runner. To divert from other duties, Nicholls had strung a line to his superior about a tip-off from a regular whiddler about some stolen goods. There was one officer of the watch assigned to go with him, it was all that could be spared.

As the footman passed by the shambling figure by the railings, he sniffed and gave the man a wide berth. Sheridan whistled the tune to 'Rule, Britannia!', which had been prearranged as a signal that the tail was in place. The footman paused momentarily, and then walked on with a wry, thinly disguised smile.

The streets were crowded at this hour between those finishing their labours and those setting off to find entertainment. The lamplighter and his boy were busy lighting the oil lamps along the thoroughfare, the reflected light spilling down onto the pavement and adding to the sense of impending gaiety. Matthew veered off the Strand and stopped for an ale at The Nags Head. There he was approached and greeted by another tidily dressed young man. After a brief, whispered conversation with this acquaintance, the other man scurried away and Matthew was left to drink alone. Sheridan would have welcomed a beverage himself but stayed out of doors. He was now more than ready to curse Joey's liberal hand with the fish oil. Thankfully, he had brought a pipe as part of his disguise and breathed in the fumes so that he might clear the scent of mackerel from his own nostrils.

The rest of the evening followed the same pattern; Matthew slowly walked through the area of Covent Garden and stopped at the occasional tavern to refresh himself. Sheridan would idle on a corner sucking at his pipe and scanning each passer-by from beneath the brim of his hat. He was starting to weary of the task. When would Wallis show himself? *Would* he show himself? Was he truly the man who Matthew had sensed was stalking him? Or was that fellow just some ordinary footpad? Or, more likely, a figment of Mr Simpson's nervous imagination. The hour was getting late but the streets were still crowded when Matthew ambled up Russell Street and then detoured into a narrow alley. This was the route discussed should Simpson feel that he had been observed and might be followed.

Sheridan's heart thumped. The game was on! He dodged down Bridges Street to enter from further down the warren of alleys which would place him ahead of the footman's agreed course. Here the well-lit streets of the West End were left behind and that poverty which so readily rubbed up against the wealth of the city was more in evidence. As he arrived at a junction to turn left, his way was barred by a large man sporting a cocked hat.

'Oi, mind out! — where's the blaze?'

'Le'me through if you would, sir — I 'ave business.'

'Not around here you don't — not without my say so.' The ruffian emphasised his point by striking the short truncheon he held in one hand into the palm of the other.

'What d'you want then?'

'What d'you think, you stinking cull?'

Sheridan rooted in his coat pockets to no avail; he turned them inside out to show their doleful state and shrugged.

'Looks like you ain't got no business 'ere after all.' The lout raised his truncheon.

Sheridan took the pipe from his mouth. ''Ave this then.' He shoved the hot bowl of the pipe into the man's empty palm and had dashed by him even as the lout let out a sharp yelp of pain.

Sheridan didn't look back but swerved by a cackling old crone, knocking her basket of faggots to the ground.

'Apologies, ma'am!' he yelled as he sped on.

He crossed a moonlit courtyard and dived into the dark opening of another alley, hoping he was not followed. At the end of that narrow passage he was about to step out into a deserted thoroughfare when he noticed a figure turning in at the top. Straining his eyes through the gloom, Sheridan recognised the footman. He caught his breath and hung back.

Matthew had covered half the distance before Sheridan spied a man in a black cloak and low-brimmed hat flit swiftly along the shadows behind the footman. In the next moment Matthew cried out and lurched to the side, revealing the figure poised for attack at his rear. Sheridan caught the glint of steel from the blade in his hand.

Nicholls and his fellow Runner appeared at the top of the alley and sped towards Matthew and his would-be assailant.

'Hold there, villain!'

The hue and cry was up!

For a moment Sheridan caught the startled look on Wallis' face before the clergyman leapt in the opposite direction from his pursuers — directly towards the opening where Sheridan was lurking.

In an instant Sheridan had stepped out to block the reverend's way. For a moment Wallis was drawn up short. The two men starred at each other. Wallis' nose twitched and then he frowned in half recognition and jabbed with the knife. Sheridan jumped backwards, avoiding the cut of the blade. It was at this point that he was struck violently from behind by what he later imagined was a short truncheon.

When he came around, his head was still ringing from the blow and Nicholls was standing over him.

'Wallis?'

'We lost him.'

Sheridan buried his face in his hands. 'So nearly did I have him!'

Nicholls grunted and reached out a hand to pull Sheridan to his feet.

'At least we know that he is here, he has not fled to France; and he is still about his grisly business.'

'And Matthew?' Sheridan enquired anxiously.

Matthew leaned in then. 'Only a little shaken, sir. I was on my guard and when I felt his breath I knew to leap aside.'

Sheridan winced as he took off his hat and tentatively touched his head. A lump was already swelling to noble proportions, the pain presaging what he knew would be a real corker of a headache.

Two days later Nicholls arrived at the theatre and found Sheridan ensconced with Bob Fairbrother agonising over his accounts. The company's demand for their salaries had been renewed with increased vigour since the arrival of the new season. He should have to borrow from Peter to pay Paul. Only, that had been done the month before, so on this occasion it should have to be borrowing from Paul to pay Peter — or could there be somebody else he might turn to? Mr Harte! He would have to cultivate the tea merchant; persuade him to increase his subscription. Promise him a box next to the Duke of St Albans in the new theatre.

The Runner held out a letter which the esteemed journalist of *The Daily Enquiry*, Mr Brockenhurst, had delivered into his hand; with the insistence that any story that might be attached to it should be his first.

'Mr Brockenhurst tells me you told him to pass on any missives from "Anonymous". This came today and he believes it is from the same author, although in this instance he signs himself, "The Thirteenth Apostle". I have made comparison with the other letters still in my possession and I am certain it is the same hand. But neither I nor Mr Brockenhurst can make head nor tail of the man's scribblings. I fear our Reverend Wallis is now entirely deranged.'

Sheridan's frown deepened as he read through to the end.

After urging Mr Brockenhurst to publish the letter in full in the national interest, the writer of the letter spoke of one who, like the favourite of King James I, was "a minion of the crown". Sheridan assumed that would be a reference to the Duke of Buckingham, who was rumoured to have been the king's male lover. Further into the text were references to the ancient warriors Nisus and Euryalus, whose intimate friendship had been described in *The Aeneid*. The letter then led on to an assertion that the highest in the land had held another "Alexander's feast". With horror it began to dawn on Sheridan that all these allusions had featured in the speeches which he himself had made in the House of Commons. Denigrating jibes most particularly at Mr William Pitt the Younger. He was reminded to his shame that he had on more than one occasion insinuated that the Prime Minister was impotent and lacking in manly attributes, the insinuation being that he was not a fit person to lead the government.

'This means something to you, Mr Sheridan?'

'Yes, I rather think it does.'

He could feel his heart thumping. For the letter went on to speak obscurely of the Last Supper, of Judas Iscariot and the betrayal that had led to the sufferings of Christ. His death on the cross and resurrection. The time was nigh for the coming of the Anti-Christ, the writer claimed. War and desolation would herald the end of days when all men would be resurrected for the Final Judgement.

He very much hoped that he had rushed to a wrong conclusion but everything in the letter pointed to one appalling possibility. The Prime Minister, Mr Pitt, was cast in the role of the Anti-Christ and the Reverend Peter Wallis wanted the world to know that he intended to crucify him.

'If he has not already done so,' Sheridan murmured under his breath.

CHAPTER THIRTY-SIX

Sheridan knocked loudly at the door to number ten Downing Street.

'Open up, if you please!'

The door was at last answered by the same supercilious manservant who had responded on the previous visit.

'Mr Pitt is unavailable, sir.'

'Damn you — I know that already! You will let me pass; I must speak to those within!'

'Sir!' The manservant's hackles rose but before he could shut the door in his face, Sheridan had barged through, followed closely by Constable Nicholls.

'Who is it, Williams?'

It was Henry Dundas, the Secretary of State for the Home Department, more recently appointed War Minister; he emerged from the front reception room and was taken aback to see Sheridan before him.

'Dundas, a word!'

'Sheridan! Devil take you! You damn traitor! Seize him! Seize the villain!'

A footman came from the back of the vestibule, with some measure of caution, Sheridan noted.

'We see your true colours at last!' Dundas continued to splutter. 'Do you come to invade the Prime Minister's residence and proclaim your Republic — you Jacobin!'

Sheridan held out a placating hand. 'We come, sir, to —'

The footman, seeing that the intruder held no weapon, took the opportunity to pounce and grapple Sheridan into an armlock. At the same instant, his fellow at the entrance clapped a hand on Nicholls' shoulder.

'I wouldn't do that, sir, I am an officer of Bow Street.'

The manservant hesitated and then thought better of his action.

'Let me go at once, man!' Sheridan grimaced.

'A Bow Street Runner?'

It was Charles Long who appeared beside the Home Secretary in the doorway and peered into the vestibule.

'Ah, Sheridan — thought I heard your voice.'

'Long! Tell this fellow to unhand me.'

Another servant appeared from the rear of the house, awaiting orders.

'What do you do here, Sheridan?' Dundas blustered.

Charles Long looked quizzically between Sheridan and Constable Nicholls.

'I rather fancy Sheridan may have come to be of assistance, Dundas.' Long nodded to the servant wrenching Sheridan's arm. 'You may release Mr Sheridan. He has not been invited — but he may be welcome nonetheless.'

Sheridan rubbed his shoulder and winced. 'Your friend, Mr Pitt? He is gone?' he asked keenly.

'How the devil does he know, Long — if he is not one of the conspirators?'

'Gentlemen, I suggest we continue this discussion within — and Williams, you might bring another bottle of claret.' Long looked then to the constable. 'Officer, we have not been introduced.'

'Constable Nicholls, sir, of the Bow Street Public Office.'

'Charles Long, friend of Mr Pitt.' The politician smiled and steered Henry Dundas back into the reception room. 'Come, Dundas, you have made a fine John Bull but we have not yet been invaded by the French, have we?' He glanced back with a show of nonchalance at Sheridan.

Taking a stance by the fireside Dundas glared at Sheridan. 'What is it you know, Sheridan? Is this some conspiracy of the Radicals? In league with the French?'

'What the Secretary means to ask, Sheridan, is how you are privy to the disappearance of the Prime Minister when myself and Dundas have only discovered it an hour since?'

'Some signal to Revolution here in England, is it?' Dundas continued his assault.

'No!' Sheridan exclaimed impatiently. Trust Henry Dundas to imagine a Radical under every bed. 'I fear for Mr Pitt it is something far worse.'

'You might as well know, we have sent for Major-General Stanhope in case we should need the military on the streets.'

Long peered at Sheridan. 'You must explain yourself, sir —' his gaze shifted to the constable — 'and why you have brought a Runner with you.'

Williams entered at that moment with a decanter of claret and proceeded to pour three glasses.

'From what hour has Mr Pitt been absent?' Sheridan enquired of the man.

Long nodded to the manservant. 'Williams, repeat to us what you know.'

'Sir.' Williams stood straight. 'A boy called at about eleven o'clock last night with a note for Mr Pitt. Shortly afterwards Mr Pitt called for his coat and hat, but not his carriage.'

'Did he say where he was headed or when he would return?'

'Neither, sir.'

'He did not return?'

'No, sir.'

'You assumed, no doubt, Williams, that Mr Pitt might have gone to his club and stayed away the night?' Long prompted.

'Yes, sir.'

Long looked to Sheridan. 'But Mr Pitt was not at White's. Dundas was there all that time. It is only late this morning that any anxiety has arisen. However —' and this was clearly for the ears of the servants in the household — 'it may simply be the case that Mr Pitt visits elsewhere and we are all in a tizz for nothing and he shall be highly amused.' He turned back to the manservant. 'Thank you, Williams, that will be all.'

'One question, if you please, Mr Williams.' It was Nicholls.

Long nodded permission.

'Can you describe the boy that came to the door?'

Williams sniffed. 'He was a boy.'

Nicholls waited.

'A street urchin. Small. Grubby.' Williams sniffed again with distaste. 'I could see his fingers had smeared the paper. I had to wipe it with a handkerchief before presenting it to the Prime Minister.'

'Did you recognise the hand?'

'No, sir, it was not familiar to me. Crossed his T's very high.'

Nicholls shared a quick look with Sheridan.

'Did the boy await a reply?'

'No, sir. He ran straight off. Didn't even wait for a tip.'

Nicholls looked disappointed.

'Is the note still here?'

'I saw Mr Pitt place it in his pocket as he departed.'

Nicholls nodded. 'Thank you, Mr Williams.'

When the manservant had quit the room Long turned to Sheridan.

'You believe this note is connected to Mr Pitt's disappearance?'

'It is most likely.' Sheridan reached for the claret.

'You still have not answered how you come to know that Mr Pitt may be missing.'

'We have received an anonymous letter, passed to us from Mr Brockenhurst of *The Daily Enquiry*. It is signed The Thirteenth Apostle. The hand is familiar to us. It is connected to a series of murders which Constable Nicholls here has been investigating. One victim being an actor of my own company, Mr Marson.'

Long frowned. 'The Bagnio Assassinations?'

'I understood the fellow was caught for that,' Henry Dundas proffered, draining his glass of brandy.

Sheridan shook his head. He looked squarely at Long. 'The real perpetrator is now known to us and was once your friend up at Cambridge and was in lodgings with Mr Pitt there.'

'Peter Wallis…' Charles Long paled. 'He is missing also, is he not? I have read so. Feared to be insane. Oh, good God!' Long raised a hand to his brow.

'Yes, sir.' Nicholls confirmed. 'And Mr Sheridan believes that our Prime Minister was always his first object.'

'But why? Why in God's name?'

'He hopes to bring about an End of Days. The Apocalypse.'

'Well it should certainly be that if the Prime Minister is assassinated.' Dundas puffed out his cheeks and reached for the brandy with a shaky hand. 'What is to be done?'

Long answered. 'If the news is spread abroad that Mr Pitt is missing, abducted, possibly even assassinated already, there would be chaos, gentlemen, there would be riots in the streets. And the war at such a precarious stage. It might signal catastrophe!'

Sheridan nodded and looked pointedly at Henry Dundas, who was widely blamed for the debacle at the siege of Dunkirk and the woefully underprepared state of both British army and navy. The French Revolutionaries had been underestimated. They were more proficient and aggressive in the field than anyone could have imagined. How they would cheer and feel emboldened if anything were to happen to Mr Pitt. That the people of Britain should know their Prime Minister was murdered, Sheridan shuddered at that thought — it was not to be countenanced.

'What is to be done?' Dundas repeated his question.

Nicholls shook his head. 'Our only hope has been to find where Mr Wallis hides. His description is already given out to every Public Station and at every port. But we believe that he is still within the vicinity of London, and this note last night to Mr Pitt, the letter to Brockenhurst, would seem to confirm that. We have hoped for some sighting but we have had nothing since he slipped through our hands.'

'You had him?' Long exclaimed with a fury unusual to his urbane nature.

Sheridan touched the back of his head. 'Almost.'

'The Knightsbridge barracks must be called out immediately, every man should hunt for Wallis!' Charles Long looked to the constable. 'Every Runner!'

Sheridan nodded. 'Well, let it be so.'

'Thank you, Sheridan.' Dundas drew himself up pompously. 'You need concern yourself no further in this business. Mr Pitt will be found and this rogue shall be hung, drawn and quartered.'

After parting from Nicholls, Sheridan had felt disinclined to proceed to the theatre, or to Nerot's or to the house in Grosvenor Street or anywhere else for that matter. He wanted to be alone and could feel a deep melancholy descending on him. There was but one venue which came to mind. He wandered up the Strand and eventually turned into a tavern where he spied a snug corner and ordered brandy. He wanted not to think and a surfeit of brandy might be the recipe for that.

It was well after midnight when the landlord, who knew his customer, tapped him on the shoulder to say that he had called an honest hackney to have Mr Sheridan taken to his residence. Sheridan lifted his head from where it rested on the table. He regarded the landlord with bleary eyes.

'End of days ... my good fellow.'

'That it is, sir. End of the day. Time you was abed.'

Sheridan raised his glass. 'Here's to the Last ... Last...' The remains of the brandy spilt from his glass before it reached his lips.

The landlord and his servant helped Sheridan to his feet and half-carried him outside into the vehicle which had been called.

'Nerot's Hotel, isn't it, Mr Sheridan?'

Sheridan's head lolled into a nod.

The landlord glanced up to the jarvey. 'And be quick and smooth about it, Jemmy, or you shall have to sluice out your carriage.'

The cab set off at a brisk pace. Sheridan rolled from one side of the rear quarter to the other. An idea had begun to swirl about in his head.

'Bath ... yes, bath...' He banged loudly on the roof of the hackney, which after some moments drew up.

The jarvey opened the latch. 'Sir?'

'Bath...'

The driver shook his head impatiently. 'Happen they will have a tub for you at the hotel, sir.'

'No.' Sheridan shook his head in a wide swerving motion. 'Near Covent Garden. There's a bath house…' He gave the address.

The man shrugged. 'If that's what you want, sir.' He clicked to his horses and pulled at the reins to turn about but had to wait until a troop of Life Guards on horseback had passed up the Strand.

'Not that you'll be up for much jiggery pokery in a bagnio tonight,' the jarvey muttered.

The hackney pulled up outside Mr Culpepper's establishment and the driver jumped down to help Sheridan out.

Sheridan snorted, half asleep from the motion of the carriage.

'We're here, sir. Looks to me like it's closed for business. Been boarded up.'

Sheridan nodded. 'That's right. S'left empty … empty.' He pulled himself through the door and staggered down the step.

'Sir,' the jarvey growled. 'I cannot leave you here. You will be robbed.'

'S'all right. Nothing left in my pockets anyway.' He slapped the jarvey on the chest. 'You come to Nerot's tomorrow, my dear fellow, ask for Mr Sheridan. I shall pay you handsomely.'

The jarvey shook his head. 'Just my bleedin' luck!' He turned away to climb back up into his seat.

Sheridan pointed a finger after him. 'Be assured.'

Moments later Sheridan was alone. He shivered. The moon was full in a clear night sky and a frost was in the air. He was dressed only in his tailcoat. He rubbed at his face. He must think. The house seemed tightly boarded, just as the hackney's jarvey had said. But there must be some way in. Of that he felt sure. He reached out to the brick wall for balance and followed it under an arch into a narrow, covered passage which led towards the rear of the building. His footsteps echoed in the close space.

At the next corner where it widened into a small courtyard he noticed an iron grille over an opening. An outlet of some kind. From underground? And then it came to him. The bagnio. Some sort of ventilation or flue for the heating system? A chimney for the boiler Culpepper had boasted of? He scraped his fingers on the wall. There was no more soot than one would expect in a London street. A vent then. To let out foul air.

He knelt down and yanked at a bar in the grille. It seemed solid. But something rattled. He felt about and found that two of the iron bars were loose, the brickwork crumbling. One by one he prised them out. And with a bar as leverage, bent another. There was a gap now into the entrance of the shaft. Sufficient for a boy, certainly. Enough for a man? Sheridan peered into the hole. It was dark. Fathomless.

He leant forward, gauging whether he might squeeze through. It was madness to even think of it; his mind was befuddled. There would be another way. Had to be another way. He should get help. Nicholls could break down the door. He should have sent for him, sent the jarvey to fetch the Runners. It was not so very far to Bow Street. Not so very far to where they had last seen Wallis. Was that why he had thought of it? Remembered that the bagnio was now empty, since Culpepper had fled to France. A good place to hide. This place where the nightmares had begun. He could feel his head begin to spin. And then he heard it, a faint cry. From somewhere down below. Had he heard it? He shook the fug from his head and strained closer, pressing into the gap. Yes, there it was. A man crying out. Mr Pitt, he thought. Master Billy. He must go to him.

And then, before he had quite realised it, he had pushed his shoulders through the grille and was pulling himself down the sharp incline of the vent by the edges of protruding bricks into a space so tight he feared at any moment he should be stuck. There was no way to turn and go back. He must go forward. And he was suddenly very awake to the danger that he faced.

'Damn and blast you, Sheridan!' he cursed himself.

He tried to kick with his feet, which was when he realised that he had lost a shoe at some point. The downward tilt had made the blood rush to his head. He knew he skirted the very edge of panic. The darkness was profound. The air foetid. Hunching his shoulders tight, Sheridan strained forward for purchase on the brick lining of the shaft. Slowly he inched down the slope, thankful for whatever force of gravity aided his descent.

And then there was the merest suggestion of light ahead. His fingers were raw with the effort of grasping each sliver of brick and dragging himself forward, but he renewed his efforts and was rewarded with the edge of what must be the opening to the shaft. He flexed his hands and, gripping the mouth, heaved himself forward.

Sheridan gradually emerged into what he realised from the sudden draught was an open space. His eyes began to adjust to the faint light afforded by the reflected glimmer from the water of the natatio. Which meant that he was above the hot spring pool, emerging from a recessed shaft in the vaulted ceiling. And then the law of gravity had its inevitable consequence and he was plummeting through the air with a wild cry, arms flailing. He gulped a great mouthful of foul water and found himself floundering in the pool, spluttering, coughing and heaving out a lungful of water whilst trying to suck in the breath of life.

'Good God! Is that you, Sheridan?'

Sheridan blinked the water from his eyes and looked up into the astonished face of Mr William Pitt.

To his horror, the Prime Minister was bound, hands and feet, to a large wooden cross. Above his head a sign on the crucifix read, *Anti Christus*.

CHAPTER THIRTY-SEVEN

Sheridan stood dripping wet and minus one shoe in front of the Prime Minister. He shook his head in amazement and staggered about in an ungainly fashion, trying to keep himself upright and straight. He was dizzy from the downward trajectory of his journey and the temples at his brow were now throbbing with the excess of the evening.

'You're alive, Master Billy! Thank all tha's good — you're alive.' Sheridan grinned inanely.

'Good God, man, you're drunk!' William Pitt hissed.

'A tad, jus' a tad.'

Bound as he was at the shoulders as well as the wrists, Pitt had to look down his nose at Sheridan. 'And keep your voice down. I won't ask how the devil you come to be here, Sheridan — like some irregular Jack-in-the-box — just untie me, I pray you, I'm damned uncomfortable.'

'Of course, your servant, sir.'

Sheridan could see that for all his apparent calm, Pitt's eyes were alive with fear. He lifted the lantern which had been left hanging on one of the pillars and moved closer to inspect the bonds which lashed the Prime Minister to the cross.

'What happened to you, Pitt? Note from Wallis, yes?'

Wallis had made a good job of the ties. He wished that he had a blade and could simply cut through the rope.

Pitt nodded his head. 'Yes. It was Wallis. I had heard that he was unwell, in his mind, that his family searched for him. He begged me to meet him. Said that only I could help him. What a fool I was!'

'You went alone?'

'The rendezvous was very close. A street away.' Pitt hesitated. 'And he had signed himself Mattie.'

'Mattie?'

'It was my fond name for him, when we were students in lodgings together. I thought that I could persuade him to be helped.'

Sheridan shook his head; he could not reach the wrists and would have to find a ladder or chair.

'And instead?'

'Instead I found myself knocked unconscious, bound and gagged.' Pitt shuddered. 'I came to in a wheelbarrow, with a filthy canvas on top of me.'

'A wheelbarrow? Yes, that is clever. No one should stop a man with a wheelbarrow, no matter the hour.'

Sheridan kicked off his remaining shoe and turned away with the lantern. 'I must find a ladder. I will return soon.'

He shivered involuntarily, his clothes were damp from the dousing in the pool and it was cold in the baths, damnably cold.

'Be quick about it... Wallis may return at any moment...'

As Sheridan made his way along the passage, he heard Pitt's tremulous voice behind him.

'...and I do not like the dark.'

He passed a number of chambers. With a jolt the vision of Mr Marson's mutilated corpse came to him. Here was a place of death. He was going the wrong way, there should be nothing of use in this direction, he must find his way back and to the stairs, as if to confirm this he saw in front of him a dead end; but quite fortuitously a ladder was propped up against the wall leading to a sizeable gap in the brickwork.

Out of curiosity he climbed and peered through the gap. Raising the lantern, Sheridan found another large underground space. It was filled with the rubble of centuries. Loose earth banked back against the wall. Culpepper had mentioned that the renovation of the Roman bath house was still a work in progress. Here was another section. He had found a ladder — might he also find some workmen's tools? Something sharp? Sheridan swung the lantern around. His eye caught on a metal object.

As he hastened back to the mineral pool, Sheridan felt his spirits lift. All would be well. It should be a simple matter to break out of the house from the inside. He had followed his instincts, now he was poised to rescue the Prime Minister and he felt a satisfying swell of heroism.

When he arrived back at the foot of the cross, Sheridan noted the look of relief which greeted him before he leant the ladder against the rear and clambered up the structure.

'Well, Sherry, it seems the role of saviour is reversed in this moment,' Pitt attempted with fainthearted wit as Sheridan arrived on a level.

The crucifix swayed very slightly. It had been roped to two adjoining pillars in a fairly crude fashion to keep it upright. Sheridan settled himself into position at Pitt's shoulder and retrieved a stone from one pocket and a chisel from another. The angle was precarious and he could wish that he did not feel so suddenly nauseous, but he began to work at the rope binding Pitt's right shoulder, using the stone to hammer at the chisel. It was harder than he had imagined, the tool not being so sharp as he could wish. Slowly, gradually, the rope began to fray under his exertions and then at last it fell away. Pitt groaned and flexed his free shoulder. Moving the ladder along, Sheridan began to work on the ties binding the wrist. The steady rhythm of work allowed other thoughts to resurface.

'You said, Pitt, that you thought you might be able to help Wallis. He had said that only you could help him. Why would he imagine that?'

Pitt shrugged. 'We were at Pembroke College. I suppose we were friends for a time. He seemed so ... without friends, very studious, Divinity, Hebrew and Greek — I believe he was one of the few to attend those lectures. We were a lively crowd, Wilberforce, Long, and the others. We met, we drank, we debated, all quite boisterous as any fellows of eighteen or nineteen are wont to be and I suppose I must have invited Wallis to join a party, and after that he was always there. Though he never spoke much. I learned his second name was Matthias and I called him Mattie one day, I was probably a little drunk, but his face — well, it lit up; I had never seen him look so ... happy. He explained that his mother had called him by that name and he should be very pleased if I were to do so. To be honest, Sherry, I didn't really think anything of it.'

'But he did, didn't he, Pitt?'

'He did rather. He kept talking about David and Jonathan, about how one might have a pure and heroic love, it was all a bit biblical, he talked as though we were very particular friends. But he seemed harmless, I liked him well enough. I suppose I may have pitied him and even humoured him...'

'Perhaps you enjoyed being the object of his adoration? I have found that it is always very welcome to be worshipped — until, after a time, it becomes tiresome.'

Sheridan whacked at the chisel. It was becoming blunt, damn it.

'Is that what happened?'

Pitt hesitated. 'In a manner.'

'But something happened, he told me once that —' Sheridan strained to recall — 'your paths diverged. I did not get the sense he was alluding to your career choices, but to something rather more personal.'

'Some youthful disagreement, no doubt.' Pitt shrugged his right shoulder and groaned with stiffness. 'I am sure I cannot remember.'

'Oh, but I am sure you can, Mr Pitt.'

Wallis' voice coming from the darkness startled both men. Sheridan wobbled on top of the ladder and the chisel slipped from his grasp, clattering onto the stone tiles below. He grabbed for the frame of the crucifix to steady himself.

'Mr Sheridan, you are here. I am very glad of that; indeed, I do believe I have been waiting for you.'

What the devil! What could Wallis mean? And where was he? His voice seemed to come from all sides out of the darkness.

'You have been chosen — I knew it. You are the witness. And you shall record these events — as the prophets did of old.'

'What exactly am I recording, Wallis? This is all —' he stopped himself before the word *madness* escaped him. He must not provoke; he should try and keep calm. 'You must let us go at once, Reverend. We want only to help you, don't we, Mr Pitt?'

'Most assuredly,' Pitt hastened to concur.

'I need no help. I am God's instrument. This is His will.'

'Wallis — it is the devil's voice you hear. Desist, I pray. Think of your child,' Sheridan pleaded.

'Child? What child?'

There — across the other side of the pool — Sheridan could just make out a pale visage.

'Your wife is expectant.'

Wallis laughed cruelly. 'Then it is no child of mine! I have not touched her — it is the Devil's spawn and she is his harlot!'

Sheridan groaned inwardly. There seemed no way to reason with Wallis now.

'Mr Pitt is the king's Prime Minister, we are at war, he is needed, Wallis. Our country needs him. He is not the Anti-Christ.'

'Then he has fooled you, Sheridan, as he has fooled everyone. It is as foretold. He has risen from the very pit of Hell. He wields a tyrant's sword and leads armies to war and destruction. He heralds our end.'

'Wallis, this is war with France — it is not Armageddon!' Sheridan shinned down the ladder and then pointed up to the Prime Minister. 'And Master Billy here wouldn't know one end of a sword from another. Yes, I agree the government is heavy-handed and at times repressive —' Sheridan paused, batting away the vision of his friend Thomas Walker languishing in prison for nothing more than a call to electoral reform — 'but Mr Pitt is no bloody tyrant. All told, he is a decent fellow, an English gentleman.'

Wallis stepped forward so that his pale face loomed out of the shadows. 'Tell him, Pitt. Tell him what happened that night in your rooms.'

Sheridan frowned as he observed William Pitt twitch nervously.

'Or shall I?'

'We were boys, Wallis! We were very drunk. I certainly was most inebriated. From what I do remember I collapsed on the bed.'

'As did I. And when you awoke in the night?'

'Was I awake? I think I dreamt...'

'That you held me in your arms — that you embraced me. That is when I awoke. And thinking only of our great friendship I welcomed that embrace ... as though I were Jonathan and you were David.'

'I was befuddled ... I scarcely knew...'

'You knew what you did. And I had thought you so above other men I allowed it! But you were the snake, the devil who snared me into sin. And now I am stained forever!'

'Nothing happened, Wallis, nothing!' Pitt repeated, insistent.

Wallis was shaking his head. 'Nothing? Only all that is unnatural. Though one may never act upon the urge — to be so aroused, only by the male. There is no greater sin. You have done that to me. And then you tossed me aside, as if in horror.'

'We were innocents, Mattie, innocents.'

'No.' Wallis stepped forward into the beam of the lantern. 'I have read the signs. Everything you are. The times that we live. I have been made God's instrument to call that end of days. I am the thirteenth Apostle. You are elect. The Anti-Christ. There will be judgement. We shall both suffer in Hell, you and I — but we shall be saved! We shall be saved by the righteous. All will be forgiven. Don't you see? Our love will be cleansed and purified!'

Pitt was shaking his head, all colour drained from his face. 'I beg you, Mattie, do not do this.'

'For both our sakes, for all humanity, I must. We all die to hasten that day when we might yet live together in paradise.'

Whilst the reverend addressed himself thus to the Prime Minister, Sheridan had inched around the pool towards him. He now stretched one hand out in a placating gesture. 'Wallis, this is all a sad delusion. And for this falsity you have murdered most savagely so many good men and would have done the same to my dear, good boy, Tom. That is not God's work. Surely, Heaven can wait.'

Wallis shook his head. '*I shall have pity on men.* God is all goodness, you see. Pity on me.' His eyes gleamed. 'And on you too, Sheridan.'

A knife flashed between them.

Sheridan flinched, but he was puzzled too. 'You use the left hand?'

Wallis smiled. 'Ever observant.' He looked at his left hand clutching the blade. 'I have trained myself. This is work for the sinister side.'

Sheridan shook his head in wonder. It appeared that Reverend Wallis had almost literally split himself in two, the dark side and the light. He had embraced that darkness as a path towards eternal light. He longed for the light, with every part of his being and sought to hasten its coming. What a poor, deluded soul.

'Well, let's not delay any further, shall we? Pitt is uncomfortable, it would seem.'

As Wallis moved to pass, his blade outstretched, Sheridan swung around with the rock clasped in his right hand and brought it down on Wallis' crown. The reverend crumpled beneath the blow, the knife slipping from his hand.

Sheridan snatched the weapon. For a moment he hovered over Wallis, uncertain. But there was no movement. He hastened to William Pitt, the blade slicing through his bonds with a disturbing ease.

'The devil, Sheridan, the devil!'

Pitt was trembling as Sheridan helped him down from the cross. Behind them they heard a low moan and turned to see Wallis staggering back onto his feet. Blood trickled down his forehead. He looked toward them, his face both bereft and puzzled.

'William, you must understand, I act only to save our eternal souls.'

'Mattie…' Pitt spoke gently and with a hint of anguish. 'I place myself in God's hands. I will be judged. But not today.'

'Then what must I do?' Wallis pleaded.

Sheridan stepped forward. 'You must come with us, Reverend.'

Wallis shook his head. 'No, no. Here is an end.' He sprang for the knife still in Sheridan's hand and plunged them both into the waters of the natatio.

The speed of the move caught Sheridan entirely by surprise. He swallowed a mouthful of water even as he thrashed about to break free from Wallis' grip. He strained upwards and his face broke the surface. He tried desperately to gulp in air but Wallis was dragging him down again, yanking violently at his wrist. He must not let go of the knife. Whatever else, he must not let go. But neither should he drown!

And then Wallis' face was looming in front of his own, his grip like iron, and he was pulling himself towards Sheridan with grim determination. No, not towards him but towards the object in his hand. With horror Sheridan realised that Wallis was thrusting himself onto the blade. The clergyman's eyes opened wide as the sharp point pierced his chest and moments later a thin trickle of blood issued from between his lips. Sheridan let go of the knife in revulsion and pushed upwards before his lungs should burst.

As he broke the surface, Sheridan flailed about wildly for the edge of the pool, coughing and spluttering. The Prime Minister stood frozen at the foot of the cross, as if transfixed.

'*On all sides round horror spread wide; the very silence breathed a terror on my soul*,' Pitt whispered, so that Sheridan only just caught the quote from Virgil. Virgil again, he thought momentarily.

They were not silent, however. From above, Sheridan heard loud sounds of banging and then voices calling. Moments later, boots were thundering down the stairs into the bagnio.

Then there were lanterns and faces that he recognised. Constable Nicholls for one and by his side Major-General Stanhope with two guardsmen. One of whom, Sheridan noticed wryly, held his other shoe.

CHAPTER THIRTY-EIGHT

It was reported in *The Daily Enquiry* that the body of The Very Reverend Peter Wallis had been recovered from the Thames that morning near the mouth of the Fleet, having been spotted by a troop of the Life Guards. The article went on to recount that the good reverend had recently succumbed to fits of mental disorder and either by accident or design had fallen into the river, suffering a number of injuries in consequence before drowning. Mr Brockenhurst went on to record that the reverend, the younger son of Sir Edward Wallis of Cranby Hall, had been a Hebrew scholar of some note and well known for his probity and sobriety. Furthermore, the clergyman had been a friend to Mr Pitt whilst studying at Cambridge. The Prime Minister, the journalist suggested, might honour the memory of this poor unfortunate Christian soul by pressing for improvements in the accommodation and treatment of the insane, who were often exhibited to the public as little more than objects of entertainment. He then went on to offer a number of salacious accounts of practices at Bedlam and other asylums.

Sheridan threw the newspaper back onto his desk. Well, it was to be hushed up. He was glad of it. They had all agreed, standing there in the bagnio, he and Pitt, Stanhope and Nicholls, that the less said about the affair the better. There had been justice of a sort, he supposed. A wretched end. Sheridan reflected that Wallis had been a man so at war with his own nature that he had created a whole narrative of salvation based on his discovery of the Revelation to the Apostle Peter. *I shall have pity on men*. He could not but feel pity for Wallis until, that is, he thought of what might have happened to Tom.

Earlier he had called in to the debate at Westminster. Pitt was so drunk he had barely been able to stand. But The Friends of Mr Pitt had rallied in his place, loyal as ever. Sheridan had caught the Prime Minister's eye across the floor of the chamber. He had seen it then. That in some measure, Pitt took responsibility and blamed himself for Wallis' fatal attachment. He had nodded an acknowledgement. It would never be spoken of. They were political opponents, but Mr Pitt should know that Sheridan was a Gentleman first before he was a Whig.

There was a knock at the door and without waiting for a reply Kemble poked his head around.

'Ah, Sheridan, you are in residence.'

'In body if not in mind, my dear Kemble. How may I serve you?'

'Well, it is not for myself, Sherry.'

It would be his damn sister, Mrs Siddons, wanting her arrears.

'Pray tell.'

'Young Mr Blackett is below.'

'Blackett? Ah, yes the young actor.'

'Fine Iago, I thought. Wonders if he might return to us? From…' Kemble looked vague.

'Edinburgh,' Sheridan supplied. 'Those dank, grey airs did not suit his sunnier disposition I would surmise. Well, make room for him.' Sheridan clicked his fingers and pointed at Kemble. 'I propose he play Romeo next week, let him earn his keep.'

'Capital, I have always enjoyed the part of Tybalt, myself.'

'Good. Good.'

As Kemble retreated there came then another knock and Monsieur Dubois burst in.

'Dear Hercules is poorly again?' Sheridan enquired before Dubois could speak.

'I 'ave seen a llama.'

'A what?'

'From Peru. We must buy this llama for the pantomime.'

'Believe me, Monsieur Dubois, if "we" had the funds —'

'You will pay!' Monsieur Dubois glared at Sheridan.

'I will pay.' Sheridan nodded. 'There is no creature in the world we need so much as a llama.' He heard a cough then from behind Dubois. 'Ah, is that good Mrs Petty I see at your coat-tails, Monsieur Dubois?'

'It is, sir.' The wardrobe mistress bustled into the room.

Sheridan settled back into his chair. It was business as usual.

Sheridan was entertaining Mary with funny faces and sounds of the farmyard, each taking turn, when Mrs Canning came to call with Bessie in tow. Bessie immediately swept Mary up into her arms and they settled down to dressing and undressing the infant's favourite raggedy doll. Mrs Canning had come to assist Sheridan in the arrangements for the ball which he was planning as part of the celebrations for Tom's eighteenth birthday. That morning he had collected the silver pocket watch which had been completed by the horologist, Mr Inigo Hughes. Sheridan felt its pleasing weight in his hand and admired the craftsmanship, it was a marvellous piece and he hoped it would enable his son to keep better time than he was wont to do.

In between discussion of the practical matters such as guest lists, musicians, menus, the hiring of extra servants and so on, Mrs Canning was full of gossip. She had recently been invited to lunch with Lady Priscilla Soersby and expressed her pleasure that they had become better acquainted again thanks to the Epping Forest expedition. Unfortunately, however, the Soersbys would not be spending so much time in London in the future. It seemed that Sir Jonas had decided to retire from his judicial duties. Mehitabel expressed her surprise. It had been widely rumoured that he would be appointed to the King's Bench.

'Such an honour. One would imagine that it would crown any man's career in that field to be so appointed. And he is no great age.' Mehitabel shook her head, unable to fathom why any man of Sir Jonas' standing would abandon his ambition. She scrabbled in her reticule for a lozenge to help with her dyspepsia.

Sheridan nodded to himself. Soersby had clearly realised how close to exposure he had come. And in so public an office. He felt a twinge of disappointment. There was no denying that Sir Jonas had been a good man and a fair judge.

'Apparently,' Mehitabel continued, 'he wishes to devote himself to the supervision of his estate in Somerset. Also, to various charitable works — of which Lady Priscilla was most enthusiastic in favour. It is her husband's notion that this new colony at Botany Bay should thrive. He has a vision, Lady Priscilla informs me. Sir Jonas imagines the Antipodes not merely as the prison colony at Botany Bay to where we send the undesirables in our society, but, as there is a vast hinterland, he believes it a destination offering opportunity to industrious men of the poorer sort. He has been talking to a pastoralist about sheep — it appears they might do well in the Antipodes. Sir Jonas is keen to promote a scheme to aid the poorer agricultural families in Somerset to settle there.'

'Sheep farming? That does sound a very woolly cause; I wish him every success and shall write and tell him so.'

'Theirs is such a happy marriage.' Mehitabel smiled wistfully. 'As mine was.'

Sheridan nodded in concurrence. Yes, perhaps it was a happy marriage, for all of Soersby's sexual predilections.

'I must be thankful that I had so many years with Stratford. Poor Mrs Wallis. To be widowed so young! And in such tragic circumstances. Her husband being so disturbed and then for him to drown in the Thames.' Mehitabel sighed. 'Oh, perhaps it is a blessed relief. And Cecily does have one comfort.'

'Oh yes?'

'Well…' Hitty bristled with the news she was to impart. 'Would you believe it — she has announced that she is some months expectant with child! I know how she has longed to have an infant of her own. Apparently, Sir Edward is agreed to granting her a very pleasant and substantial villa which edges the estate at Cranby and he will of course provide handsomely for his grandchild.'

'I am glad to hear of it. Mrs Wallis deserves to be happy.'

So, some fellow had breached the walls of the clergyman's young wife after all and with more success than he himself had managed.

'That is exactly what George said on hearing the news. He has been most solicitous. My nephew is a very considerate young man. I realise that I have been rather hard on him this past year. It was simply the shock that he should become one of The Friends of Mr Pitt.'

Was George Canning the lothario in question? The young rogue! Well, well, Mrs Wallis had courted disaster. If her husband had survived, he should have denounced her and sued for 'criminal conversation' with another man, leaving her

357

reputation in tatters. And if George had been dragged into the affair! Sheridan smiled wryly. Perhaps there was a little more of the recklessness of both his parents in George's nature than the young man might care to admit. Though, come to think of it, Mrs Wallis might simply have claimed that her husband's accusations were simply a symptom of his madness. Nevertheless, he hoped that George might learn from this a greater sympathy towards his own poor mother, Mary Ann Costello, and perhaps try to do something for his wretched half-siblings.

'He is his own man, Hitty, more seducer than seduced, and I do believe he shall go far.'

'I rather think he will, Dick.'

A note was brought in at that moment by one of the servants and delivered into Sheridan's hand.

He nodded to Hitty. 'If you will pardon me…'

She waved a hand. 'No ceremony, we are all family here.'

It was a missive from Constable Nicholls which announced the birth of a daughter, Elodie-Therese, mother and baby both in good health. Louis-Pierre and his wife should be very honoured if Mr Sheridan would agree to being a godparent.

'Well, that is excellent! I am to be a godfather!'

He felt a surge of well-being. All was right with the world. After so much death, it gladdened his heart to hear of a birth, of new life. Mary ran over to him and squirmed in between his knees, wanting to be lifted up into his lap.

'Pa! Gee-Gee! Pa!'

He obliged and lifted his demanding little daughter up onto his knee, his arms extending into reins as he mimicked the motion of a galloping horse.

Mary squealed and laughed with delight.

A NOTE TO THE READER

Dear Reader,

The term 'homosexual' was not coined until 1868, and 'gay' is of even more modern usage; earlier times used terminology which is today rightly deemed offensive. In the eighteenth century, same-sex relationships were subject to the vilest of insults and a plethora of ripe euphemistic descriptions. There is a level of authenticity which I have had to circumvent or eschew in writing for a contemporary readership. You might dip into Grose's *Dictionary of the Vulgar Tongue*, first published in 1785 and frequently updated thereafter for a goodly sample of general Georgian slang. I do not think, however, that we should shy away from the consequences of this level of vitriol and the prejudice it represented; it resulted in very real societal exclusion and punishment. Hanging might be the most dire outcome of discovery, but the pillory could be every bit as lethal and nasty; we aren't talking about a few rotten eggs and tomatoes, or even manure hurled at the distressed occupant, but stones and brickbats resulting in real physical harm and in some cases fatality.

Homosexuality has existed in every age and where not accepted has been forced underground or led to closeted, damaged lives and a constant fear of exposure and blackmail. Women were not immune, as Sheridan's star performer Eliza Farren discovered, and charges of same-sex relations were amongst those levelled at Marie Antoinette at her trial. The theatre has often been a haven for people who have stepped out of rigid societal norms. Women acting on stage was still a relatively modern innovation in the eighteenth century and serious performers like Mrs Siddons were concerned to move away from the stigma of harlotry which had been attached to many females appearing on stage. It was an age when one in five women in London are reckoned to have resorted to prostitution in order to survive. Men in positions of wealth and power were notoriously loose in their morals and flesh was bought and sold as any other commodity.

It is against the backdrop of these times that I decided to explore forbidden sexuality and the hypocrisy and double standards of the age. It also allowed me to take my Sheridan on a journey confronting his own prejudices. He did fling insults at William Pitt the Younger across the floor of the Commons. There has long been speculation about Pitt and his inclinations, but nothing concrete to say he acted upon them. Given that Sheridan lived within the more tolerant world of the theatre I have liked to imagine that his prejudices against homosexuality were not so entrenched as society at large and that he may have come to regret his slurs against the Prime Minister.

Did Princess Elizabeth have a secret child? This may never be known with any surety but the rumour certainly evolved and spread. Eliza Ramus was a real person and the legend persists that she was the child of the king's third daughter and the son of a senior royal servant following a clandestine and unlawful marriage. Eliza was then purportedly adopted by her uncle Henry Ramus, a writer for the East India Company. Subsequently, the child was brought up in India and later married there. I own to having taken complete dramatic licence with this titbit of Georgian Royal gossip.

I hope you enjoyed reading the novel, and I thank you for taking the time to do so. Reviews are really important to authors, and if you enjoyed the novel, it would be great if you could spare a little time to post a review on **Amazon** and **Goodreads**. Readers can connect with me online, **www.facebook.com/rosiewriter1** on Facebook and **@rosiewriter** on Instagram and you can find out more about my writing via my website: **https://rmcullenauthor.wordpress.com**

Thank you!

R M Cullen

Sapere Books is an exciting new publisher of brilliant fiction and popular history.

To find out more about our latest releases and our monthly bargain books visit our website:
saperebooks.com

.